HEREWARD: THE FURY OF THE NORTHMEN

by Marcus Pitcaithly

MMIX

"From the fury of the Northmen, deliver us, o Lord."
~ the "Fury Litany",
apocryphally said to have been used in English churches
during the Danish invasions

The word "Northmen" ("Normanni") can apply to either Scandinavians or Normans.

To Patrick and Susanna.

First published by Marcus Pitcaithly, May 2009
© Marcus Pitcaithly 2009
ISBN: 978-0-9556864-1-2

CONTENTS

MAP OF EASTERN ENGLAND

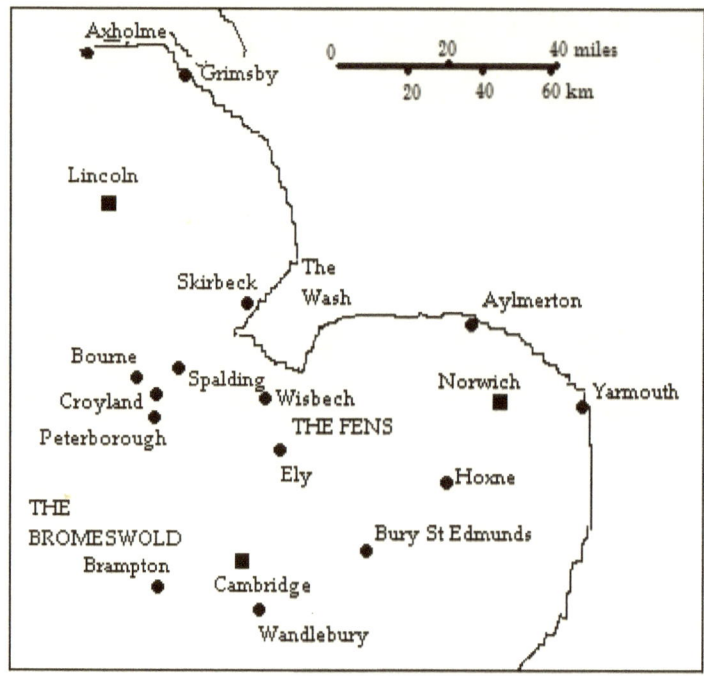

Hereward's part of England is still a wetland area: but in the eleventh century the Fenland was more marsh than dry land. The Isles of Axholme and Ely really were islands, and flat-bottomed boats were most likely the principal means of transport.

England as a whole was also very much a rural environment. The total population was between one and two million, of whom barely 10% lived in urban surroundings. Towns such as Spalding differed from villages more in amenities than in size; even London probably housed no more than 15-20,000 people; York, Norwich, and perhaps Winchester and Lincoln, 5-10,000; and probably all other cities fewer than five thousand each.

4

Acknowledgements

As acknowledged in *Hereward: Sons of the White Dragon*, Prior Herluin was created by Charles Kingsley, and some other characters made use of here (Godard, de Manville, Mariana) owe part of their inspiration to *Fair Em, the Miller's Daughter of Manchester*.

Girolamo di Salerno was created by Charles MacFarlane in the first modern Hereward novel, *The Camp of Refuge* (1844).

Names

I have as a general rule employed the forms of proper names most familiar, or easiest, to modern English speakers (e.g. Edward, not Eadweard). I have also tried to minimise duplication. The Norman name Turold was at this time used interchangeably with Thorold, a form closer to the original Norse Thorvald: later, as Norman French became closer to the French of Paris, the forms Turoud and Turaud appeared: presented with two prominent enemies of Hereward who shared this name, I have called one Thorold and the other Turaud.

Chapter 1: *Over the Sea*

Bruges, May, 1069.

Torfridel gurgled contentedly and closed her eyes. Her mother stroked back the wisp of hair that had fallen across the infant's face, and laid her in her crib. As she did so, the child's hand grasped her finger: even in sleep, she had a considerable grip, and it was not easy for Torfrida to extricate herself.

"So strong," she murmured. "Just like her father."

"Really?" said her guest. "I'd say her father had failed to keep his grip on you."

Torfrida looked up sharply. She would not normally hear any criticism of her husband, however much milder it might be than what she said – and shouted – herself when closeted with her old nurse Kolfrosta: but the Countess Richildis said what she pleased in Flanders. Her husband's accession to the title had not made Richildis better company.

"He has been detained by the war," Torfrida replied mildly. "But now that Torfridel is old enough to bear the voyage, I mean to join him as soon as I may."

"After a year?" said Richildis. "What makes you think he'll even remember you?"

"I am his wife," said Torfrida simply.

"A wife whom he left behind – and sent back when she followed him."

"He did not send me back." A hardness had entered into Torfrida's voice: she was beginning to lose patience with the carping Countess. "I chose to return in accordance with my family traditions, as I had chosen to follow him. And I choose now to go again to England."

"Is England any place to bring up a child? Let alone a noble child, with the blood of princes in her veins. Here Torfridel could have the pick of our knights for her husband,

6

as you could have done – even my son might not be above her reach. What is there in England? Norman bullies decked out in stolen finery, and the men they took it from reduced to paupers."

"It's a little early yet to worry about my daughter's marital prospects," said Torfrida crisply. "By the time she is grown England may be a very different place. So may Artois. So may Flanders."

That last remark was pointed: England was not the only country ravaged by war. As they spoke, an invading army was encamped on Flemish soil: the Vicomte de Picquigny was plundering at will in the south, unopposed by Richildis' husband Count Baldwin, who was confined to his bedchamber with a shaking fever. The doctors were divided on whether or not the Count would live. When his father had suffered such illnesses, as he often had in his later years, Baldwin himself had always been there to take over his duties: but his own son, little Arnulf, was much too young. Baldwin's brother Robert had with the Count's consent assumed command of the army, but had yet to stir out of the city: and every day more refugees arrived from villages burnt by the Vicomte's rampaging men, with fresh tales of Picquignard brutality.

"Flanders has endured worse than this before and will again," sniffed Richildis. "It's a raid, nothing more, a low piece of brigandage. England is being torn to pieces between the Normans and rebels like your Hereward: there'll be nothing left of it before they're through."

Torfrida was about to offer a heated response when there came a knock at the door.

"Enter," she said. A page sidled into the room, and bowed low before announcing:

"The Lord Hereward Askilsson and his attendant, my ladies."

Torfrida started to her feet as Hereward and Martin entered the chamber. Their cloaks were stained with both salt and mud: they had not paused to change or wash since they had left their ship. Hereward had aged, it seemed to her, by longer than the year they had been apart; and he had new scars. But what was strangest to her was the doubt writ plain on his face – doubt and fear over the reception he would meet. That was not like Hereward: and in that moment she pitied him. All the joy, relief and anger she had expected to feel were there: but pity took her by surprise.

She would not, however, give Richildis the satisfaction of seeing her react emotionally.

"Welcome, my lord," she said, somehow managing to keep her voice from trembling.

"My lady," he said quietly. There was a tense pause before Richildis finally had the grace to excuse herself and depart.

When the couple finally broke from their crushing hug, Torfrida got enough breath back to say:

"You have a daughter."

"We have a daughter?" exclaimed Hereward. He started towards the cradle, making to snatch the child up and embrace her too.

"Easy, now, don't wake her," said Torfrida.

"That's a bonny girl," he said, marvelling at the tiny perfection of his daughter. "She looks like you."

"She has your strength," said Torfrida. "She's not had a day's illness, may God continue her in health."

Hereward looked round.

"Was it... very hard?" he asked.

Torfrida's mind flashed back to the hours of agony, the blood, the semi-delirium, the dimly heard discussions of her chances of survival. She had hated Hereward for not being with her, but she knew well enough that it was not his fault. She shrugged.

"It is over now," she said. "You're not disappointed, that I didn't give you a son the first time?"

"There will be time enough for sons," smiled

Hereward. "As long as you don't have to go back to St Omer for every child."

"Only the firstborn," she reassured him, returning his smile. Kolfrosta, hunched in her corner, bit her withered lip. She had never seen as bloody a birth as Torfridel's: despite all her care to prevent it, she suspected somebody – whether through carelessness or malice – must have left a knot tied somewhere in the house that stayed the coming of the child. She had treated Torfrida's injuries, nursed her back to health, and said nothing to her that was not hopeful: but in her own mind, she did not believe that her mistress would ever have another baby.

Once they had washed, eaten, and donned fresh clothing, Hereward and Martin went to present themselves to the Count. While they were in Bruges, they were Baldwin's guests; Hereward and he, moreover, if hardly close, were old acquaintances. Baldwin, however, turned out to be seeing nobody: his very physicians were afraid to enter his room for fear of infection. The civil rule of Flanders was effectively in the care of Richildis: but, reasoning that the Countess had already seen him, Hereward decided to present himself instead to the Count's brother.

The Lord Robert was found in a side chamber, studying a chart that showed the major towns of Flanders and the distances between them; more detailed maps were hard to come by, and even this one had probably been expensive. He wore a primrose yellow linen tunic, his cloak and supertunic shed in the summer warmth. Closeted with him were a worried looking clerk with a sheaf of letters, and a harper endeavouring to distract him from his cares. A jug of wine sat on the table before him, from which he was refilling his cup as the new arrivals were shown in.

"By the chains of St Bavo," he exclaimed when he set eyes on Hereward, "it's good to see you again!"

"It's good to see you too," said Hereward.

"You'll have heard the bad news?" said Robert.

"About your brother? Yes. May God grant him a speedy recovery."

"Amen," said Robert, "but I meant about the Picquignards. A courier arrived this morning from the Bishop of Cambrai: his estates have been ravaged and he is holed up in the town, practically under siege and without the men to defend it. And the Vicomte's chief captain is an old friend of ours: Sir Ascelin de St Valéry." Hereward grimaced at the name of the Norman mercenary who had preceded him as the Count of Flanders' champion. After his attempt to murder Hereward was foiled, Ascelin had fled the county: but now it appeared the two had chosen the same moment to return to Flanders.

"Ascelin!" Martin spat. "Last time I saw that fine feathered jay I put an arrow in his shoulder. It should have been his heart, and next time it will be."

"This is not like fighting Frisian pirates in Scheldtmeerland," said Robert. "Picquigny's men may be running wild at the moment, but they're an army. I ride against them as soon as I've gathered enough men: I'd be honoured if you'd come with me, Hereward. And Martin, of course."

"I?" Hereward raised an eyebrow. "I have no troops to lend. And not much of my experience has been gained in open battle."

"You have your name," said Robert simply. "The man who killed Holbert of Guines would be welcome on any campaign; and we've heard plenty about your exploits in England too. You're becoming a legend. It will put heart into our men and fear into the enemy's if Hereward the Wake rides with us."

"I'm not my own man in this," said Hereward uneasily. "I have other responsibilities now."

"If Cambrai falls, St Omer will be threatened," Robert pointed out. "The Lady Torfrida can hardly object to you defending her own." She could and would, but it was not Hereward's place to point that out.

"There is not only the Lady Torfrida," he said. "There are my men at Ely. If I were to be killed in a quarrel which is none of theirs I should have betrayed them."

"And what if I made the quarrel theirs?" said Robert shrewdly. Hereward looked blank.

"What do you mean?"

"What if I made it profitable to your people in England that you should join me in repelling the Picquignards?" said Robert. "How many weaponsmiths have you at Ely? How much iron?"

"We are short of armour," Hereward admitted.

"Then this is my offer. If you and Martin Lightfoot will ride under my command against the Vicomte de Picquigny until he and his army are either off the good earth of Flanders or under it, then when that is done I will provide a shipload of arms and armour to further your campaign in England." The clerk stifled an exclamation. The Count's treasury could ill afford such reckless promises. The County kept a stable of weaponsmiths who worked morn till night in the heat and smoke, for no other purpose than to equip its armies, at considerable expense: months of their finest work were on offer: but then, Lord Robert was surely the best judge of what this foreigner was worth.

Hereward looked at Martin.

"We will have to consider this further," he said. He was not going to make any commitment before he had spoken with Torfrida. "But you may take it that we are… interested." Robert grinned.

"I thought you would be," he said.

"May I ask who your own chief officers are?" said Hereward.

"Second below me is the Lord Frederick van Oosterzele," replied Robert. "I've also hired an Italian engineer, Girolamo di Salerno. He's full of Roman learning, says a book can show you how to bring down a castle: and if half what they say about him in Paris is true then he's worth a hundred men."

"Van Oosterzele?" said Hereward, curling his lip. "That's a name we know too well in England." Gerbod van Oosterzele and his sister Gundrada were two of King William's closest cronies, and were not loved by the English vassals he had given them. "Is this Gerbod's brother?"

"Yes," confessed Robert. "But Frederick's never been to England."

"Does he hold land there?"

"He might. He has served William in the past, against the King of France. But it's my brother you'd be fighting for, not Frederick. For Christ's sake, man, my own sister is William's wife, and you serve with me readily enough."

"Remember the shipload of armour," Martin added. Hereward swallowed hard.

"If I have a sworn and witnessed promise for the armour," he said at last, "I think I can fight beside Frederick van Oosterzele."

"Why, Hereward," said Robert, "you're beginning to sound as if you didn't trust me."

Bourne Hall.

Sir Ogier fitz Ungomar turned a chess piece over in his hands, appearing to examine it closely.

"Who are you, exactly?" he asked casually, in English. Sir Ogier had a facility with languages and had mastered the tongue quickly; it made dealing with the natives much easier. The huge man in front of him pushed back his thick black hair.

"A man of the Fens," he said.

"I can smell that," said the knight.

"An enemy of Hereward the Wake."

"I need a name."

"My name", said the stranger, "is Starkad."

Ogier raised an eyebrow.

"Starkad the Gyrvian?" he asked.

"Once. No more."

The previous year, the island base of the brigands known as Gyrvians had been destroyed by Hereward's men, and their leader Grendel killed. For once, most Normans were grateful to the rebels. Grendel's lieutenant, his brother Starkad, had vanished, although his name had still been whispered when a dark shape was seen in the woods or livestock had disappeared. The widespread belief that the brothers were of trollish blood, and possessed with demonic powers, had not gone away, in spite of their defeat.

"I heard of your proclamation," Starkad went on. "You want men to take the Camp of Refuge. I am willing to lead them." The moment the news of Hereward's absence had reached Peterborough Abbey, the Norman prior, Herluin, had alerted his compatriots: and the opportunity to wipe out the rebels was not one to be missed.

"Lead them?" said Ogier. "Why should I entrust the task to you? I hear you attacked Ely before and failed to take it."

"That was a raid," said Starkad. "This will be a destruction."

"You are a wolfshead," said Ogier, "like Hereward. I could have you hanged here and now."

"But you won't," said Starkad. "I know the Fens. I know the approaches to Ely. You need me."

"Arrogance is a failing, wolfshead," said Ogier. "It will get you killed one day."

"But not today." Starkad fixed the knight's eyes with his, and Ogier smiled.

"No," he agreed, "not today."

"The Lord Frederick van Oosterzele; Master Girolamo

di Salerno; and Azecier de Sarton, his assistant." Hereward looked from one face to another. The most striking was certainly Girolamo, swart and saturnine, his black beard only half concealing the angry scar on his left cheek; though he was unobtrusively clad, in a dark brown quilted tunic and loose-tied turban. Azecier, a restless youth, shifted from foot to foot; Frederick, the tallest and most richly dressed of the three, looked down his long nose and offered Hereward the barest twitch of a smile.

"Lord Frederick." Hereward inclined his head. "How is my lord the Earl of Chester?" Gerbod's usurped title hung in the air for several heartbeats before Frederick answered:

"Well."

Robert shot Hereward a warning look.

"If the Vicomte decides to lay siege in earnest to Cambrai, the town will fall within days," he said. "And then he would have a base from which to forge north, perhaps to attack Bruges itself. But if he does not, then we cannot be sure where to find him: and while we hunt for him Bruges would be all but undefended."

"The latest reports suggest that his army is an undisciplined rabble," said Frederick. "They will still be raiding the Bishop's lands and we shall take them by surprise. They will be scattered easily enough."

"Master Girolamo, what are your thoughts?" The Italian shrugged.

"These questions of tactics are not where my experience lies," he said. His voice was deep and his accent guttural; it was for his benefit that they were conversing in French, since he had no Flemish, but he was still difficult to follow. "If the Lord Frederick is right, then I do not see how I will be needed."

"Lord Hereward?" said Robert. Frederick sniffed loudly at the title that he had accorded the outlaw, but said nothing.

"We cannot afford to remain here," said Hereward.

"The worst that can happen if we ride out is that we fail to find the Vicomte, and he lays siege to Bruges. Well, if that happens, at least our army will be clear of the city and able to return and attack his camp. At most, Bruges would have to hold out for three or four days; even with a skeleton garrison that shouldn't be hard."

"Then we are agreed?" said Robert. "We ride for Cambrai at dawn."

"Putting out advance scouts, of course," added Frederick, "to forewarn us of the situation there."

"Of course."

"Your proclamation will have warned the men of Ely that we're coming, obviously," Starkad pointed out. "But even if you hadn't said what the mission would be, they'd have worked out that it was aimed at them." The former bandit had been given a wash and a new suit of clothes, and was now lounging in one of Sir Ogier's chairs, drinking Sir Ogier's wine, while one of Sir Ogier's minstrels played. The knight flicked the harper a coin.

"They'd have been on the defensive at any time," said Ogier dismissively. "But without Hereward they lack their head. I was able to drive them out of Bourne when he left them before; Ely is better defended, but the outlaw's deputies are the same men." Starkad toyed with a small dagger.

"I'd rather he were here, all the same," he said quietly. "But the day will come." He paused. "I hear Ely was infiltrated last year," he said. "Why was Hereward allowed to live?"

"Because Ivo Taillebois is an idiot," sneered Ogier. "But I can understand why his agent didn't kill the wolfshead. Stealing a sword is one thing: if they'd caught him in the act he'd have been killed, but once he got off the island all they cared about was getting the sword back: but if he'd stabbed Hereward in his sleep, his life wouldn't have been worth a piss in the wind, no matter how far he ran."

"Death would be delicious if I could take Hereward Askilsson with me." The Gyrvian squeezed the blade in his hand, and a single large drop of blood splashed onto the table.

"No doubt," said Ogier. "But not everybody feels as you do. Now, you say you know the approaches to Ely..?"

"The easiest way to land men in any large numbers would be to come from the south, through Aldreth," said Starkad. "But that's a long way from Bourne. What's more, Hereward's men know it's the best way in, so they'll guard it like a gold mine. They'll watch the rivers, too, and the spot where we attacked last, in the east. But if we were to come from the northwest, they wouldn't expect it. The ground's muddy round there – most of it's too soft to march over but too thick for boats."

"So how do we cross it?" demanded Ogier.

"It's hardly rained in a month," said Starkad. "That's not usual at this time of year. The mud will be drying out. It'll be almost solid."

"Won't Hereward's men know that?"

"*Almost* solid. Strong enough for a fowler and his dog, though he may still need his mud-shoes; not to bear the weight of armoured men, never mind horses. But if we lay down planks, we can do it."

"Planks?" echoed Ogier. "Across what, a mile of fens? Two miles?"

"Probably more," admitted Starkad. "But that's just why they won't expect it."

"I think you're right," said Ogier slowly. "There is just one other thing. That route will take us very close to the monastery. My men may object if they have to attack Holy Church."

Starkad shrugged.

"The shavelings are harbouring rebels against your King," he said. "But if your men are that nice of conscience, I'll find you some that aren't."

16

"You're sure you can?" said Ogier. "These English may not love Norman monks, but they seem attached to their own."

"Maybe so. But since you came, more and more of them are hungry. When a man's belly is empty enough, he'll make war on Heaven itself for a crust of bread."

"So you will ride for Cambrai with the Lord Robert?" Hereward looked into Torfrida's eyes.

"Not if you ask me not to," he said. "I am not committed. I owe Robert nothing, yet."

"But you need the arms he has promised," she countered. "Of course I'm not happy to see you ride off again when you've only just come back to me, but I don't want to go back to England without the means to fight any more than you do. I've seen what you face there, remember. Gwynnog's hand cut off, and poor Rowena kidnapped… Of course you need armour, and weapons. And if this is the price of them then this is how it must be." She paused. "Don't get killed," she said softly. "If you are, I'll never forgive you."

Hereward pulled her close: but a moment later they were interrupted by a sharp cry from Torfridel. He looked round, concerned.

"What's wrong?" he asked. Torfrida smiled.

"She's just hungry," she said. "You'd better leave us; you'll need your sleep if you ride at dawn."

And at dawn the army of Flanders set out from Bruges. Before they departed, Robert paraded his officers up and down before the men, making speeches about how lucky they were to be led into battle by such famous heroes, in particular Hereward, the vanquisher of Holbert de Guines. That got a cheer; there were many men there who had witnessed Hereward's famous duel. Frederick glowered silently.

"Looks like a monk at a Maying," observed Martin.

The cavalry rode in the vanguard: if all went well, and the invaders were still roistering on the Bishop's ruined farms, they would be able to mop them up without needing any assistance from the infantry. Nevertheless, at Robert's insistence, Girolamo and Azecier rode with them. The engineers were unlikely to be needed, but Robert wanted to speak with them as they rode. Girolamo was not a naturally talkative man, but he had done what he did for twenty years, in any number of sieges and assaults across Italy and France, and any stories that could be drawn out of him would be of interest to a commander like Robert. Moreover, of course, if their expertise did prove to be necessary, the sooner they were apprised of the fact, the sooner they could devise something.

Girolamo obligingly recounted the undermining of city walls in Aquitaine, the burning of ships off Messina, and the like: but his accounts were clipped and curt, and he plainly found the subject of his past battles disagreeable. Before very long, Robert gave up, and instead attempted to discuss with Hereward and Martin the recent revolt in Northern England. Girolamo showed mild interest at the mention of the ram with which the Normans had brought down the gates of York: but the defeat was no more favoured a subject for them than victories were for the Italian. Nor did Hereward care to discuss his campaigns in front of Frederick: while the latter remained aloof, above talking to these foreigners.

The result was that, though the sun smiled overhead, a cold cloud had settled over the Flemish van by the time the fields and plains of Flanders gave place to the undulating ground of Hainault, and the advance scouts reported back. Their news was that the Vicomte and Sir Ascelin were in full control of the Picquignard force, which was settled into a palisaded camp before the walls of Cambrai, and reported to be nearly a thousand strong.

"Then the Bishop had reason to fear more than the

looting of his farms," remarked Hereward.

"What the Bishop is really afraid of", said Robert, "is the council of burghers which is trying to relieve him of the government of Cambrai. As long as the city doesn't fall, he'll have gained more from this invasion than he's lost: he may be a little poorer, but he'll have rallied the people behind him."

"For which God be praised," added Frederick. "If these tradesmen are allowed to run cities they'll start to think they can run kingdoms."

"That's as may be," said Robert. "We had better make camp ourselves. By the time the infantry catch us up it will be dark."

"All the better cover for an attack, surely," said Hereward.

"Against a palisaded camp?"

"William of Normandy took York by night, and that's a walled city," Martin pointed out.

"Despite your best efforts to defend it," retorted Frederick. Hereward dug his nails into his palm; he wanted to strike the supercilious Fleming.

"I agree with the Lord Hereward," said Girolamo unexpectedly. The engineer had not spoken for hours. "Surprise is our best weapon. As for the palisade... well, if there is an eminence overlooking it, it should not present a difficulty."

"In this country?" said Frederick. "We have molehills, not eminences. And if there were such a feature, do you imagine the Picquignards would have made their camp below it?"

"Even a gentle slope would do," said Girolamo. "Anything a stone might roll down."

"And where are we to get stones of that size by tonight?" Frederick demanded.

"I never said we would use stones."

In the depths of the Bromeswold, the sun seldom

penetrated the branches even at noon: now, as it sank, the gloom was complete. Starkad brandished his torch, and peered into the looming, flickering shadows.

"Uluncas?" he said. There was no answer, save a rustle from the mouldering leaves. "Uluncas," he repeated. "I know you can hear me. I've come to offer you freedom."

This time, there was a distinct sound, a deep sigh from somewhere in the darkness. But Starkad still could not swear that it had been made by a human voice.

"Sir Ogier fitz Ungomar needs men," he said. "Men to sack the Camp of Refuge. We get all the plunder we can take, and a free pardon from the Sheriff of Lincoln if Sir Ogier can take control of Ely. No more skulking in the forests; no more hunger gnawing our guts; no more fear whenever we hear a hoof fall or a dog bark." He paused. "I know your bolthole is beyond the oak tree, Uluncas. I'd have let myself in by now, if I didn't know you'd have booby-traps up."

"Go away," hissed the voice. "Let me be."

"Freedom," repeated Starkad. "Freedom, and revenge." Slowly, Uluncas moved into the torchlight. His ragged clothes, his hair, and the dirt that covered them had all but merged into one another; dead leaves were stuck in his beard; the blood of whatever he had last eaten was congealing on his face. "Thunor's hammer, you look three weeks dead," exclaimed Starkad. "Hereward's people did this to you. They took our home from us – took the Fens from us. You are a Gyrvian, not a beast of the woods. Be a man again."

"Are the others with you?" asked Uluncas, uncertainly. It was months since he had spoken to any other being than the tree spirits whom he heard whispering around him when the woods were quiet: and if they replied, he had never understood them.

"Brokk is. And Halfrek, and Grimbald. We'll find more." Starkad gripped Uluncas by the shoulders. "We'll be the Gyrvians again. And the Camp of Refuge" – he spat on

20

the ground – "will be wiped from the face of the Fens."

Hereward was amazed at how quickly, under Girolamo's direction, the Flemings were able to turn a pile of beams and branches into vicious-looking siege weapons. The core of each was a straight beam about eight feet long, with five rows of regularly spaced holes let into it: and into these holes were fixed sharpened stakes. Tied to the stakes and woven between them were pieces of coarse woollen cloth soaked in pitch. In all, there were ten of these fearsome devices.

"I only hope these work," muttered Frederick. Girolamo grunted.

There was, as had been predicted, no real hill overlooking the Picquignard camp: but the ground was uneven enough to provide several points which were at least higher than the palisade. These positions were uncomfortably close, and the Flemings creeping up to them did not dare bear torches: but every party had flint and tinder.

Below them were the campfires of the Picquignards; as they held their breath for fear of making a sound, they could dimly hear the men on the first watch chatting easily over their supper.

"And all the children of the east lay in the valley in a multitude, like locusts," whispered Girolamo. "Arise, for the Lord has delivered into your hand the host of Midian." He rose from his crouch by the nearest roller, and shouted "Now!"

It took some of the Flemish parties a few seconds to strike a light, and one was not quite in position yet: but those seconds did precious little good to the Picquignards. Before they had any idea what was happening, all ten rollers were lit, and launched. Ten bursts of flame hurtled towards the camp. One stopped still halfway to the palisade, and lay there uselessly; another rolled through a patch of muddy water and was only smouldering by the time it thudded dully into the fence; but eight struck home, one spitting two patrolling sentries on its stakes. They died screaming, pinned to the palisade: and, by the time the camp was awake, the fence itself was afire along more than half its length. As portions of it cracked and fell in, the Flemings surged through like a flood. They were on foot: horses would have been too noisy to bring so close before the trap was sprung, and too afraid of the fire: but even without the advantage of cavalry, they met little resistance. Hereward had been among the first into the camp, but before long he drew back: it was not his way to kill helpless men, even robbers and ravishers like these, and the scene brought back unquiet memories from the war in England. Instead, he hovered near the edge of the camp: one or two Picquignards trying to flee that way made to attack him, and were quickly cut down, but he attacked nobody. He saw Robert and Frederick in the thick of the battle – if such this massacre could be called – but did not join them.

By morning the field before Cambrai was red. The Picquignard dead numbered in the hundreds: the Flemings had lost only thirteen men. But the Vicomte, and Ascelin, the leaders of the invasion, had escaped.

"They won't come back to Flanders in a hurry," said Robert. "And I doubt Ascelin will last in Picquigny's service after this. It'll be back to Normandy for him. Back to the life of a hired sword." He spat. "Good riddance. And the Bishop of Cambrai can sleep easy too. We've done a good night's work."

Hereward looked round at the smouldering camp and the heaps of corpses, and bit his tongue. This good night's work had saved Cambrai, but it still smelt foul, and it would not compensate those who had already lost everything in the invasion.

"It is grievous to see so many of God's creatures slain," said Girolamo quietly. Hereward looked up, startled: he had not heard the engineer approach. "But it is His will." Hereward frowned. The night before, the engineer had quoted Scripture, though in Norman French, not Latin: men of war were seldom so devout.

"Were you trained for the priesthood?" he asked.

"Not exactly." Girolamo turned away. It was plain that he would say no more, at least at present.

The lowering grey sky had begun to spit. Ogier glanced upwards.

"It's raining," he observed.

"This isn't rain," said Starkad. "It'll make no difference."

"It will if it gets heavier."

Ogier had had great rolls of planking constructed, portable wooden roads. As his company advanced across the mud plain, they unrolled these, and proceeded slowly along them: so far, they had borne their weight, sinking only an inch or two. In most places, the surface of the mud had dried out altogether, though it cracked and shifted when weight was placed upon it. But it was slow progress, and there was little cover, only a scattering of small, hardy wetland trees. The few birds that nested in these were agitated and on guard; those without eggs to defend had already fled the approach of the armed men. They knew what it meant when humans ventured onto the flats.

Once the attackers were sighted, the men of Ely would be roused to defend the island: there was no way of knowing how close they could come before that happened. But this was their best chance of springing a surprise trap.

"We're within half a mile of the island," said Starkad. "There's more mud behind you than ahead."

"There's a path behind us," the knight pointed out. "We're advancing by inches." A heavy raindrop splashed into his eye. The planks beneath his horse's hooves juddered; a soldier swore. Ogier's Normans were looking apprehensive. Most of them spoke little English and were not sure what their lord was saying to the outlaw: but they knew enough to fear the treachery of the ground beneath them. Another drop struck Ogier's helmet. He looked around: the rain was getting heavier, and quickly. "Back!" he barked. "Every man in armour, retreat along the path!"

"And what about *my* men?" demanded Starkad, catching hold of Ogier's bridle. "What about our pardons?"

"You'll get them when you've earned them, wolfshead," snapped Ogier. "But no Norman goes with you today." He jerked the bridle out of the outlaw's hand, turning his horse on the planks. The movement made them slide a little further. The men at arms were already in retreat: the English recruits, many of them beggars or poachers freed from Ogier's cells, exchanged nervous glances. They had all come here ready to face death in battle, but not a choking end in the ooze of the Fens. Most would rather go back and hang.

"On," barked Starkad. He turned to rally his men. "We're enough to take this isle without these yellow Norman bastards. The mud's not melted yet. Think of the gold of the shaveling monks. Think of food and wine and warm beds. Think of vengeance on the men who broke the Gyrvians. Forward! Charge like the Devil's behind you, or on my oath I'll send you to meet him!"

It did not work on all of them, but it worked on enough. The former Gyrvians among them, whipped up by the memory of what they had lost, drove the others forward. Off the edge of the planking they went, splashing and squelching through the rain as they ran for the island, drawing their weapons. The ground bore them up well enough, and they took heart: and it was not until they were within a stone's throw of the monastery that the old bandit Brokk slipped and fell.

Halfrek turned and reached out to his comrade: and, as he stopped moving, the mud came over his shoes. He cursed, but thought little of it; he took Brokk by the arm, and heaved.

The mud sank away beneath Halfrek's feet. By the

24

time Brokk had found his again, both were up to their knees. The rain was now beating down hard as hail, and puddles and pits appearing all over the flats; the men who forged onwards were wading now rather than running, but the mud was claiming ever more of them, liming them like trapped birds: and the horrible realisation was creeping over them that this fen would be their grave.

By the time Winter and his hastily assembled band arrived, alerted by an abbey tenant who farmed a strip of land to the north of the monastery, they could see no attackers still alive. Here and there, on what was now to most purposes a lake, there floated hoods and hats, but there was little other sign that men had been there.

Then, suddenly, with a great slurp, at their very feet, there lurched out of the water something more mud than man. Spluttering and wheezing, it collapsed before Winter.

"I yield," it managed to say. "I yield."

"What is your name?" demanded Winter suspiciously, levelling his sword at the prone figure.

"Uluncas."

"Well, if you must go, you must," said Robert regretfully. "Flanders will miss your services." Hereward and Torfrida had just entered the great hall and announced that, now that the promised arms were at last loaded aboard the *Gannet*, they would be leaving with the morning tide.

"I've done little enough service this campaign," said Hereward. "Precious small return for your shipload of arms."

"A bargain is a bargain. I wish you good luck with your campaign."

"My campaign against your lordship's brother-in-law?" said Hereward drily. "There's no need to say things you don't mean. My greatest regret is that I can't take our Italian friend back with me; I've a feeling he'd be worth ten times the arms and armour you've given." Girolamo bowed.

"It would be an honour," he said.

"Unfortunately, he is bound to my brother," Robert smiled.

"That is not so," said Girolamo unexpectedly. "My bond was given only for this campaign; now that the Vicomte has left Flemish soil I am a free man." Robert frowned. Surely the engineer could not actually be contemplating giving up Flemish service for what would effectively be the life of an outlaw?

"But you will remain a retainer to the County of Flanders," he prompted.

"I think", said Girolamo, "that I should like to visit England. It is a land I have never been to. A visit only, of course; I shall return to Flanders in good time; but with your lordship's permission I should like to accompany the Lord Hereward." Robert breathed easy again. It was curiosity, nothing more: he would see the harsh life of the rebels and return a wiser man.

"Of course," he said, waving his hand. "We cannot deny you: as you say, you are a free man."

From the reeds at the edge of the Isle of Ely, a stolen boat slipped forth. Huddled over the single paddle, ragged, muddy and stinking, was a huge man, shivering as much from rage as from cold. This time he had nobody to be angry with but himself: but that very knowledge only redoubled his hatred for the Camp of Refuge and every human soul within it.

They would hear again from Starkad the Gyrvian; and they would wish he had died.

Chapter 2: *The Shrieking Pits*

Ely, June, 1069.

"Aylmerton," said Winter. "Aylmerton will give us a second base, and a harbour, well out of reach of Ivo and Ogier."

"And within reach of the Sheriff of Norfolk and Ralph Guader," Methelgar pointed out.

"The land round that coast's flatter than the sea," added Gwynnog. "We'd never be able to defend it. Besides, we should wait until Hereward gets back."

Hereward was at that moment on the sea, and due to touch English soil before night fell: but his men, crowded in the hut of an abbey tenant on the Isle of Ely to discuss their plans, did not know that. And the idea of expanding from the Isle to a second base was an appealing one. When they had lost their last headquarters they had had to flee all but blindly: that they had reached Ely at all had been extraordinarily good luck. And if Hereward truly meant to fight a war from here, then in time they *must* spread their wings.

"The earthworks at Aylmerton are their own defences," insisted Winter. "What's more, they say there's treasure hidden there."

"They say that about Wandlebury and a score of other sites," snorted Leofric the Deacon. "Wherever there's a hole in the ground men's imagination fills it with fairy gold."

"And they say it's fairy gold indeed at Aylmerton," put in Wulfric. "That or worse. The Pits are haunted; we'd be meddling with magic there." That hit home: Winter crossed himself, though he still did not look ready to give up his plan.

"Tell us the story of the Aylmerton Pits," suggested Methelgar, hoping to make peace. "I've not heard it before." Most of Hereward's men were local, but Methelgar hailed from the far west and had as yet only a shaky grasp of the lore of this strange corner of England: and he knew that Wulfric could never resist an invitation to tell a tale.

"There must be a dozen different stories," said the tumbler. "Some say the earthworks there are just what's left an old castle, built to defend the coast when the Danes came – or when the Saxons came, or when the Romans came. Others say they're abandoned iron workings, or else the tombs of kings going back to before the Flood, who were buried in armour of solid silver. But most would have it that they're fairy mounds, and the little people come out of them when the moon is full to dance in rings atop them. The people round there leave food and drink out, so that the little folk won't molest them, and it's always taken.

"But as for the haunting, what I was always told was that back when my grandfather was young or longer ago than that, a child wandered into the Pits chasing a butterfly. Now maybe he went into one of the mounds of his own will, or maybe he was bewitched from the moment he set foot on enchanted ground: but the Fair Folk took him.

"Now, such things happen, and the folk of Aylmerton made up their minds to forget the boy, though all of them had been fond of him: but a mother can't forget. And it so happened that he was an only child, and his father had been killed in the Danish wars, so he was all his mother had: and she made up her mind to go into the Pits and bring him back, and she would not be dissuaded.

"She took a crucifix and an iron blade, and a torch lest she should have to enter the mounds, so she should have been well protected against all magics: but she was never seen again, no more than her son. But her wailing is still heard by those as venture near the Pits, the anguished cry of a soul lost.

"So that is why the folk of Aylmerton have stayed away from those Pits longer than any man living can remember: and treasure or none, I've little mind to go there myself." There were gasps at that. Wulfric was the finest swordsman among them, and none would ever question his courage. If even he feared what lay in the Pits, it was doubtful if even Hereward could lead the men there: Winter realised that he would have little chance.

"Lysir," he said suddenly. "The one-eyed man; the one who speaks to Hereward. He'd know the truth about the Pits, if any man does."

"And, of course, you know where to find him," said Gwynnog. Winter shook his head glumly: he was not sure if even Hereward knew that, or if it was always Lysir who found him. He was defeated: but Leofric's interest had been aroused.

"Wulfric," said the deacon, "have you ever been to Aylmerton?" The tumbler shook his head.

"Not I."

"Has anyone here? Have any of you met anyone from that part of the country, even?" All shook their heads.

"Then don't you think the tales may have grown in the telling? For all we know these shrieks are just the wind. Now, I agree we shouldn't be trying to settle a second base before Hereward returns: but it'll do no harm to scout out places we *might* use. And, besides, who knows – the story about the silver armour might even be true, or based on truth. The treasure of St Edmund was real enough. I say a small party should be sent to Aylmerton, to see the lie of the land."

"Agreed," said Winter, glad to have the decision taken for him. "I'll lead it. Wulfric, since you don't want to risk the wrath of the fairies, you can take command here."

Aylmerton.

Ralph Guader, Seigneur de Montfort et Gaël, surveyed the Aylmerton Pits and wrinkled his nose.

"Is that it?" he asked. "Are those the famous

earthworks of Aylmerton? I thought there were ditches, mounds, something fortifiable. I was told I could build a castle here that would be unassailable. And what do I find? An empty field, that looks as if it's been taken over by peculiarly large moles."

"Them ain't molehills, begging your pardon, m'lord," mumbled the village headman, peering out fearfully from beneath eyebrows like battlements. Guader looked down his nose, finding it hard to believe that this decrepit old skeleton was the best spokesman Aylmerton could produce. The Seigneur, whose father had served in this benighted country under King Edward, had, like Ogier the Breton but unlike most, made a point of learning English after King William had granted him lands here: but it often struck him that the natives had not made the same effort. "Them's the Pits."

"So I understand. But they're of no use to me."

"I can't think who told your lordship they would be," said the old man, distressed. "Ain't nobody round here would ever build on the Pits. They're cursed."

"Elves and goblins?" scoffed Guader. "Whatever those pits are, they were made by men."

"I know that, m'lord," said the headman. "Them's the old iron workings. I remember when we were still usin' 'em, though there's none else as does. And I remember when the ore ran out and we had to move the workings, and when poor Adswith went into the Pits, her as became the White Lady. She's the one as haunts 'em still."

"So," said Guader, "there are no silver suited kings. Well, God knows, if I were a king, I'd want better tombs than these." He turned to his lieutenant. "Can't hurt to take a look, though," he said. "We've wasted the day already; at the very least we'll lay this ghost to rest. Get shovels from the houses and set the men to breaking those heaps of dirt open," he ordered. "See what you can find."

"No, my lord!" protested the headman. "Adswith's spirit will be angry!"

30

"*I* am angry already," replied Guader. "Which do you really fear more?" The headman bowed his head, and said nothing. "Get on with it," the Seigneur barked at his soldiers.

They at once scattered throughout the village to find tools. Doors were kicked in, shelves pulled down, spades snatched from the hands of men digging their little strips of land. The women preparing for the Midsummer celebrations, building the bonfire and hanging wreaths of St John's wort to scare off the wraiths that walked on the saint's eve, muttered darkly that evil would come of it. Finally, the now fully equipped soldiers lined up before Guader.

"Into the Pits," he ordered, and into that strange knobble-surfaced field they advanced, spreading out and positioning themselves in twos and threes on top of the disappointingly small mounds, until all had begun to dig.

They had been at it for less than a hundred heartbeats when there arose an unearthly, eldritch shriek. It sounded more like a wounded beast than a human voice, and it seemed to come from all around them. The soldiers turned pale; many dropped their tools: more than one set of teeth were chattering by the time the scream died away.

"I did tell you, m'lord," said the headman unhelpfully. "'Tis Adswith."

The soldiers were mastering their fear, picking up their tools, and trying to tell themselves that what they had heard was the protest of a limed bird or the wind whistling through a cracked rock, when one suddenly shouted:

"I see her! The White Lady!"

Pandemonium followed, as some men made to flee from the Pits, while others shouted and argued, some swearing that there was no Lady, others that they had seen her in quite another direction. But when a second flash of white from the largest, central pit was followed by another shriek, every man of them turned and ran back towards the village. In vain did Guader curse them for cowards, and strike at those who passed near him: the Lady now held more

31

fear for them than their lord.

With an oath, the Seigneur turned the head of his horse towards the Pits, pushing aside the headman who caught at his bridle. He fumbled for the hilt of his sword, declaring:

"I'll bring back this White Lady's head!" But when he reached the edge of the Pits, his steed stopped dead, so suddenly that he jolted in the saddle. He applied the spurs, but the beast would not move, even when he dug so deep that the blood was pouring down its sides: it gnashed on the bit and turned aside. Many of Guader's men were crossing themselves and muttering prayers, while the headman allowed himself a grim, private smile. The Lady's anger might yet hurt Aylmerton, but at least these Norman interlopers had been taught to respect her.

So too had four Englishmen, who had landed at Aylmerton not long before the Normans had ridden in, introducing themselves as fishermen on their way to Yarmouth, and had seen the whole affair from the table before the tavern where they sat drinking. Their eyes had widened at every shriek.

"That's Adswith," the innkeeper told them. "The White Lady. She bore a Dane's bastard back in King Ethelred's day and her husband threw the child into the Pits, and she's haunted 'em ever since."

"Now, that's not the story as old Saethryth tells it," another customer, a round-bellied, red-faced man butted in. "She said it was Adswith herself that the husband murdered – and she ought to know, she was alive at the time. We'll have a bad Midsummer now, with the Lady angry. She'll make our cattle fall sick, I shouldn't wonder, and our sheep waste away."

"Saethryth's addled in her wits," insisted a third man. "Now Redwald told me -"

"Redwald!" exclaimed the fat man. "How can you believe anything that old liar says?" As the squabble grew fiercer, and louder, and the danger of attracting Norman attention greater, Winter called over the innkeeper and quietly paid the bill: and shortly afterwards the four false fishermen slipped out of the village and down to their boat. Nobody was watching closely enough to observe that they turned west instead of east.

The Wash.

The *Gannet* nosed slowly towards the shore, Hereward standing impatiently in the bow.

"Why do we not go faster?" he demanded. "The sea's no more than choppy, and we've a good wind behind us."

"This coast is treacherous," said Brunman. "There are sandbanks everywhere. And there are strange things round these parts, that can draw a ship off course. I've heard tell of mermaids and the like, though I've never seen such: but I *have* seen things here that weren't there, and heard 'em too. It's dangerous for a sailor to trust even his senses sometimes."

As he spoke, there reached them against the wind the distant echo of a cry.

"What was that?" exclaimed Azecier, who had been clinging to the rail looking green ever since they had left Antwerp; at least after the first hour he had had nothing left to throw up.

"Someone in pain," said Hereward. "Dying, by the sound of it. It came from the shore, there to the east."

"It sounded like the southern shore to me," said Martin.

"It's a trick of the finfolk," insisted Brunman. "Them or whatever other evil spirits haunt these waters. I tell you, I've heard it before."

"Then what's that?" said Hereward suddenly, pointing ahead and a little to starboard. A dark shape was clearly splashing in the water not a hundred yards from shore, struggling, fighting to stay afloat. Brunman shielded his eyes, and gave a low whistle.

"By Aegir's kettle," he said, "it's a woman." He turned to his crew. "Veer to starboard!" he ordered. "We'll pick her up before she drowns."

Sheets were hauled on and the steerboard turned, and the *Gannet*'s course set towards the floundering woman; as always, Hereward was amazed by the ease with which Brunman's ship moved. She handled better than any other vessel he'd set foot in.

"Can you still see her?" asked Brunman.

"There – damn it, that's not where she was before! We'll have to veer larboard again."

"She can't have moved that fast," said Martin. "There must be more than one."

"I see only one," insisted Hereward. "It *is* the same, I'm sure of it."

"Where?"

"There – no…" The woman had disappeared again.

"Dragged under, perhaps," said Martin. "St Maughold grant we're not too late."

There was a sudden grating crunch, and the whole body of the *Gannet* shuddered; Hereward was thrown off his feet, and Azecier began to gasp as if he were the one drowning.

"Hell and damnation!" cursed Brunman. "We're aground."

"Aground?"

"I told you these shallows were dangerous; and I told you we couldn't trust what we see. Do you see your drowning woman now? No; the finfolk have got what they wanted." Martin peered back towards where the woman had been seen. A largeish grey seal, head erect, was bobbing through the waves: but he kept quiet. If that was truly all they had seen – and he could have sworn he had glimpsed long dark hair and a dress floating wide – it would please nobody

34

to have it pointed out. Brunman was right about one thing, whether or not there were any finfolk: at sea, a man could not always trust his eyes.

"Are we holed?" demanded Hereward urgently. With Torfrida and their daughter aboard, in a makeshift cabin erected aft, he was acutely aware of every danger to the ship. He preferred even the raw fear of battle to this constant anxiety.

"No," said Brunman, "we'd have felt that. Nothing cracked. This is just a sandbank. It doesn't make us any the less stuck."

"Will the tide lift us off?"

"Who knows? But there's nought we can do until it does. And high tide's not till dusk."

Hereward spat on the deck.

"The Normans may patrol the shore," he pointed out. "Are we to sit here like lobsters in a pot, waiting for them to come and get us?"

"We have no choice."

"You were right," Winter told Wulfric. "Aylmerton's not worth facing the ghosts. We couldn't build on it anyway – it's just an old ironworks." The sun had sunk and the campfires been lit by the time the four spies had arrived back, and dozens of the folk of Ely had gathered round to hear their story.

"So the ghosts are real?" said Leofric.

"We heard them," Winter insisted.

"And saw them," added one of the men who had accompanied him. Those who stood around listening muttered hasty prayers.

"If there are truly unquiet spirits at Aylmerton," said the deacon, "they should be exorcised."

"You do it, then. We're not going back to that accursed place."

"I'm only a deacon; it's a priest's business," said

Leofric.

"It's not *our* business," said Winter. "I should never have gone there."

"If you hadn't, we wouldn't have known it wasn't suitable for a second base. Now we do, and we can think on matters at Ely again. Such as: what do we do with the Gyrvian?"

"Kill him," came a fierce growl from a couple of rows back. There was a muttering of assent. Winter recognised the speaker, a stout, dark, scowling man, as Hogor, a lay brother who served as the abbey cook, and had entered into the counsels of the rebels from the day they had arrived at Ely.

"The decision is the Lord Hereward's," Winter declared.

"Why have we kept him alive this long?" demanded Hogor. "Why was he not cut down the moment he came ashore? He's an invader, a foe, a thief and a killer. The Gyrvians near starved us when they came to steal the grain last year. The Lord Hereward himself said that we couldn't share the Fens with them. But we're taking food from our own children's mouths to feed this scum."

"He was unarmed and helpless," said Gwynnog, stepping in to defend Winter. If the authority of Hereward's lieutenant were undermined, Ely would never stand. "We are men of honour. We don't kill in cold blood. Uluncas the Gyrvian is a prisoner of war."

"Forsooth, there is not a man
Over earth so high-mooded," chanted Hereward,
"Nor in giving so good,
Nor in youth so forward,
Nor in deeds so doughty,
Nor to his thane so close
That in his seafaring
He has no sorrow,

36

No fear of what his Lord
Will do to him.
Not for him is the harp's note,
Nor the ring-giving,
Nor a wife to win,
Nor the world's highness –
Nor ought else,
Save the waves' rolling:
But he has ever a longing
Who toils on the waves."

At the end of every line, Brunman's men gave a heave on their oars. It had not been possible to get any purchase on the sandbank itself, which was under the water even at low tide: but as the tide rose and they began to loosen, the captain had ordered the sweeps out in the hope that they might pull free. The ship creaked and groaned at first, but did not move: but as they continued, it began to seem that they were indeed beginning to slide by fitful inches off the bank. Then, with a sudden lurch as Hereward reached the end of the verse, the *Gannet* freed herself. She had been held so low in the water that now she shot up like a cork, throwing Azecier off his feet; Torfridel, after a gasp at the first shock of the movement, giggled excitedly.

"Well," said Brunman, "at least we know we're not holed."

"Will we be able to make our way upriver by night?" asked Hereward anxiously. "Those waters aren't safe."

"We have no choice," said the captain. "At least the dark'll keep us out of sight of the Normans. If we go slow, we shouldn't run into any more banks, though we may graze them. You can't cart these arms overland, and I can't put in at any Norman port to see what the damage is. The river's the only way for both of us."

They arrived at Ely early the next day. While the ship

was being unloaded, bundles of swords, piles of shields, boxes of helmets and even a dozen rolled hauberks carried into the abbey, Hereward saw Torfrida and Torfridel ashore, and ordered that a room be prepared for them. Abbot Thurstan tutted and clucked: he would have no women within the abbey: but Hereward pointed out that the pilgrim hostel had been erected outside the gate for this very reason. The hostel had been out of use since the Conquest, but it should not take too long to put it into some kind of habitable order, and in the meantime they and Kolfrosta could surely be found a berth in some tenant's house. When this was done, Hereward sought out Winter, to receive his report on how things had befallen in his absence.

"So," he said, when he had heard all, "this Uluncas is still a prisoner here?"

"He is," Winter confirmed. "He's kept in a monk's cell with the door bolted; it's more secure than anywhere in the camp; but I doubt he could escape anyway. He wrenched his leg coming ashore and it hasn't healed; he drags his left foot when he moves."

"It could be a ruse," said Hereward.

"That's what Hogor says," remarked Winter. "He thinks we should have killed him."

"Are we taking counsel from the cook now?"

"Many of the men resent having to keep an enemy, especially with the hungry time coming."

"That's understandable," said Hereward. "But you did right to take him alive. He may even prove of use to us yet. I should like to see him."

"It won't be safe to enter his cell," warned Winter. "He nearly had Wulfric's fingers off once when he took him some food, and he threw his slop bucket at my head. He's a vicious bastard."

"I think I trust myself with an unarmed cripple who's been a week in durance," said Hereward with a grimace. "Take me to him."

The cells were spare and gloomy but serviceable; most monks spent little time there when they were not sleeping. They were not designed to be lived in. The hard monkish plank bed might be easier to sleep on than the floor of the Bromeswold, but Uluncas missed the sun. The surges of anger that had burst out of him in the first two or three days of his imprisonment were past now; they had been replaced by a dull ache of resentment. He agreed with Hogor: they should have killed him.

He recognised Hereward the moment he entered the cell. He had seen the commander of the Camp only briefly, and at a distance, when the Gyrvians' island had fallen: but the torch Winter bore shone full on his leader's face, and illuminated his famous odd eyes, one blue, the other grey.

"Hereward Askilsson," said the captive flatly. "Here to inspect the guest rooms? Do they meet with your approval?"

"And you are Uluncas the Gyrvian," said Hereward. "Stand up." Uluncas, who was sitting slumped in a corner and had not moved when his captors entered, braced a hand against the wall and struggled upwards, wincing. Hereward hesitated for a moment, then held out his hand. Uluncas looked at it in puzzlement. "Take my hand," said Hereward. "I'll help you." Tentatively, suspiciously, the Gyrvian placed his hand in Hereward's, and was hauled to his feet. He flinched again as his left foot touched the ground: then, suddenly, he hurled his weight forward, bearing Hereward off his feet, his left hand scrabbling for his throat. Winter seized him by the collar of his filthy tunic and hauled him off Hereward, slamming him against the wall.

"I warned you, my lord," he said. Uluncas smiled.

"I had to try," he told Hereward.

"Against two of us? Poor choice. But yes, I suppose you had to try." Hereward dusted himself off, and fixed his eyes on the prisoner's. "Why did you come to Ely?" he demanded. Uluncas shrugged.

"We were offered money, and a pardon," he said. "Starkad, may snakes eat his bones, brought the message from Ogier of Bourne." He spat, aiming at the floor; but the spittle caught the wrist of Winter, who was still holding the Gyrvian back, and who made a disgusted noise.

"Starkad?" said Hereward. "Grendel's brother? What became of him?"

Uluncas shook his head.

"Don't know; don't want to know. I hope he's under a thousand tons of mud. I've never known his like, not even Grendel, and God grant I never do."

"But you didn't see him die?" pressed Hereward.

"No."

Hereward looked at Winter.

"Did anybody else?" Winter shook his head. "But the rest of the Gyrvians were drowned?"

"Most of them weren't Gyrvians," said Uluncas, "just folk who needed the money. There are a lot of hungry people in these parts. And Ogier's own folk got away. He pulled them back when the rain began." He was calmer now, and for the first time looked Hereward in the eye.

"First Ivo Taillebois and now Ogier," remarked Hereward. "The barons round these parts seem to make a habit of hiring Starkad to do their dirty work."

"Makes sense," shrugged Uluncas. "He knows the Fens. But he's failed twice now, and there can't be many of the old Gyrvians left. Maybe just me." Hereward nodded.

"So, tell me, Uluncas, Last of the Gyrvians," he said, his hand resting on the hilt of his dagger, "can you think of one reason why I shouldn't kill you now that you're in my power?"

"Not one," said Uluncas. Hereward nodded.

"That's the difference between us," he said. "Come on, Winter, there's nothing more to be gained here today."

That evening, a council of the leading men of the

40

Camp of Refuge was called in the abbey's refectory: Hereward had an important announcement. At his own insistence, despite the Abbot's disapproval, Torfrida was present; Kolfrosta was minding the baby, assisted by Wulfric's wife Rowena, who would herself be a mother before long.

"Brunman has learned", he declared, "that a war fleet has assembled on the coast of Denmark. There is some doubt about its aims: some have said it is designed against Scotland, or Poland; and none know why it has not yet sailed, with the summer waxing late: but most say that King Svend plans to invade England." A ripple of gasps ran round the room as this sank in. "We do not know", Hereward went on, "if Svend comes for plunder or something more; if he aims against the Normans or against all of us; if we should fear his coming – or welcome it. But I have a plan." He took a deep breath. "There is one way to ensure that the Danes will rest friends to the English; to turn this war, if war there must be, to our advantage and William's confusion. And that is to offer Svend the Crown of England." The stunned silence seemed to last an age, before at last Abbot Thurstan spoke up.

"That is unthinkable!" he declared. "Edgar Edwardsson is the rightful King. He is the next in line and was elected by the Witan. You are bound to uphold his right, not to swap one foreign tyrant for another."

"Edgar Edwardsson was a disaster," replied Hereward fiercely. "Norman William thrashed him twice and now he's hiding in Scotland or God knows where with his tail between his legs. Svend is a king tried and tested. The union of England and Denmark worked before, under Canute. It worked because Canute respected our laws and customs and never robbed an Englishman to pay his cronies; it worked because our land wasn't flooded with new sheriffs and lords and priests who don't even speak our language. William isn't a tyrant because he's foreign, he's a tyrant because he's William. And the Danes are coming anyway. Would you rather they plundered and sacked their way along the coast and then went home? Would you rather we had to fight them and the Normans both?"

"If you appeal to Svend Estridsson, you will regret it," insisted the Abbot. "Will you be another Berne Bucecarle? Berne was a wronged man: he had a just quarrel against his king: but in pursuit of that quarrel he brought in the Danes, and he brought decimation on England."

"I know the story," said Hereward. "Things were very different then. Svend is a Christian and a man of law. The Danes are no longer the people they were in Berne's day."

He looked around the table for support.

"You weren't at York, Father Abbot," said Martin. "We've seen what happens when Edgar tries to lead an army."

"If the Lord Hereward thinks it's the best course," agreed Wulfric, "we'll take a chance on Svend."

"It's the best hope we've been offered yet," added Methelgar. "And the enemy's still in disarray after the Northern rebellion."

"We are at war," the old priest Wulfwine said heavily, "and we need an ally. We need the Danes; let us pray that they do not fail us."

"If I may speak?" Torfrida was on her feet; the men fell silent, and Hereward inclined his head towards her. "At the court of Flanders I heard much of this Svend, and most of it good. He has ruled for twenty years; he defeated Hardrada himself in war, and has kept the peace well with the Obodrites and the German dukes; he can read and write; he found the Danish Church in chaos and has reformed it root and branch. The Danes who come to Antwerp and Bruges praise him and call him the only true heir to Canute. They all agree that he is an excellent king."

"Thank you, my lady," said Hereward, nodding. "Now, it is my intention to send Brunman of Skirbeck to King Svend, with a message assuring him that he has our goodwill and will have our support if he comes to overthrow the usurper William. Brunman will be able to argue our cause well enough; he can sell anything to anyone. But he will require payment. We have enough gold here, taken from the Norman thieves: does any man object to this use of it?" A few hands were raised, but they were a clear minority. "Then it is decided. We will invite Svend Estridsson to be our King."

"Did I do right?" he asked. He was sitting in a dell on a wooded corner of the island, where he had gone to be alone and bathe in the dappled green light: but Lysir had come to him there. The one-eyed man never failed to find him. In wood or fen, on the Isle or off it, Lysir in his grey cloak and broad-brimmed hat would appear. Hereward had long since given up asking how.

"In the matter of Svend?" Lysir shrugged, and stroked his beard. It had grown longer and more tangled than Hereward remembered. "You will know when he comes."

"If it is not that which has brought you to me," said Hereward, flicking away an insect that had settled on his hand, "then what?" Lysir was silent. "Is there something else? The prisoner Uluncas? The ghost at Aylmerton?"

"So your men have been to Aylmerton," said Lysir. "I heard as much."

"What is it that haunts the Pits?" pressed Hereward. "Does it threaten us here?"

Lysir shook his head.

"I do not know," he said. "I have not seen what is there: but I know that there has been a great wrong suffered."

"By whom?" said Hereward. "By the woman Adswith? By… the elves? Do they exist? What wrong? Whose task is it to right it, and how?"

"I do not know," repeated Lysir.

"I never thought to hear you say those words."

"I see much," said Lysir. "More than most men with two eyes. And I hear more still. But the Pits of Aylmerton are dark to me."

"You are not sending me back there?"

"I can send you nowhere, Hereward. You come and go at your own will, as you have always done. And in this case I cannot even advise you. Perhaps the Shrieking Pits are meant to remain a mystery; but whether you go there or no is your own free choice."

Hereward smiled.

"You know me by now," he said.

Hereward appealed for one companion to go with him to Aylmerton; but after the reception Winter had met, the men were reluctant. Martin declared that he believed in no ghosts, but did believe in Ralph Guader, and would need better reason than Hereward's curiosity to put his neck under the Seigneur's sword; Gwynnog offered to volunteer, but his missing hand would have made him a mark for any Norman patrol. The same was true of Methelgar's accent.

"I could come," said Wulfwine. "If you need an exorcist…"

"I also need a man who can fight if we are cornered," said Hereward. "You're a brave man, Father, and I'm thankful for it, but you're not a warrior."

"But *I* can wield a cudgel and wear a cassock," said Leofric the Deacon with a grin. "Take me to Aylmerton; I've a mind to see these famous ghosts."

It was mid afternoon the next day when they arrived in Aylmerton: since Guader's territory was not a safe place to spend the night, they would need to ride back by night. As merchants were more likely to be robbed, they had adopted their old disguise as pilgrims, which had served the folk of the Camp of Refuge so well in the past; the day's food they carried was not worth attacking two armed horsemen in open country for.

"I'd imagined something more impressive," remarked Hereward when the Pits came into view. "But there's an eeriness about them, right enough." There was indeed. These iron workings, where men had quarried and smelted, shouted and laughed within memory not yet quite dead, were now not merely tumbled in but so overgrown that nobody could tell what they had been: but although the grass had returned, it seemed that animals had not. The field was silent as a cemetery, and it would be long before the print of mankind's hand wore away from it altogether.

For now, however, no mortal was near. Wreaths of flowers had been hung up on posts at the entrance to the field, to appease the Lady and the little people, and bread and milk left out: but the people of Aylmerton had all gone to the bonfire. Ghosts or no ghosts, they were not going to miss the dancing.

"I don't think the horses will enter," said Leofric.

"You mean you don't want to," retorted Hereward; he tried to accompany the remark with a grin, but found he could not. "But you're right; you should mind them. And be ready to come in after me if I call for help." He dismounted, handing Swallow's bridle to Leofric. The mare made a whimpering noise and nuzzled her master; he stroked her mane and whispered "There, now. I'm not taking you in there; and I've come back from worse than ghosts before, haven't I? That's my brave girl."

And Hereward stepped into the Pits.

He half expected to feel a chill as soon as he put his feet on the haunted ground: he felt no different, but once he was a few yards in, and the low green mounds were rising all around him, he fancied he did begin to feel cold. The path seemed to be leading down towards the centre of the field, where the grass was darker and a deep depression lay between the mounds. It was in perpetual shadow, and even so late in the day a thin wreath of morning mist lay over it.

"Often he who is alone
Bides in grace," he declaimed,

"Finds the Lord's mercy,
Though he, care-laden,
Along the lades
Long by hand must scull,
In the rime-cold sea
Tread the path of loss.
Wyrd goes ever as she will."

Ahead of him, something groaned.
"Who's there?"
Another loud sigh.
"Adswith?"

A white shape flitted across the corner of Hereward's vision: and he understood.

"Adswith," he said, softly but clearly, "I know you are here. I know you are no ghost. I know it's you that takes the food the villagers leave out for the little people; I know you've never stopped looking for your child. Come out."

There was no sound. Hereward advanced to the edge of the central depression: in the shadow ahead, he could make out a deeper darkness, the mouth of a tunnel leading into one of the mounds. The mist wound itself around his feet; he could hear his own heartbeat, but no other sound, no twitter of birdsong nor rustle of grass.

"Adswith," he repeated. "Come forth."

Slowly, from the depths of the tunnel, something began to move, a grey shape seeping out into the dim light. As it separated itself from the shadow and moved forward, it began to take form: a bent and haggard figure, thin, shrunken, swathed in tattered woollen blankets and with a mat of dirty white hair, and a face – a face as worn and ancient as the Pits themselves, out of which stared two watery blue eyes. The figure whimpered like a wounded dog; and Hereward stretched out his hand.

"Come," he said again. "Come out of the Pits. It is over." Slowly, fearfully, Adswith raised her withered hand,

and placed it in his: then, with a howl, she collapsed onto Hereward's chest, and began to weep. Cradling her as he would Torfridel, he picked her up, and carried her forth from the Pits: she weighed no more than a bundle of dry sticks.

Eleven days later, he delivered her into the care of his mother at Croyland Abbey; she was accepting food and beginning to talk a little, and would be better off there than at Ely. The same day, the *Gannet* put forth from the Wash, lighter by a load of arms, and bound for Denmark. The seed of war had been planted: it was time to see what would grow.

Chapter 3: *The Muster*

Ely, July, 1069.

"When will we be going back to Flanders, master?"

Girolamo grunted, and continued to polish his sword.

"In good time," he said. "I am not yet ready to leave."

"Why not?" demanded Azecier. "What is keeping us here?"

Girolamo sighed, and looked up.

"These English interest me," he said. "I am learning their language, and I should like to observe them in battle."

"In battle!" exclaimed Azecier. "We aren't here to fight! We aren't being paid!"

"I said observe, not fight," said Girolamo mildly. "And we are being fed and housed, no doubt at some expense. We do owe a debt to the Lord Hereward."

Azecier bit his lip.

"How do you intend to pay it, master?" he asked.

Girolamo set his sword down. He did not want to be drawn into this conversation.

"I have watched him training his men," he said. "It is fascinating, but hardly in accordance with the precepts of Vegetius. They need the advice of the ancients."

"So we're to stay while you teach him the whole of *De Re Militari*?" scoffed Azecier.

"There is another matter," said Girolamo, more sombrely. "I have fought beside and against Normans, in Sicily and Calabria, in Brittany and Maine, and I have seen the manifold cruelties of their knights: but this country seems to have suffered more than any. These people here at Ely have lost everything but their lives; if I can help them strike at least one blow against the invader in return for that, I shall be glad of it." It was the longest speech he had made in months.

"And then we'll go home?" said Azecier hopefully.

48

"We will go back to Flanders," said Girolamo, who had no home, "before the winter. But a couple more months here will do us no harm."

Roskilde.

Even in the speedy *Gannet*, it had taken more than two weeks crawling up the dangerous coasts of the North Sea, evading sharp rocks and Frisian raiders, to get Brunman from the Wash to the court of King Svend: now he had been there eight days more, and had made no progress.

On his arrival he had been taken almost at once into the presence of the King in his hall, which had seemed to bode well: but the hall was full of shouting men, many of them Obodrites in fur cloaks and long whiskers, jabbering in their alien tongue, and Brunman had not got near the King. Over the succeeding days, he had at first struggled to learn what was afoot: the servants and shield-bearers he managed to talk to understood little, and the one member of the court he knew, Svend's brother Asbjorn, had always been busy, striding from hall to hut, fuming against this or that Obodrite lord or recalcitrant priest, with no time to speak to the English sailor. His crew back at the creek must be growing impatient; Hereward had not paid them enough for a long stay. With individual rooms only for the greatest nobles and no space left in the hall, he slept in the kitchens, and lucky he was to get that.

At last, however, he was shaken awake one morning to find himself looking up at a young man in an embroidered cloak of scarlet wool, who proffered him a cup of ale.

"Brunman of Skirbeck?" He nodded. "I am Harald Svendsson. My uncle Asbjorn noticed you; he regrets that he cannot attend to you himself..."

"What is it that has the court in such an uproar?" Brunman interrupted. "Why are the Obodrites here?"

"Lord Krakus and his train have come to demand that we give up Prince Henryk," said Harald. Brunman looked blank. "Three years ago," the prince explained, "the Obodrites had one of their civil wars, and Kruto of Wagria ended up as the new leader of the Confederacy. He calls himself Prince of all the Obodrite Nations, and most of his rivals were driven into exile. One of those was Prince Henryk, who came to Roskilde and sought shelter from my father. Now Kruto wants an alliance with Denmark, so he's sent his brother Krakus to negotiate it. He could have chosen better: Krakus is charmless and difficult: but we need some sort of accommodation with the Confederacy, and Kruto knows it. So he demands a royal bride for Krakus, and Henryk sent back to Wagria in chains."

Brunman blinked, and sipped his ale; it was a little early for him to try to follow such complicated matters.

"Henryk", Harald went on, "demands that we should go to war to restore him as Prince of the Obodrites. That's why the court is in such turmoil."

"Would your father do it?" wondered Brunman, realising too late how sensitive this question might be: but Harald merely shrugged.

"Nobody knows," he said. "The Church is on Henryk's side because he's a Christian and Kruto's a heathen, but the bishops will do as my father tells them. We have a war fleet ready to sail, but -" He stopped himself.

"But it was intended for England," Brunman finished, "and now you can't leave Denmark until you're sure Kruto won't invade while your backs are turned." Harald looked at the floor and said nothing. "You know, of course, the English will welcome your father," Brunman went on, peering into the prince's face. "I was sent here to offer him the Crown."

"You were?" Harald gripped Brunman's arm. "By whom? Gospatric? Waltheof? One of the bishops?"

"By Hereward Askilsson," said Brunman. "The one they call the Wake." Harald shook his head.

"I don't know the name," he said. "Is he an earl?"

"No," admitted Brunman. "He's the son of a thane from Lincolnshire, though Earl Leofric was his uncle by marriage. He leads the resistance in the Fenland."

"How many men has he?"

"A hundred, maybe more," said Brunman. "And, of course, there will be many more soon. He has called a muster -"

"Only a hundred," said Harald disappointedly. "They say the Norman William can field thousands." He paused. "Has this Hereward the support of any of the earls?"

"There are no English earls left that I know of," said Brunman.

"But the former earls?"

"I don't know. But their fathers were happy to serve Canute. Why should they not rally to Canute's nephew?"

"Well," said Harald doubtfully, "this is certainly a matter that deserves to be heard. I'll see my father gives you an audience before today is out. But I can promise you nothing."

"Ulric Grogan, champion of Mercia!"

Grogan bounded into the centre of the ring. He was a squat, heavy man, and his massive beard was streaked with grey, but he still moved like a cat. Hereward remembered him from Earl Leofric's mead hall, when he was a boy: the Norse-Irish mercenary had been as fierce at board as in battle, and if the years had mellowed him it was not by much. He grinned, and swung his battleaxe under the noses of the men nearest him: though seasoned warriors, there was none who did not flinch. They had gathered to welcome the day's assignment of new recruits to Ely, and to see their skills put to the test: though, in truth, there would be none turned away unless they were taken for spies or had some horrible crime in their past, though Hereward might seek to dissuade some. The Camp of Refuge sheltered the helpless as well as warriors: many had nowhere else to go. At this hungry time of year, when the last of the old year's harvest was running out and the next not yet begun, it might be foolhardy to invite new mouths: but many had brought all the food they could carry, and in a few weeks the crops would be in.

"Have you a champion to set against me, Hereward Askilsson?" crowed Grogan. Hereward shook his head.

"I know you can fight, my friend," he said. "I remember you. There wasn't a man dared face you when you were the Earl's champion, and I wouldn't like to now."

"That was twenty years ago and more," muttered somebody near the back of the crowd. Grogan's face darkened, and he shook his axe.

"Who said that?" he shouted. "Which snivelling little whelp dares call Ulric Grogan dotard? Come out and show yourself!"

Through the crowd, there pushed the hefty form of Hogor, the monastery cook. Grogan looked him up and down with a sneer.

"Soft," he said scornfully. "Fat as a corn-fed pigling." It was true that Hogor ate well in his kitchens; but there was muscle under his fat, and he was taller and younger than the old Earl's champion. He grinned.

"If you'll put that cleaver down, old man, this pigling will show you how to fight with your fists – if your bones aren't too stiff."

Grogan scowled, and handed the axe to the man who happened to be standing nearest; he nearly dropped the unexpected weight. As Grogan went to unclasp his cloak, the cook struck, lunging at his face: but before the onlookers even had time to gasp at this unsporting attack, the older man had sidestepped the blow. Carried forward by his own weight, Hogor staggered past, and Grogan kicked him to the ground before he could regain his balance.

"You'll have to be quicker than that to get the better of Ulric Grogan, boy," he jeered. "If you're going to fight dirty, try and look like a decent man first. If your enemy can see you're a dirty dog he'll be ready for you to behave like one."

Hereward stepped forward. He could not afford ill feeling in the Camp of Refuge. Helping Hogor to his feet, he said:

"Well done, Grogan; welcome to Ely. Now embrace and part as friends." Hogor bit his lip, then winced, for it was as bruised as his pride from the fall: but Grogan, after a momentary hesitation, threw his great arms around the cook as if greeting a lost brother.

"No harm done, lad," he said. "When I've taught you how to use that right properly it'll be as deadly as a sword."

"Who is next?" asked Hereward. A tall, thin man with untidy dark hair, wearing an ill-fitting woollen tunic and too-short cloak in a muddy green, and carrying a pair of sickles, stepped forward.

"Lewine the Sickle," he said. "From Croxton."

"And are you a fighting man, Lewine, or were you dispossessed? Or both?"

"I can fight," said Lewine, sticking his chin out with what struck Hereward as undue defensiveness. "Well as any noble."

"Were you a soldier? Do you use the sword or the axe? You don't look like a man who fights with his hands."

"I fight with these," said Lewine, holding up the sickles. "I'm the best in Croxton. That's why they call me the Sickle."

"I... see," said Hereward. "Are you a serf, Lewine?"

"No, I'm freeborn."

"Do you have a family?"

"I've no wife yet; I live with my parents in Croxton."

"And you're not in any trouble? Accused of poaching, behind with your rent, anything like that?"

"No indeed, my lord," said Lewine stoutly. "We're respectable people. But that don't mean we like living under the Normans."

"No," agreed Hereward. "But it seems to me you've more to lose, your family has more to lose, from you being here than from you staying at home. Your parents may suffer if you join us."

"Oh, they know I'm here," said Lewine airily. "It was them as sent me."

"Well, I'd still strongly advise you to go back. We've not much call for sickle-fighting; it's a game, isn't it? A sort of a dance? Have you ever been in a fight for your life?"

"No, my lord," admitted Lewine. "But I reckon I could."

"You do, do you?" Hereward gestured to Wulfric. "This man is the best swordsman I've ever known," he said. "Let's see how you and your sickles do against his blade. Try not to carve each other up too badly."

Shrugging off his cloak, Wulfric took up his sword and buckler, and stepped into the ring. Lewine shambled forward – then, suddenly, struck with both sickles at once. Wulfric blocked the blows, and tried to twist the left hand sickle out of Lewine's hand: but, instead, he found that the peasant forced his sword slowly down towards the ground. Then, unexpectedly, Lewine released the pressure, and slid his sickle off Wulfric's blade. The sword leapt upwards, and Lewine, at the same time, dropped to a crouch and swung his sickle sideways, stopping it a mote's length from the tumbler's unprotected leg.

"There," he said. "You see?"

"By God," exclaimed Wulfric, "I've never seen the like." He turned to Hereward. "It's the shape of the blade," he said. "I never quite knew what it was going to do, which way it would glance. A man who'd faced a sickle-fighter before might stand a good chance, but raw recruits from Normandy who only learned to hold a sword three months ago? He'll cut them to pieces."

"It seems we need your skills after all," said Hereward. "Welcome to Ely. Who's next?"

54

"I'd have thought you'd have recognised me, Hereward." The speaker was a slender, sandy-haired young man in a supertunic of russet linen and a light cape. He did look familiar, but Hereward could not place him. "It may have been a long time, but I *am* your cousin."

"Geric?" Hereward peered again at the young man's face. Geric Sigurdarson had been a child when Hereward had gone into exile. "Geric!" He hugged his cousin fiercely to him. "By the bones of St Edmund, it's good to see you!"

"It's good to be here," answered Geric. "But I nearly didn't make it at all."

"What happened?" demanded Hereward.

"I was travelling with Egen of Burwell; he was one of King Harold's housecarles, and he's itched to be rid of the Normans since they came here. We were ambushed on the way. The Normans were on foot, and I managed to outride them, but Egen and his shieldbearer were killed."

"Do you think you were betrayed?" asked Hereward.

"I don't know. I don't think so."

"If the Normans knew we were mustering men," Wulfric pointed out, "it wouldn't matter who was using which routes. They could set ambushes on every road to Ely."

"Is there a spy in this camp?" demanded Grogan. "If there is I'll make him eat his own brains."

"I don't believe there could be," said Hereward. "Enough people knew about the muster; more likely one of the men I sent for betrayed us. Or one of my messengers was captured; there are two who haven't yet returned. Or maybe the Normans simply noticed warriors leaving the villages."

"What about that foreigner?" Hogor piped up. "The Moor or whatever he is, that you brought back from Flanders? He's a mercenary; he speaks the Normans' language; I don't trust him."

"Aye," muttered a few voices.

"That's absurd," said Hereward firmly. "Girolamo is our guest, and he's an honourable man. Besides, what opportunity has he had to communicate with the Normans?"

"Let him prove himself," said the cook.

"I will hear no more of this!" insisted Hereward. "There is no spy!"

"Master Brunman, I am sorry I did not welcome you earlier to Roskilde." Svend's speech was precise, his voice silky. A pile of letters and charters lay on the desk before him; he must be the only monarch north of the Alps who attended to such matters himself. At first the nobles had mocked him as a clerk in a crown, half king and half monk: but his victories in war had silenced them.

Brunman bowed low.

"Your Grace owes me no apology."

"I have been acquainted with the offer you bring from the Lord Hereward. Can he deliver the throne?"

"Alone, no," admitted Brunman. "Lord Hereward is a fine captain but no general, and his following is small enough beside the hosts of King William."

"And the former earls?"

"Think they're generals," sniffed Brunman. "Gospatric still supports Prince Edgar; he has a strong following in the Border country. Waltheof is in King William's peace. But the thanes remember Your Grace's uncle well. And the common people are sick of Norman rule."

"Sick enough to support mine?"

"Certainly in the North," said Brunman. "The Danelaw folk are as much Danes as Saxons anyway, and the Normans barely venture north of York these days. You'd be welcomed with open arms."

"And how will we support our troops?" Asbjorn butted in. The prince was a burly, red-faced man with light hair: Brunman would not have guessed that he and the slim, dark King were brothers.

"The harvest will be in soon. The villages will be glad to feed their liberators; the Norman manors will be easy

56

prey."

"If we mean to rule the English," said Svend, "we cannot begin by robbing them; we must proceed carefully." He paused. "Are you aware that an emissary from Earl Gospatric has already been here?" Brunman shook his head, unable to conceal his surprise. "His offer was less generous than Lord Hereward's, but also rather more solid. Five thousand pounds in silver if we would help to place Edgar Atheling on the English throne. What do you think of that?"

"Er, I knew nothing of this," said Brunman, flustered. "But as King Your Grace would have the revenues of all England."

"If the South accepted me."

"Nowhere in England loves Norman William."

"Some loved him more than Irish Diarmait and the sons of Harold, I've heard," said Svend.

"That – that wasn't the same. And you'd have to wait until after the war was won to get your money in any case – there's no way Gospatric could raise five thousand now."

"Perhaps not. But I've only your assurance that we'd be welcome. How do I know that isn't the Lord Hereward's wish speaking?"

"Your Grace didn't summon the fleet to play ducks and drakes," said Brunman impatiently. "What's it costing you to feed and maintain them all?"

"We don't have to take them to England to make them pay for themselves," snapped Asbjorn. "There's the whole of the North Sea and the Baltic to play in. We could show these damned Wagrians who's master."

"Peace," said Svend, holding up his hand. "We will… consider the Lord Hereward's proposal."

"Your Grace had best consider quickly, then," said Brunman through gritted teeth. "The sailing season's halfway over."

"I know that," retorted the King, showing signs of temper for the first time. "I am not entirely without experience of the sea. We will discuss this matter again in a day or two."

Brunman bowed, and withdrew. Svend looked up at his brother, and smiled.

"I told you, did I not?" he said. "The Danelaw is ours for the taking. And in time Southern England will follow. The empire of Canute will live again."

"Can it be done quickly?" asked Asbjorn doubtfully. "I've no stomach for long wars, and neither have the men."

"It *must* be done. If you'd learned to read, Asbjorn, you'd have a better grasp of the state of our treasury. England is the richest kingdom this side of Miklagard, and Denmark needs it."

"And the Obodrites?" pressed the younger prince.

"Perhaps if you were to invite Lord Krakus to accompany you to England..?"

Asbjorn grinned.

"He might not return."

"I didn't say that," said Svend sharply. "I haven't decided yet what to do about the Obodrites. But sending Krakus to England is at least a way to put off the decision a few months more, and spare Mariana from marrying the brute just yet, without antagonising his brother. At least, until I choose to antagonise him."

The birds were singing as Torfrida strolled through the monastery garden alone. The buildings might be forbidden to women, but Thurstan had conceded that no such ban ran here. Torfridel was sleeping under the ever keen eye of Kolfrosta, and Hereward was busy training his recruits; Girolamo had had the monastery librarian dig out a copy of *De Re Militari*, which he thought would be of assistance.

"My lady."

"Martin," she said, surprised: she had not seen the squire approach.

"Have you heard the news?" he asked. Torfrida shook

her head.

"Nothing new today."

"Byrhtred of Yaxley was ambushed last night by Ivo Taillebois's men. He was on his way here."

Torfrida put her hand to her mouth.

"Another one?"

"Another," Martin nodded. "And two of the messengers who went to proclaim the muster haven't returned. Lord Hereward still insists there is no spy at Ely; I hope he's right, but it looks bad. The people in the camp are angry and afraid, and Hogor has openly accused Girolamo di Salerno."

"Girolamo?" echoed Torfrida. "Surely you don't believe..?"

"No," said Martin, "I don't. Or at least, I don't think it likely. It doesn't make sense. But we'd be foolish to blind ourselves to the possibility."

"Then you think there is a spy?"

"I think there might be," he said simply. "I think that these ambushes are hurting more than our numbers and morale, they're hurting the Lord Hereward's authority. If there is a spy he must be caught."

"Or she," added Torfrida.

"I've considered that. But all the chief suspects are men."

"Are you saying that we should try to hunt out this spy ourselves? When he might not exist? Hereward doesn't believe it."

"If Hereward will not, then somebody must. Winter and Wulfric and the others listen to Hogor too much; I needed to speak to somebody with a clear head, that Hereward would listen to."

Torfrida considered the matter.

"Very well," she said. "But not here. It's too open."

"I can hardly go to your ladyship's chambers when the Lord Hereward is absent," Martin pointed out. "It wouldn't be proper."

"Kolfrosta will be there. I receive guests all the time."

"I think out here will suit better. We'll see anyone approaching long before they see us."

Torfrida fixed her eye on Martin's.

"Then tell me whom you suspect," she said.

"There are the missing messengers, Withold and Wulfstan," he said. "Then there are the ones who did return. Maybe the messengers were taken by chance and the news of the muster tortured out of them; in that case there really is no spy. But they're the only folk who've been off the island, apart from Father Wulfwine." The priest had departed a few weeks before to study some manuscripts in the library of Peterborough Abbey.

"It couldn't be him?"

"Never," declared Martin firmly. "Every monk in this place from the Abbot down I might suspect if they'd left the island, but not Wulfwine."

"Is there anybody else?" asked Torfrida.

"Well, there is Girolamo, of course; and then..." Martin paused.

"Yes?"

"Then there's Geric Sigurdarson."

"Hereward's cousin!"

"Lord Hereward has scores of cousins," said Martin. "Most of them he hasn't seen in fifteen years. Even Sheriff Turaud is kin to him. Would you trust family as distant as that? The first man to be killed was Egen of Burwell, travelling with Geric. Geric escaped. And since he came to the island the Normans have taken four more. That's suspicious by any lights."

"You're right," said Torfrida thoughtfully. "It could be Geric."

"Geric and Girolamo are both close to Hereward," Martin pointed out. "They'll most likely be there when you dine with the Abbot, or go hawking, or what have you."

60

"I'll keep watch for anything untoward," promised Torfrida. "And you keep an eye on the messengers." A thought struck her. "We've forgotten somebody," she said. "Girolamo's assistant, Azecier de Sarton. He's as likely a spy as his master, maybe more so. We'd best watch him too."

Krakus peered at his dim reflection in a sheet of polished copper, and teased a bone comb through his thick moustaches. He wanted them to bristle their fiercest at the banquet, that Princess Mariana might see what sort of men were bred in Wagria.

"The felt cap, master?" asked his body-slave.

"No, the circlet. I am here as a prince." The slave handed him a gold coronet, then held back his hair while he put it on. Krakus frowned at his shimmering image: yes, that would do. That was princely.

There was a sharp knock at the door. Krakus scowled.

"Who is it?" he snapped.

"The Englishman Brunman, my lord," came his guard's muffled voice.

"What does he want?"

"He won't say, my lord, except to you."

"Show him in." This was intriguing. What could the Englishman want with him? Was this some plot of Asbjorn or Svend? Certainly they would know Brunman was here: Krakus had quickly learned that there were spies behind every door in the Danish court: but that didn't mean they had sent him.

Brunman was ushered in. Krakus paced around him, eyeing the Englishman critically, as if he were a new horse he was thinking of buying. This was, Brunman realised, not too far off: he was there to sell something.

"Why have you come to me?" he asked in guttural Norse.

"Your lordship is aware, of course," replied the Englishman, "of the fleet which King Svend has mustered?"

"To subdue one of the old territories," Krakus shrugged. "Norway, or your England. It is no concern of mine."

"You do not think it could be a threat to the Obodrite Confederacy?"

"Ha! Svend would not be so stupid. He knows we would be ready for him."

"Really? With Henryk to set at the head of his forces, and you as a hostage?"

"He'd have to take me alive first," said Krakus darkly. "But if you really thought Svend meant treachery you'd have found some more secret way to warn me. You wouldn't be here openly. What's your game?"

"I want the fleet to come to England," said Brunman simply. "And I want your help."

"Ha, you do, do you? And why should I help you? And why do you want your country invaded, anyway?"

"My country has already been invaded," said Brunman. "Don't you know?"

"England is a long way from Wagria," said Krakus. "We're not a seafaring people. Why should I care who rules in England?"

"Well, today it is William of Normandy. And the people I represent would rather have Svend. And you can help persuade him."

"I can?"

"Yes," said Brunman emphatically. "You can. Svend wants peace with the Obodrite Confederacy, whoever rules it. But he won't give up Henryk if he can help it."

"Then it's war," said Krakus.

"Need it be? Is Henryk really such a threat?"

"With a Danish army at his back he would be."

"Exactly. So as long as Denmark's attention is elsewhere, Henryk presents no danger. It's in your interests that Svend should sail against William: but he won't until he secures his alliance with Prince Kruto."

"So?"

"So," said Brunman patiently, "forget Henryk. That's the only real sticking point, isn't it? Let Henryk alone and you'll get your alliance. And once Svend knows the Confederacy is his friend, he'll feel safe sailing off to England. His fleet will be gone, and without it Henryk will be no more threat than if he were dead. Isn't that what you're here to achieve?"

Krakus grunted.

"It all sounds very pretty," he said. "But with or without Henryk, there'll be no alliance if I don't get Mariana."

"'The first thing new soldiers should be taught'", read Leofric, "'is the marching step, which can be perfected only by constant practice undertaken together. Neither is there anything of greater importance than that they should hold their line, both marching and in the field, with the utmost precision: for troops whose marching is irregular stand in great peril of defeat.'" Hereward had not set foot in the Ely library before: it was a strange place. In the outer copy-room, scores of lamps flickered on the desks of transcriptors, and the monks scurried and whispered, while others ground charcoal, and many-coloured minerals which Hereward could not begin to name, to make ink. That was a living place: but here in the stacks, where Girolamo had brought them, there was only dusty silence.

"When are my men ever going to be attacked on the march?" demanded Hereward. "We slip through the shadows, melt into the woods when the enemy comes. Being able to run, now, or fight from cover, that matters more."

"They'll never be an army if they can't march in order," insisted the engineer.

"They'll never be an army at all," said Hereward. "They're fine fighting men, but they're not a shield wall. They're skirmishers, ambushers, dagger-men. Get onto the use of weapons; we might learn something useful there. Read what he has to say about the sword." Leofric sighed, and leafed through the ancient manuscript.

"Here we are: 'With the sword, one should not cut, but stab. The Romans laughed at those who fought with the edge of the blade, and easily conquered them. For a blow with the edge seldom kills, however great the force, for both bones and armour protect the vitals: whereas even a shallow stab can be mortal: moreover, raising the arm to strike with the edge exposes one's side -'"

"Roman swords must have been much smaller than ours, then," Hereward interrupted.

"They were," conceded Girolamo.

"Ours are too long to stab with in close combat, but they're heavy enough that a blow with the edge can kill. What more does he have to say?" Leofric glanced at the Italian, who frowned, and recited from memory:

"He recommends daily training at the posts with javelin, bow and sling; that all men be taught to vault, climb and swim; that they be accustomed to the weight of armour by wearing it every day..."

"That's good," said Hereward. "The armour. It's a good point. And more training at the posts would certainly help. There's something in this Vegetius after all."

"That's about the whole of the first book. He deals with military organisation in the second, engagements in the third, siege engines and war at sea in the fourth."

"The second book will be like the passages on recruitment in the first, yes? Aimed at imperial generals, no use to me."

"Yes," Girolamo admitted, "so far as I remember, it mostly is."

"But engagements... there could be some real matter there. Does the library have the third book?"

"The catalogues are in a shocking state," said Leofric.

"I'll find it," insisted Girolamo. "The abbot is being very helpful; I've offered to translate some Greek texts for

64

him."

"Good; good. Who'd have thought you could learn so much about soldiering from books?"

Krakus got unsteadily to his feet, and banged his cup on the table. The feast hall fell silent; even the dogs fighting over a beef bone that had fallen among the rushes stopped growling.

"My friends," he slurred, struggling to remember the Norse words for what he wanted to say, "my friends... I came here to make a pact of friendship between the Ob- the Odrobite Conf- between us and Denmark. And that is still my desire. We have wasted enough time wrangling over details. Let the pact be made tonight. No quibbles. No conditions. Let me marry the Pr- the Princess Mariana." The King's daughter could not suppress a gasp. Others also reacted: Henryk and Harald had leapt to their feet, protesting, while the bishop who sat at the King's side wrinkled his nose at the term "Princess". Like all Svend's vast brood of children, Mariana was illegitimate: but, dependent on the King's favour, the Church tended to keep quiet.

Svend rose, and bowed his head politely towards the Wagrian.

"I am most touched by the warmth of our guest's feelings," he said. "I agree, we should make fast our pact *without conditions*." He gave Henryk a significant glance; the Obodrite prince frowned, puzzled, for a long moment, before he realised what was meant. "Let us indeed solemnise the betrothal of Prince Krakus and my daughter this night." So, thought Brunman, marriage becomes mere betrothal and nobody bats an eyelid. Of course, to acknowledge the contradiction would be to acknowledge that Svend had just denied, and effectively insulted, his Obodrite guest: and that could prove very ugly.

There was a pregnant pause. Svend looked pointedly at his brother, and coughed. Asbjorn, remembering his part, lumbered to his feet.

"Ah, in, um, in honour of this happy alliance," he rumbled, sounding very far from happy, "I should like to invite Prince Krakus to sail with the Danish fleet, and fight alongside us, who are to be his new family, in England, against the usurper William." That, at last, roused some cheers. The warriors and thanes of Denmark had not known how to react to the declaration of betrothal: but that their long idle fleet was at last going to be put to use, and to recover what had been the richest part of Canute's empire, pleased them. Krakus looked surprised: but he could hardly now decline.

"I accept," he said, and hiccupped. "Gladly."

"Excellent," smiled Svend. "We will hold the wedding on your return. Now, for the betrothal. Come up here, both of you – we have the crowns ready, and the bishop to cry the banns…"

So, thought Brunman, it was decided. Now there would indeed be a war. God save King Svend; and God help England.

"Girolamo hasn't been in contact with anyone outside the island," said Martin, "I'll swear to that; and I doubt if Azecier would have the initiative."

"And the returned messengers?" wondered Torfrida.

"They know nothing. And since Byrhtred there've been no more ambushes."

"I've learnt nothing from Geric," said the lady. "Perhaps there never was a spy."

Ready at last to leave Peterborough, Father Wulfwine had packed his meagre possessions for the trek back to Ely. He took his affectionate farewell of Abbot Brand and Brother Benedict, and his many other friends there, saddled up his donkey, and took up his staff.

"God go with you, Father Wulfwine," said Brand

warmly. "Visit us again soon; and bring us all the news you can of Hereward."

"I will, Father Abbot," said the priest. "I promise."

In the shadow of a doorway, Herluin, the Norman prior, watched, and smiled. He had learnt enough from eavesdropping on his abbot's conversations with the priest from Ely to keep Ivo Taillebois well posted on the outlaw's plans; his friend Drogo, commander of the guards the Bishop had appointed to protect the abbey, had been more than willing to carry his messages. What they had not managed to learn was *why* Hereward was mustering men; he could have no design of leading a national revolt himself from Ely. But no doubt they would learn soon enough.

Spalding, September, 1069.

The Sheriff of Lincoln looked at the poor, ramshackle huts lined higgledy-piggledy along the road, and wrinkled his nose.

"So this is Ivo's domain," he said. "Maybe he really is as poor as he claims at tax time. The fields look fertile, though, and the beasts are fat."

He was used to Ivo Taillebois descending on his household in the city, uninvited and often unannounced, to quaff his wine and gorge on his beef. Barons of Ivo's stamp were a necessary evil: Sheriff Turaud needed allies, and could not be choosy about where he found them: but he preferred to hold them at a distance. Unfortunately, Ivo had somehow picked up the idea that they were friends, and regularly insisted on inflicting his company on the Sheriff, often bringing trouble with him in the shape of rowdy soldiers or fresh reports of Hereward's doings in the Fens. Never before, however, had Ivo thought to invite the Sheriff and his family to Spalding. It was an unwelcome interruption to Turaud's routine. He was buried under work. England under King Edward had possessed the most sophisticated administration north of the Alps: much of that had been swept away in the Conquest, innumerable documents destroyed either in the course of the fighting, or deliberately, by Normans wanting to obscure the rights of the original English owners to the lands they had seized. King William wanted the system restored, and his sheriffs were kept working sun-up to sundown trying to achieve it. Turaud glanced nervously at the rotting body dangling from the roadside gallows: he was squeamish about death, and disapproved of the summary justice exercised by the barons. It might be necessary to keep the King's peace in these wild parts, but in his view it did nothing for the law's authority.

Of course, Ivo wanted to show off the rate of progress on his new stone keep, which was nearly half built: given the state of King William's relations with the King of France, he had been unable to summon masons from Paris, but the finest Rouen could supply were at work there: yet Turaud could not help wondering whether there was something more to it. He mopped his bald head, and wished he had chosen a lighter cloak: but it was not only the autumn sun and his fox fur trim making him sweat.

Ivo was waiting in the courtyard of his old Saxon mead hall to welcome the Sheriff's party.

"Turaud!" he exclaimed. "My old friend, how good to see you." He had got fatter, the Sheriff observed: he had the beginnings of a double chin.

Behind Ivo were, as well as his usual guards, three men who caught Turaud's eye. Over what looked to be fairly ordinary tunics and breeks, they wore long, cowled cloaks in black wool, the hoods pulled forward so that their faces were in shadow. All three bore stout staves which they held out in front of them, their hands folded around them as if in prayer; and each wore on the little finger of his right hand a pewter ring set with a vicious, tooth-like triangular shard of dull green stone. Standing in grim stillness all in a row, they looked like some diabolical parody of plaster apostles in church. The middle one towered over the other two; he was quite the tallest man Turaud had ever seen. The Sheriff shuddered, but managed to muster what he hoped was a friendly smile.

"Ivo, my dear fellow," he said. "To what do we owe your hospitality?"

"Oh, I've been meaning to ask you for months," said the baron, a touch too airily. "You've entertained me often enough." He was not a good liar.

"We're very grateful," said Turaud, "but you did mention that there was also business you wished to discuss..?" Ivo's face darkened.

"Hereward," he spat. The Sheriff groaned. It was always Hereward. It seemed that almost every day he was besieged by indignant landlords from the Fens, bewailing some new enormity committed by the rebels.

"What has he done now?"

"It's not what he's done, it's what he's going to do," said Ivo. His steward leant over and whispered in his ear. "But I'm forgetting my manners," said Ivo, rather forcedly. "Let my men take your horses, come in, and we'll talk about this over a drink."

A few minutes later, with the horses stabled, the Sheriff's wife and daughter ensconced in the guest house, and his soldiers mixing uneasily with Ivo's, the baron addressed Turaud directly.

"You've heard about the Danish war fleet?"

"I have," said the Sheriff guardedly. He was not sure how Ivo knew about it, or how much he knew: King William's agents had been careful not to let anything get out that might cause panic.

"Hereward is mustering men at this minute to greet and support a Danish invasion, and he's sent word to Svend's court to assure him that the Danes will be welcome. He's even summoned Gospatric and Waltheof from their rat-holes in the North."

Turaud could not conceal his surprise. The King's agents had learned nothing of this, or, if they had, it had been kept secret even from the King's own officers.

"How do you know this?" he asked.

"I have my spies," Ivo shrugged. "I've sent word to London, of course. But something must be done *now*. We must deal with Hereward before ever the Danes get here."

"Now?" said Turaud. "Are they really likely to sail before the winter?"

"If they don't, so much the better," said Ivo. "But we should still strike now." Silently, the Sheriff damned him for dressing this up as a social occasion. He had brought his family to Spalding: they might now be in danger.

"The problem is", he said carefully, "that Ely is not under my jurisdiction. I'm happy to assist, of course, in any operation against the rebels, but this is primarily a matter for the Sheriff of Cambridge. At the very least we should seek his permission."

"The Sheriff of Cambridge is one of these damned natives," Ivo sneered. "God knows why the King kept them on. I don't trust him." Turaud bristled.

"I was born in this country myself," he reminded Ivo sharply. "My mother is English. And, as a matter of fact, it happens that Hereward Askilsson is my first cousin. He is still a traitor to the Crown, and I will do whatever is necessary to bring him to justice; and I am quite sure that Sheriff Ordgar will do the same."

"Hmph," sniffed Ivo. "There's no need to take offence."

Turaud forced himself to smile again.

"Do you have a plan?" he asked.

"Yes," said Ivo, "but that can wait until after dinner." He changed the subject. "Young Lucy is growing into the image of her mother. In a few more years you'll be beating suitors away from the door."

"I'm not ready to think about that," said the Sheriff fervently. "She's quite enough trouble already."

"Well, perhaps you should make ready for it," said Ivo. "You've no son, and your wife's an heiress too. Whoever marries Lucy will inherit a fair estate. Some men might be willing to do much for that."

"The Lords Gospatric and Dolfin."

Hereward, who had been overseeing a bout of the slingshot training recommended by Vegetius, turned to greet his guests. It was slightly awkward that Waltheof Siwardsson was already his guest on the island: Waltheof and Gospatric were rivals for the wealthy earldom of Northumbria. Nor, indeed, were they the only ones: one of Hereward's innumerable cousins, Morcar Alfgarsson, likewise claimed the mighty fief, vacant since the assassination of the Norman Earl Robert Comyn. There was, of course, always the danger that more than one of them would demand the title from Svend before committing men to the campaign: getting them to cooperate would be a delicate business.

Gospatric had brought his eldest son, Hereward noted, but the rest of the family were nowhere to be seen. Well, he would not miss the sharp-tongued Lady Ethelreda, and the fewer young children in an armed camp the better. As for Dolfin's wife, Elfthryth... it was perhaps as well that she was not here.

"Welcome, my lords," he said, with a slight bow, "welcome to the Camp of Refuge."

"Let's come to business," said Gospatric briskly. "Will you talk here or shall we seek somewhere more private?"

Hereward shrugged.

"I'll not be telling any secrets," he said, "but if we're talking terms perhaps we should go inside. I'm sure Abbot Thurstan will let us have the use of the refectory."

A few minutes later, they settled down to the refectory table with a jug of wine and a platter of honey cakes. The place felt eerie in its deserted state, as if there were something unnatural about its emptiness: the monks were at terce: but at least it was suitably private at this time of day.

"Prince Edgar is in Scotland," Gospatric began, "but I've sent him word of your summons. I have twenty men with me, and nearly a thousand more encamped only a few days' march away. But what do you plan to do from here that we couldn't do when we took York seven months ago?"

"Prince Edgar?" Hereward frowned. He had not reckoned on this. Edgar Edwardsson was indeed the lawful Atheling, proclaimed King after Harold's death at Hastings, only to be hastily pushed aside in favour of the Conqueror.

The previous winter, Hereward and Gospatric had fought side by side to place Edgar on the throne, and had been crushed by the Normans at York. In Hereward's eyes, Edgar's kingship had died there: but not, it seemed, in Gospatric's.

"Yes, Prince Edgar," said Gospatric impatiently. "Whatever you think of him, he's the only King we've got. Would you rather try and rout out the sons of Harold from their lairs in Ireland? Or were you thinking of trying for the throne yourself?"

"I have already offered my allegiance," said Hereward.

"Yes," said Dolfin hotly, "to Godwin Haroldsson *and* Edgar Edwardsson, and probably every man else who isn't William –"

"To Svend of Denmark," Hereward interrupted.

Gospatric was speechless.

"Svend?" echoed Dolfin. "An outlander, a viking? What sort of king is that for England?"

"One who's proved himself an able king already," said Hereward. "Tried in war and peace. Canute's nephew. His fleet will be here in a matter of days. England must be ready to receive him."

"Is William of Normandy not bad enough, that you must invite another foreign invader?" demanded Dolfin. Hereward sighed; he had always got on well with the young man before. But then, Dolfin and Edgar were close.

"We need aid from outside," he said.

"A million English against ten thousand Normans, and we need aid?" scoffed Dolfin.

"A million peasants!" retorted Hereward. "The people have no training. How many soldiers can we muster? You have fewer than a thousand, I have barely a hundred. Even with the King of Dublin's men, the sons of Harold were beaten at Bristol; we might have won at York if the Scots had joined us, but they didn't. Now we have the Danes ready to help us – our kith and kin. Half the families in the North are of Danish stock -"

"Including yours."

"Including mine," agreed Hereward.

"And what of the South? Down there a Dane's as foreign as a Norman."

"They remember Canute," said Hereward.

"They remember the battles against him."

"But he proved a good king in the end. He respected English laws and English customs. William wants to sweep them all away, replace the law with the King's word. Svend will swear to restore every law as it was in King Edward's day. If he doesn't, he'll forfeit our support, he knows that."

Gospatric hung his head wearily. For the first time Hereward noticed how much older he looked than when they had last met, only a few months before.

"By the time the Danes arrive, Edgar will have joined my army at Goole," he said. "More likely than not he'll have Scottish troops with him. What am I supposed to do? Send them home? Say 'Sorry, sire, you're not my King any more'? You're right, we do need help from outside. I know that. That's why I offered Svend five thousand pounds to help put Edgar on the throne. That offer stays open, and I'll make it again when the Danes come. I'll be happy to fight alongside them: but not to make Svend King." He placed his hand on Hereward's arm. "I'm sorry, Hereward," he said. "I can't do it. If you can give us the hospitality of your camp tonight, we'll be very grateful: but tomorrow we'll ride back to Goole."

Slurping down the last of his fifth baked pear, Ivo turned to his guest. Turaud tried not to grimace: the baron's breath reeked of wine, and his face and tunic front were slimed over with the various juices of the meal.

"And now," he slurred, "it's time to show you what you – what I – what I asked you here to see." He banged his cup on the table, slopping wine into his lap. "Gentlemen," he announced, "I give you the Toadmen of Wisbech!"

Into the centre of the room stepped the three cowled men. They bowed curtly to Ivo and the Sheriff.

"Are they not going to show us their faces?" wondered the Sheriff's wife.

"It is best not," said Ivo, and winked. Turaud bit his lip: he knew well enough that the barons on the edges of the Fens were not above engaging the services of outlaws when it suited them, but he had not expected that they would go so far as to involve a sheriff in their shadowy dealings.

Ivo clapped his hands.

"Bring in the hounds!" he ordered.

Servants and soldiers hastened to clear a path, as Ivo's growling dogs were brought in. They were Norwegian elkhounds, half a dozen of them, tall and muscle-bound, their thick brown fur glistening in the torchlight, their bristly tails curled upwards: and hunger glowed fiercely in their eyes. The heaviest of them pawed the ground like a bull, and bared its teeth; its handler bit his tongue and looked at Ivo.

"Release them," he ordered. The chains were unfastened from the six brutes' collars. They looked around, suspicious: they were not used to being unchained indoors.

Ivo nodded towards the three cowled men.

"Kill," he said.

As if with one mind, the hounds turned, and crouched back on their haunches, ready to spring: but as they did so, the three men raised their staves before them, and pushed back their hoods so that their eyes were visible. Levelling their unblinking gaze at the dogs, they began to mutter softly in what sounded like Norse: and, one by one, the elkhounds quivered, whimpered, looked away, and slunk back to their handlers. The hooded men smiled, and bowed towards the baron's table. Ivo, his eyes gleaming, his drunkenness apparently shrugged off, turned to the Sheriff.

"There you are," he said. "What do you think of that?"

"Remarkable," said Turaud.

"Remarkable? Damn it, it's miraculous! Those hounds hadn't eaten in two days, and they always obey me. If I'd sicked them on a bear, they'd have brought it down or died trying."

"So what did we just see?"

"The power of the Toadmen," declared Ivo in a dramatic whisper.

"And who are the Toadmen? What are they?"

"Native cunning men," said Ivo. "They have a power over animals like nothing I've ever seen. Oh, I know it's hard to believe; I didn't, at first: but you've seen what they can do."

"And they can help us with this jugglers' trick?"

"Jugglers' trick?" spluttered Ivo. His steward, Hubert Gervase, leant forward.

"Imagine, my lord," he said, "the outlaws' horses throwing them and trampling them. Imagine every cow and sheep they try to steal turning on them or leading them into the mire. Imagine hawks and ravens flying at their faces in the woods."

"And these men can really do all that?" pressed the Sheriff.

"What you've seen is just a taste," Hubert promised.

"I'm willing to put my troops behind the Toadmen," said Ivo. "Are you?" The Sheriff chewed his lip.

"You truly believe we can destroy the rebels?"

"At least we can weaken them," urged Hubert. "We have to do something before they join with the Danes."

"All right," said Turaud. "I'm with you." Ivo grinned broadly.

"Good," he said. "You've made the right decision." He turned and barked at a servitor: "More wine for my lord Sheriff! And the Lady Beatrice, of course." He inclined his head to Turaud's wife, who smiled politely. "We should drink to the furtherance of our friendship."

"Not a hare nor a pigeon in sight," grunted Winter. "It wasn't worth the risk."

"We could pick some berries," suggested Wulfric. "They'll make a nice pudding for a few of us, and we don't have any on the island."

"Are we risking our necks for berries? Supposing a patrol comes by?"

"If any Normans show up, we'll have purses as well as berries to take back," retorted Wulfric. "Nobody's looking for us here." They had ventured into the woods north of the Fens with a view to varying their diet; Winter had been regretting the decision from the moment they had left their boat. They had brought with them Ceawlin, an experienced local poacher: but he had wandered off to check his traps.

"What's that?" he said suddenly. Both men stopped, and listened intently. It was unmistakeable: the brush of grass, the snapping of twigs – there was somebody unused to woodcraft coming along the overgrown path. Somebody small, from the lightness of the tread, and alone. Craning, they peered through the trees.

"Mercy on us, it's a child," breathed Wulfric. "And a rich one, too, to judge by that dress. I wonder what she's doing out here alone?"

"She won't be alone," hissed Winter. "A rich man's child, alone in the woods? There'll be her parents and half a dozen stout armed servants in call. I told you we should've gone back."

"Can you see them?" demanded Wulfric. "Can you hear them? Look at the state of her. She didn't get like that with her parents watching." The little girl was muddy and grass-stained, her mantle, if she had been wearing one, lost, her hair disordered, her face scratched from pushing through low branches. It was almost as if – "She's running away," he realised. "We've got a little Norman fugitive there. A miniature outlaw." He straightened up, and stepped out into the path. "Stop where you are, miss," he said. "I won't hurt you."

The girl plodded on, ignoring him.

"Do you speak English?" he asked.

"Go away," she said, without looking up. Her English was good, her accent slight. Either she was a very good learner or she had grown up on this side of the water.

"Where are you off to all on your own, then?"

"York."

Wulfric laughed aloud.

"York?" he exclaimed. "Saints and angels, you wouldn't get there in a week if you were going the right way, and you're not."

Finally, she stopped, and turned to face the outlaw. It was remarkable, he thought, that anyone could look down her nose at somebody so much taller than herself, but this child managed it.

"Then show me the right way," she said. "I don't care how long it takes."

"You shouldn't be out here on your own," said Wulfric. "Why do you want to go to York?"

"To live with my grandfather," she said.

"And who's your grandfather?"

"He's the Sheriff," she declared proudly. Wulfric stared.

"The Sheriff of York is your grandfather?" he said.

"I just told you that."

"What's your name?"

"Lucy," she said. "What's yours?"

"Wulfric," he said. "They call me the Heron." Lucy's eyes widened.

"You're the Heron?" she exclaimed, impressed for the first time. "You're the man who burned Ivo's castle down?"

"Well, not exactly," admitted Wulfric. "I was a prisoner there; the fire started when I was rescued by Hereward the Wake. Would you like to come and see him?" The child's jaw hit her chest.

"You know Hereward?" she said excitedly.

"Of course."

Suddenly, Lucy broke into a sprint. She pushed past Wulfric and tore up the path, only to career straight into Winter after a few yards. He held her at arm's length while she struggled and kicked.

"I won't go to Hereward! I'll die first!"

"Now then," laughed Winter, "he won't eat you. I don't know what your parents have told you, but we don't hurt children." She stopped kicking, but narrowed her eyes suspiciously. "But we can't let you go, either."

In another part of the wood, a poacher moving through the undergrowth stopped stock still. He had seen something move ahead, something on the path – a nobleman's hound, perhaps? A dark, slinking shape, in any case. He heard a low growl. Slowly, silently, he edged forward. There, on the path, there lay the bloodied body of a man; a great dark beast was sitting on his chest, its slavering jaws so close to his face that its saliva was dripping onto his chin; the poacher heard him gasp, and realised with shock that he was alive. Another such animal, bigger and more ferocious of aspect than any dog he had ever seen, slunk nearby – but there was no sign of any huntsman or verderer.

Then he heard it – low, faint, but unmistakeably a human voice, chanting in a level monotone: he could not make out the words, but suspected that the language was foreign; he would surely have discerned something had it been English. He could not tell where it was coming from.

"Who's there?" he shouted. To draw attention to himself in this place might be very dangerous, but he strongly suspected whoever was chanting had no business in the forest either: and, besides, he was a big man and handy enough in a fight. There was no answer, but the nearer animal looked up, and hissed. The poacher reached down, picked up a stone, and threw it: his aim was true, and the hurt beast yelped and scampered off: another stone took care of the one sitting on the fallen man's chest. From somewhere in the bushes ahead there came the crashing of a man forcing his way through branches at speed, and the poacher thought he glimpsed the edge of a black cloak: but, although he shivered, there was a wounded man to tend to. He knelt by the stranger, and lifted his head. The man's breath quickened, and his staring eyes locked onto the poacher's face. He raised his hand, and tried to grasp at his rescuer's tunic, but had not the strength.

"The eyes!" he gasped. "My God, the eyes!"

"The child's story rings true," said Hereward. "Turaud married Malet's daughter Beatrice, and they do have a child named Lucy; and Turaud arrived in Spalding yesterday."

"Daughter and granddaughter of sheriffs, eh?" grinned Geric. "We've got a real prize there."

"She's also my cousin," Hereward added. "Turaud's mother and mine are sisters."

"Another cousin," muttered Hogor, "and a Norman one at that! How many more do you have?"

"I couldn't rightly tell you myself," admitted Hereward. "We're a large family."

"Well," said Winter, "what are we going to do with her?"

"We'll have to release her," said Waltheof. Everybody looked at him. The deposed earl was still a newcomer in the Camp of Refuge, and very young, but he had a habit of speaking as if he commanded there. "We don't make war on women and children," he insisted. "It isn't honourable."

"Nobody's suggesting we harm her," said Hereward. "But we need to know why she was running away. She's said nothing since she was brought in. And it might not be safe to let her go now that she's seen the island."

"Ivo's spy had a better look round last year, when he

stole your sword," Winter pointed out. "And he's not managed to bring down the soldiers on us."

"We can't just let Turaud's only child walk out of here," said Geric. "Could we hold her to ransom?"

Hereward shook his head.

"Turaud would never pay," he said. "He knows I wouldn't hurt her, and even if he thought I would, he has too many principles to negotiate with rebels. But just the fact of holding her might be enough. As long as Turaud knows she's on the island, he's hardly likely to attack us here." Waltheof grimaced.

"And what about finding out why she was running away?"

The men looked up: they had not heard Torfrida enter the hut.

"Do you think you could get her to talk?" asked Hereward. Torfrida shrugged.

"She might talk to a woman," she said, "and one who speaks French to her. Or she might not. But I believe I've as good a chance as anyone else."

"Good luck, then," said Hereward. "She's in the monastery garden, with Rowena." He turned to Wulfric and Winter. "How long is it since you saw Ceawlin?" he asked. "He should have been back by now."

At that moment, there came a hoarse cry from outside.

"My lord Hereward!"

"Enter," called Hereward. Ulric Grogan pushed into the hut.

"My lord Hereward," he said, "you must come at once. Ceawlin is dying."

Hereward started to his feet and hurried after Grogan, who was already striding out of the door and back up the path towards the monastery.

"What happened?" he asked.

"Wolves," said Grogan curtly.

"Wolves?" echoed Hereward incredulously. "In clear

81

daylight?"

"Ceawlin knows a wolf when he sees it," snapped Grogan.

Ceawlin had been found a bed in the infirmary, where the infirmarian, Brother Thomas, was attending to him. He had already washed the poacher's wounds with wine, and was now binding sprigs of comfrey into them with linen bandages. Ceawlin's arms were the worst affected, torn until the skin below the elbows was all in tatters, but there were deep scratches on his chest as well. He was moaning faintly. Father Wulfwine had been summoned; and there was another man in the chamber, a big, awkward fellow in a woollen tunic, forced to stoop slightly because the ceiling was too low for his great height. Hereward had seen him before: it was Hiccafrith of Wisbech, the contumacious serf who had helped him destroy the Gyrvian camp.

"What's he doing here?" Hereward demanded.

"I found your friend," said Hiccafrith. "I was bringing him here when I met Lord Grogan."

"On your way to Fulney again, to see your sweetheart?" Hiccafrith nodded. "Well," said Hereward, "we can thank a good Providence for bringing you so often to our side of the Level. Whatever would we do without you?"

"They'd've killed him if I hadn't been there," said Hiccafrith.

"Who would?"

"The wolves."

"Wolves," scoffed Hereward. "Whoever heard of wolves abroad with the sun still high in the sky? And this far south, at that?" He looked at Wulfwine. "When was a wolf last seen this side of the Trent?"

"Not since I was a boy," admitted the priest, shaking his head "or not for certain; though there were rumours of some surviving in the Bromeswold. And Ceawlin did say when he was brought in here..."

"How is he?" said Hereward, turning abruptly to

Brother Thomas. The infirmarian, unperturbed, continued with his work.

"He is calmer," he said, "and his breathing more regular. I've ordered a simple of pulped apple and valerian; it should help him sleep. If he lives till dawn he should recover, unless an infection takes hold: but he may never get his full strength back in his arms. And there's still no saying he won't die tonight."

"We'll discuss this somewhere else," decided Hereward. "Wulfwine, Hiccafrith – come with me."

"Hullo, Lucy."

The little girl dropped the toy horse that Rowena had given her, and shot a suspicious look at the tall lady who had entered the garden.

"Who are you?" she said.

"This is the Lady Torfrida," said Rowena, in English. She had more or less understood the few words of French that had passed between them, but felt uncomfortably excluded nonetheless.

"Hereward's wife?" said Lucy apprehensively.

"Hereward isn't an ogre," said Torfrida gently, "and nor am I. Nobody here wants to hurt you."

"Then why was I brought here?" asked Lucy.

"For your own good," said Torfrida, feeling a little guilty at the half lie. "You wouldn't have made it to York on your own. You were carrying less than a day's food, and there are all sorts of bandits and wild beasts between here and York."

"Not worse than here," insisted the Norman girl.

"Much worse," said Torfrida. "You're safe here." She paused. "What did you want to go to York for, anyway?" she asked. Lucy bit her lip.

"I wanted to live with my grandfather," she said.

"What was wrong with your parents' house?" asked Torfrida. The girl frowned, then suddenly burst out:

"They wanted me to get married."

"Married?" echoed Torfrida. The girl could not be more than ten, probably younger.

"Not now – Mother said it would be in four or five years – but I don't ever want to marry him, not if I live to be a hundred!"

"Who?" asked Torfrida. Lucy wrinkled her nose.

"Lord Ivo," she spat.

"Ivo Taillebois? The baron of Spalding?"

"Yes. He's horrible! He's fat, and he shouts, and he smells like wet dogs, and he has hair growing out of his nose -" Horrific though the prospect might be of this child being married off to the gross Ivo, it was all Torfrida could do not to laugh at this description. She had never seen the baron, but this would, she was sure, tickle Hereward – and it was certainly not unlike what she had heard about the lord of Spalding. They said that Ivo had been a handsome youth once; but his mode of living had not been kind to him.

"Did she mention the Lord Ivo?" asked Rowena uncertainly. Her limited French had failed her some time previously.

"Yes," said Torfrida, still stifling her laughter. "She is to be his wife." Rowena gasped; then, impulsively, she reached out and folded Lucy tightly in her arms. The laughter died in Torfrida's throat as she remembered what Rowena had suffered at the baron's hands. Ivo truly was a vile man: falling into the clutches of the rebels might indeed prove Lucy's salvation.

"I suppose they could have been dogs," said Wulfwine doubtfully. They had gathered in his rooms off the monastery church to speak in secret without alarming the camp; Martin had been sent for, and had joined them. "Some breeds are not unlike wolves, though I don't know of any such round here. Also dogs would be more likely to attack a man. Wolves are afraid of humans, unless they can see they're helpless, wounded or trapped. And Ceawlin said something about a hooded man – if there was a man directing them, they won't have been wolves."

"A hooded man?" said Hiccafrith. "Did he say anything else?"

"Only 'the eyes'," said the priest. "The wolf's eyes, I suppose – if it sat on his chest they'd have been right in front of his face."

The big serf crossed himself.

"The Toadmen," he breathed.

"The what?" said Hereward.

"The Toadmen," repeated Hiccafrith. "They come from Wisbech, same as I do. They say there are three in every generation, and they have the power to command birds and beasts to do their bidding."

Hereward snorted.

"Have you ever seen this?" he asked. Hiccafrith shook his head.

"No," he said, "but some of the old folk in Wisbech have, back in King Canute's days. Nobody knows who the Toadmen are now; but they wear each a toadstone ring that's the source of their power, and they have only to look a beast in the eyes to put it under their spell."

"Is there anybody missing from Wisbech other than yourself?" asked Martin sceptically.

"Not that I know," admitted Hiccafrith. "But who else but the Toadmen could set wolves on to attack a grown man, and him wide awake, with the sun still in the sky?"

"Nobody I ever heard of," agreed Hereward. "But anybody can train a dog. Or even a wolfcub, if it's taken young. And tame ones wouldn't be afraid of men."

"I've heard of the Toadmen before," put in the priest. "There are enough folk here from that side of the Fens that the name might mean something to them. And if it were put about that the Toadmen were against us, were working for the Normans perhaps, and that they had real magical powers…"

"I see," said Hereward grimly. "You're right, that would put fear in our people's hearts indeed. It's too clever for Ivo, though."

"Perhaps," agreed the priest. "But his steward's no fool. And there are others around him with brains in their heads."

"It might have been Turaud's idea," Martin suggested. "Maybe the girl knows something about it."

"Maybe," agreed Wulfwine with a grimace. Like Waltheof, he misliked the idea of holding Lucy.

"I wonder if they went back to Spalding," mused Hereward. "Of course, we don't even know if they came from there – it could as easily be Ogier the Breton who's behind them, or Gilbert of Ghent – but they might still be in the woods. Attacking just one of my men isn't very fearsome; they may be planning some sort of blow against Ely."

"What could they do here?" wondered Wulfwine. "Three men?"

"A lot of damage, if they could get onto the island undetected," said Hereward.

"Or maybe", Martin pointed out, "they were trying to lure us *off* the island. Draw us into the woods, or provoke an attack on Spalding. That would give them a chance to defeat us in front of Ivo's tenants and serfs – or else to attack the camp while we were gone."

"None of us stirs off the island tonight," said Hereward firmly. "That includes you, Hiccafrith. If your master objects to you going missing you can say I kidnapped you; it'll be no more than the truth."

"I daresay he's got some ready answer, anyway," said Martin. "He spends enough time away from Wisbech." Hiccafrith coloured, but said nothing.

"Lord Hereward." Hereward looked up: Waltheof Siwardsson was standing in the doorway.

"My lord Waltheof," he answered, wondering how

86

long he had been there. As a self-proclaimed earl, Waltheof could be considered the highest ranking man on the island, and might well resent having been excluded from this conference.

"I hope I am not interrupting," said Waltheof, entering the room and sitting down without waiting for a reply. "I have reached a decision. My men and I will leave the island tomorrow, and ride for Goole to join with Gospatric."

Hereward blinked.

"But the Danes will be here any day now," he said, puzzled.

"I know," said Waltheof simply. "But Gospatric is right. Better Edgar Atheling on the throne than Svend. We have all of us sworn oaths to the Atheling. And the Danes are sea raiders – they will need help from men used to inland fighting, men who know England. Gospatric has ten such men to every one of yours. The best chance of beating the Normans lies with him."

"He failed before," said Martin.

"At York he let himself be trapped. I cannot pretend to like Gospatric, but he is too intelligent to let that happen twice." Waltheof spoke quietly, calmly, with absolute certainty. Hereward sighed.

"So be it," he said heavily. "I cannot keep you here against your will." Waltheof had only a dozen followers with him, small loss to the military might of the Camp of Refuge: but his name, and more particularly his father's name, the great, the dreaded Earl Siward, had been worth many more. With Waltheof and Gospatric gone, Hereward himself would be the only nobleman left in the Camp of Refuge, a landless thane whose family had risen from nowhere and seemed now to have fallen just as abruptly. Such petty persons seldom shook thrones.

"Thank you," said Waltheof. "We will leave an hour after dawn."

Hereward barely slept that night. He lay outside, by a campfire, gripping Brainbiter to him, his eyes periodically flickering open whenever he thought he heard a sound. When he did sleep, he dreamt of wolves, a great grey mass of them overrunning the island, tearing to pieces all who stood before them: and after them came snakes, slithering across the corpses, their scales rustling against iron hauberks, their bodies twining with dead men's hair. And behind the snakes were the Toadmen, yellow eyes glowing under their sable hoods as they chanted the evil spells that drove the animals on. He had seldom in his life been more glad to see the sun rise.

After he had breakfasted and had a cup of ale, he went to seek Waltheof, to bid him farewell. He had been allotted a room in the pilgrim hostel: but now it stood empty. The blankets the monks had provided for him had already been cleared away.

Hereward left the cell and headed for the stables. These had been extended since his arrival: one good side to having few horses was that there was no need to build new stables outside the monastery walls. One of the stalls was open, the gate left swinging: Waltheof's horse was gone. The earl and his men had slipped away early, and were already off the island.

It made, of course, good sense. The earlier they left, the easier to evade Norman patrols. But Hereward did not care to be deceived, and it was in a sore temper that he stomped back to the hostel to see Torfrida and Torfridel. The child was asleep in her crib; Torfrida was sitting watching her, with a beatific smile which vanished the moment she saw Hereward's expression.

"What's wrong?" she asked.

"Waltheof," he growled. "I gave him permission to leave and then he sneaked away like a thief."

"Where has he gone?" said Torfrida.

"To join Gospatric at Goole."

"Gospatric?" she exclaimed. "I thought they hated each other."

"They do," sighed Hereward. "But they'd rather fight together than serve Svend. If the rest of the nobles think as they do, then he'll never be King."

"They'll come round," she said. "It's him or William." Torfridel opened her eyes, then screwed them up against the light, and whimpered; just as her mother was lifting her out of the crib, Kolfrosta pushed into the chamber, out of breath. Torfrida had not noticed the Lapp woman's absence: she usually slept in the room with them whenever Hereward did not: but here she was, bristly brows drawn, speaking rapidly in her own sing-song language, a sure sign of agitation.

When she had calmed down enough to remember her French, she managed to say:

"The Norman child is gone."

"Gone?" echoed Torfrida.

"Waltheof," Hereward spat. "God damn him."

"Waltheof? Why should he take her?"

"He hated the idea of keeping her here; he's probably sent her back to Turaud."

"The sentries and some of the monks will have seen his men go," Torfrida pointed out. "It wouldn't be easy just to ride out with Lucy under his cloak. Maybe she escaped on her own."

"Maybe," agreed Hereward. "But either way, I have to go after her. We need that surety. And in God's name, she's better off here than betrothed to Ivo Taillebois!"

Swallow was quickly saddled, and horses provided too for Martin and Wulfric. Leaving the island with horses was always a slow business, especially now, with the water too high to take any of the safe routes: they had to be floated on rafts: but the beasts had learnt to endure this calmly, and at last they reached dry land.

There was an eerie quietness in the woods. It took

Hereward some time to realise what it put him in mind of: but then it struck him – it was like the Pits of Aylmerton. There were no birds singing.

"You can see Waltheof's men passed this way," said Martin. "Only a dozen, and they've made enough of a trampling for fifty – worse than Normans. But at least it should be easy to track them."

"Assuming they have the girl," replied Hereward.

"And assuming it wasn't some other fifty men who came this way," added Wulfric. All three glanced from side to side: there might at any point be a Norman ambush waiting.

"Where would she go, if she did escape on her own?" wondered Martin.

"York," said Wulfric. "Same as she was trying to when we caught her."

"The Lincoln road would be best for York," mused Hereward, "but that's the last way she'd go. Turaud's men are bound to be looking for her, and she's not stupid."

"Well, then, she might -"

"Hereward Askilsson!"

All three reined to a halt, reaching for their weapons. There was no sign of the man who had spoken: it was undoubtedly a single voice, deep and doomladen, but it had seemed to come from all around them.

"Who's there?" called Hereward, half-drawing Brainbiter from its sheath. "Show yourself!"

Where he came from, Hereward could never afterwards say: but down the path ahead of them came striding a cowled man of massive height, bearing before him a wooden staff. About him there seemed to hang an air of terror and despair; the very horses lowered their heads as if fearing to look on him. Even under the shadow of his hood, the glint of light in his eyes was visible, almost as if they glowed from within.

"The ring," whispered Wulfric. Hereward blinked. The cowled giant was indeed wearing a ring just as Hiccafrith

90

had described.

"Who are you?" demanded Hereward. The Toadman ignored him, but stared unblinkingly into the eyes of Swallow, speaking softly. The mare whinnied uneasily – then, quite suddenly, reared up, pawing the air. Hereward, caught by surprise, tumbled from his saddle and fell on his back. Martin instantly spurred forward, drawing his axe: the Toadman dived into the bushes, and Martin's horse refused to follow. The man was gone. Turning back, Martin swung down from the saddle, and knelt by Hereward, who was struggling to get up.

"Starkad," he gasped. "It was Starkad."

By the time they got back to the rafts Hereward had recovered his breath and his composure. It was too dangerous now to go after Lucy: if Starkad was working for the Normans again, his masters – and his fellow Toadmen, if there were truly three – could not be far away. The only course was to return to the island, and redouble their watchfulness: for surely some kind of assault was now planned.

On the island, however, there were already strangers. The returning warriors, as they led their horses into the monastery courtyard, found an anxious Winter awaiting them, shifting from foot to foot as he announced:

"The Danes are here."

They were waiting in the refectory: two dozen men in coats of mail and brightly dyed woollen cloaks, and two handsome youths at their head, while Abbot Thurstan stood to one side all but wringing his hands. The taller of the youths gave a slight bow when Hereward entered.

"My lord Hereward," he said. "I am Prince Harald Svendsson; this is my brother Knud."

"Is the rest of your father's fleet waiting offshore?" asked Hereward abruptly. Harald glanced at his brother.

"Not exactly," he said. "Lord Asbjorn decided that the

Isle of Axholme would be a better place to make landfall. The attention of the Normans is directed here, and at Axholme we should control the mouth of the Trent -"

"Asbjorn?" Hereward interrupted, ignoring the angry growls with which the Danes greeted his disrespect for their prince. "Where is the King?"

"His Grace remains in Roskilde," said Knud, "where he has responsibilities to his own people. He will join us in the spring if our campaign has been successful."

"I asked for a king and they sent a viking," said Hereward disgustedly. "This is supposed to be a war for the crown of England, not a raiding party! The King should be here. Is Brunman with you?"

"We expected more gratitude," snapped Knud. "No, Brunman is not here. He is at Axholme with the Lord Asbjorn. The people there have come out to welcome us, even thrown feasts in the villages. We thought you'd be happy here too. You asked us to come – or have you changed your mind?"

Hereward grimaced; what he might have said had Torfrida not wafted into the hall at just the right moment was more than he cared to think about. Thurstan's jaw dropped open in shock.

"Of course we are happy," she said. "We merely weren't expecting you so soon. And we shall have a feast." Hereward blinked, and the Abbot's face collapsed into horror, but the Danes cheered and stamped, and even Knud allowed himself half a smile. Harald blushed and looked at the ground, and Hereward reminded himself that these were only boys, who for all their bravado were silenced by the presence of an attractive woman.

Torfrida steered Hereward out of the hall, leaving the flustered Abbot to make the Danes welcome.

"A feast?" Hereward hissed. "What do we have to feed them?"

"Lord Ogier's cattle," she said, as if it were the most

obvious thing in the world.

"What?"

"Ogier is experimenting with grazing cattle on the fields of Bourne. I hear he has eight beasts; that's enough to feed them all."

"But the Toadmen," objected Hereward. "Driving cattle from Bourne to Ely will..." he tailed off.

"Will draw them into the open," Torfrida finished, smiling. "Wulfric told me what happened. Well, our Danish friends have come here to fight. It would be discourteous not to take them with you." Grasping her head between his hands, Hereward kissed her on the forehead.

"By God," he exclaimed, "what would I do without you?" He turned to Martin, who had followed them out of the hall. "Tell the princelings to make ready for a raid," he said grimly. "We're going reiving."

Martin nodded, and said nothing: but he had not missed what everybody else apparently had. The Isle of Axholme lay so close to Goole that it was all but impossible for Asbjorn's army not to meet Gospatric's: but there was nothing the men of Ely could do now to forestall it. They must merely await tidings.

"Meanwhile," added Hereward, "I'm going to have a word with Uluncas."

"So he's alive."

Uluncas' cell, although Hereward had ordered it cleaned, was in a poor state. The buzzing of flies was as constant as out on the Fens, and an ugly sore had developed on the prisoner's still dragging leg. But although he had been muttering to himself when Hereward came in, he had quickly composed himself, and seemed rational enough.

"You should have Brother Thomas look at that leg," Hereward advised him. Uluncas snorted.

"What for? In case I want to run away on it? I'd have thought it would suit you to see me lose it altogether."

"Starkad," Hereward prompted him. "Do you remember him as having any special affinity with animals?"

"Starkad?" Uluncas stared. "He was good at killing them. That was about it. But he preferred to kill men. Grendel, now, Grendel used to talk to the birds. I don't know if they understood him; the gods know we never did. But they weren't scared of that face of his, and he liked that. I think if he was ever happy it was with his birds. But I don't remember Starkad having much to do with animals. He could quiet an angry dog or a frightened horse if he had to... why do you want to know?"

Hereward took a deep breath.

"Starkad is leading the Toadmen of Wisbech."

Uluncas gave a loud bark of a laugh.

"Ha! So Starkad's turned cunning man, has he? Folk always said their mother was a witch; maybe he's a sprig off the old bough." He looked into Hereward's face. "Good luck," he said, suddenly very serious. "If Starkad and the Toadmen are against you, you'll need it." Grimacing, he added: "If you do send the shaveling in, I promise not to kill him."

There were few horses to go round, but the Danes were swift and quiet runners, even in armour: and it suited Hereward's plan that they should not reach Bourne till dark. Thus should they go unobserved, while the Normans would most likely be preparing to repel an assault on Spalding. Besides, if the Toadmen were abroad, horses would be a liability: so even Swallow was left behind. If they stuck to the woods, any Norman horsemen would struggle to gain an advantage over the fleet-foot Danes. In any case, the favoured weapon of the Northmen was the axe – not hatchets like Martin's, but great wicked double-bladed iron beasts: and these were best wielded by a man on foot.

As predicted, they took Ogier's men entirely by surprise. He had placed a guard on the cattle, but only of two soldiers, who were dispatched before they knew what was happening; the cowherd was quickly knocked out by Hiccafrith, who had insisted on accompanying them, before the Danes should think to kill him.

It was all over in minutes, without one sound that could have reached Ogier in his hall, and the beasts proved docile, going where they were herded with little objection. Hereward began to wonder if it had not gone too smoothly: how were the Toadmen to know that there was anything amiss? But then, Starkad had probably been trailing them since they left Ely.

Then the chanting came. Out of the darkness, low, soft, in Norse. The cattle stopped as one in their tracks, and began to snort and toss their heads; the two men leading and guiding them had jogged on a few paces before they realised what had happened, and turned – only for one to be tossed aside and the other trampled as the two leading beasts hurled themselves forward. The ones behind began to make frightened, angry noises; Hereward stayed Knud's hands just in time before he could hamstring the nearest with his axe.

"Better let them run loose than have to carry one," he cautioned. But by now, the hindmost animals had made up their minds to charge into the night after their fellows, and there was no stopping them. They were lost; and somewhere in the dark, Starkad chuckled. Then, from the darkness ahead, there came an unmistakeably human scream. Hereward drew Brainbiter. "Stay here," he hissed to the princes. "Hiccafrith, come with me." A man who knew what they were dealing with would be more use than one who did not, though he might not have the training of a warrior. Hiccafrith nodded, and hefted his cudgel.

They did not have to go far. A man was lying in the path, trampled like the Dane, but this one had not been wearing a steel hauberk and helm. His tunic and breeks were sodden with blood; his black cowl had fallen back from his head, and he was breathing in short, painful gasps.

Hiccafrith's mouth fell open.

"Dag?" he said.

"You know him?" said Hereward.

"Yes, this is Dag Tovason. He's a sokeman; his uncle's the Reeve of Wisbech. I never thought -"

"Well, it seems the Toadmen's power over animals isn't so absolute after all," said Hereward. He leant over Dag. "Where are the others?" he asked urgently. It was all the injured man could do to move his head, let alone shake it, but he managed. "You're dying," said Hereward abruptly. "I can make it quick, or I can leave you to wheeze half the night until you drown in your own blood. I've seen men die that way. Have you?"

"They're... behind... you." Dag expelled the words as if each one was a barb pulled from his flesh. Hereward raised his sword, and the wounded man nodded, asking for death. Hiccafrith looked away as Brainbiter fell.

"So, they're behind us, on the path," said Hereward. "Two left against two dozen, and the cattle gone, in the other direction. Why they didn't drive them *back* against us -"

The dog hit his chest as he turned, knocking him clear off his feet. He dropped Brainbiter in the fall; but as he hit the ground, winded though he was, he wrapped his arms around the great hound, and rolled, so that, even as it snapped at his throat, he landed on top of it.

"Kill," hissed Starkad's voice.

As the beast continued to snarl and snap, grazing Hereward's chin, he tried to force the breath from it; but something struck him on the head, and he slid off it, dazed, trying to reach for Brainbiter but unable to command his hand, while the hound regained its feet and its wind and loomed towards him, slobbering at the mouth.

Whether Hereward would have come to his senses in time to defend himself had Hiccafrith not batted the animal aside, he did not like to guess. As it was, the big serf helped him to his feet just in time for him to see a second dog running off into the trees, with a man close behind it. Hereward frowned: why were they fleeing? Then he saw the Danes advancing along the path – and what had struck him.

Between Dag Tovason and the stunned hound lay the body of another man, the side of his skull smashed open by Hiccafrith's cudgel. Hereward vaguely recognised him: of course, he had been a Gyrvian. So they hadn't all perished: were there yet more for Starkad to lure forth and set against him? The so-called magic rings might not have been able to stop rampaging cattle, but Grendel's brother had escaped yet again.

Hereward grimaced. The cattle could be rounded up again easily enough; and it appeared that the Toadmen, though they could make dogs attack and kine stampede, had no more than a facility with animals – no real magic. But it all seemed too easy. For all this to end in just a skirmish... something was wrong. And then there was Starkad. The Gyrvian might have run out of Norman allies, now that he had failed them so often: but whether he would ever stop was another matter. If he was going to continue seeking his vengeance, that was one more thought to trouble Hereward's sleep.

Deep in the woods, Starkad stopped running, and turned. Twisting the ring on his finger, he muttered:

> "The first night I slept
> Where the sheep ate the wolves;
> The second night I stayed
> Where the wolf ate the cart
> And the horses escaped;
> The third night I lay
> Where the mice ate the blade
> But spared the haft of the axe.
> The bees are dazed
> And the dog is dead."

An owl screeched, and Hereward made the sign of the cross. Starkad, he knew, was still out there, watching.

York Castle.

William Malet shook his white head in amazement.

"But how did you come here?" he asked.

"Richelm brought me," said Lucy matter-of-factly.

"Who's Richelm? And where is he now?"

"Lord Waltheof's shield-bearer, of course. And he's gone. He left me at the bottom of the hill, pointed the way to the castle and rode off."

"He did, did he?" The Sheriff looked to his captain, who was fiddling with his dagger on the other side of the hall. "Did nobody see this Richelm?"

"No, my lord," said the officer uncomfortably. "But our intelligence -"

"Of course," Malet interrupted, and turned back to his granddaughter. "Where was Lord Waltheof when you saw him last?"

"He'd just left Ely," said the child, with an air of infinite patience, "and he was on his way to Goole." She beamed proudly. "I escaped from Ely, after I escaped from my parents. I saw Hereward! You know, he's shorter than they said. And his wife is very pretty."

Malet whistled.

"That's my little hero," he said.

"This matches our information," said the captain. "Waltheof met with Gospatric and Asbjorn at Goole. And now..." He tailed off.

"And now," said Malet heavily, "they move inland." He chewed his lip. "There are too many who will welcome them, if they come to York. As Gospatric was welcomed before."

"The Archbishop will take ill at any exaction against

the city," the captain pointed out. "These are his people."

"The Archbishop has placed himself under the rule of King William," said Malet. "He must do what is necessary to maintain the King's peace. As must we all, however distasteful we may find it."

"Grandpa?" said Lucy, frowning, with the first look approaching fear that her grandfather had ever seen on her face.

"Run along and play, dear," he said softly. "We have grown-up things to talk about." Dolefully, she began to trudge towards the door. "You can tell me all about your adventures at supper," the Sheriff called after her. She brightened, and skipped out of the door.

Only once she was safely out of earshot did he turn back to the captain.

"We cannot risk an insurrection here while a hostile army sits outside the gates. If the enemy does make for York, then we have no choice: the Danish quarter must be destroyed."

Chapter 5: *The Pilgrim*

Ely, October, 1069.

"So York burns," said Hereward. "But Malet still holds his castle. Our own people suffer, and what do we gain?"

"They say the Archbishop died screaming curses on the Normans," said Winter.

"Three years too late," retorted Hereward. "He knew well enough what kind of King he was giving his allegiance to." Eldred of York had, it was said, been felled by a broken heart when he heard of the order to burn the Danish quarter. That he had such an organ might surprise the men of Ely; but they had not been present in the King's Council after the last revolt, when the Archbishop had begged the clemency of the King. Whatever he thought of the rest of his countrymen, he cared for the citizens of York.

But other parts of the realm were in an equal ferment. While the north began to wonder if it was time to repent its welcome to the Danes, who had destroyed most of the rest of the city when they arrived and were now draining the resources of the county while they laid siege to Malet there, the south had troubles too.

"They say another King Harold was hanged in Sussex," Methelgar reported. "A monk, this time. The Bastard's taking no chances."

"How many does that make?" wondered Martin.

"Four, by my count."

"I make it five," said Geric. "Looks like every one-eyed man in the kingdom's decided he's Harold. God knows why. Who wants Harold back, even if he could prove who he was?"

"If Harold were alive," said Martin, "he'd have gone to his sons in Ireland, not declared himself here just to get

100

strung up. They're madmen; all they want is a name, even if they have to die to get a false one." He looked at Hereward. "It's a wonder my lord's friend Lysir hasn't declared himself yet." Hereward's forbidding scowl silenced him: but in the corner of his chief's eye, Martin could see as well a glimmer of curiosity. Hereward had suggested once before that Lysir might be the lost king: what if Harold Godwinsson really had survived?

"I don't think they need be mad," said Gwynnog. The Welshman had not spoken so far, but sat in a corner munching on an apple. "The rumour's going round everywhere that Harold *is* alive. The Danelaw may not care for him, but the South is different. They want to believe in Harold there: if one pretender could stay unhanged long enough, he might soon have an army behind him."

"An army of fools," said Hereward. "They might help us by distracting the Bastard for a month or so, but they'd end up cut to pieces. It wouldn't be worth it." He peered out of the window: it had begun to rain. "A fine day the princes have picked for their hunting," he remarked. "I wish them joy of it."

In the northern tip of the Bromeswold, Harald and Knud were chasing King William's deer – with, so far, no luck. The last leftovers from Ogier's cattle were long since devoured, and the Danes were beginning to eat into the island's winter stores; furthermore, they were restless, the only action they had seen since their arrival being an ill-conceived attempt to raid the Norman fort at Norwich. Ralph Guader had seen them off after a brief skirmish, and had been trumpeting his own praises ever since, making it sound as if he had won a battle as great as Hastings. That they should be sent to bring in food made good sense, though they went heavily armed for fear of Norman patrols. One such, by the sound of it, was coming up the road now, and the Danes had been forced to hide themselves in the sodden undergrowth, much to the chagrin of the younger prince.

"We do nothing until we've seen their numbers," Harald told him firmly. "If we have the advantage, then we attack."

The Normans clanked into sight, singing as they came.

"Battle grows harder yet,
Franks and pagans on are set,
Each strikes each, defends himself;
Shafts break, stained with blood,
Torn are flags and pennants good,
Young Franks lose both life and pelf,
No more will see mother or friend,
Nor French hosts that still attend..."

There were twelve of them, four each in van and rearguard, while the central four surrounded two prisoners: a grey-bearded man in a broad-brimmed hat, his right eye covered with a leather patch, and a tall woman in a dark kirtle and mantle of strange design, the mantle falling forward so that they could not see her face.

"That must be Lysir," breathed Knud. "Hereward's one-eyed counsellor. They've got Lysir!" Without waiting for his brother to reply, he leapt to his feet, brandishing his axe, uttering a ululating warcry. An instant later, every Dane had joined in, and they fell upon the Normans from both sides.

The soldiers were taken completely by surprise. Here, west of Peterborough, far from Ely, Hereward's men had never attacked, and they had expected no trouble. No flank guards had been put out. In minutes, it was all over, and the two prisoners stood before the princes, while the Danes finished off the dying. The woman's eyes were cast down, but the man faced them squarely.

"Is your name Lysir?" asked Harald.

"No," he answered, frowning. "Men call me Christian. Are you Hereward Askilsson's men? We were on our way to

Ely when the Norman filth took us."

"We are guests at Ely," said Harald. "We will take you to Hereward: but what is your business with him?"

"It is for Hereward's ears alone."

"Do you know who we are, Englishman?" demanded Knud hotly.

"My rescuers, and I thank you for it," said Christian. "But I will not disclose my business to you."

"This is Harald Svendsson, and I am Knud Svendsson. Our father is the King of Denmark!"

"But not yet of England," said the one-eyed man, a smile playing on his lips. "Bring me before your father and I may speak to him; but before that, to none but Hereward."

Harald shrugged.

"It can do no harm," he said. "They're obviously enemies to the Normans, and besides, there are only two of them. What could they do to hurt us?"

"They were prisoners," Knud told Hereward, "this one-eyed brute and the Egyptian or whatever she is. He won't speak except to you, and she doesn't seem to speak at all." Hereward looked over the rescued pair, holding up a torch: they had been brought to him in one of the huts in the Camp of Refuge, where the air was thick and smoky, and outside it was night. The man could not help but remind him of Lysir, but the resemblance was superficial: this Christian was burlier, slightly shorter, his visible eye smaller and less bright. The eyes of the woman were large and liquid, and lent a haunting quality to a face which would otherwise be unremarkable but for one thing: its colour. Many of the men of Ely referred to Girolamo, behind his back, as "the Moor": but the woman was a far deeper brown than the engineer.

"So," said Hereward, "you are before Hereward Askilsson now. Speak."

"To you and your trusted English officers only," said Christian stiffly. "Not before Danes."

103

"These are my honoured guests, pilgrim," said Hereward.

"I will say nothing while they are here." The one-eyed man folded his arms. Hereward glanced at the princes: both were clearly angry, Knud probably only moments from violence.

"If I were to send them away," said Hereward slowly, "I could not possibly give you a guarantee to keep from them what you should tell me."

"Tell them or not, at your own discretion," shrugged Christian. "But hear me before you decide."

"We'll get nothing out of him if you stay," Hereward had to tell the Danes. "I must ask you…"

"We will go," said Harald through gritted teeth. Knud was about to add something, but his brother seized him by the elbow and steered him towards the door.

"Thank you," said Hereward. Once the Danes had gone, leaving him, Martin, Girolamo and Winter alone with the prisoners, he looked quizzically at Christian. "So?" he said. "Who are you, really?"

"I am the King of England," declared the pilgrim simply. "I am Harold Godwinsson."

"There are plenty more of those where you came from," said Martin, "and there still will be when you're rotting and forgotten."

"Do you scoff at me?" said Christian dangerously.

"Yes."

"Peace," said Hereward. "Sir, you must understand, there are always pretenders. Why should we believe you? How did you escape from Hastings?" Christian took a deep breath.

"I was struck down and thought dead, but loyal men of Wessex exchanged my body for another lest the Normans should mutilate it. As they bore me away, they realised that I was still breathing, and they took me to this good woman, Zainab of Palermo, for healing. I was in her care some weeks, but Norman agents heard of my whereabouts and came seeking to silence us both. We fled, and since then have lived in the guise of pilgrims, moving always from one place to the next before the Normans can catch us."

"Palermo?" said Hereward. "That's in Sicily, yes?"

"I was a slave," said Zainab softly, "bought in Brindisi by a Norman knight named Bernard de Norville. He later joined King Edward's bodyguard and brought me to England. In his will he set me free, and I set up as a healer in Winchelsea." Like Christian, she spoke the Saxon English of the south, quite fluently though with a heavy accent. Her speech sounded less rehearsed than the pilgrim's, Hereward noted. But then, Christian might have been expected to prepare for this moment, whether he was Harold or no.

"We could do with another healer round here," remarked Winter.

"Hmm," said Hereward. That was hardly foremost in his mind. "But what are we to do with him?"

"The princes are here to make their father King," Martin reminded him. "How do you think they'll take it if they hear this King Ragged here calls himself Harold?"

"Asbjorn's here to fight for Svend too," Hereward pointed out, "and it hasn't stopped him joining Edgar's army. And most of the Danes are with him. The boys don't carry much authority."

"Not here, perhaps," said Martin. "But what weight might they carry with their father?"

"We won't see Svend this side of March," replied Hereward. "But you're right, it would be foolish to alienate the Danes."

"I do not object to Danish help, of course," said Christian loftily. "They are my mother's people, after all; and I have been three years in the wilderness – I will hardly reject aid that could set me back on my throne. But I need hardly say that I will support no pretenders. Edgar Edwardsson is my subject, Svend Estridsson my brother monarch: but neither is above me, nor ever will be."

"I will tell you what I am going to do," said Hereward at length. "You will be placed under guard while I consult with the princes of Denmark. Your claims will not be kept secret; I am not in the habit of deceiving my men. But I cannot promise you any support."

"You'd have gained more advancement from the Sheriff," remarked Martin: "at least as far as the scaffold." Christian scowled, but said nothing. Hereward realised suddenly that Martin had spoken in Norse. Had the pilgrim understood, or was it only the tone that he was responding to? Harold had known his Norse, but years without practice might dull a man's facility in foreign tongues. Of course, Norse and French were common enough accomplishments. He wondered if the King had spoken Gaelic, or Welsh: certainly he had sojourned in Ireland and Wales, and those might be harder tests to set Christian.

Hereward called for Ulric Grogan, who was standing guard outside, and the big Dubliner squeezed himself into the hut.

"Guard this man until I relieve you," said Hereward. "The woman is free to move about the camp." Turning to Zainab, he added: "I'll get you a bed with one of the abbey tenants, or have a hut made up for you in the camp. I'm afraid the monks won't offer room to an unbeliever, even in the hostel." She inclined her head in acceptance.

Harald and Knud laughed aloud when told of Christian's claim.

"If you want a madman in your camp, by all means let him wander," they told Hereward; "whatever he tells your people is so much baying at the moon." Hereward wished he could share their confidence, but it was not worth keeping the pilgrim under guard, so he ordered his release before leaving the island. He went alone: he had to speak with Lysir.

As usual, it was the one-eyed man who found him, in

a coppice at the northern edge of the Deeping Fen, only moments after Hereward had tied up his boat in the reeds. They were dangerously close to Ogier's territory here, but these were the parts which Lysir seemed to haunt, with no apparent difficulty in staying out of Norman eyes. Hereward had long since learnt the futility of asking how it was done.

"You seek knowledge," said Lysir. It was a plain statement, requiring no confirmation, but Hereward nodded.

"A man has come to Ely who claims to be King Harold. I want to know the truth."

"What makes you think that I would know it, or tell you if I did?" asked Lysir, one bushy eyebrow cocked upwards.

"Maybe because I think you've drunk of Mimir's Well," said Hereward. "Maybe just because you tend to have answers, even if you aren't always ready to give them up."

"And maybe because I might be Harold myself," finished Lysir. "I remember you asked me that once before."

"And I remember you did not deny it."

The older man chuckled, and stroked his beard.

"If I were King Harold," he said, "why would I be here? Why risk my life by living among the Normans, without ever trying to regain my throne?"

"You help me to fight the Normans, though," said Hereward. "Perhaps revenge is enough for you."

"When have I ever spoken in favour of revenge?" Hereward frowned, unable to remember if he had or no.

"Well," he said, "Harold or no, tell me: who *should* be King of England?"

"The choice of the Witan, the natural heir, the best man," said Lysir. "The one who is followed."

"The Witan chose Edgar and then William," Hereward pointed out. "Edgar is natural heir to the House of Wessex, Godwin Haroldsson to the House of Godwin. The best man is surely Svend. And they are *all* followed by thousands."

"You knew all this before you asked me," rejoined Lysir. "Why ask a question when you know it has so many answers?"

"I meant, whom would you follow, if you had to choose?"

Lysir smiled.

"I am not a follower," he said.

"You are hardly a leader," Hereward pointed out. "And nor are you being helpful."

"I don't see that you need any help from me," said Lysir. "Be wary of this Christian. Keep your wits about you. Do not lose the loyalty of your men. Have I said anything that was not already in your mind?"

"No," admitted Hereward.

It was only when Lysir had gone that Hereward realised he had never mentioned the pilgrim's name.

Zainab was crouching by the round hearth in the centre of her hut, watching the flickerings of the new fire and hoping that it would catch this time, when there came a tentative knock at the door.

"Enter," she said. The door opened, and the dark man who had sat silently by Hereward while he questioned Christian peered round it.

"You do not object to being alone with me?" he said. To her surprise, he spoke the dialect of southern Italy.

Zainab shrugged.

"I am a widow," she replied in the same language, "and as a healer I am alone often enough with my patients. Besides, these are hardly the most formal surroundings."

Girolamo entered the hut and closed the door.

"*A-salaam alaikum*," he said with a bow. Zainab blinked.

"*Alaikum salaam*," she replied. "But surely you are not a Muslim?"

"'A Muslim is he from whose tongue and hand

108

Muslims are safe,'" quoted Girolamo. "No, I am not a Muslim, nor have your people always been safe from my hand. I served in Sicily; that is where I learned a little of your tongue. My name is Girolamo di Salerno; you will be safe from all hands here, I promise you." He had quoted the hadith in Arabic, but then reverted to Italian; now he added: "I'm sorry, my Arabic is very poor – do you mind if we speak Italian, or would Norman French be better?"

"Italian will be very well, thank you," said Zainab a little stiffly. He might know the hadiths, but he had still served in the army that had enslaved her. "What do you want with me?"

"I want to know what you know of your companion," said Girolamo, seating himself opposite her. The turfs of peat between them had caught, and were beginning to burn merrily, though as yet giving off little heat.

"His story is true, as far as I know," replied Zainab. "He was brought to me the night after the battle, with an arrowhead in his eye and a sword cut to the chest, and I was bidden to mend him in secret. I did so. Then one day we were told that the Normans were coming for us and we fled."

"Why together?" asked Girolamo. "Does it not make you more noticeable?"

"We are not lovers, if that is what you think," said Zainab. "We left together because we were together when the danger came and it seemed the natural thing to do. I stayed with him at first because he was not yet well, and he needed me. I have stayed with him since he mended because I have nowhere to go and need a protector. We live from what I earn by mixing potions for peasants."

"So you believe he is King Harold?" pressed Girolamo.

"I know no more than I have told you," said Zainab simply. "The men who brought him said he was an important man who must be hidden. They gave me no name. He has hinted from the first that he was Harold but the first time I have heard him declare so openly was today."

Girolamo got to his feet.

"The Lady Torfrida will visit and make sure you are comfortable," he said.

"I have been on the road for nearly three years," replied Zainab flatly. "To sleep under a roof, let alone the same roof more than two nights running, will be comfort enough."

"The Camp of Refuge is a welcoming place," said Girolamo. "You will find it so. I have found friends here."

"You have been fortunate. I have disadvantages."

"Healers are welcome everywhere," said Girolamo. "Is it not enjoined: feed the hungry, care for the sick, and free the captive?"

Zainab blinked. This curious Salernian was well read; she had not heard another voice speak the hadiths since she had been taken as a slave.

The next day was bright and crisp; and Christian, whose story was by now known throughout the island, sat in the centre of the camp, telling tales of his – or Harold's – adventures to an admiring circle of Hereward's people and the islanders, while their work went by the board. Lewine the Sickle was sitting at his feet; Geric and Ulric were also in the crowd. Christian had made use of the monks' bath-house the night before, but had rejected new clothes, instead putting on his grey pilgrim robes and hat again.

"It was then", he declaimed, holding up his right arm as if to brandish an imaginary sword, "that I charged into the thick of the fighting..."

"He's a plausible villain, I'll give him that," remarked Martin.

"Are you sure he's lying, then?" asked Winter. "He certainly knows his story. Maybe he really is Harold."

"What did you learn from the Saracen woman?" Hereward asked Girolamo.

"She doesn't know," replied the engineer. "His story is consistent, but that doesn't make it true."

"You're sure *she's* not lying?" said Martin.

"Entirely sure," said Girolamo emphatically.

"So he was at Hastings," said Hereward. "And if it is a lie, it's one he thought of that day."

"Perhaps he's one of the nobles supposed to have died at Hastings," suggested Winter. "One of Harold's brothers, maybe."

"She hadn't heard him say openly that he was Harold until yesterday," added Girolamo.

Ulric Grogan, clambering over young people who were crouched on the ground to listen to the pilgrim, stumped over to Hereward and his huddle of men.

"There's a man who doesn't understand battles," he growled. "If he's Harold Godwinsson I'm the Pope."

"Why, what did he say?" asked Hereward.

"He was talking about Hastings, and when the line broke to chase the Norman feint. Oh, I don't doubt he was there, probably charging down the hill with the rest of the idiots, but he didn't know what was happening and he still doesn't. Him a general! Him a king! Pah!"

"You were at the battle?"

"Of course. I was there in Earl Edwin's fyrd."

"So you saw Harold?"

"Not close," Ulric admitted. "I can't say as I'd recognise him. But I'm sure that man's a charlatan."

"Methelgar was there too," Winter pointed out, "and he says Christian looks like Harold."

"'Looks like' isn't 'is'."

"We've nothing solid to go on…" Hereward tailed away, as to his surprise he saw Torfrida approaching.

"Is that the famous Christian?" she asked abruptly, without greeting them.

"Yes," said Hereward.

"And do you think he's telling the truth?"

"No. But we've no proof."

"Well," she said, "if I were you I'd find some quickly. The Danes aren't happy."

"But they brought him here," Winter pointed out.

"I know that," she said impatiently. "But that was before he started spinning his tales and enchanting the young folk. Asbjorn may not mind fighting alongside Svend's rivals but Harald and Knud are another matter. They're in the refectory now – they arrived before the monks had finished their midday meal, and started talking while the rule of silence was still in place; Abbot Thurstan was scandalised. They're swigging mead and muttering about leaving Ely."

"Maybe we should make a move soon," said Hereward. "King William's bound to move north again; we don't want a repeat of the last revolt."

"Not we," said Torfrida, "*they*. They'd go without you, take their men up to Axholme or to the siege of York Castle and leave us mouldering in the Fens."

"Break up our forces and hand victory to the Bastard," said Martin. "We need to put a stop to this. Soon."

Bourne Hall.

Albert fitz Guy shuffled from foot to foot, his eyes on the ground. He had been stumbling alone through the rough, wet countryside, not seriously wounded but bruised enough to feel it, since the Danish attack: but he had almost decided to stay on the road rather than face his master.

This was not what he had come to England for. Albert was a younger son of a free farming family, Normans settled on the Breton border; he had always known he would have to make his way by the sword or in the Church, and when his village had been called upon to provide shieldbearers for Ogier and his knights he had eagerly volunteered. He had welcomed the news of the invasion: people were saying that the whole of England was to be parcelled out to pay the Duke's army. It was an opportunity for a man like Albert to make himself rich, perhaps even rise to see his sons knights, his grandsons barons. England was the wealthiest kingdom in Western Europe, and he had heard that its soil yielded two harvests a year. And the Pope had blessed the enterprise, so God was on their side. Wading through mud-sodden paths, sleeping in puddles in his rusting armour, seeing his comrades cut to pieces three years after the war was supposed to be over, and at the end of it having to stand under the gaze of Ogier fitz Ungomar, was enough to make a man wish he had become a priest after all.

"And just how did you come to be taken by surprise?" asked Ogier, dangerously calm, appearing to study his fingernails intently. Gilbert of Ghent, his neighbour and guest, watched the soldier with a half smile as he poured himself a cup of wine.

The soldier gulped.

"There were only a dozen of us, my lord," he said. "To put out guards would have reduced the strength of the centre and slowed us down. Besides, Hereward's never ventured that far west…"

"He ventured as far as Bristol last summer," said Ogier. "And he keeps popping up miles from Ely. Just because those woods aren't a regular haunt of his is no reason to let your guard down – particularly when you have such important prisoners."

"I, ah, I brought away this," said Albert hesitantly, holding up a little silver cross. Ogier shrugged dismissively.

"What is it?" he asked indifferently.

"The prisoner Christian was wearing it when taken. It's a rich thing for a poor pilgrim – we thought –"

"You thought you'd sell it off, and now you think you'll buy my mercy with it," said Ogier. "Well, give it to my steward. But it's the prisoners I care about, not their trinkets."

"Is it certain that they were Hereward's men?" asked

Gilbert. "Did you see him there?"

"Not to recognise," mumbled Albert.

"Could they have been ordinary bandits?"

The soldiers shook his head.

"They wore armour," he said. "Byrnies, round shields and helmets, every man."

"What kind of weapons did they carry?" asked the Flemish knight.

"Axes," said Albert with a shudder, remembering helmets split and arms sheared off. "The biggest and sharpest I'd ever seen."

"Danes," realised Ogier with a smile. "By St Armel the Dragon-Drowner, Christian's fallen into the hands of the Danes!"

"Who are Hereward's allies and guests," Gilbert pointed out.

"If you were one of Svend's sons," retorted Ogier, "would you let the pretender live?"

"Probably not," admitted Gilbert. "But can we afford to rely on that? If Hereward does have him, who knows what they could be plotting?"

"If Hereward has him, he's beyond our reach," snapped Ogier. "I've tried to assault Ely, and I'd not go back without a thousand men."

"We may not be able to get onto the island," said Gilbert, "but we might man the main routes off it."

"In every direction? There must be five or six different roads, and when you count the deer-tracks in the woods that's a hundred more. Even manning the major roads would take more men than you and I together could muster."

"Then we should think about which way Hereward and Christian might go, if they do strike out together. They might come here or to Spalding, to land a blow on you or Ivo Taillebois. They might set out to join Asbjorn's army at York, or in his base camp at Axholme."

"Or they might head south to rouse Harold's

114

supporters there," said Ogier. "It's still too many routes to cover."

"But I think", continued Gilbert, "that we can rule out Axholme and York. To judge from our reports, this false Harold is a proud man; he'd not want to join forces with Asbjorn. And by that token he's unlikely to come here, either – because where would he go afterwards except north? My money's on them going south – and south means the Cambridge road."

"It would take us days to get there," Ogier pointed out. "We'd never be in time. No, if he does go south he's Sheriff Ordgar's problem. All we can do is patrol the northern roads." He looked at Albert, who had been sidling towards the door, hoping that he was forgotten. "Get out," he exclaimed disgustedly. "Out of my house, out of my service. See if Ivo will take you on. Or Hereward."

Albert left, silently thanking the saints for his escape and promising them that, whatever he did, he would find himself a peaceful profession, far away from Lincolnshire and Ogier the Breton.

"Your people are flocking round that beggarly rascal," complained Harald. "Do you even control them any longer?"

"My men are mine," said Hereward calmly. "Christian has a honeyed tongue, but that is -"

"Poisoned, more like," exclaimed the prince. "Have you any notion how hard it has been to keep my brother from cutting his head from his shoulders? I wish we'd never brought him here."

"But you did," said Torfrida. "And now he is our guest. What can we do?"

"Challenge him for the liar he is," said Harald.

"That could be dangerous," said Hereward. "Divisive. Until we have proof -"

"If you will not," Harald interrupted again, "I will."

"Highness," said Hereward as patiently as he could,

"I must ask you to give me time. Ulric Grogan has noticed inconsistencies in the man's story. We are looking for the means to disprove his claims. If we can do that we can denounce him without dividing the camp." Harald frowned.

"Let it be by tomorrow, then," he said reluctantly.

At that moment, there came from outside shouts and the clash of steel. Hereward and Harald rushed out of the hut; a circle of angrily clamorous young men had formed on the grass, through whom they had to push to see what was going on at the centre. There they saw Knud, axe in hand, fury in his eyes, facing Christian, who had from somewhere picked up a sword: but the pair had been separated. Holding them apart, each at arm's length, straining until his neck looked fit to burst asunder, was Ulric Grogan.

"Enough!" barked Hereward. "I will not have this in my camp!" Scowling, looking like petulant children, the two men lowered their weapons, and Grogan relaxed. "What is the meaning of this?"

"The Norse whelp called me a liar," snarled Christian.

"A liar he is, and I'll prove it in battle," Knud spat back.

"Whoever heard a Dane give the lie to an Englishman?" the pilgrim sneered. "You who come of a race of liars! Have at you, I don't fear you! God will defend the right."

"You will make peace," said Hereward.

"No," replied both in unison.

"Take his hand, Knud," ordered Harald. "Now."

"No!" snapped Knud. "Would you make peace with this? As well shake hands with Bastard William."

"If he will not apologise," said Christian, "I will not remain in this camp with him."

"Then go," said Knud. "Nobody's stopping you."

Christian looked to Hereward, and narrowed his single eye.

"Would you have it said that you had the true King of

England in your camp but turned him forth?" he demanded imperiously. "Send away the Danes. They are the enemies of England; I am her anointed sovereign."

"I have seen no proof of that," said Hereward quietly.

"Dear God," said Christian, "will you side with the Northman? With a viking?"

"God damn the pair of you for forcing me to take a side," said Hereward. "You are doing William's work for him, and he will laugh if he hears of what has happened this day. But since you have driven me to the choice, it is no choice at all. Either show me some proof that you are Harold Godwinsson, or forfeit my protection."

"The proof was taken from me by Ogier's soldiers," said Christian.

"How convenient," said Knud.

"If the man who took it escaped, he will have gone to Bourne," insisted Christian. "We could get it back."

"Attack Bourne for a phantom?" said Hereward, shaking his head. "It would be too great a risk for something we don't know is there."

"I mean to have my revenge on Ogier for my captivity in any case," said Christian. "I had meant to lead the men of Ely beside you and the Danes: but it seems I must go without you."

Hereward stared.

"You're mad," he said. "You'd go alone against all Ogier's men?"

"Not alone," said Christian. "I fancy I can find followers enough here." He turned back to the crowd. "Who's with me?" he shouted. "Who'll follow King Harold?"

There was a long pause; then Lewine stepped forward.

"I'm sorry, Lord Hereward," he mumbled. "But he's my king."

More followed, mostly the younger sort, recent arrivals; Hereward bit his lip when he saw Geric join them.

Feeling someone touch his arm, he looked round, and saw Methelgar by his side.

"Somebody should go with them," said the Marcher quietly. "Keep an eye on them, and try to hold them back from destroying themselves."

Hereward nodded.

"Go," he said. Methelgar stepped up to Christian, and bowed his head.

"I am with you, my prince," he declared.

When eighteen men had pledged themselves to Christian, and it was clear there would be no more, he went to fetch Zainab. He barged unannounced into her hut; she was cooking a dish of eels given her by Wulfric and Rowena, and looked up without registering surprise.

"We're leaving," said Christian.

"Farewell," she replied, inclining her head.

"We," he insisted. "You are my companion on this road." Zainab shook her head.

"The road led us to Ely and ended here," she said. "This is where God has brought me, and this is where I shall stay."

"You were charged to protect me," the pilgrim reminded her.

"Until your wounds were healed. I fulfilled that charge nearly three years ago."

"Damn it, woman, I am the King!"

"When you wear your crown again," said Zainab levelly, "return and command me, and I will obey. Until then my service will belong to those who have put a roof over my head and food in my mouth, things you only ever took from me."

Christian glowered.

"I will not forget this," he growled.

"God go with you," replied the healer softly.

The pilgrim's party made little attempt at

concealment. They were, after all, not near habitation; time enough to hide themselves when they drew near Bourne, in preparation for their night attack upon Ogier's manor. Methelgar alone glanced fearfully around, and fingered the hilt of his sword. But when he suggested that they should go more circumspectly, Christian laughed, and asked scornfully:

"Are you afraid?"

"Afraid of stupidity," retorted the Marcher. "Afraid of dying needlessly and not being able to take any enemies with me. The Harold I followed at Hastings knew the difference between courage and folly."

"The Normans are louder than we," shrugged Christian. "If they are on the road, we'll hear them long before we meet them."

"Let us at least move in formation," insisted Methelgar, "and not shout or sing."

So it was that some semblance of military order was bestowed on Christian's men: and it was as something approaching a unit that they rounded the next bend and walked almost into the Norman roadblock.

There was an immediate outcry, and both sides began tugging at their swords, Lewine astonishing the foe when he produced his sickles; but fighting had hardly begun when a tall man in polished byrnie and helm, his long shield painted in a bright zigzag pattern, stepped out before the roadblock, handing his green woollen cloak to an attendant, and held up his hand. The English glanced at him suspiciously; none lowered their arms, but such was the natural authority in his unblinking grey eyes that they did pause.

"You are Christian?" he asked in English, with a stiff nod to the pilgrim.

"I am Harold Godwinsson," replied Christian, jutting out his chin. "Who asks?"

"Ogier fitz Ungomar, as I think you know. I must ask you to surrender, in the name of King William."

Christian gave an expression that was half grin, half

grimace.

"I'm afraid that won't be possible," he said.

Ogier gestured at the men around them, poised for battle.

"You would prefer bloodshed?" he said.

"If you choose," said the pilgrim, "I will fight you alone. A duel to the death, the loser's men to retreat before the winner's; but they will be allowed to go free."

Ogier frowned.

"You would truly submit yourself to such a test? Against a younger man, better armoured, with both his eyes?"

"I have mail and helm," replied Christian calmly, "and I fight better without a shield. I fear nothing: God will protect me. It is not my wyrd to fall this day."

"Sheathe your swords!" Ogier barked to his men. "And you, Englishmen, stand back! I accept your king's challenge; I will fight him."

There was much muttering at that: but both sides did as they were told. A circle was formed around the two leaders; Christian shrugged off his cloak, under which he already wore a coat of mail, and exchanged his hat for a helmet; and the two began to circle one another, blades bared before them, eyeing each other intently.

Christian struck first, but Ogier caught the blow on his shield. The sword bit deep into the wood; as the pilgrim wrenched it out, the baron hit back. His blade glanced off Christian's hauberk without penetrating it, but the blow had been heavy, and the shock jarred through the pilgrim's left arm. Christian fell back a pace, and Ogier stepped forward, striking him on the helmet. The pilgrim reeled, dizzy, and only feebly held up his sword as the baron lunged again. This time, the point of his blade caught the pilgrim low, and drove through the front of his mailcoat and into his abdomen. Gasping, gurgling, Christian staggered, and crashed backwards onto the ground, Ogier's sword sliding out of him.

120

He sat there, wheezing, dribbling blood, unable to rise; Ogier reached out and knocked his helmet off his head.

"This is your King of England!" he declared. "This pitiful old beggar! Is this wretch the man you want to follow?" He raised his sword for the final blow.

"I – am – the – King!" Christian gasped; and Ogier's sword descended.

Methelgar's blade was out before the pilgrim's body hit the ground.

"Now," he said quietly, "we will retreat in good order – and unmolested."

"I promised you nothing," spat Ogier.

"Are you sure you want a fight?" asked the Marcher. "We're evenly matched, more or less: it'll be bloody. Ask yourself – is it worth it?"

Ogier glanced suspiciously around. There could be more English following; he had no reinforcements to call on – and Hereward was not here. It was not worth throwing away the lives of his men to kill these nobodies.

"You may go, Englishman," he grated. "But the body of your king remains with us."

"No king of mine," replied Methelgar. "If he was Harold once, he was Harold no more by the time he came to Ely. His mind was gone." He looked down at the pathetic crumpled heap that had been Christian, and murmured: "Wyrd goes ever as she will."

"Was he the true Harold?" pressed Hereward. Lysir shrugged.

"Does it matter?" he asked. "He has died twice now. And you yourself said he was not fit to lead men."

"No," admitted Hereward. "But if he had let others lead... Harold might have united us. Even a false Harold."

"Did the real one achieve that when he was King?" asked the one-eyed man. Hereward shook his head.

"The last king to do that was Canute."

"Who began", Lysir pointed out, "as a foreign invader. Whether or not Christian was Harold, it is not who men *were* but who they *are* that matters: kings no less than any other."

"So who should be King?"

Lysir smiled.

"Are you sure that is the right question?" he countered.

"Then what is the right question?"

"That", said the older man, "is for you to discover." Hereward gave up, and walked away.

"So," said Gilbert, "do you think he was Harold?"

Ogier shook his head, and proffered another morsel of duck to his dog, who gulped it greedily down.

"No," he said. "That duel was insanity; Harold would never have agreed to it." He reached into his scrip, and, after a little fumbling, pulled out the silver cross which Albert had found. "Although", he went on, "I am a little puzzled by this. What do you make of the marking on the back?" Most unusually for a man of his rank, Gilbert of Ghent could read.

Taking the cross between thumb and forefinger, the Fleming peered at it. Where the shaft and beam joined, there was on the back a small X-shape scratched into the silver.

"It could be a maker's mark," he said, "or just decoration. Or it could be a Greek *chi* – for Christ, perhaps: or Christian."

"It doesn't stand for Harold, then," said Ogier. Gilbert was not sure if he had imagined it, but he thought the Breton knight looked relieved.

"No," he replied; "but if it is an English rune, it would be a G. And Harold's parents were named Godwin and Gytha."

Chapter 6: *The Abbot*

Peterborough, November, 1069.

Abbot Brand propped himself up on his elbows, wheezing with the effort. It was dim in his cell: although it was daylight, the windows had been shuttered against the fever-laden air of the Fens, and only a single candle aided his failing eyes. The tallow it was made from stank, but the old man would not have an expensive wax candle wasted on him: they were for use in the church.

"I'm glad you are here," he said. His guest was Father Wulfwine, the priest from Ely who served as go-between for Brand and his nephew Hereward. Hovering behind the priest was Brand's last surviving brother, Godric, more than twenty years his junior and a monk like himself. Godric had insisted on taking on the care of his brother under the direction of the infirmarian, and had gone about his duties stoically and silently; he had scarcely rested since Brand had fallen ill. "With Norman soldiers here," the abbot went on, "it's difficult for Hereward to visit... it's good that he should have word from me, should hear the truth and not rumours..."

Wulfwine bowed his head.

"He will hear of your serenity and courage."

Brand smiled, though it made the dry skin at the edges of his mouth crack painfully.

"You flatter me, old friend," he said. "For myself I fear nothing; I have confidence in the mercy of God. But for Peterborough..."

Ely.

"So," said Harald, "Asbjorn has returned to Axholme." Hereward's war council had appropriated a barn

123

at the western end of the isle as a meeting place – though, with the Camp of Refuge so full, they needed more barns in use, not fewer. Little storage huts were springing up all over the island. It was cold, draughty, and the rain pounded on the roof, but it was better than cramming everybody into a cottage or trying to talk outdoors in this weather.

"And Edgar to Scotland," added Knud. "This is what comes of trusting the English!" There were angry mutterings at that from English and Danes alike. "Gospatric and Waltheof have failed us."

"It's your uncle who's retreated, not Gospatric!" retorted Geric Sigurdarson angrily. "He's still besieging York Castle, without Danish help!"

"Peace!" said Hereward. With his uncle's illness to worry about, and winter descending on the island, he had no wish to be distracted by dissension among his own people; but the war would never let him be. Torfridel had taken her first steps alone a few days ago, and he had not been there. "Whatever the rights and wrongs of the Lord Gospatric's quarrels with our Danish allies, there is no reason to let them spread here. We are sworn subjects of King Svend -"

"Not of King Christian, then?" jeered Knud. Geric shot a fierce glance at him, his hand going to the hilt of his knife.

"Of King Svend," continued Hereward determinedly. "We should reestablish contact with Prince Asbjorn and find out what exactly is the truth in these stories. At present we do not know what is happening north of Lincoln. Where is Edgar Edwardsson really? What's happening in Durham? Who remains at York? Most important of all, where is William and his army? We've heard they were marching north, but no word further this past week and more. It's all rumour and speculation."

The door clattered open, sending a sudden blast of wind up the tunics of those unfortunate enough to be standing nearby; and the priest, cowl and cloak wrapped tightly round him, pushed into the building.

"Wulfwine?" exclaimed Hereward. "Is something amiss? Why didn't you wait for better weather?"

"The sky was calm enough when I left Peterborough," answered Wulfwine. "But I had to see you, Hereward."

"What is it?" asked Hereward. "Is Brand - ?"

"Your uncle is dying," said the priest heavily. "I am sorry."

Prior Herluin watched sourly as the two cowled pilgrims, heads bowed, entered the gates of Peterborough. He knew well enough that, when he heard Wulfwine's news, Hereward would come straight here: but the Norman guards were few, and still under Brand's authority. Furthermore, the outlaw very possibly had more men lying in wait. It would have been different before, when the mere fact of Hereward's presence would have been useful, a tool he could turn against Brand: but what good would that do him, now that the Abbot was dying? All that the Prior could do, and all that he need do, was wait. Soon enough, time would deliver Peterborough into his hands: and once Brand was dead, let Hereward beware.

The guests were shown into the Abbot's frugal cell. Though the infirmarian had scattered dried lavender on the floor, it had done little to relieve the smell, which already smacked of death. Brand tried to sit up, but the effort was too great, and he fell back upon his pillow: normally he slept without one, but Godric had convinced him that Christ would understand.

Not until they were within the cell did Hereward and Martin push back their hoods: the fewer could attest to their presence here the better, and Hereward's mismatched eyes and white-blond hair made him very recognisable.

"Hereward?" croaked Brand. Hereward dropped to his knees by the bed.

"Uncle," he said.

"You shouldn't have come," Brand wheezed

125

painfully. "Too dangerous. Drogo…"

"There's no danger," said Hereward reassuringly. Martin, fingering the short-hafted axe at his belt, wished he felt so confident. The soldiers would surely have been told that two hooded strangers had entered the monastery; whether they would see anything suspicious in that, he did not know, but Martin did not feel safe. He knew the prior here was a Norman, and an enemy of Hereward's youth. He would feel happier once they were clear of the abbey grounds.

"There is… danger… to the abbey," said Brand. His voice seemed to be growing fainter. "When I die… I fear… disaster." Suddenly, he did manage to sit up, grasping the front of Hereward's supertunic. "The relics," he hissed. "The relics of St Peter, and the abbey plate – don't… let…"

Whatever the abbot had been about to say, he did not finish. The effort was too great; and he fell back, the breath leaving his body in one last groan.

"*Requiescat in pace*," said Godric dolefully. Hereward reached gently out, and closed his uncle's eyes, before clambering to his feet.

"We should leave," said Martin. "It isn't safe to stay here."

"Ah, of course…" Godric's mind had understandably been on other things. "There is a postern gate – it'll be more discreet – I'll have Brother Benedict show you out."

The postern gate, which led off a little used secondary courtyard, was kept locked; and Benedict was sliding back the last of the stiff, rusty bolts when Prior Herluin entered the yard. Ranged behind him were Drogo fitz Dudo and four more armoured guards.

"Stop!" ordered the Prior. "Those men are outlaws. They are under arrest, on my authority as acting Abbot of Peterborough."

Pushing Benedict out of the way – all the better for the young monk if he appeared not to know them – Hereward tore open the door, and plunged through it. Martin was right behind him: and he tore on, west, not east, making for the Bromeswold. There they could hide, and make their way back to Ely by night...

Hereward stopped. He could not hear pursuit. For several seconds his own footsteps had been the only ones in his ears. He looked back, towards the forbidding shape of the abbey, silhouetted against the grey sky: there was nobody behind him.

Martin had been taken.

"It's my fault," muttered Hereward, "my fault. I should have gone alone." He was sitting slumped on Torfrida's bed, in her quarters at Ely. Little Torfridel was playing with a horse on wheels he had carved for her, gurgling happily.

"Hush," soothed Torfrida. "You know Martin would never have let you go alone. And if you had, you'd have been taken. We can rescue him."

"What if they've killed him already?" said Hereward. "He's an outlaw, he's owed no trial." Torfrida sighed.

"If they'd killed him on the spot they'd have kept on pursuing you," she pointed out. "And if they took him alive, they'll want to milk it, get glory from his capture. That means a hanging. Which shrievalty is Peterborough in?"

"Cambridge," said Hereward – then suddenly struck the wall with the flat of his hand. "You're right! Herluin doesn't have the authority to hang men; they'll send him to Sheriff Ordgar. We do still have a chance!"

"Is there anybody within the abbey who might still help us?" asked Torfrida. Hereward frowned.

"Most of the monks were well disposed enough," he said, "especially Brand's secretary, young Benedict. But now that Herluin's in control I don't know if any would still be willing to take the risk, if we could even get word to them."

"How long will he be in control, anyway?" said

Torfrida. "Doesn't the chapter elect a new abbot?"

"Some election," grunted Hereward. "King William will make the decision. And nothing would please him more than to have my enemy as Abbot of Peterborough."

Technically speaking, the new abbot should be elected, subject to confirmation by ecclesiastical superiors; it was not supposed to be the business of secular authorities. But in effect all senior offices of the Church in England were in the gift of the King. William, who had won the Pope's support for his invasion by promising to bring the messy, disorganised, and frequently corrupt English Church to heel, had in the event subjected it not to Rome, but to himself; and he kept tight grip on the reins. He had not yet managed to depose Stigand, the fractious Archbishop of Canterbury: but he had curbed his power – and another of William's holy victims was at that moment arriving by barge on the Isle of Ely.

The barge, the top of its prow sheathed in gold leaf and its canopy of the finest purple, had been sighted as it approached, although word had not yet got back to Hereward: and Ulric Grogan was waiting as it nosed its way in to the shore, with two stout men at his back.

"Ahoy!" he called. "Who seeks to land here?"

"My lord the Bishop of Durham," came the unexpected reply.

"Durham?" exclaimed Grogan. "He's a long way from home."

"We humbly beseech the Abbey of Ely to offer us sanctuary," answered the speaker, whom Grogan could now see, a young priest, some kind of clerk, perched in the bows of the vessel.

"Sanctuary?" echoed Grogan. "What crime is the Bishop accused of?"

"Treason."

"Ha!" roared Grogan. "Then come ashore, and welcome! We're all traitors here; all honourable men are these

128

days."

"We thank you," the priest called back. "Send to the abbey and bid them make ready to welcome their lordships, and to have men ready to bring their treasure ashore."

"Lordships?" Grogan frowned. "Is there more than one Bishop of Durham, then?"

"Of course. My lord Ethelwine, and my lord Ethelric."

"Ethelric," mused Wulfwine. "I'd forgotten he was still alive. We'd hardly heard of him since the treasure scandal."

"What scandal was that, father?" asked Torfrida.

"While a church was being renovated they found a hoard of Roman coins; Ethelric sent the gold to Peterborough. He'd been a monk there. But it wasn't his to take, and certainly not to send out of his diocese; so he was dismissed, and used his influence with King Edward to get his brother Ethelwine appointed in his place. Since then he's been living idle in a wing of Ethelwine's palace."

"I remember him too," said Hereward darkly. "A friend of Prior Herluin, and well matched, from all I heard."

"Now, now," reproved the abbot, "we shouldn't speak ill of our guests. Whatever they have done, they are princes of the Church – and now, it seems, fellow enemies of King William."

"And they bring treasure," remarked Martin. "Another Roman hoard, perhaps."

"We shall see," said Hereward.

Into the abbey courtyard, with as much dignity as they could muster, strode the brother bishops, both in full finery of their office, albeit now somewhat spattered with mud at the lower extremity; between their tall, broad frames and florid faces there was little difference to be seen, save that one had a heavier paunch than the other. Behind them trundled a donkey-cart, provided by the monks to bring their luggage off the barge. Their few servants trudged alongside.

Abbot Thurstan and Father Wulfwine bowed low; Hereward and his people made a rather more perfunctory obeisance.

"Which is which?" wondered Torfrida.

"My lords the bishops Ethelric and Ethelwine," declared the clerk, not adding "of Durham" – to name but one diocese would only highlight the absurdity of calling both bishops.

"My lords," said Thurstan. "You are welcome to our humble house; we are honoured."

"We claim the right of sanctuary," declared one of the bishops curtly. "We shall of course expect decent accommodation." The law stated that sanctuary men should sleep in the church, before the altar whose holy protection granted them asylum; but, of course, King William's law did not run on the Isle of Ely, or else traitors could never have been offered sanctuary in the first place. Besides, no bishop, or even ex-bishop, had ever officially claimed the right before, so precedent was lacking.

"We shall also need storage," said the other, "for the relics of St Cuthbert and the cathedral plate."

Thurstan gasped; Wulfwine mouthed to Hereward: "They've stolen them!"

"My lord..?" faltered the abbot.

"These treasures", said the bishop testily, "have been preserved only by a miracle from the ravages of the Danes. You have doubtless heard how the viking Asbjorn meant to march on Durham, and was diverted to York only by a vision of the holy Cuthbert warning him to spare his city?" They had heard no such thing, nor did it sound much like Asbjorn: but nobody contradicted the bishop.

"Therefore," continued the other, "it is our solemn duty to keep them likewise out of the hands of the Normans. King William has decreed my brother's deposition: therefore, to preserve the plate and relics in English hands, we were obliged to remove them." So this was Ethelric, and the slimmer one Ethelwine.

"They will be safely guarded here, I assure your lordships," promised Thurstan, bowing still lower than before.

"My lords," interjected Hereward, "I would have you remember that on Ely you are as much my guests as the good abbot's, since your safety here depends on me and my men."

"Who is this?" sniffed Ethelwine.

"The wolfshead Hereward," answered his brother. "I heard all about him when I was Bishop. A profligate, a delinquent, a robber of Holy Church."

"I am what stands between you and King William's justice," retorted Hereward. "He has never been a respecter of sanctuary, and now you are his enemies he will hunt you without mercy. If you are to remain on this island, you will behave with courtesy to me, my wife, my men, and my Danish allies."

"Danes!" exclaimed Ethelric, turning purple. "You have Northmen here, at Ely? In this holy place?"

"The Danes have been a Christian people for three generations," said Wulfwine mildly.

"They are the more at fault, then, that they remain ravagers and pirates! Tell the people of York that the Danes are Christians, and your allies!"

"York was sacked by William in March, and Malet burned most of what was left before ever Asbjorn got there," said Hereward. "I doubt he can have done much more harm than they."

"Impious, intransigent, and a fool," sneered Ethelric. "You have not changed, Hereward Askilsson."

"You do not know me, my lord," said Hereward. "Whatever Herluin of Peterborough has told you, you do not know me."

"Nor do I wish to." Ethelric turned to the abbot. "You do not house this bandit within the monastery?" he asked.

"Not regularly, my lord," said Thurstan unhappily. "But his wife and child are housed in our pilgrim hostel – and

131

we can hardly deny entry to our protector."

"We shall have to tolerate it," said Ethelwine hastily, before his brother could speak. "I am sure there is room for all." Hereward doubted that; what, he wondered, would the sons of Svend think of this? But for now, he inclined his head towards Ethelwine, and said nothing.

They found the Danish princes practising their axe-throwing, with a cowhide nailed to a dead tree for a target. The throwing axe had long since all but passed out of use in actual combat, superseded in Denmark by the larger battleaxe designed for hand-to-hand fighting, but the sport remained popular. Knud was taking aim as Hereward and Winter approached.

"Who are the shavelings' guests?" he asked, without looking round.

"The Bishop of Durham, and his brother the ex-Bishop Ethelric," said Hereward. "King William was going to depose the Bishop, so he fled with the cathedral treasure." The axe thunked into the cowhide, about a span and a half off centre.

"Treasure?" said Harald. "The Durham plate?"

"And the relics of St Cuthbert," said Hereward. Harald whistled.

"We could do with that silver," he observed. "To buy arms and supplies."

"Don't think I hadn't thought of that," agreed Hereward. "But we're safer not crossing the bishops, at least for now. The Abbot wants to stay on the right side of them, and we need his goodwill."

"Why?" demanded Knud. "We occupy Ely whether your Abbot Thurstan likes it or not. They need us, not we them."

"There's no sense in antagonising the monks," insisted Hereward. "It's hardly as if we're in urgent need of the silver. What we need to do is plan for the rescue of Martin Lightfoot; but I don't ask you and your men to have any part in that."

Harald hefted his axe and let fly. It struck the target almost exactly on the centre line; Knud grimaced.

"We'll play our part," said Harald. "We're your guests here too, and we know our obligations, even if the Bishop doesn't."

"Thank you," said Hereward, "but I haven't a plan yet. If they mean to take him to Cambridge, we should attack the convoy as they pass through the Bromeswold, but we don't yet know what Herluin intends or where to attack."

"You say there are only a handful of Norman guards at Peterborough?" said Knud. Hereward nodded. "Well then, this Herluin must know you'll plan a rescue; so he'll send for more men from Cambridge. When they come, you'll know he plans to send your friend to die the next day."

"But Cambridge is far away," said Hereward, "and Herluin and Drogo know that I'll have men watching the roads. They'll be more likely to seek help from the local barons – Ogier, Ivo, Gilbert of Ghent."

"And we can't be sure we'll hear of their coming in time," added Winter.

"Could we lay siege to Peterborough?" wondered Knud. Hereward shook his head.

"They'd just kill Martin as soon as we turned up. They wouldn't fear revenge – who'd slight a monastery? And besides, we'd be exposed to attack."

"Then we lay an ambush on the Cambridge road now," said Knud. "It's sure to be soon; what's a few days' wait?"

"Life and death, perhaps," said Hereward, "especially when they may not even take the main road. Sheriff Ordgar will have patrols in the Bromeswold. No, I don't believe we can plan our ambush until we've made contact with Brother Benedict. But thank you for the offer of help; we may need it."

He walked away, looking at the ground. Winter was about to follow when Harald caught him by the arm.

"Many men may die in this attack," he said. "Is it

worth it? For one man?"

"That's why Hereward didn't want to ask your help," replied Winter. "Ideally, he'd take only his friends. There are enough of us who'd be willing to die for Martin. Besides: Hereward doesn't let his men hang."

"Then that's good enough for us," said the Dane. "We're with you."

"So," said Martin, "why haven't you hanged me yet?"

"Be quiet," snapped Drogo.

A cellar of the abbey had been turned into a makeshift dungeon; but on Herluin's assistance Martin was guarded at all hours. He had heard too much of the cunning and daring of Hereward's men to risk an escape. It was damp and dim, lit by one hissing torch, and the soldier hated it, not least because the prisoner would not stop talking to him.

"I know, I know, I'm to be sent to Cambridge. Very fine and grand; but is it wise?" Drogo shivered.

"You're not going to be rescued," he insisted.

"Maybe not," said Martin. He would have shrugged had his arms not been pinioned. "But if you think you'll be safer when I'm dead, you're a fool. If I'm not rescued I'll certainly be avenged. Be glad if I do escape: it'll mean you just might survive."

"I told you to be quiet!" The Norman's voice was quavering.

"These are things you should think about," said Martin. "Come on – loosen my bonds, and let me go. You'll only have to answer to the Prior; whatever he does, it'll be better than answering to Hereward."

Drogo strode over, and struck Martin in the face. The Norman, who had never seen combat, was slightly built, and not used to employing his fists; and Martin rolled with the blow as well as his bonds permitted; but he was knocked off his feet, and fell jarringly to the floor.

"I told you," muttered Drogo. "I told you. You've not

got long left now; Abbot Herluin's sent to the Lord Ogier. As soon as he can spare the men to take you, it's off to Cambridge with you, to stretch your neck."

"Yes, I'm certain," said Lewine breathlessly. "A guard from the abbey rode into Bourne at dusk."

"Then Ogier will set out as soon as he can raise the men – tomorrow, if he can," said Hereward. "They'll spend the night at Peterborough, and leave with Martin in the morning, unless we do something."

"We could ambush them before they got to Peterborough," suggested Geric. "They won't be expecting that."

"And what good does that do?" demanded Hereward. "Martin will still be a prisoner. Unless we storm the abbey he won't leave without the guard."

"Then we provide the guard." Everybody looked round, startled. They had not heard Girolamo di Salerno enter the barn. He moved forward, into the torchlight, into the circle that had gathered around Hereward.

"What do you mean?" asked Geric.

"A detachment pins down Ogier's men at Bourne, long enough to delay them from getting to Peterborough; and a guard of men not known to Herluin or his soldiers turns up at the abbey, says Ogier couldn't come, and marches out with Martin under guard and with the Prior's blessing." Speaking rapidly as he was, Girolamo's English occasionally failed him, and he substituted snatches of French: but Hereward, at least, was understanding him.

"The men who went to the abbey would need to take all our mail and half our helms and shields," mused Hereward. "There'd be precious little armour for the ones who attack Bourne. And how many men do we have who can pass as Normans?"

"I can," said Girolamo. "We only need one or two to speak. Azecier and I are fluent in Norman French, and

135

nobody at Peterborough has seen us. As for armour, the Danes have byrnies enough: even if they won't lend men, they can lend mail."

"You'd be prepared to do that?" said Hereward. "It would be a terrible risk."

"I don't think so," said Girolamo. "So long as Ogier's men don't come, the worst that can happen is a fight with the abbey guards. And how many are they? Five? Six? We'll be twenty."

"Thirty," corrected Hereward. "It must look convincing, as if Ogier's sent every man he can raise: after all, they're expecting an ambush in the Bromeswold." He grasped Girolamo's hand. "Thank you for this," he said. "I know you didn't come here to fight; and this is a mission for none but volunteers. I won't forget what you've done for us."

The Italian shook his head.

"There's no we and you," he said, "not now. I want nothing more than to be one of you."

It was the coldest hour of the grey dark before dawn when an arrow hissed out of the mist. The solitary sentry guarding Ogier's stables had not worn his aventail, hating the weight and coldness of the metal and expecting no attack: and the arrow pierced him through the throat. He fell without a sound.

Led by Wulfric, half a dozen men hurried forward. It was the work of moments to drag the corpse aside, unbar the door and get inside: but while it would have been easy simply to turn the horses loose, getting them away without waking the house was another matter. This would take delicacy, and time; the beasts would have to be woken and led away without startling them; there would very probably be a groom sleeping above the stable. While the others set about waking the horses as gently as possible, Wulfric – the quickest, with his tumbler's training – scaled the ladder.

"Wh-?" was all the bleary groom managed to say

before he was knocked out. He would sleep past dinner now.

Meanwhile, in a copse on the Peterborough road, Hereward and the Danish princes were overseeing the dragging of a massive tree trunk into the path, while another, a few yards further back, was hoisted on ropes, ready to fall. Anybody who got that far, with no horses and the axle of the condemned cart hacked through, would be trapped, with archers and slingers on both sides. Ogier, even assuming that he had been ready to set out, would not be seeing Peterborough today.

"Master, we are going into the jaws of death," grumbled Azecier. "Surely we don't owe this to these English."

"You owe it to me, this once, at least," said Girolamo curtly. "After this you may go back to Flanders or whither you will. I stay with the Lord Hereward."

"But why, master? What has changed? Why is he different from the Counts of Flanders or Brittany?"

"Answer me this, Azecier: what is the purpose of this mission?"

"To rescue the Irishman," said Azecier.

"Which I and every man here have chosen to do – even you, for all your complaints. Lord Hereward asked us, because he would not abandon his friend: but he did not require us, because he would not have others fight his battles, unless they choose, like him, out of friendship. That means more to him than land or gold or even reputation. Do you not find that admirable?"

Azecier grunted. It was not for Hereward's or Martin's sake that he was here, but for his master's; and if he had been able to persuade Girolamo to remain at Ely he would have been happy to stay there with him.

Remarkably, they had managed to fit out thirty men in decent enough armour to look like Norman soldiery: and, thanks to *De Re Militari*, they were well enough drilled to act the part, as long as none but Girolamo and Azecier had to speak. They marched three abreast, making short work of the roads; and had Girolamo not held them back, they would have arrived at Peterborough so early that even Herluin, ignorant in such matters, would have wondered how they had covered the ground from Bourne so fast.

None of Ogier's people thought to check the stables before they had breakfasted; it was only when a new sentry went out to relieve the man who had been shot that the raid was discovered. The baron was quickly called up, and swore by all the saints of Brittany: he had been fond of his horses, and they would be expensive to replace.

"Hereward," he spat.

"You're sure it wasn't ordinary bandits?" faltered Herluin's envoy.

"There are none left," said Ogier. "The ones Hereward hasn't recruited, he's killed or driven out."

"Then what do we do?"

"He must mean to slow us down. That means he's going to try some raid on Peterborough – with my horses, God damn it! Well, we can't get there ahead of him; all we can do is pray that Drogo and his men can hold him off. We will go, as planned; all this means is that I'll have to walk beside the men." He grimaced. "One good thing will come out of this," he said. "If Hereward does attack a monastery in force he may well be excommunicated. Then we'll see how long he keeps Thurstan of Ely's favour." He turned to his steward. "Round up twenty men and have them arm as quickly as possible. I'd have liked to take more, but there isn't time. If we can, I want to catch Hereward at Peterborough."

Twenty men were found, and set off at a quick step: but the baron himself soon struggled to keep up, unused to going on foot in armour. Every step of the way he cursed Hereward, and longed for his horse; and before noon he had called a halt for food and rest. Guards were put out on every side; but no trace of any ambush was found. It was some time before they proceeded into the wood, and into Hereward's trap – and their baron, his feet aching, was at the back of the column.

When the tree came down, Ogier, and the last five men, instinctively dived backwards, not forwards. One was too late: the trunk fell clean across him, pinioning him, his legs crushed and oozing blood and marrow. The baron and the other four formed a circle, drawing their swords, and waited. A few moments later, the hail of arrows, darts and stones began – but not onto them. They were falling onto the men caught between the two trunks, whose screams rent the stillness of the copse, sending up flights of startled birds.

"We will retreat," said Ogier through gritted teeth. "There's nothing we can do here."

Thus it was that, when Hereward called out of the trees for Ogier, the baron was already gone.

"He's not here," one of the soldiers yelled back, breathing heavily and nursing an arrow wound in his upper arm. "Whoever you are, we surrender; cease your attack." Of twenty-one men including the baron, five had fled, and one lay under the fallen tree; four more had taken arrow wounds from which they could not recover, and nearly all were in some degree hurt.

"Lay down your weapons and take off your armour," called Hereward, "and we'll let you carry your wounded back to Bourne."

"And lay ourselves open to your arrows?"

"If you don't, I promise every one of you will die. You may be able to take one or two of us with you, but will that be worth it against the chance to live?" He had spoken in crisp, clear Norman French; every soldier had understood him. They began to mutter among themselves; some were saying "Don't trust the English bastard", "We can break out", but soon it became clear which way the mood tended.

"We accept your terms."

While Ogier's men were stripping off their coats of mail, Girolamo and his column had arrived at Peterborough. The gates of the abbey were closed and barred; townsfolk had not been admitted to the services since Brand's death. A slat in the left hand gate was moved back when Girolamo knocked, and a nervous-looking monk peered out. Drogo had wanted to replace the monastery doorman with one of his guards, but Herluin had pointed out that rebels would be charier about killing an English monk than a Norman soldier.

"We come from Ogier fitz Ungomar at Bourne," said Girolamo in clear French. The monk frowned uncomprehendingly, and he repeated the statement in English, with his best Norman accent. "We are here to relieve you of the prisoner Martin."

"Is the Lord Ogier himself here?"

"Alas, no," said Girolamo. "He was detained at Bourne."

"I will fetch Drogo fitz Dudo," said the doorman, eager to pass on responsibility, and scurried away. The wait could not have been long, but it felt like an age before Drogo's face appeared at the slot, eyes narrowed suspiciously.

"The Lord Ogier sent you?" he barked, in French.

"Yes."

"Did he send any token that you are who you say you are?" Girolamo smiled broadly, and took off his helmet.

"Who else should I be?" he asked. "Do I look English? Do I sound it? You see a man burned by the Sicilian sun, you hear a Norman tongue, and you ask whether I come from Lord Ogier? Are you a fool?"

"I'm sorry, sir," said Drogo, "but we can't be too careful. Might I ask your name?"

"Certainly," replied Girolamo affably. "I am Aubrey de Raffetot. *Sir* Aubrey de Raffetot. Is that good enough for you?" Aubrey de Raffetot had been a Norman adventurer Girolamo had known in Apulia; there was a chance that the

140

soldier would have heard the name. From the look on his face, it appeared that he had not: nevertheless, he looked suitably impressed to be addressing a knight. "The Lord Ogier could not be here, as there was a raid on Bourne last night; all our horses were stolen, and poor Herbert Berengar was killed. Doubtless the wolfshead Hereward planned to slow us down so that he could prepare a rescue for this Martin Lightfoot: but we will be ready for him." The mention of Berengar, one of Ogier's soldiers, was calculated to allay Drogo's suspicions: and, indeed, he could not see how the well spoken de Raffetot, with his Mediterranean tan, could possibly be one of Hereward's men. The guard looked over his shoulder, to where Herluin stood watching over him.

"Shall I let them in, Brother Prior – I mean Father Abbot?" he asked. Herluin nodded curtly, and Drogo slid back the bar and let the gates swing open.

The thirty men marched into the abbey courtyard and formed up in good Norman order, and Drogo wondered how he could ever have suspected these men of being outlaws.

"Fetch forth the prisoner," Herluin ordered him.

"What is happening, Father Abbot?"

Girolamo maintained his composure, but Azecier looked round in surprise – for the voice had been female. A young woman in a plain, nun-like blue kirtle had entered the courtyard; her severe white mantle failed to hide her golden hair, and Azecier caught his breath at her beauty.

"It is nothing, my lady," said Herluin sternly in English. "You may return to your chamber."

"Nothing?" The lady gestured at the thirty soldiers.

"They are here to take the prisoner to Cambridge."

"Then I will stay and see your prisoner," she said. "I haven't been allowed to see anything or anyone since I've been here."

"Your husband -"

"My husband left me in your care, not your custody," she said. Herluin bit his tongue: he hated having a woman in

141

the abbey at all, but the lady was noble, and Abbot Brand had insisted that the rule of hospitality was more sacred than the rule against the admission of women. Furthermore, since her husband's family was in rebellion against the King, she might yet be of use as a hostage: although Herluin did not dare place her under guard yet. For the moment, then, her insolence must be endured.

It seemed a wait as long as years before Drogo dragged the blinking, dishevelled Martin out of the dark recess that led to the cellar and into the light of day.

"Sir Aubrey," he said, with a little bow. "Your prisoner."

"Martin!" exclaimed the woman. "Martin Lightfoot!"

Martin looked up, frowning curiously, as his eyes became used to the light, and she came into focus.

"Lady Elfthryth?" he said. He blinked again. Whatever she might be doing in Peterborough, there was no mistaking her: she was Elfthryth, the wife of Dolfin Gospatricsson.

"You know the wolfshead?" said Herluin, unsurprised. "Well, make your farewells, my lady; he is to hang."

"No..!" Elfthryth exclaimed, but Martin interrupted her.

"I've had time enough to prepare myself, my lady," he said, trying not to smile as he glanced at Girolamo, "and I have no fear. At least I am leaving the hospitality of that hooded crow there that calls himself a man of God; I advise you to do the same."

"Thirty men to escort one?" said Elfthryth to Girolamo. "Are you so afraid of him?"

"We mean to put his fate beyond doubt," replied the Italian.

"Cowards! Cowards all!" She stepped up to the prisoner, and looked into his eyes, tears beginning to fall from her own. "Goodbye, Martin," she said softly. "I will pray for you." Then, leaning in, she added in a whisper: "I will see that Lord Hereward hears of this."

"Don't worry, lady," Martin hissed back. "He'll be hearing from me first." And he winked.

Girolamo ordered his men into a square around Martin, saluted the abbot, and marched them out: and that, almost too easy though it seemed, was that. Martin was free.

Hereward and the others met them less than an hour from Peterborough. By the time they arrived back at Ely, the relief of escape had sunk in, and they were laughing and joking as they stepped ashore from the barges: but in Hereward's throat the laughter died the moment that he looked on the face of the waiting Gwynnog.

"What is it?" he demanded. "What has happened?"

"A courier has come from Prince Asbjorn," said Gwynnog.

"From Axholme?"

"What does uncle say?" interrupted Knud. The Welshman shook his head.

"Not from Axholme," he said. "Asbjorn's fleet is in the Wash. There has been a battle..." He tailed off, and bit his lip. Hereward looked quizzically at him.

"And?" he prompted.

"William has taken Axholme."

Axholme.

The Danes had fled so quickly that they had left their tents and huts up, and half their supplies still in them; William had appropriated Asbjorn's pavilion, and was now standing before it, sampling the Danish prince's mead as he surveyed the deserted camp in the moonlight. A few snowflakes were beginning to fall, settling on the unroofed huts, the overturned benches, and the few bodies not yet removed. The Danish scramble for the ships had allowed the

143

Normans to take the island with little loss, but had also meant that they had killed few of the enemy, and that all of the long ships had escaped. This would not do. The English population, of course, had been less fortunate: with no ships to fly to, they had been obliged to weather the Norman landing: but as the camp was outside the town, they had not been directly in its path, and not many had been slain outright.

"Sire!"

Two men were approaching, a sentry escorting a courier in boots and riding cloak.

"What news?" asked the King.

"Word from Peterborough, sire."

"From Peterborough?" William frowned. "Come in." He turned and strode into the pavilion; the courier followed. Inside, the King's clerk was pottering about, trying to make sense of the jumbled chest of letters and charts they had brought from the south, which had been emptied pell-mell onto Asbjorn's table; it had not been cleaned first, and puddles of beer and mead were soaking through several of the documents. Two knights stood by, awaiting the monarch's orders.

William turned back to the courier.

"Well," he said, "what is your word from Peterborough?"

"The Abbot Brand Tokason is dead, sire," announced the courier with a bow, sweeping his cloak back with a flourish so that his bright particoloured tunic was displayed. "The acting Abbot Herluin sends you his compliments."

"Brand's death was already known to us," said William brusquely. "As too was the capture of the Irishman Martin, known as Lightfoot. Is he hanged yet?" The courier faltered.

"Alas, no, sire," he said. "The Irishman was rescued."

"Rescued?" exclaimed William. "From under the noses of Herluin and his guards?"

"The English came in strength and with guile, sire -"

"Shut up," said the King. "What is your name?"

"Drogo fitz Dudo, sire. I command the abbey guards."

"Then you are as culpable as that cuckoo Herluin. And he thinks he is fit to run an abbey!" The King turned to his clerk. "What did I do with Thorold of Fécamp?" he asked.

"Your Grace made him Abbot of Malmesbury," said the cleric. "There is a pile of letters half a yard high back in London, begging Your Grace to find him another appointment." William frowned, surprised.

"From Thorold?" he said. "That's not like him."

"From the Prior of Malmesbury," said the clerk. "And the Sub-Prior. And the cellarer, the librarian, the infirmarian..." William broke into a grin.

"Then it is time we heeded their prayers," he declared. "Thorold always did enjoy a scrap; he deserves an enemy worth the fighting, and we shall give him one." He snapped his fingers at one of the knights. "Waryn," he said, "as soon as I can spare you from this campaign you will take your troop of cavalry and ride to Malmesbury Abbey. There you will inform the Abbot Thorold that he is to be the new Abbot of Peterborough, and you will accompany him thither with all your men as soon as is convenient. You will serve as the Abbot's steward and captain of the garrison of Peterborough until further notice." He pointed at the clerk. "You," he said, "prepare the necessary papers, and make sure the chapter of Peterborough and the local bishop understand my will. I want no opposition to Abbot Thorold. I want him confirmed in his office by the time Waryn is free." And, finally, the King turned back to Drogo fitz Dudo. "And you..." he said softly. "Get out. I ought to hang you for this failure, but somebody has to command at Peterborough until Thorold and Waryn get there. Be warned, though: I am giving Abbot Thorold full authority over the life and death of any who oppose, hinder or fail him in his journey to Peterborough. If he is disappointed he will not show mercy to you or any other.

Now go. Be off the Isle of Axholme within the hour." Drogo nodded, gulped, and scurried out of the pavilion.

"What is our next move against the rebels, sire?" asked Waryn.

"We do not yet know where Asbjorn's ships have gone," said William. "He's not likely to have headed back to Denmark, not at this time of year; the crossing's too dangerous. He may mean to winter in Scotland, or he may be planning to keep raiding along the coast. We will need to move more troops into the North, as many as can be spared, to wipe out every pocket of rebellion here once and for all. Some men will have to remain in these parts to mind the coastal defences. Myself, I will go to York, to deal with Gospatric. You will accompany me." He turned to the other knight. "For you, Alan, I have another task."

Alan de Penthièvre inclined his head. He was the only one of the Penthièvre brothers King William entirely trusted. The Breton patriot Geoffrey had refused to accompany the invasion of England, claiming the need to defend his own lands – most likely against his Norman allies; Brian, the King's general in the West, was an able enough commander but had a delicate streak, an unfortunate tendency to attacks of conscience; the youngest, Black Alan – at the time of his christening, his brother had not been expected to live, and the name had been reused with typically Breton economy – was callow and inexperienced. Alan the Red was another matter. Owing everything to William, he would do the King's bidding without question or hesitation, and thus far he had pleased his monarch well.

"We need to make the suppression of this rebellion a lesson the English will never forget," the King went on. "Common folk in the villages of Yorkshire welcomed the Danes when they landed, staged feasts and dances for them. Gospatric remains loved in the further north. It is not only the nobles who need to be taught the consequences of defiance."

"A harrying, sire?" asked de Penthièvre.

"A harrying," agreed William.

"Of which region?"

"Everywhere," said the King. "The whole of the North between Humber and Tees, and beyond if necessary. Burn the fields and barns, destroy the livestock, slay all who resist. This will be the harshest winter England has ever known: and the world will see the fate of traitors in my realm."

York, January, 1070.

Apart from the twin bailies facing one another from their heights, there was little left of York. The very walls had been pulled down; most houses that had survived the firing of the Danish quarter and the subsequent onslaught of Asbjorn had now been burned. Wherever the ground showed through the thin covering of white snow, it was black, charred and dead. In places thin plumes of smoke still rose. Many of the dead, soldiers and civilians alike, lay unburied, food for stray dogs and carrion birds; at the western gate, facing the woods, even a few wolves had entered the city, driven by hunger.

Amid these ruins, King William had made his camp. In summer it would have been unbearable, but as it was, the cold kept the smell from growing too bad: and he wanted to inspire awe and fear in those who came to his Christmas court to do him homage. There were plenty of these: thanes whose lands were burning, and whose tenants and serfs had fled the harrying, came hoping to salvage some sort of living; greater nobles, fearing perpetual exile, came to renounce Svend and Edgar and beg the King's clemency; the poor came in hope of nothing more than a crust to put in their bellies. Red Alan, who had been named Earl of Richmond for his pains, had done his work well: there was a famine beginning all over the North, and it would get worse. Some had voluntarily outlawed themselves, preferring to shiver in the woods and steal the King's game rather than try to resurrect their farms; some had struck out for Scotland in the hope of building new lives there; and rumour said some had already resorted to eating human flesh. Certainly, many thousands had died, and the black smoke from their blazing stores and the pyres where their cattle and sheep had been piled high still hung over the whole of the North. Run-off from these pyres had contaminated those streams and wells which the Normans had not already poisoned, and in many areas there was only rain to drink. Even the King shuddered at the suffering he had seen, and vowed to endow at least three monasteries when he had the time, that Masses might be sung for those he had sent untimely to their graves.

But today was special. Today, there had returned to York the biggest fish William had angled for. As the supplicant's steed picked its cautious way over the rubble in what had once been the city's widest street, the reek stung his eyes, pricking forth the tears that he had sworn he would not let them see him shed; his son, riding behind him, was openly weeping.

Gospatric and Dolfin had come to surrender.

The King was waiting for them, on his own Franconian destrier, more than two hands higher than the Englishmen's mounts, in full mail but with a crown in place of his helmet. As they drew near him, soldiers took the reins of their horses, and motioned for them to dismount. Stiffly, they did so, and, at a gesture from the King, got down on their knees. Dolfin's face was crimson with shame and anger; William permitted himself a half smile before demanding:

"Where are the rest of your family?"

"My wife and youngest son are in Carlisle," mumbled Gospatric, looking at the ground. "My son Waldeve is in Scotland."

"So all are in lands hostile to us," said William. "Tell me, why should I believe in your good faith?"

"I have summoned them," said Gospatric, struggling to control the catch in his voice. "Ethelreda and Patrick will come, I promise you. If Waldeve does not…"

"If Waldeve does not, he will be outlawed in the realm of England, that I promise you," said William. "But you are his father. And you have betrayed me once already." Gospatric gritted his teeth. He knew exactly why William had to trust him: because there was nobody else left who could control the wild Borderers, or who was even willing to be Earl of the ruined remains of Northumbria: but to say so might be to risk his life and his son's.

"I own my fault in that," he said, "and submit myself most humbly to Your Grace's mercy."

"As do I," said Dolfin, almost inaudibly under the whistling of the wind.

"Our allegiance", Gospatric went on, "we pledge entirely to Your Grace, now and for ever: and this we swear in the name of Our Lord Jesus Christ."

"Amen," added Dolfin. William paused long, before declaring:

"We accept your allegiance."

The brother bishops had departed in disgust from Ely as soon as they heard of the approach of Asbjorn, taking refuge instead at Peterborough, where, for the moment, Herluin had reluctantly afforded them shelter: although now that word had come of Abbot Thorold's appointment, it was doubtful how much longer they would be welcome there. For the moment, the monks were resisting electing William's choice: but all knew they would sooner or later have to submit. They could elect an alternative abbot, but the King would only block his confirmation: and as long as they were without a head it was all but impossible to conduct business and collect revenues.

One guest at Peterborough had not waited for the election. The moment word had come of the King's decision, Elfthryth had left the abbey and ridden east, to seek shelter in the last place south of the Border where she felt safe: and so the wife of Dolfin, a matter of days before her husband and father-in-law surrendered, had come to Ely.

Hereward had welcomed her warmly, Abbot Thurstan solicitously, and a chamber had been prepared for her in the hostel, near Torfrida's. Torfrida welcomed her with

150

a degree of polite suspicion: but they had settled into a kind of friendship. Elfthryth was warm and open to all, and good with Torfridel, who beamed whenever she appeared, and quickly learned to say "Eff-riff".

Asbjorn's men kept themselves mostly to their ships, though he and a few of his captains were occasional visitors to Ely, coming to get drunk with his nephews and seek for female company. The monks were scandalised, but could do nothing.

It happened that Asbjorn was entertaining Harald and Knud aboard his ship when a strange vessel arrived in the Wash. She was a dragon ship, but smaller, narrower, and of an older style than the Danish ones; her sail was dyed in a zigzag pattern, her sides hung with shields, and she bristled with armed men.

The outlying Danish ship hailed her as she nosed in towards the fleet.

"Ahoy," called her helmsman. "Who goes there?"

"The Atheling Edgar Edwardsson, lawful King of England," came the unexpected reply, in perfect Norse.

"Edgar Edwardsson on a dragon ship?" said Asbjorn when the news was brought to him. "This I have to see."

"We'll come with you," volunteered Knud, who was curious to meet his father's rival. Asbjorn smiled and nodded, but Harald disagreed.

"Not all of us," he said. "We don't know if we can trust this Edgar."

"Well, stay here if you're afraid," his brother jibed. Harald's eyes narrowed.

"If you don't know the difference between cowardice and good policy, God help the men you lead to war," he spat.

Edgar's helmsman was duly informed, and gave permission for Asbjorn, Knud and a small guard to come aboard. The smaller vessel drew up beside Asbjorn's *Sea Wolf*, and the Danes, disdaining gangplanks, leapt across the narrow gap as if they were a boarding party. When they had got their balance back, they found Edgar standing before them, in full hauberk and helm. The effect, with his bright blue eyes staring out from either side of the nosepiece, and his high cheekbones framed by the top of his aventail, would have been most impressive, had not his posture betrayed the fact that he found the armour uncomfortably heavy.

The Atheling was flanked by two somewhat more natural-looking warriors, likewise armed from helm to heel. One, broad-chested and dark-haired, was only a little older than the prince himself, but carried himself with an air of command. This man was known to the Danes: he was Waltheof Siwardsson. The other, an older man with ruddy colouring and a scar on his cheek, was a stranger to them: but he wasted no time in introducing himself, speaking good Norse but with a strong Scots-Gaelic accent.

"I bid you right welcome aboard the *Orca*, princes," he said with a smile. "The lords Edgar and Waltheof I believe you know; my name is Melmuir mac Duncan, Mormaor of Atholl."

"Mor..?" Asbjorn frowned, puzzling over the unfamiliar word.

"You would say Jarl, or Earl; it is close enough."

"Wait." Knud snapped his fingers. "I've heard of you." He turned to his uncle. "This is King Malcolm's brother!"

"Correct, my lord," said Melmuir. "We have come to pay a visit to my old friend Hereward Askilsson."

"With a shipful of armed men?"

"Is that not what Hereward needs? Since Axholme fell and Gospatric surrendered, Ely is the last stronghold of the Bastard's enemies this side of the Lakes."

"Gospatric has surrendered?" echoed Asbjorn. "We have heard nothing of this."

"Whether you have heard it or not, it is true," said Melmuir, some iron entering his soft voice for the first time. "The loss of Gospatric and the harrying of the North has brought the war to our borders. Scotland is not prepared to sit still and become the Bastard's next prey when he has devoured England. We are here to fight."

"How many of you?" sneered Knud. "Fifty? Forty? Is that the greatest army Malcolm Canmore can raise?"

"My brother the King", said Melmuir calmly, "is in Northumbria with twelve hundred men. The Bastard will be caught between our forces, if you will cooperate."

"And your price?" said Knud sharply.

"Why, no more than the acknowledgement of England's lawful King: our kinsman, Edgar Edwardsson."

Lumphanan, 1057.

"There they are, my lord," said Melmuir, pointing. "At the top of the rise. There can't be three dozen left."

"Even so," said his brother, "they have a defensive position, and Macbeth is not a fool. If he means to sell his life he'll make us pay dearly for it."

It was now three years since the princes had ridden across the Border to claim their father's throne; three years since the victory at Dunsinane, three years of advance into the north; their English allies had all gone home, save for Hereward, who, outlawed in his own country, saw Scotland as his best hope to build a new life. But through Scotland there ran a fault. For more than a century the men of Atholl and of Moray, the two greatest provinces of the kingdom, had been at feud, their Mormaors struggling for power: Atholl's victory had seemed decisive when Duncan mac Crinan, one of their own, had become King, but his high-handedness had driven the men of Moray to rebellion, and their Mormaor, Macbeth, had slain Duncan and seized his throne. Now the sons of Duncan were home, and the men of Atholl rejoiced: but the men of Moray clustered around Macbeth. The King might be cornered, he might be outnumbered: but he was still

King of Scots – and this was his country.

"When this is done," muttered Malcolm, "there will be no more of this bickering. I won't rule as an Atholl man, to be King of Atholl alone; I will be a true King of Scots."

"Well, boys?" came a shout from the heights ahead. "What have you got?"

"It's him," breathed Melmuir. "It's Macbeth."

The King of Scots had stepped out before his line of soldiers. He was on foot, but stood half a head taller than any of them; he had taken off his helmet, displaying his ruddy face streaked with blue warpaint, and his famous mane of red-gold hair, now shot with grey. He wore the ancient dress of the men of Moray: a long fringed tunic, a bronze torque upon his neck and another on his forearm, and a square shield, sheathed in iron, with swirling spirals embossed upon it: and he brandished a boar spear. He seemed like some vengeful ghost from an elder age.

"Does he not realise we could shoot him down?" wondered Melmuir. "Or does he not care?"

"It would be quite a shot, at this distance," remarked Hereward. "Our bows aren't powerful. I'll try if you like."

"No." The cold voice belonged to the Mormaor of Fife, whose eyes had taken on a wild glitter when Macbeth had appeared. "He is mine." The roots of MacDuff's hatred for the King, Hereward did not know: none of the Scots would speak of it: but hate him he did.

"How are we to attack?" he asked. "We cannot come behind them, and I see no way to draw them down the slope."

"So," said Malcolm, "we must make a frontal assault. It will be costly, but we are easily enough to take their position – and at least they have no bowmen."

"We could lose twice their numbers before we win through," objected Melmuir. "If we encamp here, where can they run to? They have no food, no shelter and no way down." Malcolm shook his head.

154

"We cannot let Macbeth escape again," he said. "As long as he is loose, this war will not be over. And the only way to be sure of taking or killing him is to attack today, before dusk."

"We may not be able to come behind them in force," said Hereward, "but if just a few men made it to the upper slopes, they could provide a distraction while the main force attacked from below. I don't know the land here: is there a way to get a handful of us round behind them before dark?"

Melmuir turned to their local scout, and repeated the question in Gaelic. The man thought for a moment, and nodded.

Over the next couple of hours, Malcolm and his men made three feints up the hill, falling backwards as soon as the men of Moray began to hurl their rocks and darts. There were a few bruises and grazes, but no serious wounds on either side. Finally, over the crag which loomed behind Macbeth's men, there waved a white flag: the signal.

"Charge!"

The princes' men poured out of their woodland cover in fullest strength for the first time, and surged up the slope, like a tidal bore rushing up a river. The men of Moray had not so far seen the full numbers of the Southerners; many gasped.

"Hold," barked Macbeth. "Keep your courage firm. Be ready to meet them."

Suddenly, rocks were raining down on the men of Moray from above. They turned: a dozen men were skidding down the slopes above them, pelting them with sharp stones. Two had already fallen with cracked skulls. Darts were thrown back, one well-aimed one bringing down the scout, who somersaulted down the rocky slope and landed in a bloody heap at the feet of the King.

"Keep the line!" shouted Macbeth. These men behind the line were gadflies only; they must not be allowed to distract from Malcolm's attack. He ordered six spearmen to turn, to be ready to repel the men coming from above: but the attackers were by now almost upon them. Meanwhile, those coming from below had crashed into the Moray line. The line wavered: the attackers on the slope skidded into the Moray men, Hereward cutting down two of the defending spearmen with one sweep of his sword: and the line crumpled and broke.

There was now no order left in the battle, just a bloody shambles of milling men, stabbing, slashing, struggling desperately to survive. Now only numbers would tell, and numbers were on the side of the princes: but many good men would die before it was over.

The princes themselves were in the thickest of the fighting, back to back, holding off the Moray men, while MacDuff hacked men down like inconvenient undergrowth, trying to carve his path to Macbeth. Stones were still flying: and, suddenly, one caught Melmuir on the side of the head, and he slumped stunned to the ground. Seeing the gap at Malcolm's back, a wild-haired Moray man leapt forward, swinging a battleaxe: but it never fell. Hereward, who had fought his way to the princes' side, drove his sword into the axeman's chest, and he tottered, swayed, looked down in shock at the blood dribbling down the front of his leather cuirass, and managed to mutter *"Diabhol!"* before he crashed to the ground.

"Aiee!" There were many screams on the slopes of Lumphanan, but that one rose above all the others. Men stopped in mid fight, and looked up. MacDuff had mounted a rock above the Moray position; he was covered from head to toe in blood, most of it not his own, and brandished before him a gory trophy: the hewn-off head of the King of Scots. "Behold the tyrant! Behold the Herod, the butcher, the usurper, the man of blood! He is slain! Macbeth is slain!"

A sepulchral silence fell over Lumphanan, broken only by the groans of the wounded and the cawing of the first crows already beginning to gather. Out of this silence, there arose a single high, keening voice, a Moray man mourning his fallen lord:

> "Poison is this weapon,
> Poison he who owns it,
> Poison the hand that cast it,
> Poison for him that fell by it:
> If it stays within the *rath*,
> Plague will lie on the land."

Ely.

"Melmuir!" Hereward exclaimed, opening wide his arms to embrace the Mormaor of Atholl. Melmuir returned the hug; but when he stood back, he detected a slight tone of suspicion in Hereward's question: "What brings you to Ely?"

"The right of Prince Edgar," said Melmuir simply. "King Edgar, as should be. And will be."

Hereward frowned.

"The time for that is past," he said. "Edgar had his chance, at York. He failed."

"My brother failed to destroy Macbeth at Dunsinane," Melmuir reminded him. "Yet you stayed by his side, and we won in the end. A rightful king is still a rightful king."

"Malcolm was my ring-giver," said Hereward. "That was personal. But now I have more than my honour to consider – there is England's good."

Melmuir raised his eyebrows.

"And England's good lies with the Danes?"

"Svend is no more foreign than Edgar," Hereward pointed out. "Even to the Southron Saxons – Edgar was raised abroad, by a Hungarian mother. And we in the Danelaw are more Norse than Saxon to begin with. But blood doesn't make a man. If there were a Greek or a Saracen who'd make a better King of England than Svend, he'd have my loyalty."

"What about a Norman?"

Hereward grimaced.

"If he would give back English lands and treasures, restore the English law, pay the wergild for all the thousands the Normans have slain, then yes, even a Norman. But there is no such man. Svend is all we have."

"Things were different at York, though," said Melmuir. "You had no allies."

"So now Scotland deigns to help us?" said Hereward, raising an eyebrow. "What has changed? What did it take to make Malcolm realise William wants his kingdom too?"

"The Normans have raided and harried our borders," said Melmuir. "But there is also the matter of kinship. Edgar is now one of our family. His sister the Princess Margaret has consented to marry my brother; our houses are one."

Hereward bit his lip.

"And Malcolm is prepared to bring an army in support of Edgar?"

"It is already in England."

"The Danes are my guests," said Hereward slowly. "In the autumn they cooperated with Edgar and his allies at York, but you know how that ended. They will not be eager to fight beside him again; and Svend himself will be here when the spring comes."

"The Danes fight for gold, not land," said Melmuir. "They have been bought off before and they can be bought off again."

Hereward shook his head.

"Things are different since Canute's day," he said. "He made his family kings in England; they have not forgotten. Melmuir, I welcome you and your men, aye, and Edgar Edwardsson; and for any help you can give us, we will be grateful. But I cannot give my voice again to Edgar for the kingship."

There was a long, tense pause.

"Well," said Melmuir at length, "at least we can hurt

the Normans."

"Goll slew Lugaid of the Hundreds
On the field of Knock, I tell you true:
Fair Lugaid of the shining valour
Fell by the hand of Goll mac Morna.
By his hand fell Cumhal the Great,
On the field of Knock, among the hosts:
It was to lead Ireland's warband
That they bravely fought the fight."

It was usually Wulfric who sang in the Camp of
Refuge; but, with Gaelic-speaking guests, Martin had
volunteered – or, more accurately, Hereward had volunteered
him. His voice did not compare to the English tumbler's, but
the Scots did not care; they were delighted just to hear a song
they knew in this strange land, and clapped and hooted
wildly. Hereward, who sat by Melmuir with the women – for
such an occasion as this, Torfrida could not but join the
company, leaving Torfridel with Kolfrosta; while Elfthryth,
who had known the Mormaor when she was a child in
Lothian, had been happy to renew old acquaintance – joined
in the applause; but the Danes did not.
  "A heathenish language," muttered Harald; to which
Knud added, none too quietly,
  "And a devilish voice."
  "Come, Lord Asbjorn," called Melmuir in Norse, "sit
with us." They were outdoors, in the heart of the camp: it was
a frosty night, but a bonfire had been lit, and was keeping
them warm enough. Wulfric and Rowena were holding up
their little son, Octha, younger even than Torfridel, letting
him watch logs pop and sparks scatter; he gurgled happily.
  Asbjorn stalked over; Krakus followed behind him,
smoothing his moustache. They took their seats, the Dane
stiffly, the Wagrian carelessly.
  "My lord Melmuir," said Asbjorn, with a curt nod.

159

"Do you mind if we speak English?" asked Hereward. "The Lady Torfrida has but little Norse."

Asbjorn grunted; if Torfrida had little Norse, Krakus had less English, but he did not particularly care whether the Wagrian prince understood them or not.

"When may we expect the company of King Svend?" asked Melmuir.

"As soon as the sea is passable," said Asbjorn. "Before April; maybe much sooner."

"I shall look forward to it," said the Scot. "Your brother's prowess is sung of in Scotland, as elsewhere. It will be an honour to fight alongside him."

"Indeed," said Asbjorn. "We hear little of King Malcolm in Denmark."

"Well, Malcolm has not been so blessed in his enemies. We cannot all be granted a Hardrada."

"We could not all defeat him."

"Maybe not," conceded Melmuir. "But Svend wasn't alone in that. Harold of England beat Hardrada, and slew him: and William the Bastard beat Harold."

"Are you saying William's a greater warrior than Svend?"

"We will not know that until they meet," said the Mormaor mildly. "But let us say, a greater challenge than any of us has yet faced, including King Svend."

"Harald Hardrada was the greatest warrior in Europe," insisted Asbjorn. "He commanded the armies of Kiev, and the Varangian Guard in Constantinople. He reconquered Bulgaria for the Eastern Emperor and cleared the robbers from the pilgrim road to Jerusalem. He suppressed the feuding nobles of Norway -"

"Nobody disputes his valour," said Melmuir. "The fierceness of the Norwegians is but one more reason why Scotland and Denmark should be friends: they are a danger common to us both."

"By the four faces of Svantevit!" Krakus interjected. "I

wish I had known this Hardrada."

"He slew the Bulgar Khan with his own hands," said Asbjorn. "But when he heard his pitiful nephew had taken the throne of Norway, he desired to go home, and to take with him his lover, the Princess Maria – but the Empress her aunt would not hear of it, and threw the hero in jail. Men say she secretly lusted for him herself. But by the intercession of St Olaf, he was rescued from his dungeon by a noblewoman of the court whom the saint had once cured of a wasting sickness; and his Varangians helped him to abduct Maria from her chambers and make it to their ship. And they raided all around the Mediterranean, and filled their hold with treasure, before they returned to the North."

"I heard this story," remarked Melmuir. "I wondered what had become of Maria, since I had never heard that he brought her back to Norway. And then I spoke with a Varangian from Orkney who had served under Hardrada, and he told me Maria was no princess but a waiting gentlewoman, and Hardrada was imprisoned for plotting to steal the Empress' jewels, and the girl did not come to Norway because he left her in Constantinople when he escaped. A great warrior, certainly, but let us not exaggerate his deeds."

Asbjorn was turning purple when Hereward intervened.

"He does not compare to your lordship's own ancestors, after all," he told the Dane. "Your uncle Canute, and your grandfather Svend the First with the forked beard, were more successful in war." Asbjorn smiled.

"Conquerors of England and Norway," he said proudly. "They were unbeaten."

Melmuir muttered something under his breath.

"What did you say?" snapped Asbjorn.

"Oh, nothing," said Melmuir. "I was just wondering if you had heard of the Battle of Luncarty."

"No," growled the Dane.

"Eighty years ago, your grandfather decided to add Scotland to his empire. He landed at Montrose with fire and sword, and laid waste to Angus. When word was brought to the King of Scots, he drew up his army on the plain where the Earn and Tay flow together, at a place called Rhynd, and they marched out to face the Danes. They met at Luncarty, and it looked as if the day would go Svend's way; the Scots were in retreat; but then a farmer and his two sons, who had disdained to join the battle earlier, took up their stand on a rise in the centre of the field, and called out, 'Turn again, Scotsmen! Do not flee!' And the Scots rallied, and the Danes were put to flight, and to this day that rise is called the Turn Again Hillock; and Svend decided England would make easier prey."

Asbjorn glowered.

"I never heard of my grandfather losing a battle," he said.

"Is it necessary to fight over these long gone wars?" asked Torfrida. "We have a war here and now. We are all on the same side today, Scots, Danes, and English. If we do have differences we can surely put them aside until the Normans are beaten."

"Need we talk of war at all?" wondered Elfthryth. "Can it not wait for day?"

"War never waits," said Hereward gruffly. "But you're right," he added, nodding to Torfrida. "We are friends here."

"If I have caused any offence, I apologise," said Melmuir. "None was meant." He held out his hand; Asbjorn regarded it suspiciously for a long moment, then took it, limply, with an expression of extreme distaste, but took it nonetheless.

The last remnants of the fire were dying down, and frost reasserting its grip on the camp, as a cloaked and cowled figure picked its way through the debris of the celebrations.

Despite the cold, a few warriors too drunk to make it back to their huts lay asleep outside, wrapped in their cloaks, shivering occasionally in their slumbers, their extremities glowing red as the embers; but most had found shelter. The Scots had been housed in the barn which served as a meeting place; the old year's rotting hay might smell noxious, but at least it provided some warmth. For tonight, Edgar slept among them, although Abbot Thurstan had promised that a chamber would be found for him at the monastery, or at least in the pilgrim hostel.

Approaching the barn from the side, avoiding the gaze of the sentry on the door – who was, in any case, leaning on his spear in a half-doze – the hooded figure burst into a sudden spurt, running straight at the wall, and leapt. With the tips of his fingers he just managed to catch hold of the edge of a window some eight feet up, that led to the loft: and, slowly, gritting his teeth, gasping, he hauled himself up by his fingertips, until his chin was over the window, and he was able to reach in, gain purchase with first one elbow, then the other, and heave himself forward, the sill scraping painfully against his chest, until he tumbled into the loft. It was deserted: they were all down below. The cowled man drew his dagger. The hatch was open; he leant over it, peering down into the gloom below. He could see no movement, nor hear anything but snores. The Atheling would be near the centre, protected, surrounded by men – but sleeping men. With luck, they would be soundly sleeping still when the cowled man escaped.

His own breathing now sounding monstrously loud in his ears, the hooded man swung down, and dropped to the floor of the barn, wincing less at the impact than at the noise it made. Yes, there was Edgar, only three bodies away: to step over them and reach him would be little trouble, but getting away would be another matter. Eight or nine more men lay between him and the door; it would be easier to go back the way he had come. The trapdoor was lower than the window

163

outside had been; he should have no difficulty in jumping that high – it was only a question of getting enough time to pull himself up.

"Who's that moving about?"

The hooded man blinked, and glanced around in the darkness. He had seen nobody awake. There seemed still to be nobody – no, wait, there was someone propped up. The man had spoken Gaelic, which the intruder did not understand, but the import was plain. He had no choice: he dropped his dagger and jumped for the trapdoor.

"Hoy! Wake up! There's a damned outsider here!"

The Scots began to stir, as the hooded man swung back and forth, hauling himself upwards; the man nearest to him awoke to find a foot dangling above his face, and made an instinctive grab for it, but missed. The stranger disappeared into the loft, and a moment later a thud was heard as he leapt down from the window to the ground outside. By the time they had got the door open, he was long gone: but he had left behind his dagger.

It was not distinctive enough to identify the man: a very plain, unadorned iron weapon: but it spoke eloquently of his intent. Every man in the barn could see that what had just been thwarted was an assassination.

"There must be a score of such knives on the island," said Hereward, turning it over in his hands. "It tells us nothing of the man who wielded it."

"We know he was no Scotsman," said Melmuir. "Some of my men have been muttering about English treachery: but I don't believe he was any man of yours. He was there to kill Edgar, and it's the Danes who want Edgar dead."

"We don't know that," insisted Hereward. "I'd hate to believe it was any man of mine, but I couldn't swear it wasn't. And there were forty men in that barn besides Edgar."

"Only one that anybody here had reason to kill,"

164

insisted the Mormaor.

"I think you do yourself an injustice."

For the sake of privacy, they had prevailed upon Abbot Thurstan to lend them a chamber, well away from eavesdropping ears in the camp; even the Abbot himself had withdrawn, leaving the two leaders alone with Martin and Father Wulfwine. The narrow slit window provided little light, so a guttering lamp had been lit, and the smell pervaded the bare little room.

"The only one who'd have any grudge against me was Asbjorn."

"And Harald. And Knud," said Martin. "And any other Dane who heard you tell the Luncarty story. And there may have been quarrels enough in drink last night. Any one of your men might have picked a fight with one of Asbjorn's, or ours, or one of the islanders."

"Prince Edgar is still the most probable target," Wulfwine pointed out. "What is most regrettable is that now the whole island knows what happened. It will make for more ill feeling between the Scots and the Danes. We cannot afford to have our allies fighting each other, on the very soil of Ely."

"It may be too late to prevent it," said Martin. "Listen." Somewhere far outside, angry voices were raised. They could not hear the words, but the tone was clear enough.

Hereward's hand went instinctively to Brainbiter's hilt as the door of the cell was flung open: but it was Deacon Leofric who pushed his way in.

"You must come at once, my lords," he said abruptly, "before all falls into chaos."

They had no sooner left the abbey than they saw the crowd gathered in the open space before the gates: a circle of whooping, jostling men, surrounding they could not see what. Ulric Grogan, at a nod from Hereward, moved forward to join him, and together they shouldered their way through the crowd to the centre, Melmuir pushing behind them: there, unarmoured, circling around one another with long dirks in their hands, crouched, eyes narrowed, were a Scottish warrior – and Prince Knud. The Dane slashed suddenly forward at his opponent's face; the Scot leapt backwards, landing sure-footedly, the tip of the knife missing his nose by the breadth of a shrew's tail. With startling speed, he then threw himself forward, and might have deprived Svend of a son then and there, had not his own prince waded into the ring. He did not even see Melmuir's fist before it struck him on the temple, and he slumped heavily to the ground. There were angry yells from the crowd, and Knud shouted:

"I need no Scots to fight my battles for me!"

"Our battle is with the Normans!" snapped Melmuir. "The Bastard is laughing while we fight amongst ourselves!"

"Ourselves?" sneered Knud. "You're not us. We're not the same."

"We're on the same side," insisted Hereward.

"Are we?"

"Go back to the camp," Hereward ordered loudly in Norse. "Anybody who knows or guesses anything about the attempt on Prince Edgar's life, bring word to me at the pilgrim hostel. And if there is any more trouble between Scot and Dane, or Scot and English, or English and Dane, those found fighting will be flogged – whoever they may be." He shot a dark warning glance at Knud, who stared sullenly at the ground. Melmuir repeated the warning in Gaelic, and the crowd, muttering ominously, began to disperse.

It was good to have an excuse to wait at the hostel, without feeling that he was deserting his men; he sat quietly by Torfrida's side, his arm round her, stroking her hair, and watching Torfridel chase a wooden ball around the floor. Elfthryth crouched down, laughing, batting the ball back to the child; she looked carefree as an infant herself. Hereward wished the quarrels, and the war itself, were as far away as they seemed right now in this still gloom, under the light of the torches: but they were doomed always to intrude on his peace. It was not long before there came a knocking, and Kolfrosta scuttled crab-like across to open the door. The man she admitted, cowled and cloaked, looked so furtive that Hereward's hand dropped instinctively to his dagger, in fear that the would-be murderer had come for him: but as soon as the door was closed, the figure straightened, and pushed back his hood. At the sight of his face, Hereward started to his feet in surprise: it was Harald Svendsson.

"Prince Harald," Hereward exclaimed.

"Shh," hissed Harald. "Nobody knows I'm here, not even my brother."

Hereward's face darkened.

"Is that *why* you are here?" he asked. "Was Knud involved?" Harald shook his head.

"If I thought that I'd not have come to you," he said. "No, I don't believe Knud had anything to do with it, nor Asbjorn neither, whatever they thought of Edgar and his Scots friends."

"They are my friends too," Hereward pointed out. "But you obviously know something. Speak up: who was it?"

"I know nothing for certain," said Harald. "But I know who had a motive. Krakus."

"The Wagrian?" wondered Torfrida. "Why?"

"Krakus wants to marry my sister Mariana," said Harald, pacing nervously back and forth. "The Obodrites are trying to negotiate a concord with my father, but he's putting them off. To buy time he said that they could marry after this campaign, once he's King of England. Edgar threatens that, the marriage and the alliance."

"He also threatens your own hope of being King here one day," Hereward pointed out. "Not to mention every Dane's loyalty to your father."

Harald frowned.

"If Edgar becomes King, my father will claim the

silver Gospatric offered him," he said. "All the Danes know that, and they know Edgar wouldn't dare not pay. Why should they care about the crown? As for me, Denmark's enough. I've never wanted to be an emperor."

"So if the Normans offered more money for you to go home, you'd take it?" pressed Hereward. "You and all the Danes?"

Harald bridled.

"We're here now," he said, "and we're sworn to fight by you. We're men of our word. But the Obodrites..." He trailed off.

"I see," said Hereward. "But you have no evidence? Would you be prepared to challenge Krakus publicly?"

Once more, Harald shook his head.

"Not until some proof comes to light," he said. "But now you know where to look for it."

"I?" said Hereward, arching an eyebrow. "What if it's not there? I can't afford to be wrong; it would be a mortal insult. No, somebody needs to watch Krakus unobserved, perhaps search his belongings: and no Englishman can do that. It has to be a Dane."

In the event, it was neither Englishman nor Dane who found the damning evidence, but Krakus' own body-slave. He would have hidden it again had he been alone, but Krakus and Asbjorn had been placed in the same single-roomed house, and while the slave was making his master's bed Asbjorn's shield-bearer was sharpening his lord's axe. So it was that the shield-bearer saw the slave find a black, cowled cloak stuffed into the straw mattress, and hold it up in puzzlement, wondering whence it could have come; and it was the Dane who noticed that, as well as straw, there were stalks of hay sticking to the black wool. That a man in a black cowl who had crept through the hayloft was responsible for the bad blood between Danes and Scots was already well known; and the shield-bearer was instantly on his feet, hollering to all in hearing to come and witness the guilt of the Wagrian.

First into the room was Asbjorn himself, who shook his head sadly, and declared:

"We must show this to the Lord Hereward. And the Lord Melmuir, of course." Some of those Danes who had arrived behind him muttered angrily, saying that Krakus had tried to do them a favour: but Asbjorn was insistent. "We have a duty to show our goodwill," he said. "We owe it to our allies, and our King."

So the leaders were rounded up, and the men of the camp assembled, under a lowering sky, already spitting with rain. Krakus was there at the front of them, dark eyes flashing fire, brandishing his falchion and furiously protesting his innocence, swearing by all the gods of his people and calling on the wolves of Dazbog to rend his accusers' flesh; in his excitement he lapsed frequently into his own language.

Seeing Asbjorn, who bore aloft the damning black robe, he exclaimed:

"By all the curses of Marzanna! Do you dare outface me?"

The Dane shrugged.

"I don't want to believe it," he said. "But the proof..."

"Is nothing!" spat Krakus. "That thing was planted in my bed! I've never seen it before!"

"Do you wish to accuse anybody?" asked Hereward, calmly, speaking Norse.

"Yes," growled Krakus. "I accuse my accuser, Asbjorn Estridsson. I demand the right to trial by combat."

"The ordeal by combat isn't English law," said Hereward.

"The law doesn't run here," Asbjorn pointed out. "I am willing to fight Prince Krakus: but others have an equal claim. It was Prince Edgar he tried to kill, and the Lord Hereward whose hospitality he abused. If either of them wishes..?" Edgar squirmed. The muscular Slav was certainly stronger than he, probably more experienced, had a longer reach and looked dangerous. Hereward frowned.

"I won't fight my own guests," he said. "There'd be no unity left in Ely."

"I will fight on behalf of Prince Edgar."

Hereward looked round, surprised. Waltheof Siwardsson had stepped forth from the crowd.

"I will fight," he repeated, "if the Lord Hereward will permit it, and Prince Asbjorn will yield me the right." Hereward glanced round at the crowd. If he forbade the duel there was no telling what might happen. He sighed, and nodded.

"Fight him with my blessing," said Asbjorn.

A circle formed, and helms and bucklers were brought. Both men were already wearing their hauberks, and neither objected to fighting sword against falchion: perhaps they reckoned that the keener edge and greater swinging weight of Krakus' broad blade offset the longer reach and backhand potential of Waltheof's. And the fight began.

Krakus launched the first assault, bounding forward and swinging his blade down in a motion that would have split Waltheof's skull to the teeth had it struck his helmet; but the Englishman sidestepped, blocking the stroke with his buckler. The edge of the shield was sheared off as easily as if it had been made of vellum. As the falchion descended, Waltheof swiped sideways, striking the edge of it with a deafening clang. Krakus, not expecting this, staggered slightly as a painful jolt shot up his arms: and Waltheof punched him in the face with the boss of his shield. Bloodied, a little stunned, Krakus stepped back: Waltheof stepped forward, and struck at his head, but Krakus blocked the blow, catching it on his buckler and stepping forward into it, forcing Waltheof onto the back foot. He slashed at the Englishman's belly: Waltheof skipped backwards only just in time. But Krakus was wheezing slightly now. Waltheof came back with a double attack, striking from left then right: he didn't expect to draw blood, but intended merely to batter and tire the Wagrian further towards defeat. Krakus gurgled, and spat a gob of bloody matter at the Englishman. The blood from his nose was now congealing in his fine moustache, matting it into a disgusting mess. He raised his falchion, and again struck downwards. It met the upraised blade of Waltheof's sword – and shattered.

For a long moment, Krakus simply stared at the useless hilt in his hands: then, as the meaning of it sank in, he dropped the splintered weapon, turned, and, spotting where the crowd was narrowest, dived into it, hurling people aside as he ran for escape, for any way out.

"Stop him," ordered Hereward, then turned to reassure his fellow leaders: "He won't get off the island."

Asbjorn did not care if he did. Things could only have worked out better if the Atheling had actually died; but his shield-bearer had bungled that. The important thing, however, was that Krakus was now gone: if he did not die, he was as good as dead in Denmark, and in the Obodrite Confederacy. No marriage, no abandonment of Henryk, but no insult to Kruto either: he would see to it that, in the version that reached the Obodrite Prince's ears, it was the English who had accused his brother. He had done Svend's will.

Bourne, two days later.

"It looks more like a beast than a man," remarked Ogier, "and smells like it, too. What are you? You're no beggar with those rings, and if you were a thief you'd hardly have come to me."

"Another Gyrvian straggler," sneered Ivo, "come to sell us a tall tale of how we can take the Camp of Refuge. String it up, set an example."

The strange figure, hirsute, scratched and scarred,

swathed in mud-encrusted furs, made a low, animalistic rumble. He did not understand French, but the tone of the noblemen was unmistakeable. The three of them were ranged behind the table, gazing at him with a mixture of curiosity and distaste, as if one of their dogs had found him in a ditch. The dogs themselves eyed him warily.

"Where do you come from?" asked Gilbert in English. "What do you want here?"

"Do you speak Norse?" the stranger growled.

"A little," replied Gilbert, and repeated his questions. The other two squinted suspiciously: but the stranger straightened up, and pushed back his filthy hair.

"My name is Krakus," he said. "I am the Prince of Wagria; and I want to destroy the Danes."

Ely, February, 1070.

"It's certain," declared the courier. "Malcolm and MacDuff have retreated from Monkwearmouth, towards the west. They've burnt a few of Gospatric's farms, but done little harm to the Normans. They've hardly met any bar a few patrols, and now Red Alan's marching that way with more men than they can face."

Hereward scowled.

"Burning English farms?" he said. "Is that what you came south to do?"

Melmuir sighed.

"I wouldn't have done it," he said. "But I understand it. Gospatric's a traitor, naturally Malcolm wants to hurt him. The reports say the farms were mostly deserted; there wasn't much left that Red Alan hadn't burned already. It sounds more like MacDuff's doing than Malcolm's, anyway. You know how he is when he's angry."

Hereward did; but he also knew King Malcolm's habit of raiding into Northern England for cattle and slaves. Burning farms out of spite did not sound like the King of Scots, but sacking them for profit was another matter.

"But if Malcolm's in retreat, what becomes of your pincer attack?" Hereward demanded.

Melmuir shrugged.

"It's useless trying anything on land now. The Normans probably know we're here, and we can't rely on the Danes for help after all that's happened. I think the best I can do to help Malcolm is to return to my ship and raid the Norman coastal bases, see if I can draw Red Alan into dividing his forces, maybe stop William from joining him, or at least sting the bastards a little."

"You're leaving Ely, then?"

"What else would you have me do?" asked Melmuir, spreading his hands. "What good are we doing sitting here on our arses? If you have a better plan, tell me."

"You know we can't form a plan until we know where William is," said Hereward.

"By which time the Breton might have driven Malcolm back across the Border," Melmuir pointed out. "William could be making ready to invade Scotland as we speak. If we could just land one solid blow on the Normans, then we could come back south in the summer, resume the campaign. But right now we're doing no good in Ely, just eating your food." Hereward could not deny, it would be a relief not to have to feed the Scots any longer. The Fens were almost fished dry, the Bromeswold hunted bare.

"You're right," he conceded. "Will Edgar stay here? He'd be safer."

"Among those Northmen?" retorted Melmuir. "I doubt it. Besides, Malcolm won't look kindly on me if I go back without him."

"Well," said Hereward, "if you're leaving, you're leaving."

Melmuir inclined his head.

"I think it best. We can still part friends, even if our alliance has been less fruitful than we hoped."

The Scots returned to their ship with little ceremony; the Danes were glad to see them go, and most of the English indifferent. The islanders had other things on their minds: with the St Valentine's celebrations out of the way, and March now only a few days off, they were preparing for the sowing. Already honey cakes preserved since the autumn for the purpose had been buried in the fields to encourage fruitfulness; the mattocks and hoes were being cleaned and sharpened. As long as Hereward and his men kept the Normans off the island, and did not eat into their stores, they mostly contrived to ignore their presence: though when

Asbjorn and his men were on the island, this proved difficult. Fortunately, the Danes had, now that the weather was letting up, largely returned to the sea, to pick off Norman ships and raid coastal estates.

Occasionally, still, new people would arrive at Ely. Some had fled the famine in the North; one or two were native officials purged from their positions by the increasingly suspicious Normans; but only two days after the Scots had left, there came to Ely, on a barge with his horse and a page boy, the last person Hereward had expected to see there.

"Van Oosterzele?" he exclaimed incredulously. "Frederick van Oosterzele?"

"The very same," said Martin. "He rode openly into the camp, bold as you like, and asked to see you."

"What can it mean?" wondered Hereward.

"An overture from King William," suggested Torfrida. "He must have something to offer you."

Hereward shook his head.

"Surely the Normans are beyond trying to buy me by now."

"They've never tried it before," Torfrida pointed out, "and force has failed. They want the stone out of their shoe, so they turn to a man who knows you."

"A man I never liked," said Hereward. "Why not send Gilbert of Ghent? Or one of the English nobles – one of my kinsmen?"

"Because an Englishman who comes in William's name is a traitor, and you wouldn't hear such a man out. And you know Gilbert well enough that you might have learned to tell when he's lying." Hereward could deny none of this, but he was still unconvinced.

"Do we know he does come from King William?" asked Elfthryth. "Has he said so?"

"No," said Martin. "Only that he must see Lord Hereward."

"Then see me he shall," Hereward decided. "I'll meet him outside: he can say what he has to say before the camp."

Frederick van Oosterzele was waiting a little way from the hostel, guarded by Hogor and Ulric Grogan. He wore a rich scarlet tunic under his riding cloak, and carried his highly polished helmet in the crook of his left arm; his page, a tousle-haired boy in a russet supertunic, held his horse for him. At the sight of Hereward and Torfrida, the Fleming wiped the impatient scowl from his face and bowed his head.

"Lord Hereward," he said. "And Lady Torfrida."

"My lord Frederick," replied Hereward in Flemish. "Welcome to Ely. But what would you have with me?"

Frederick glanced around at his unwanted attendants.

"May we speak in private?" he asked.

"We will speak here," said Hereward. "It is private enough; these men speak no Flemish, and you know that Martin and Torfrida will hear soon enough whatever you tell me anyway. What are you doing in England?"

"I am the guest of my sister, the Baroness Gundrada de Warenne," said Frederick stiffly.

"Your sister and her husband are no friends of mine, or of any man's here," said Hereward. "I have people here they have driven from their land and left to starve. William de Warenne was the Bastard's second in command a year ago when York was sacked; I saw his men ravish women and dash out the brains of the greybeards. You keep bad company."

Frederick visibly bridled, but kept his temper, and answered evenly:

"Whatever you think of them, you may have interests in common."

"I know of none."

"What if I told you that King William was expected at Castle Acre within the week?"

Hereward shook his head.

"William's still in the north."

"The couriers say he's confident Red Alan can beat the Scots without any more help from him. He plans to leave the main army and bring a few hundred men south to deal with you."

Hereward frowned suspiciously.

"And you tell me this why?"

Frederick smiled.

"He's not bringing the whole force round into Norfolk. He'll leave them in Lincolnshire and ride on to Castle Acre through the Bromeswold, with only a bodyguard of maybe a dozen or twenty men – and my brother-in-law is away on his southern estates, and may not be back in time to greet him."

Hereward began to understand.

"Go on," he said.

"The Norman barons want only to keep their English lands," said Frederick. "You must realise by now you could never get rid of them. Some were here before the Conquest, after all. William Malet, Sheriff Turaud -"

"In lands they'd won through marriage, or that were taken from dispossessed traitors," Hereward pointed out, "not stolen."

Frederick shrugged.

"The point is, they don't care if the monarch is a Norman or an Englishman, or a Dane. What they want is a king who'll end the wars with France and Scotland. King William's campaigns cost them heavily in money and men, and they can't afford it."

"I weep for them," said Hereward drily.

"And what I want", Frederick continued, ignoring his interjection, "is silver. My lands in Flanders are mortgaged to the Bishop of Cambrai and I cannot pay him."

"So now we come to it," said Hereward. "What exactly are you offering to do?"

"To kill the King," said Frederick simply.

Hereward blinked.

"To kill the King?" he echoed. "And this – you say de Warenne is with you?"

"No," said Frederick. "But other barons are."

"Who?"

"I am not at liberty..."

"Do you thing anyone here will tattle to the Sheriff?" Hereward interrupted impatiently.

"I have given my word," said Frederick haughtily.

"And the word of a man who'd betray his King is worth what, exactly?"

"He is no King of mine."

"But he is your sister's. And you are her guest." Frederick glowered, but said nothing. "How much do you need to pay off the Bishop?"

"A thousand shillings."

Hereward whistled.

"Can you stay here tonight, or must you return to Castle Acre?"

"I will not be missed for one night," Frederick shrugged. "But I will need an answer tomorrow morning."

"I'll make no deals with the barons," said Hereward. "For one thing, I don't deal with men who hide behind their friends. For another, I've no right to offer them anything – and I'd have little inclination to if I had. If we reach any agreement, I will promise nothing to any man but you."

Frederick inclined his head.

"That is acceptable."

Hereward turned to Hogor.

"Make up a room in the hostel for the Lord Frederick and his page," he said. "And Ulric, would you stable his horse?"

"There's no need to go to the trouble of making up a room," said Frederick. "A cell in the monastery will suit me very well, and on a monk's bed I won't oversleep in the morning." Hereward looked at him curiously: he would not have judged Frederick an ascetic: but it would make many matters easier if he did sleep in the monastery, so he raised no objection.

Though the hostel now held no danger of being overheard by Frederick and his page, Hereward, Martin and Torfrida repaired to a hut in the main camp to discuss the offer, rather than be disturbed by Torfridel. Winter and Deacon Leofric joined them at Hereward's invitation. Around a low turf fire, they spoke quietly.

"Do you believe him?" asked Winter. Hereward frowned uncertainly.

"It's so incredible it just might be true," he said. "Though I think he's bluffing about bringing the barons along. If he does mean it, he's just doing it for the money."

"That doesn't sound like Frederick," said Torfrida. "I know what you think of him, but by his own lights he's honourable enough. I can't make sense of it."

"I can," declared Martin. "He dropped the barons because he didn't want to name names, and he didn't want to name names because the whole plot's a lie. He's doing what he thinks *is* the honourable thing: entrapping the King's enemy by any means necessary. He lures us into a trap, Lord Hereward's removed before King Svend gets here, our revolt falls apart, and the Normans are spared a long war. Of course he'd think it honourable: we're wolvesheads. William is an anointed king."

Hereward stroked his chin.

"I know nobles like Frederick," he said. "Their honour lies in their land first and their actions second. He wouldn't readily betray William, but if he really is in danger of losing his estates, who knows what he might do? With or without the barons. If de Warenne is in the south, then Frederick can tell himself he isn't deceiving him, because he isn't lying to his face; and maybe Gundrada goes along with this for her brother's sake."

"If she cares so much for him," Leofric pointed out, poking the fire and stirring a little life out of its dull, tepid glow, "she could always raise the money herself, or get her husband to provide it."

"Her husband's away," said Hereward, "and, in any case, all the nobles are short of cash right now: William's raised the taxes to pay for his campaign in the North."

"So you do believe him?" said Winter.

"Think what it'll mean if it is true," Hereward urged. "This is the perfect time for such a blow – if William had died three months ago there'd just have been chaos, but with Svend arriving any day, we'll leave the Normans without a head just as we're about to strike against them."

"I'm sure Frederick has considered that," replied Martin. "He knows we'll all want to believe him, and that's what he's relying on."

Hereward looked to Torfrida, who shrugged.

"I don't know," she said. "It's too early to trust him, but he might be sincere."

"We should watch him," agreed Leofric. Hereward nodded.

"At least he's sleeping inside the monastery," he said. "He's not come to steal Brainbiter or slit my throat in the dark."

Frederick joined Hereward and Torfrida to dine in the hostel that evening: Rowena rustled up some salted mutton, and Abbot Thurstan sent over a jar of wine from the monastery's cellars – and even a couple of wax candles, that they might be spared the smell of tallow. Elfthryth, lacking any language in common with Frederick, elected not to join them. Away from the crowd, and assisted by the drink, the Flemish nobleman mellowed somewhat, becoming almost friendly. Having only recently crossed from Flanders, he was able to bring all the gossip of the court of Bruges, betrothals, duels, the ongoing fluctuations in Count Baldwin's health, and so forth.

"He was sick again at Christmas, though on his feet before I left," said Frederick. "It's the same complaint his father had, no mistaking it. Thank God for the Lord Robert."

"What of Lord Arnulf?" wondered Torfrida. Frederick shrugged.

"A child," he said dismissively. "Strong and intelligent, by all accounts, but too young to be given any responsibility."

"And the Countess?"

"She has learnt to stay out of the Lord Robert's way. With all respect, Lady Torfrida, it is not a woman's place. She should be caring for her husband and her child, and that is what she does – these days." Frederick took another swig of wine.

"She must be very confident of the Count's recovery," said Torfrida. Frederick frowned.

"I don't follow."

"If Baldwin were to die," she pointed out, "there must be a council of regency until Arnulf is old enough to rule. Richildis is an ambitious woman: if she thought Baldwin were going to die, she would already be planning to claim her place on the council. Stepping back from government is no way to do that."

"I don't know," admitted Frederick. "She would know better than I, I suppose, whether her husband will live or die."

At length, necessarily, the talk turned to the proposed assassination.

"You know the exact route King William will take through the Bromeswold?" pressed Hereward.

"The main road," said Frederick promptly. "Even with only a dozen men, with all on horseback the lesser roads would be difficult; besides, he is a king in a land at war. He needs to show he is not afraid."

"And the timing?"

"I will know the day as soon as he sends word to Castle Acre. It is expected any day now. I lie in wait, with a few archers – you provide those – and when he draws near I ride out to greet him, pretend I have a message from my brother-in-law. When I get close, I stab him; your men shoot down the nearest guards so I can escape; and then – you pay me."

"You don't want the money in advance?"

Frederick grimaced.

"I would if I thought I'd get it. But I'll just have to trust you." He stood up, looking slightly unsteady. "Now, however, I am tired; with your permission, and Lady Torfrida's, I will retire to the abbey."

"Well?" said Hereward, once he was gone. "Do you think he's sincere?"

"Yes," said Torfrida. "I don't think he's a good enough liar to have kept up the friendly front if he meant harm to us; and a man that proud wouldn't have stooped to bargaining unless he needed money badly. But there's still something that makes me uneasy…"

"And me," agreed Hereward. "Still, at least we are safe for tonight."

Hereward and Torfrida were asleep in each other's arms; Elfthryth lying awake a thin wall away, covering her ears; even the monks were snatching a few hours of sleep between compline and matins. Outside, an owl hooted; and, deep inside the abbey, a bolt was slowly slid back.

"Uluncas?"

The prisoner, barely visible where he lay in deep shadow, did not stir. His visitor repeated the name, still in a whisper. Nothing. The stranger bent over the Gyrvian – and Uluncas' hand shot up, seizing him by the throat. He spluttered, choking, as the bony fingers dug in.

"What do you want?" demanded the prisoner. "Who are you?"

Frederick pointed desperately at his throat; Uluncas relaxed his grip, but only enough to let him speak.

"I am a friend. I have a proposition." He had had a slave teach him English before ever he had crossed the Channel; but it had seemed wisest to conceal his knowledge before Hereward and his men.

"For me?" Uluncas gestured at his manacles. "I'm not well placed to do favours."

"I have the key."

Uluncas let go, and the nobleman staggered backwards, gasping. The air in the cell was stale, and it took him several lungfuls to feel even half alive again.

"You would release me?" said the Gyrvian suspiciously. "What do you want in return?"

"No more than you want," said Frederick. "Hereward dead."

Uluncas chuckled softly.

"Oho, I want that, do I?" he said. "And why do you?"

"That's none of your business."

"If I'm to get myself killed, I think it is."

"Nobody need die but Hereward," Frederick insisted. "Tomorrow morning, a little after the bell rings for lauds, I'll be leaving the island by barge from the southern stage." He had rehearsed this speech a hundred times. "Hereward will be there to see me off. There are bushes there where a dozen men could lie hidden. You will wait there, until you hear me say 'Until we meet again'. Hereward will be on the edge of the stage with his back to you. It will be the easiest matter in the world to kill him and step into the barge beside me."

"And then his men shoot us while we bob around two feet from the land," finished Uluncas.

Frederick smiled, and held up the bundle he carried under his arm.

"A hauberk and helm," he said. "You will be armoured. I will have a light coat of mail under my tunic; and, besides, we'll be well clear before they get over the shock."

"If it's so easy," said Uluncas, "why don't you kill him yourself?"

"If I'm to escape – if we're to escape – I have to be ready to pole away instantly, the moment he's stabbed. I couldn't leave it up to my page because it wasn't safe to trust him with the plan; the boy's a fool and he'd be sure to blab. So it needs two men."

"That sounds… plausible," said Uluncas thoughtfully. "You'll do it?"

The prisoner stood up suddenly, and put his face very close to Frederick's. The smell of his breath made the nobleman gag.

"I want my freedom," he hissed. "For that, I'll do anything."

The next day, as promised, Frederick rose early; even Hereward, who needed little sleep, was bleary when he was roused to see the Fleming off. Frederick seemed anxious to leave as soon as possible, but Hereward insisted that they should breakfast together, on rye bread, small ale, and a somewhat tired-looking lump of cheese. Only once they had eaten, and shaken hands on William's death for a thousand shillings, did they proceed, accompanied by Torfrida and several of the men, to the southern stage; lauds was under way before they even left the pilgrim hostel. Frederick was beginning to look shifty, glancing anxiously from one side to another, his look going most frequently to the monastery: but no alarm was sounded. The monks, it seemed, had not yet discovered the Gyrvian's escape. He could only hope that Uluncas would keep his side of the bargain: if he uttered 'Until we meet again' and nobody came out of the bushes, he would have to stab Hereward himself, and then what would his own life be worth? Still, he told himself, at least he would be remembered as a hero. Somehow, though, this seemed less of a comfort today than when he had first conceived the plan.

At every crack of a twig, Frederick felt his heart beat faster. What if Hereward already knew somehow of Uluncas' escape, and was playing some deep game to trap him? What if Uluncas had fled the island? What if his page, whom he had sent ahead to ready the barge and coax his horse aboard her, was slow or incompetent enough to forestall his escape? Between shock at seeing Hereward fall and their first impulse to take revenge on Uluncas, the English should be too preoccupied to stop the barge moving off – if they even realised that Frederick had put the assassin up to it – but it was a slim probability to rely upon.

They reached the stage. The barge was there, the page standing in the bows, pole in hand, the horse tethered to a rail. The water, thick though it was with mud and weeds, ruffled slightly in the morning breeze. Frederick swallowed. So far, all had gone according to plan. He measured with his eyes once more the distance between the stage and the bushes. What if Uluncas should be spotted and brought down before he reached Hereward? None of the men behind him had bows, nor were there any stones in reach, but daggers and axes could be thrown.

"So, my lord Hereward," he began rather forcedly, stepping onto the stage, "this is farewell."

"Lord Hereward!"

Hereward turned, reaching for Brainbiter's hilt, as Uluncas stepped into view. The Gyrvian was armoured, and wore a dagger at his belt – but he held his hands above his head. Nevertheless, every hand among Hereward's men went to their weapons.

"You have a traitor there, Lord Hereward," said Uluncas levelly. With a sudden wild lunge, Frederick drew his dagger and struck Hereward between the shoulderblades. The blade turned in his hand, and snapped. Torfrida screamed. While the men behind still stood in shock, the Fleming leapt down into the barge, seizing the pole from his page, and thrust with all his strength against the stage itself.

The barge slid easily away from the land: but not quite quickly enough. With a great bound from the end of the stage, the cook Hogor, brandishing a meat-cleaver, sailed through the air towards it. With a sickening crack and the crunch of splintering bone, the pole connected with his cheek; he fell like a shot fowl into the murky water, blood from his wound spreading to mingle its crimson with the dull brown of the Fen.

Frederick had by now scooped up his shield from the bottom of the barge, and was holding it aloft, warding off the shower of darts, knives and whatever else was to hand from the shore. There were no other boats at this stage or any nearby: he could not be followed. In a very short time, he would be clear of Ely: but he could see Hereward, on the stage, clambering back to his feet, grimacing and rubbing at his back. The wolfshead was alive: he had failed.

Hereward was thanking all the saints for his Saracen mail, and Torfrida's inspiration that he should wear it beneath his tunic today. Whatever had brought on her sudden intuition of danger, it had saved his life. He had seen fine coats, thicker than this, pierced by lesser blows than he had suffered, but though bruised he was unscarred. Torfrida, helping him out of it, could not but marvel at the wholeness of his skin. But now the danger was past, and Frederick beyond capture: there remained Uluncas.

"How did you get out?" he asked, still wheezing a little; Frederick had knocked the breath from him.

"The Fleming released me so that I could kill you," said Uluncas simply.

"And why didn't you?"

The Gyrvian shrugged.

"A little because you sent the monk to treat my leg. A little because I hoped you'd free me if I saved your life. A lot because I didn't trust him – he meant me to take the blame, and die for it. But mostly because I don't like doing what

186

people expect." He narrowed his eyes, and peered into Hereward's face. "Will you?" he asked. "Set me free?"

Hereward paused.

"Will you join with us?" he asked. "I think we are a man short." Ulric and Methelgar were now hauling the cook's body, limp as a wet rag, from the water: it was clear that he was dead.

The ghost of a smile played around Uluncas' lips.

"I can't think of a better service," he replied.

The southern stage had been the only plausible one to leave from, if Frederick was to maintain the fiction that he was heading for Castle Acre: but his rendezvous was not there. The same morning that he had set out for Ely, his sister had ridden to join her husband – who was not in the south, but in Lincolnshire, on his way to Spalding, as, by now, King William should be. It would be dangerous riding north through the Bromeswold, Hereward's hunting ground, and humiliating to have to admit that the attempt on the wolfshead's life had failed; worse still if the King were there to hear it. Best to ride swiftly, then: evade pursuit, and reach Spalding ahead of William, with, if possible, a new plan.

Abandoning his page, who would only slow him down, Frederick saddled up as soon as he reached solid ground, and hurried for the forest way. His mind was working furiously as he rode; ignoring the increasingly heavy rain, the wet branches whipping into his face, the dark of night and the stab of hunger, he rode on, his mind on one thing only: how to trap Hereward.

The next day was far advanced by the time the draggled, exhausted Frederick arrived at Spalding. His horse was almost ready to collapse, and he was in little better shape himself: but he brushed off the solicitude of Ivo's worried servants, and marched straight into the Baron's mead hall.

They were gathered there, a small knot of aristocrats at the high table while the rest of the hall stood empty, over a midday meal of cold roast pork and Fenland ale: Taillebois, red-faced as ever; dagger-eyed Ogier, his hound crouched by his side; Krakus, scowling mistrustfully at the others, whose language he still did not understand; and the de Warennes, richly clad, Baron William in his round deep-blue cloak with its vast shoulder-brooch, his tunic embroidered with roses; the stately Gundrada in a grey supertunic fringed in gold, and not one but two mantles, a long woollen one about her shoulders and a lighter one to cover her hair. Frederick was acutely aware of his own riding cloak, disordered hair and muddy feet. A little down the table from these four sat Ivo's retainers, the lean and grim steward Hubert, the little priest Hugo, and others whom Frederick did not recognise.

"Ah," exclaimed de Warenne, "the guest of honour arrives. Have you slain the dragon? Is our tribulation over?"

Frederick shook his head.

"I was betrayed," he said. "It was all I could do to escape."

"You let him live?"

"And I thought you were my father's son," sneered Gundrada.

"I had no choice," Frederick insisted.

"King William will be here within the week – perhaps tomorrow; perhaps tonight," his brother-in-law pointed out. "Are we to tell him that English wolves still take Norman sheep unchecked? That we cannot flush out one plaguey thief from those filthy Fens?" Ivo and Ogier exchanged glances. As Hereward's nearest Norman neighbours, they were being reproached as much as Frederick here: but they said nothing.

"There is still a way to draw him off the island," said Frederick. Ogier frowned.

"There can't be. There's nothing we haven't tried."

"Hereward's weak spot is the people he cares about," said Frederick. "His wife and child are on the island, so are all his real friends and that woman Elfthryth – but his mother is not."

188

"His mother is a holy nun," said Hugo uncomfortably. "She took her vows at Croyland with her sister Godiva, may God rest her."

"Exactly," said Frederick. "A message from the good Sister Edith would bring Hereward to Croyland like a fly to a dead dog." Ogier's hound whimpered, and he scratched its head comfortingly. "He often travels with few companions, sometimes only the Irishman Martin. I've visited Croyland: the nuns there occupy a separate house to keep them from tempting the monks to unchastity, and it's far less defensible than the main building. If we draw Hereward to Croyland, he will be in our power."

"And how do we persuade the Lady Edith to send such a message?" wondered de Warenne.

Frederick shrugged.

"We will have to take control of the nuns' house, and lay the monks under siege until Hereward comes," he said simply. Hugo stood up, spluttering.

"My lords!" he exclaimed. "I, I cannot be a party to this – it is abominable!"

"Sit down," barked Ivo. "Nobody's asking you to come with us." He turned to Frederick. "You're sure we could hold them?"

"From what I've seen of the abbey, I have little doubt," said Frederick. "Taking the main complex would be another matter, but we don't have to. As long as the monks are penned in, they can't warn Hereward: and that's all we need."

"They could shout," said Ivo.

"How are they to know when he's in earshot? Besides, by the time he is, it'll be too late."

"They could ring the bells," de Warenne pointed out. "He'd hear that for miles."

"Then we send two men into the abbey before we attack the nuns' house. They can take the belfry and keep the monks out, cut the ropes if necessary."

"We could take Croyland tonight, send the message at first light tomorrow, and have Hereward in our power by dusk," said Ogier. "It could work."

"You would all be willing to take part in such an enterprise?" said de Warenne doubtfully, looking from Ivo, to Ogier, to Frederick. The first was actually smiling, the others wore set and impassive faces: none showed a flicker of doubt.

"It's no more than duty," observed Gundrada. "It's not as if you're going to harm the sisters: just inconvenience them for a few hours, to catch a traitor." De Warenne bit his lip. He was chary of anything that smacked of sacrilege: but it would be a great triumph to take Hereward, and as senior nobleman present he could claim the greatest share of the credit. He could always salve his conscience afterwards with a gift to the abbey.

"Then we are agreed," he said at last. "We put Lord Frederick's plan into action; and God grant we may have a kingly gift for His Grace when he arrives."

Though punts and barges were usually the most convenient way to reach Croyland, the Normans approached overland. It was somewhat roundabout, and forced them to march in a narrow file – to stray from the road in armour was to risk being swallowed up by the mire – but with thirty men-at-arms, this was the easiest way. To come over the Fens would have required a small fleet.

They approached by torchlight after vespers, on foot. The men were coated in mail from head to foot, with leaf-shaped shields and long-handled axes. They would be seen, but it was hardly likely that the monks would raise any alarm: they had no reason to expect an attack. The five noblemen led the column: none had been willing to miss the taking of Hereward. Krakus was disappointed that he would not get to fight Danes or Scots, but was there nonetheless, axe in hand, sniffing the air like a hound scenting blood. Frederick bore his sword naked before him.

The path widened as they neared the abbey grounds, the grass to either side well enough trodden to show that it was firm. Croyland loomed before them. It was not a standard cruciform building like Ely or Peterborough, but a squat near-cube built mostly of wood. It had always been a small community, with few donors and little land beyond what had been granted to the heirs of St Guthlac three hundred years before: no larger building had ever seemed necessary. Frederick reckoned that even the main building would fall fairly easily, if they had to take it.

As the front broadened, the Normans changed formation. They were well drilled – de Warenne's men, hardened in war, made a rather more impressive force than Ivo's or Ogier's – and the manoeuvre would have been flawless, had they been allowed to complete it: but they were still in mid shift when the English struck.

Hereward had few archers, and it was difficult for them to aim in the dark: but he had plenty of slingers, and there was little need for precision when the enemy was all but trapped. One of the first shower of stones struck Frederick full in the face, leaving him bloodied and cursing through cracked teeth. As the Normans raised their shields, the arrows were loosed; most missed, but Ivo was winged in the arm, and one of de Warenne's men fell like Harold, shot through the eye.

"How in Hell did he know we were coming?" roared de Warenne. "We haven't even sent the damned message yet."

"*I* have a message for *you*," a voice boomed out of the darkness. It spoke good Norman French, but those who had heard it before all recognised Hereward Askilsson. "It's here." Onto the edge of the circle of torchlight, there moved a shadowy figure: they saw him raise something, though he was too deep in shadow for any Norman to tell what: then, with a sudden forward arc propelled by his whole body, he hurled it at the Fleming. It was a javelin, made in the Welsh style, but heavier, with a longer blade. Frederick raised his shield, but the vicious iron weapon punched through it as easily as if it had been made of vellum, and pinned it to his chest. The very force carried the Fleming backwards: he would have fallen flat had he not collided with the man behind him. He slid to the ground, dribbling blood as he gurgled, trying to speak: but no words came. Frederick van Oosterzele was dead.

"All that practice at the posts was worth it," Hereward murmured to Girolamo.

"You see?" replied the Italian. "The Romans knew a thing or two about war."

It was from an obscure appendix to Vegetius, on Girolamo's advice, that Hereward had drawn the new moon formation the English had adopted before the walls of Croyland. The shadow of the abbey hid them from the enemy: and the two horns of their crescent were pointed towards the Normans, ready to pinion and enclose them. Girolamo had drilled them for just such a manoeuvre; he had not expected so perfect an opportunity to use it.

"Retreat," de Warenne barked.

"But with the English behind us –" Ogier began to object; but de Warenne cut him off.

"Now!" he ordered. "Before we're all chopped to mince and fed to the Fenland eels!"

A retreat would be one way to describe what followed: more accurate would be to call it a rout. As the English closed in, the Normans fled before them; two men were jostled off the safety of the path in the stampede, and ended up mired to the waste in green and stinking mud. The nobles themselves abandoned dignity and ran: proud they might be, but they knew when they were outfaced and outfought. It was not long before English cheers, rather than the clash of battle, rent the night air; and from the abbey came an answering peal of bells.

The men were entertained that night at Croyland; Abbot Ulfkytel could offer them little enough, but managed at least to ensure that none went hungry. Edith did not join them. The nuns, Ulfkytel told Hereward, kept to themselves; Edith had been invited, but had preferred to avoid rupturing the tranquillity of her retreat.

"May I see her?" asked Hereward.

"She will be awake," said Ulfkytel, "and she won't turn you away; if you wish, you may see her."

The Abbot himself went with Hereward to admit him to the nuns' house; Edith was in the prayer room, alone. Ulfkytel tactfully withdrew.

"Mother?" said Hereward.

"Hereward," she said levelly. "My blessing upon you."

"Thank you." He stood awkwardly by the door, in embarrassed silence.

"I understand you and your men have saved us from the assault of the blasphemers," she went on, still not looking at him. "You have all our thanks."

"Mother, is – are you well?" asked Hereward, worried. Now Edith did turn to face him.

"Well?" she said. "Yes. I am as well as I have ever been. I have found peace." For the first time there was warmth in her voice. Hereward looked into the blank depths of her eyes, and saw still a spark of the mother he remembered, not the flat-voiced and distant woman who had greeted him when he came in. But he knew that something had died in her when his brother Toli was killed, and it could never be brought back. In the world outside she would have gone mad with grief: she was best off here: but there was a gulf between them. He could not bridge it; but he could see that she was indeed at peace, and that was enough. He bowed his head.

By the time the Normans trudged back into Spalding,

it had begun to rain. Pouring off their helmets, the water bleared their eyes, and ran down inside their aventails and under their byrnies; every step was a splash or a squelch. Focused entirely on the keep, and the prospect of a warm fire and a flask of wine, they did not see the pennants erected at the entrance, nor note that the guards they pushed past were not Ivo's. Only as they stomped into the hall, still dripping, pulled off their helmets and hoods of mail, and shook their heads like wet dogs, did it begin to dawn on the three barons and the Obodrite prince that all was not normal.

The fire was already lit, a great log blazing and crackling. Soldiers lined the wall, standing to attention. At the high table sat the Baroness Gundrada, wrinkling her nose as she stared down it in haughty disdain at the dishevelled men: and by her side, his helmet off but otherwise fully armoured, sat a man all three knew only too well. The tall and powerful frame might be running to fat, and the first flecks of grey beginning to appear in the close-cropped reddish hair: but there was no mistaking the long straight nose, the bright and piercing eyes.

"I take it, gentlemen, that your little jaunt has been unsuccessful?" said the King. They hung their heads.

"Yes, sire," mumbled de Warenne.

"Then you have bungled the last chance to prevent Hereward joining forces with Svend Estridsson. The Dane arrived in the Wash this morning; by now he may already be at Ely. Where is Frederick van Oosterzele?"

"He was killed, sire," said Ogier. Gundrada gasped.

"At least he will not fail me again," said William coldly. "All I asked of any of you was to kill the wolfshead before the Danes arrived. You've had months. It seems I must teach you your business."

"My lord -" Ivo began.

"Be quiet," snapped William. "You were betrayed by your chaplain; he is gone, no doubt among the outlaws at Ely. By the grace of God I am free to face this threat. The Scots

194

have retreated across the Border, and the North is in no state to rebel again; and I have word from the West that Edric of Shrewsbury has surrendered. That leaves only fleabitten Welsh bandits, the posturings of Philip of France – and Ely. This is the last real front; the last real enemy; and we have all the resources of the Kingdom of England to throw against them. This time there will be no failure."

Chapter 9: *Mariana*

Ely, March, 1070.

"I bless this field in the name of St Matthew; I bless this field in the name of St Mark; I bless this field in the name of St Luke; I bless this field in the name of St John. May the crops wax and multiply and fill this earth, by the Cross of Christ, amen."

Wulfwine crossed himself, and pushed the little quickbeam crucifix into the hole the islanders had prepared. This much he was prepared to do for a rich harvest; the second half of the charm, he had refused to speak. The abbey tenants were distressed, believing that the words would be efficacious only from a priest.

"It's remarkable," Wulfwine had told Hereward, "but even here, in the shadow of the House of God, they seem to have only half learned Christianity."

Eventually, a ploughman had been found whose father had been a deacon. That was held to be good enough, and he offered to complete the charm. Abbot Thurstan tutted and worried, misliking such heathenish proceedings on his land, but Wulfwine shrugged: as far as he was concerned, it did little enough harm, as long as he was not called on to dignify the flummery.

The ploughman stepped forward onto the turned earth, the gaggle of eager islanders and curious warriors, and a few monks, who had gathered along the edge of the field, watching intently. Spreading his hands, he bowed over the little hole where the cross had been placed, and intoned:

"Erce, Erce, Erce, earth's mother:
Hail to thee, furrow, mother of men.
Be thou growing, in God's keeping,
With fodder filled, men to succour.
Full acres of feed in folk's ken,

Bright-blooming, that thou mayest blessed be."

"That thou mayest blessed be," chorused several of the watching islanders, and one or two of Hereward's men. Some crossed themselves, apparently seeing no irony in the gesture. The hole was filled in, and the ceremony was over.

"It's the same in Denmark," King Svend remarked to Hereward. "The peasants go to Mass and love the saints, but they're not ready to give up their magic; they don't see any contradiction."

As William had predicted, Svend had been waiting at Ely when Hereward's men returned from Croyland. Leaving his sons in charge of the fleet, he had brought Asbjorn back with him; Hereward had not been best pleased to see the prince again, but had greeted him courteously enough. Also with the King was his daughter, Mariana, once the betrothed of Krakus; Svend had told the Obodrite envoys at Roskilde that the two would be married in England. The discovery of Krakus' exposure and defection had not pleased him, and harsh words had passed between the two brothers about it; it would have served Denmark's interests better had the Obodrite fallen in battle. To explain this to Kruto would be embarrassing.

Mariana had been installed in the pilgrim hostel, where she had formed a friendship of sorts with Elfthryth, who spoke enough Norse to understand her. Whenever she got an opportunity, the princess wandered off alone to explore the island; she had never been out of Denmark before, and hardly out of her father's court. She was standing now beside her father, peering in fascination at the sowing ceremony.

"Well, you've seen our strange English ways now," said Hereward, as they turned and ambled back towards the camp. "God grant they do get a good harvest; at least the frosts are over now."

"Amen," said Svend; "but man doesn't live by grain alone. I've not tasted fresh meat since I left Roskilde. What do you say to a hunting expedition in your Bromeswold?"

Hereward frowned.

"It's dangerous," he said. "With William so nearby..."

"Everything we do is dangerous," replied the King. "And our scouts say William has only a small force; he's left most of his army in the north for fear of the Scots. We can go on foot: hunt like peasant poachers with bows. It will be an adventure – and we'll be a match for any patrols." He could see that Hereward was still hesitant. "Come now," he said, "have you ever heard that I did anything reckless? Believe me, I have calculated the danger as I always do."

"May I come, Father?" Mariana piped up.

"Of course not."

"But if there's no danger -"

"There is danger. There is always danger."

"You know I'm as good with a bow as any man," she insisted. Svend sighed.

"And you know that's not what's at issue," he said. "I will not have you putting yourself at risk."

"You just said it would be an adventure."

"It will, but that's not why we do it. We do it for meat. I am to be King here: I have a right to taste the King's deer. But for you to go is unnecessary."

"For you and Lord Hereward to go is unnecessary," retorted Mariana. "You're more important to the war than I am. Anybody could bring down a couple of deer. You want to go because you enjoy hunting. So do I."

"The King forbids it," said Svend testily. He knew that he was as good as conceding the argument, but he had not the will to fight longer. Disputations with Mariana always seemed to end this way.

It was decided that the party should be limited to six, three Danes and three Englishmen: a small enough party to hide, should the need arise. Svend chose two of his housecarles, while Geric and Lewine volunteered to go with

Hereward. Both eagerly wanted to bring down the first stag, that they might boast of it to Mariana; she had made a considerable impression among the younger men at the Camp of Refuge.

The best spot for hunting deer was to the west of Peterborough, though it was also uncomfortably close to the bases of the Normans. It was agreed that they should not stray far from where their two punts were hidden at the edge of the mere, but nor should they rely on the punts for escape if they had been seen: for, despite the few waterlogged trees which dotted that part of the Fens, they would be dangerously exposed if they took to the water. Better, if possible, to hide, than to offer their backs to Norman arrows.

It was not long before Svend spotted a young buck grazing, its back to them. Slowly, noiselessly, he drew an arrow from his quiver and set it to the string: but before he could draw the bow, an arrow whistled past his ear from somewhere behind him, and struck the beast at the base of the neck. It leapt up, staggered a few paces, crumpled and fell to the ground; Svend, swearing by all the saints of Scandinavia, turned to see who had dared endanger the King's life by loosing so close to him.

"Mariana!" he exclaimed. "What are you doing here?"

The princess wore male peasant garb, a dull green cloak and hood over a russet tunic, and carried a light bow such as had been used by huntsmen before the Normans restricted the right of the chase to the nobility. Her hair under the hood was tied back, and her eyes were sparkling.

"Did you think I'd miss it?" she asked simply.

Svend was about to scold her when Hereward held up his hand.

"Hsst!" he said. "Horses."

He was right. Horses were approaching, a small group of them in metal harness. The hunters fell silent. They were far from the main roads, but there were paths criss-crossing all over the forest, many of them wide enough to ride on in single file: and one of these passed very close by. Geric was the nearest to it: he parted the bushes and peered through.

There were four horsemen. At the front rode a tall, beaky-nosed man in armour, with a heavy embroidered cloak and a brightly painted shield; behind him, a grizzled older man in a torn blue woollen tunic, his hands tied; and at the back, two more armoured men, less splendidly accoutred than their leader. A Norman knight of some consequence, then, with two guards and a prisoner. Geric drew an arrow.

"No!" hissed Hereward: but he was too late. Geric had let fly at the nobleman. The arrow rebounded off his helmet; and the Norman wheeled instantly, levelling his lance, and spurred straight towards him.

Geric flung himself aside as the powerful destrier crashed through the bushes: the Norman cursed, and reined in.

"Serlo!" he barked. One of the guards moved after him into the clearing. Hereward had dived for a hollow beneath a dying tree the instant Geric had loosed his arrow, pulling Svend with him; Mariana had hidden behind another trunk, and one of the Danes had dropped without hesitation into the mere. The others, however, remained exposed.

The knight gestured with his lance at Lewine; Serlo nodded, and, lowering his own weapon, urged his horse forward – while his master took aim at the still exposed Dane. The Dane raised his bow: but he had no time to draw it before the lance was driven through his chest. Lewine, meanwhile, moved more quickly, drawing his twin sickles and slashing the guard's horse across the neck as he dived out of its path. The animal gave an anguished, gurgling shriek as its forelegs gave way, pitching its rider over its head: as the man struggled up onto his knees and scrabbled for his helmet, which had tumbled from his head in the fall, Lewine struck with both blades at once. One bit through the Norman's byrnie into his shoulder; the other through hood and skull into his brain. As the blood trickled down his face, his eyes glazed, and he collapsed. Lewine stood unmoving, staring at the corpse in horror.

The knight, despairing of freeing his lance from the Dane's corpse, drew his sword, and wheeled again to face Lewine: but then he stopped. He had heard, or seen, something beyond the young Englishman, among the trees: and thither he now spurred. Hereward, in his hiding place, frowned, wondering what it could be.

Too late did he hear the cry as Mariana was grabbed and swung up over the knight's crupper. Too late did Svend start up to loose an arrow after the Norman, who was already cantering onward, shouting to his remaining guard to follow with the prisoner. Too late did the survivors emerge into the clearing, Geric not daring to meet anyone's eyes.

"I've killed a man," muttered Lewine. "I've killed a man." Hereward placed a comforting hand on his shoulder; but Svend was in no mood to comfort anyone.

"Stop your snivelling, boy, or I'll stop it for you," he snapped. "And you!" He rounded on Geric. "I ought to have your head. Because of you, a good man is dead, and my daughter's a prisoner!"

All that Sir Henry de Manville knew was that, while temporarily lost some way south of his path in the Bromeswold, he had captured a woman in man's clothing – a curiosity, certainly, but he did not think her likely to be important. That she cursed and spat in furious Norse was interesting, but told him little: a certain amount of Norse was mixed into the language of the Danelaw, more in some areas than others, and there were descendants of Canute's men as well as earlier Danish arrivals in the area: she could easily be from such a family. It was because of his other prisoner that he sought audience with the King as soon as he arrived at Spalding.

"His Grace is in conference," he was told.

"Tell him I've brought him Sir Oliver Godard," he

replied.

The sentry did not know the name, which was all but forgotten in Normandy: but Sir Henry's tone told him that the King would know it, and that was enough to send him scuttling off to procure the audience requested.

Nearly thirty years ago, when William had been a child and Normandy held as a regency by Count Alan of Brittany, Oliver Godard had served the Count. When Alan was murdered, he had fled, labelled a traitor: and by winding roads he had come at last with his daughter Emma to Manchester, where, setting aside all memory of his former heritage save for a gold signet that he would not part with, he had become a miller, known as Godred and passing for English. Hereward and Martin had encountered him there in 1068, and a Norman neighbour had found out his secret: but all had sworn to keep it.

The rebellion and the Harrying of the North had swept Godred's world away. He had managed to get Emma safely to Carlisle, which still owed allegiance to King Malcolm and was beyond the reach of the war: but his protector Miles de Mountney had been killed, and he himself near beggared as the farms which supplied his grain were burned, and his customers dispossessed or killed. At last he was forced to sell his ring. Recognising it as a noble emblem, the Flemish goldsmith who bought it had taken it to Sir Henry, whose steward had recognised the Godard seal, an eight-pointed star. Sir Henry had been summoned to join William's army: he had no intention, however, of removing defenders from his own house, and had therefore decided to leave behind him nearly all his soldiers. The King, of course, would be angry: but the exposure of Godard offered the perfect means to appease him. It was a gift from God, and Sir Henry took it gratefully: he arrested the miller, and dragged him in his train across England.

As he had expected, the King agreed to see him. Prisoners in tow, helmet under his arm, he strode into the royal presence, and bowed curtly.

"My lord King," he said. "I bring you a gift."

"And is that all you bring me?" asked William, raising an eyebrow. He had been disturbed at dinner, and his mouth was beslobbered with goose fat. "No men, no horses, no arms?"

De Manville did not answer, but prodded the miller forward.

"This is the traitor Godard," he said. William turned a curious eye on the old man.

"Are you so?" he asked.

"I was once Sir Oliver Godard," said the miller. "But he lies who calls me traitor."

"Give me the lie, will you, you vermin?" snarled de Manville. William held up his hand.

"Peace," he said. "Sir Oliver will have a chance to defend himself. He is a Norman and nobly born; we owe him no less."

"My lord!" interrupted the hairy, fur-swathed barbarian who sat on the King's left side. His accent was guttural and his French appalling; de Manville frowned, wondering what such a creature was doing there. William sighed.

"What is it?" he asked.

"That woman!" The man in furs was pointing at the wench de Manville had taken in the forest. The knight cursed silently, hoping she would not be taken from him to please some royal favourite, let alone one as uncouth as this. "It is Mariana – Svend's daughter!"

The King's eyes widened.

"You are sure?" he asked. The other nodded vigorously. "Bring her forward," William ordered. De Manville pushed Mariana into the light, and pulled back her hood. The man in furs began to speak excitedly in Norse; the girl addressed him coolly in the same language. De Manville understood little of it, but the man's excitement and anger and the girl's contempt for him were plain to see. "Well," said the King, "it appears, Henry, that you've brought us a greater prize than you knew. That is the daughter of Svend Estridsson, no less. Where did you find her?"

"Poaching in the Bromeswold," said de Manville, trying not to sound too flustered. "I must confess I had missed my way. There was a skirmish and I lost a man. I fear there were too many of the ruffians for us to fight to the end, but I thought -"

"You thought you'd pick up the prettiest of them," William finished for him. "Well, I'm afraid you must forfeit your pleasure; this woman is much too valuable. She is my prisoner now."

The man on the King's right, whom de Manville now recognised as the Baron de Warenne, spoke up.

"My lord," he said, "if there were survivors from this skirmish then it is known that we have the princess. The Danes will surely attack us here."

William stroked his chin.

"Perhaps," he said. "But they will know that an attack in force could place her life in danger. More likely they will try infiltration – and when that fails, negotiation. Besides, Svend's men are mostly with their ships. It would take time to gather them; if he strikes hastily, then he must do it with Englishmen, not Danes."

"Hereward has rescued captives from Spalding before," said de Warenne. Ivo Taillebois scowled at him.

"Not from the heart of an armed camp," William pointed out. "No, I think we need not fear a rescue. Nobody enters this town without my knowledge. And if it does come to an attack in force – why, then we shall have them. Hereward is a skirmisher, an attacker by night – a bandit, not a soldier. And Svend... Svend is a long way from home; his troops are restless and ill disciplined. I have never lost a battle. Such an attack is exactly what we need: it might end this war."

"The Normans will be expecting an attack," Hereward pointed out, stirring some life out of the embers of the campfire with Brainbiter's point. "I know the knight who took the princess; his name's de Manville, and his estate's away in the north-west. If he's in these parts it can only be to join King William. Our intelligence is that Krakus has joined with the Normans already: he'll identify the princess, if she hasn't identified herself."

"But if they don't know who she is yet -" Geric began. Svend shook his head.

"Lord Hereward is right," he said. "An attack in force will be expected. The only way it could be effective would be if we had enough men to overwhelm their entire camp – and we don't know how many that would be, until we learn how many the enemy has. This must be done subtly."

"They will anticipate that too," said Leofric. "It would be better to negotiate – at least it would buy time, and cover our rescue efforts."

"Negotiate with what?" snapped Svend. "There is nothing William wants that I can afford to give. He would demand at least the withdrawal of my fleet."

"We need a hostage of our own," suggested Martin.

"Who is there that the Bastard would value as high as Mariana?" demanded the King. "His wife and children are all safely over the sea in Normandy."

"There is William de Warenne," said Leofric. "The Norman depends on him in many things. If we could take him…"

Hereward frowned.

"If," he said. "Does he ever leave the Norman camp?"

"Maybe not," said Martin, "but he'll be easier to take out of it than the princess. We know the nobles stay at Ivo's hall and the houses around it; there's any number of English attend them there – retainers, slaves, folk delivering food. Getting to him will be the easy part; we just need a damn good plan for getting out again."

"We have people here who know Spalding," Leofric pointed out. "Wulfric – and Father Hugo."

"Wulfric hasn't lived in Spalding in two years," said Hereward. "And the priest would never help with a kidnap."

"So," said Martin, "we tell him we're going in to rescue the princess."

Hereward shook his head.

"I'll not lie," he said. "He's a good man, he deserves better than that. And if we lie to him he'll never help us again." He turned to Geric. "Find Wulfric; he may be able to help us."

A little way behind Ivo's hall, there stood a stone smokehouse for the curing of meat and cheese. It was stoutly walled, windowless, and had but one low entrance, and the earthen floor was long since baked hard. It was, William observed, the strongest cell he could have looked for – and already provided with chains, from which Ivo's cooks were accustomed to suspend hams for smoking. Thither, therefore, the prisoners were brought, and manacled to the chains which hung from the roof; and there they were left.

"What is a princess doing with an invasion force?" Godard wondered. His Manchester Anglo-Norse was not so different from the Norse of Denmark, and they understood one another.

"I would not be left behind," said Mariana simply. "My father is to be King of England. It is only fitting that he should have a court in England from the beginning."

"And risk your life by taking you poaching?" said Godard incredulously. Mariana hung her head.

"That was my own fault," she admitted. "I followed them."

"Well, you've learned your lesson," grunted the miller. "God pity your poor father."

"He should leave me here," declared Mariana. "I

deserve no more, and he must not give ground to William."

"It must be terrible," said Godard. "I thank God I am not a king, to face such choices; the life of a knight is ill enough. I thought I had escaped it; but it seems that it has found me out."

"The life of a warrior is a noble thing," declared the princess. Godard laughed bitterly.

"There's little nobility in war, girl," he said. "If you'd seen what these Normans are doing in the North, you'd know that. There's nothing but murder and shame."

Mariana frowned.

"But aren't you a Norman?" she asked curiously. "And a nobleman by birth?"

"I was," said Godard heavily. "I served the Duke, and I thought it was possible to be a good knight. The regent then was Alan of Brittany; I don't pretend he was a saint, he wanted Brittany's safety and that meant making sure Normandy didn't get too strong, and no doubt he took his share of Norman revenues too: but he never meant ill to the Duke himself, and he never tried to take a foot of his land. Others were worse; many wanted William dead. He didn't deserve what they did to him."

"What was that?" asked Mariana, wide-eyed.

"He was murdered," said Godard flatly. "They poisoned his wine. Back in Brittany his family was told the Duke himself had done it – a boy of eleven! That's why Alan's son Conan grew up hating Normandy; and they say William did poison Conan in the end, to prevent a war. I don't know if that's true, though from what I've seen his men do in England I can believe it. When last I saw William he was a frightened child who'd lost his father; what he's become now, I don't know.

"But after Count Alan was killed the new rulers needed to be rid of anyone who might be loyal to him; so they made up a nonsense about him plotting against the Duke, and they called all his men traitors. I lost my title and estates, and I had to flee Normandy or lose my life. Now there are hundreds of thousands like me, who've lost their homes on account of William the Bastard; I found refuge at a king's court, but most don't find the meanest hovel. They die in ditches instead. Three times now I've lost everything. Twice the corruption of courts brought me down, so I left that world behind, and built a life away from courtliness, where I did no harm. I was a miller; I fed people; better that than a cheating courtier or a murdering knight. But to do no harm isn't enough in war; it's those that do the most that come off the best. I was found, and called by a name I'd almost forgotten, and brought here to be served like a trussed hog to the King."

Mariana blinked back a tear.

"We'll get out of here," she said. "I know it. Somehow, we'll get out."

Godard shook his head.

"Not unless we free ourselves," he said. "If your father attacks Spalding hundreds will die. Did you ever see men killed, close to?"

"Not before today," said Mariana quietly.

"Today, of course," said Godard softly. "I am sorry; I'd forgotten what you had gone through. But now you know what it is like."

They heard the key turn in the lock. Mariana's whole body tensed in fear; Godard shook his head.

"They won't harm you," he said. "Not yet; they can't afford to. They'll have come for me."

But it was not a Norman who pushed into the dim light of the smokehouse: it was Krakus the Obodrite. He had come from eating, and his moustaches were shiny with goose fat; he swayed tipsily on his feet.

"My lady," he said, with a mocking bow to Mariana.

"My lord," she replied frostily. "Have you come to press your suit? You are hardly likely to win my father's approval now."

"Do I need it?" leered Krakus. "In the circumstances?"

"Don't be a fool," said Godard. "The princess is a hostage. King William needs her unharmed." Krakus spun on his heel, eyes blazing, and struck the miller across the mouth with the back of his hand; blood spattered across the wall.

"He's no need for you, though, old man," he spat. "You're worth nothing to anybody, so you can't afford to insult your betters."

"If I see them, I won't," said Godard, attempting a painful smile. Krakus scowled.

"Do you like the bargain you've made?" demanded Mariana. "You'll get no royal bride here. William doesn't need the Confederacy."

"No?" said Krakus. "Would it not suit him very well if he had an ally able to attack Denmark? Besides, this bargain was made for me by your uncle when he planted the black cowl in my pack."

"You're lying," said Mariana. Krakus shook his head.

"I never tried to kill the brat Edgar. Though it would have been a service to your father if I had. It can only have been Asbjorn or one of his people. And if he hadn't done that, I wouldn't have been in this camp, and William would never have known who you were." He stomped to the door, then turned and looked back. "Don't put too much hope on a ransom," he said. "Most like your father will try to rescue you – and that's just what William wants. Danes will die for you, in their hundreds. Think about that."

"There are vaults beneath the new tower, but they're not complete yet," Martin reported. "The priest believes they'll hold her in the smokehouse behind the hall."

Svend inclined his head.

"I thank you," he said. "And de Warenne?"

"Arrived after the priest left," said Martin. "There's nothing he could have told us anyway. So, since what he told couldn't have helped capture de Warenne, there was no dishonesty in not mentioning that plan."

Hereward growled, but said nothing. It was not worth quarrelling now; not in front of the Danes.

"So," said Svend, "can we get to this smokehouse?"

"It's in the heart of the town," said Wulfric. "But the hall and Ivo's other buildings face away from it, except for one storehouse."

"Nothing else faces it?"

"I don't think so," said Wulfric. "Unless Ivo's built anything."

"A fence," said Martin. "I asked the priest; he'd put in a length of fence. He wanted to make the storehouses more secure."

"And it's to the north of the hall," added Wulfric. "The wrong side, coming from Ely."

"But also away from the Norman camp to the southwest," Leofric pointed out. "*And* on a side they don't expect us to come from."

"So," mused Hereward, "if we enter Spalding from the east, and skirt the hall, we might be able to win to the smokehouse. But not in force. As soon as they knew we were there they'd send everything they had to defend it. I don't see a decoy working."

"Unless the rescue *is* the decoy," suggested Wulfric. "To allow us to snatch de Warenne." Hereward shook his head.

"No," he said, "we'd never get near him once the camp is roused."

"Two missions, then," said Svend. "Simultaneous and secret. Two small groups enter Spalding, one to kidnap de Warenne, the other to rescue Mariana. That way, if one fails, the other may succeed before the enemy has time to raise his guard." He paused, and looked around. "Wulfric to lead one," he said, "Asbjorn the other."

"With respect, sire," said Hereward quickly, "Lord Asbjorn does not know the area. I do. I should go."

"I am not to go," said Svend. "If I had suggested it,

you would all have said my capture could not be risked. Well, neither can yours." Asbjorn grimaced at the implication that he was more expendable than Hereward, but did not dare contradict his brother before the English.

"It is a matter of who is best for the task," insisted Hereward. "I have been to Spalding, I know the country around it, I speak French; and this is my kind of mission. Lord Asbjorn is a battle captain."

"Let it be so, then," agreed Svend. "Who will lead which?"

"I will rescue the princess," said Wulfric hurriedly. He had no intention of letting Hereward undertake what would almost certainly be the more dangerous mission.

"So be it."

The smokehouse door creaked once more. Godard, who had slumped against the wall, not quite able to sit down, struggled back to his feet; Mariana bit her lip, fearing that Krakus had returned. It was very dark: as night drew in outside, the little light that the chimney and the cracks around the door had admitted had dimmed: and the torch which was pushed in at first blinded them. But it was not Krakus' shaggy head which followed it. The hair was blond, and cut short in Norman style. Even before he straightened up, both prisoners had recognised Sir Henry de Manville.

"Sir Oliver Godard," he said curtly, "the King would speak with you."

"I am at his service," said Godard, glancing at his chains. Fumbling in the scrip at his belt, de Manville produced a key. He leant his torch against the wall; then, positioning himself behind Godard, and clasping him round the chest with his left arm to prevent his escape, he unlocked the manacles from first his right wrist, then the left: but at the moment that the lock clicked open, Godard hurled his body backwards, driving de Manville back against the wall and forcing the wind from his body. While the younger knight wheezed, Godard broke free from his loosened grip, and turned, grabbing him by the hair, and slammed his head against the wall; de Manville's eyes rolled upwards, and Mariana gasped as he slid to the ground.

Godard at once dropped to his knees, feeling around for the key. The torch's guttering light was little help, but after a few moments he found it, and set about freeing the princess.

"Quickly," he hissed, "we haven't much time. He'll have guards outside. If I go out in his cloak, and with the torch before me, it'll buy us a few moments – long enough for you to get through the door."

"And then?" quavered Mariana.

"Run," ordered Godard simply. "If there are only two or three I should be able to hold them long enough to give you a start."

"But you'll be killed!"

"Isn't that the best end a knight can make?" he retorted, as he tugged de Manville's sword belt off his prone body. "To die defending a noble lady?"

"I won't do it!"

"You must," Godard insisted, buckling the belt round his own body. It was a little tight, but no matter. "Remember what Krakus said: Danes will die in their hundreds for you. Save yourself to save them." He picked up the torch, kicked open the door, and, thrusting the brand before him, strode out into the night.

"Where's the prisoner, my l-" The sentry's question died as Godard's fist crashed into his unarmoured throat. He staggered backwards; as Mariana dashed out of the smokehouse, the second guard reached for his sword, but Godard was already drawn. The princess ran blindly away from the hall, thanking the saints for her male garb as she vaulted over Ivo's fence; behind her, she heard the clash of steel and the shouts of alarm, but she dared not stop until she came to the edge of Spalding – and was suddenly seized by the belt and pulled to the ground. She screamed, but a hand was clamped over her mouth.

"Be quiet, or – Highness?"

She knew that voice. It was English, she had heard it sing in Hereward's camp. The hand relaxed.

"You're the tumbler?" she whispered.

"Yes, my name is Wulfric. But how -"

"Sir Oliver sacrificed himself," she said, her voice trembling with shame. "Another good man dead for me."

"God rest him," muttered Wulfric. "I only hope Lord Hereward hears the commotion before he enters the town."

As the second sentry lunged again at Godard, the old knight parried, twisted his sword to one side, and struck him on the side of the head with his torch. He shrieked and fell to the ground. By now more soldiers were coming from the hall and the houses beyond, more than any one man could fight: but there was no need to any more. If Mariana were not beyond their reach by now, there was nothing more he could do. Godard turned his sword in his hand, and held it hilt upwards.

"I, Sir Oliver Godard, do here offer my surrender to the most noble William, by God's grace King of the English," he declared loudly. The soldiers edged forward suspiciously. He might be alone, grey-haired and breathing heavily, but there were two men groaning on the ground and Sir Henry nowhere to be seen. "Come on," called Godard. "Are you afraid to take me?" He cast aside both torch and sword, and spread his arms. "I am defenceless," he said. "Bring me before the King." At last, they moved forward. Five of them seized his arms and bound him; and he was lifted off the ground and carried back to the hall, where, pushing through the doors, they cast him to the ground in front of the King. William set down his wine cup and stared; chatter stopped throughout the hall.

"What does this mean?" the King demanded. "Where

213

is Sir Henry? What has happened?"

"He killed him," muttered a man at arms, looking at the ground. Godard shook his head. The motion was painful; he was beginning to feel all the knocks and bruises he had taken that night.

"He lives," he said. "He will be conscious soon enough. But the Princess Mariana is free."

"Once again you aid my enemies," said William softly. "Why do you hate me, Sir Oliver? What wrong did I ever do you?"

"I was never your enemy, sire," said Godard. "I've only tried to do what is right."

"By helping a hostage escape?"

"A girl, a child almost, of royal blood, chained up in a smokehouse?" said Godard. "It's not worthy of Your Grace. I wouldn't see her treated so."

"Indeed," said William. "There are few who presume to speak to me thus, Sir Oliver."

"Hang him," snarled Krakus. William gestured to him to be quiet.

"Maybe Your Grace needs more men who are not afraid to speak," said Godard. William smiled.

"Maybe I do," he said. "But you are already under sentence of death. You have nothing more to fear by being forthright. Should I hear the counsel only of condemned men?"

"Maybe Your Grace is asking the wrong question," said Godard. "Perhaps some of your counsellors should be condemned. If there are any left who told you Alan of Brittany was your enemy, they deserve to die."

"Then you maintain that he was not?" said the King, raising a sceptical eyebrow. "A man whose own lands stood to gain by every loss Normandy suffered?"

"He was an honourable man," declared the knight, "and would never have harmed Your Grace."

"Well," said William, "it hardly matters, after thirty

214

years. Those counsellors are dead, Alan is dead, Conan is dead, and Brittany knows who its real master is. There is nobody left but you."

"And I will be dead soon enough." Godard grimaced. The pain was beginning to flood through his limbs; probably he had some cracked bones.

"What if I were to pardon you?" asked the King suddenly. "What if I were to bring you into my court, make you first among my counsellors?"

Godard chuckled, but it gave way to an agonised wheeze. He shook his head.

"I thank you, my lord, but no," he said. "A court is no place for me, and nor is a battlefield. I am a miller."

"Without a mill," the King observed. "What would you go back to if I were to let you go?"

"I don't know," admitted Godard. "I have a daughter…"

"Who I hear is in Scotland," said William, interrupting. "Among yet more of my enemies. Is that where you will go?"

"Perhaps," said Godard. "Would you stay in a burning house? England is burning."

"The flames may spread to Scotland yet," remarked the King. At that point, William de Warenne entered the hall, a little out of breath.

"My men have searched all Spalding, sire," he announced. "The Danish princess is gone. If she had any help from Hereward's people there's no sign of them."

The King sighed.

"Since I came to this town I have found myself surrounded by incompetent fools," he said, a little too calmly. "Lock the smokehouse door and mount a new guard over it; de Manville can spend the night in there. I'll decide what to do with his guards later." He looked back to Godard. "And you…" he said. "Was there any help from outside? Outlaws? Danes?"

Godard shook his head.

"The escape was my plan," he said, "and mine alone. I saw nobody from outside the town."

William nodded.

"I believe you," he said. "Will you swear to give no more aid or comfort to my enemies?"

"I swear," said Godard. "By the bones of St Audoin and the honour of my family."

"Then go in peace," said the King at last. "You served my father well; and I trust your oath. But if you prove me wrong, you will not taste my mercy a second time."

Godard bowed his head.

"Your Grace will never find me false," he promised.

Permia, 1033.

Erik Thorbjarnarson rubbed the snow out of his eyes and peered into the whiteness ahead of him. There it was: ill-defined, blurred by fog and swirling snow, but undoubtedly a shape different from the rest of the blank plains, something like a great longhouse, a ring of dead trees around it, and a black patch showing where the snow had melted around its chimney hole.

"We've found it," he breathed. "The Temple of Ukko."

It was now more than half a month since his warband had left their ship, although there was no telling how great or little was the distance they had covered across the wastes of Permia. They had left the gloomy pine forest behind some days ago; if the land this side of it had any features, the white drifts had hidden them. The band, mostly Swedes from Sörmland like Erik himself, missed their native lakes and woods as never before: but the tales of the temple treasures had driven them on. In coastal temples and chieftains' longhouses they had taken rich furs and amber jewellery, and a little gold, but everywhere they had heard that the Temple of Ukko was the site of the greatest hoard in Permia. They had been suspicious at first, wondering why the Northern natives would so willingly betray this secret: but every Permian had given the same answer.

"It makes no difference. You'll never get there. Ukko protects his own."

But now they were here. As they approached, they saw the standards set before the temple, windsocks in the form of scaly serpents; a stiff breeze had sprung up, and they were roiling and writhing like living things. They could have done with this wind earlier, to disperse the fog, but in spite of the fog they had found their way.

Above the gate of the temple there sat what Erik had taken for a bird carved from wood: he whom so little could affright was startled to see it spread its wings as his men approached. It was a white-tailed eagle, he realised, though what it was doing so far from the sea he did not care to guess; taking in its vast wingspan, he was sure he had never seen a bigger. In that instant, the eagle launched itself from the temple top, and swooped low over the Swedes; one, trying to duck, tripped and sprawled in the snow as the eagle flapped lazily and flew away. Normally Erik would have mocked the man's cowardice, but just now he did not feel like laughing. It was not just that the eagle's claws had come too close for comfort, though he had seen what the talons of the white-tail could do: there was something about the place itself that seemed to compel a sort of awe.

But that did not change the purpose for which they had come. Silently, Erik motioned his two strongest men forward to test the doors: though huge and massy, they were unbarred, and slowly slid open. A blast of freezing air preceded the Swedes into the temple; the flame of the great brazier which burned perpetually at the centre guttered, but did not go out. The temple maidens, in their flimsy blue gowns, were already running crying from the cold before they realised there was a worse danger upon them.

"Take them all and bind them," ordered Erik, "but do them no harm. We need them virgins and unscarred if they are to fetch a good price." His men instantly scattered in eager pursuit of the fleeing women, grabbing them and binding them hand and foot with leather thongs, stripping from their arms and necks the amulets and gewgaws with which they were adorned. Suddenly, from the shadows beyond the brazier, there came a deep, animal bellow: many of the Swedes stopped, shaken, in their tracks. Erik drew his sword. "Who's there?" he barked.

Before he saw the beast, he noticed the brazier wobble. He dived aside only just in time as it crashed to the ground, sending burning coals skidding across the floor of the temple, which almost immediately began to smoulder: and over the fallen brazier, into the cinder-strewn floor, there bounded a bull aurochs. The beast's glossy coat was, save for a grey band along its spine, altogether sable; it stood higher than a man at the shoulder; its horns were like blades, and its vast body pure muscle: and it was enraged. A warrior who was standing nearby was not merely gored, but actually run through, before he so much as had time to turn: he was still screaming, and his gushing blood spurting onto the maiden he had been pursuing, as the aurochs shook its head to dislodge the inconvenience of the corpse. After a few moments, it succeeded, and his body flew off, landing crumpled on the floor. The aurochs snorted, steam rising from its nostrils, and bellowed again; a spark had caught its fur, and the pain only maddened it further. Lowering its head, it made to charge at the two men who had the misfortune to be standing between it and the door. Erik yelled frantically to them, but they had no time to get out of the way: one was hurled aside, landing with a sickening crack as his back broke, and the other fell wailing under the beast's hooves.

Only when the aurochs had hurtled out of the door did Erik gingerly begin to pick himself up: but then he heard something new. Over the crackle of the flames, the whimpers of the captives, and the moans of the dying men, he could hear *laughter*.

Straightening his bruised body up, he edged forward, sword before him – the end had broken off in his fall, but it was still sharp – through the flames which were beginning to lick across the floor of the temple, towards the laughter. There, in the dark recess from which the monster had come, there stood a dais, on which there was an altar, and a throne before it: above the altar stood Ukko, and on the throne sat his priestess.

The god himself was impressive enough: hewn from

the solid heart of a pine tree, he glowered down from under a crown topped with golden stars; his arms were bound with jewelled rings, and a silver chalice as big as a bucket was borne between his hands. But it was the living woman, not the statue, who commanded Erik's awe.

Unlike the temple maidens, she was swathed in furs from neck to ankle, wolf, squirrel, beaver, lynx, and the gods knew what: though her powerful, leathery arms were left bare, as were her feet. With bony, long-nailed hands which reminded Erik horribly of the eagle's talons, she clutched the arms of the throne. From her neck, her wrists, and the belt through which was thrust a dagger of sharpened and polished walrus ivory, there dangled more charms and pendants than Erik could count, wood, ivory, iron and silver, in the shapes of beasts real and fabulous, carven with runes of all kinds, some familiar, some extraordinary. Her head was sunk upon her chest as if in sleep: but her sharp black eyes were open, and fixed unblinkingly on Erik. She laughed again, and the Swede gritted his teeth: the noise was painful.

"Stop it!" he burst out. "Stop it! Stop laughing! Your temple's burning, you fool, your women are taken, your beast is gone – you are a slave! You will be sold in the marketplace at Novgorod; your god has failed you. Stop laughing! *Stop!*"

Ely, April, 1070.

Torfridel's whimpering slowly died away, as she closed her eyes, and fell asleep. Now that her shivering had stopped too, she looked curiously still. Torfrida caught her breath, and clung to Hereward's arm. Kolfrosta, who had been bent over the child's crib, looked up.

"She will live," she said curtly. "The fever will be gone by morning. She is a strong child. Not all will be so lucky."

Brother Thomas crossed himself.

"Praise God for that, at least," he said. "But already

220

some of the men are grievously sick."

The sky outside was overcast, and the small windows of the pilgrim hostel admitted little light at the best of times; it was now lit by flickering, smoky torches, which cast eerie dancing shadows across the faces of those who had gathered round the infant's sickbed.

"What is it, Brother?" asked Torfrida fearfully. "Have you seen it before?"

The infirmarian inclined his head.

"It is St Guthlac's Ague," he said, "though it seldom comes so early in the year. Every ten or twenty years there is an outbreak somewhere in the Fens. They say the best treatment is always had at Croyland, the house Guthlac founded, because the saint's blessing is upon it. Not that there was anything but an idea to bless: St Guthlac himself died of the ague before the house was built or the first monks took their vows." The saint's death, living as he had on a tussock of grass poking above one of the boggiest parts of the Fens, was hardly surprising: but even now, after so many centuries, there were still hermits who emulated him by retreating to the remotest parts of the wetlands – and the ague still raged.

"Should we send for monks of Croyland, then?" said Hereward. "Or nuns?"

"Father Abbot will not take kindly to women in the infirmary," said Thomas, "even the gracious Lady Edith. He might be persuaded to make an exception for her, but I think it would be better if I used the pilgrim hostel to treat the sick. I regret that the Ladies Torfrida and Elfthryth would need to find alternative accommodation."

"Why?" asked Hereward.

"Because whatever exceptions Father Abbot might make for the Lady Edith, he could never permit an unbelieving woman within the walls of the abbey," said the infirmarian. "The Saracen Zainab is an accomplished healer; I have never met one more learned. And Kolfrosta too seems to have some skill. If we do face an epidemic, I shall need their help."

Svend had been with his fleet when the ague had reached Ely; on hearing of the sickness, the Danes had promptly departed on a raiding expedition. These were increasingly common as the weather grew warmer, and where at first only Normans had been targeted, rumours were reaching Ely that the English population was not being spared. Certainly the Normans were making use of such tales, as they had of the Scottish raids earlier in the year, declaring the barbarous foreigners to be England's foes and calling on the natives to rally to their lawful King; and in some areas it was said there had been reprisals against Danish families, people settled for generations forced out of their homes in revenge for what their ancestors' countrymen were doing on the coast. But though this news might sadden hearts in the Camp of Refuge, they had more pressing worries now.

Hereward ordered word sent at once to Abbot Ulfkytel and his mother at Croyland; but it was not until the fourth day that Edith came. She was accompanied by one other nun, a Sister Aldeva; but by that time, the ague had spread across the Isle. Half the men were affected: great Ulric Grogan was weak as a baby, Winter shaking like an aspen leaf, Lewine taken so badly he could not stand; and, the day before Edith arrived, the fever struck Elfthryth.

The pilgrim hostel was full, and Thomas was making calls on the sick who could not leave the Camp and the village of the Abbey tenants between his duties there; though the women gave him all the help they could, Torfrida leaving Torfridel in Rowena's care so that she could devote her time to the stricken, it seemed the infirmarian never slept. He acknowledged to any who asked that he could not have coped without Zainab.

Kolfrosta had been useful too, but Thomas found her a less congenial colleague. She eschewed the herbs of his garden for strange scrapings of moss and bark, which sometimes worked and sometimes did not; she was apt either to ignore instructions or to reply to them with a sharp tongue; and as part of every preparation, she recited spells in her native language. It was not only that she was praying to strange gods that offended Thomas: it was that she regarded the words as being as vital, and as reliably efficacious, as any ingredient she gathered from the green world without. To both Thomas and Zainab, this seemed not only foolishly superstitious, but blasphemous: for the implication of it was, that Kolfrosta did not appeal to her deities, but commanded them. Had Abbot Thurstan been aware of the spells, he would certainly have ordered the infirmarian to dispense with the old woman's aid; but, however strange her ways, she was a valuable pair of hands, and Thomas said nothing.

Hereward stood by Elfthryth's bedside, her hand clasped in his. Her breathing was loud and laboured, and she shivered.

"Can you do no more for her?" he asked anxiously. Thomas shook his head.

"It is beyond my skill to tell the path the fever will take," he said. "But it should break tonight, if..." His voice tailed away.

"If she is going to live," Hereward finished. He looked at Elfthryth's pale face, now drawn, and shiny with sweat, and bit his lip. Kolfrosta narrowed her eyes.

"I shall see what I can achieve," she said, "if it is your wish." She seemed almost to be challenging Hereward to refuse her. He looked unblinkingly into her deep black eyes.

"Do whatever you think is necessary," he said. "Don't let her die."

Kolfrosta reached into the mass of clanking charms and amulets that hung from her robes, and unhooked one made of polished iron, in the form of a wriggling serpent with a strange, arrow-shaped head: and she set it upon Elfthryth's glistening brow, holding it in place with one gnarled hand, and began to chant in Lapp, softly at first, then rising, growing louder. Hereward caught the word "Ukko" repeated several times; Thomas crossed himself and hurried from the chamber. Torfrida, watching, bit her lip, and said nothing.

It was some hours before Torfrida left, called away to help Thomas attend to Lewine; Hereward remained until he could no longer stay awake. He slept that night alone, in a hut in the Camp of Refuge; and he awoke early, to a cold, damp morn, the monastery bells ringing in the distance.

After only a draught of watered ale, he hurried to the hostel. Zainab met him at the door.

"Is the Lady Elfthryth well?" he asked breathlessly.

"She sleeps well," she replied, "and the fever has left her." Hereward clasped her hand, and thanked her; but the healer merely stood there, her face flat and unresponsive. Hereward frowned: was she merely tired, or was there something more?

"What is it?" he asked. "What is wrong?"

"The fever has left the lady," said Zainab, "but it has gone into Kolfrosta."

Hereward hurried past her, and pushed unceremoniously into Elfthryth's chamber. As Zainab had stated, she was sleeping calmly, her breathing regular and her brow clean of sweat: but beside her upon the bed lay Kolfrosta, curled up, her body seeming shrunken, shaking with fever. The ancient Permian, who had always seemed so strong, whom Hereward had vaguely thought of as immortal, whom Torfrida so dearly loved, was as helpless as a blind kitten. To his own surprise, Hereward felt tears prick his eyes; and he left the chamber.

"Can anything be done?" he asked Zainab quietly. The Saracen spread her hands.

"All things are possible to God," she said. "But she is not young, and the fever is strong. I would not be too hopeful." From within the chamber, there came a faint moan. "I must attend to her," said Zainab. "I can at least ease her suffering. You should not stay in this place; we would all be the losers if you should die."

Hereward, his eyes bleared, nodded vaguely, and stumbled out back into the morning light. He did not want to be the one to tell Torfrida.

It was an overcast day and the sun cast few shadows; and Hereward was not sure how much time passed between his leaving the hostel and the arrival on the island of Edith and Aldeva. His mother gave him a cool, perfunctory greeting and threw herself immediately into the work of tending the sick; Thomas took the nuns first to the part of the hostel where the stricken warriors were housed. Torfrida was already there, moving from bed to bed with a pot of broth with a sort of restless urgency: she had not dared stop moving since she had learnt of Kolfrosta's illness.

She looked up when the infirmarian entered the hall.

"Lewine has gone to God," she said flatly. "There was nobody to remove him."

Thomas and the nuns crossed themselves.

"I will send for two of the brothers," the infirmarian said. "You should rest, lady." Torfrida shook her head.

"I need no rest," she said.

"Yes, you do," said the monk firmly. "When did you last sleep? Every minute awake makes you weaker, and more open to the fever yourself."

"I couldn't sleep," insisted Torfrida. "Not while – not while I'm needed…"

"There are enough of us," said Thomas more gently.

"You must rest, child," said Aldeva. "We cannot let your life be put at risk."

"So many others are dying," Torfrida sighed. "Do I matter more?" Thomas glanced pointedly at Ulric Grogan; the big warrior was awake. He let out a groan; Torfrida realised that others might have heard her. "I am sorry," she said quietly."

"Rest," said Edith. It was not advice, but a calm, authoritative instruction. Torfrida bowed her head.

"I will try," she said.

As the sun dipped, Torfrida awoke. The island woman in whose hut she had been allowed to make her bed was cooking, a stew of eels caught in the pools on the edge of the mere; she ignored Torfrida, who smoothed down her kirtle – she had slept fully clothed, as she had done for several days: caring for the sick left little time to change – and hurried back to the hostel.

Elfthryth had moved out, leaving Kolfrosta the chamber to herself, at least for the moment; Torfrida found the old woman asleep, Edith kneeling by her bed, a single candle lit. The nun's hands were clasped in prayer, her head bowed: she did not look up until some minutes after Torfrida entered.

"She sleeps," she said. "The fever has not abated much, but at least she is able to sleep. She rambles in many tongues when she is awake; I fear what she says is heathenish; but the state of her soul is the priests' concern. I can only pray."

"As we all do," said Torfrida. She paused; there was something uncomfortable in the air. It was but this day that she had first met her mother-in-law, and as yet they had hardly spoken. "Have you seen Hereward?"

Edith shook her head.

"Not in some hours," she said. "He attended the burial of the boy Lewine. So young; he reminded me of my son Toli." Torfrida bit her lip; she knew that Hereward's young brother had been murdered by Ivo's men a few years before, but they had never spoken of it. Edith narrowed her eyes, and peered into Torfrida's face. "Is all well between you?" she asked. Torfrida sighed.

"I do not know," she said. "I think so... perhaps I am being foolish. I have no reason to be jealous... of anyone." She paused again, then said, suddenly: "What is the life of a nun like?"

Edith blinked.

"It is… peaceful," she said. "Though not all find it so. It is difficult as well, and sometimes peace eludes the most serene. But I know that for me, there would be no peace outside the cloister. I have seen too much, buried too many, even before… There is much toil and prayer, and little sleep. And Croyland is not a true double house; there are few such left these days. They say that in times past the great abbesses could sway councils, speak louder than bishops: but those days are gone. Croyland is a house of monks, with only four women left: and two of us are here." It was years since she had spoken so long at once.

"But it is peaceful?" Torfrida pressed.

"Yes," said Edith. "I find it so. The routine is soothing, and I believe I am closer to God. But your path is a different one; you are a wife."

"As you were."

"And now I am a widow." *As you may soon be* hung in the air, unspoken. Both knew the dangers faced every day by the man they loved.

Kolfrosta's eyes snapped open.

"Ukko," she hissed. "Ukko!" Suddenly, her withered hand grabbed Torfrida's wrist, and she began speaking urgently in her own tongue. Torfrida, keeping her composure, smoothed the old woman's hair with her free hand, and said in Flemish:

"What is it, Kolfrosta?"

The Permian flashed a suspicious glance at Edith: but it was enough to tell her that the Englishwoman did not understand them, and she spoke in Flemish, low-voiced.

"The dragon must be protected," she said. Torfrida frowned, uncomprehending.

"The dragon?" she echoed.

Impatiently, Kolfrosta scrabbled at her belt: but she found nothing there. Her amulets were missing. Panic entered her eyes.

"It is gone!" she exclaimed. "My charms -"

"They are safe, Kolfrosta," said Torfrida softly. "They are here." She tapped a wooden box by the bed. She and Zainab had stripped the clanking amulets from Kolfrosta as soon as she had lost consciousness: she would sleep easier without such a mass of metal and bone upon her, and the monks and nuns would see less to scandalise them.

"Open it," Kolfrosta ordered, gripping Torfrida's wrist tighter. Despite her weakness, the Permian was hurting her mistress. "Find the dragon."

Avoiding Edith's eyes, for the nun did not look approving, Torfrida unlocked the box and raised the lid. There were more than a dozen different charms, some of polished horn, some of round stones worn by the sea – and, yes, there it was, a little scrap of iron, crudely shaped into the form of a wriggling horned serpent, with a hole for an eye. It did not look impressive.

"Is this the dragon?" she asked, holding it up. Kolfrosta's eyes flashed.

"Yes," she breathed reverently. "The Dragon of Ukko."

"Who is Ukko?" asked Torfrida.

"Ukko is the sky and the storm, the father of life," said Kolfrosta. "The dragon is the lightning, his symbol and his most dreadful servant. I was his priestess before I was enslaved." She smiled. "It was his will to bring me to the west," she said. "This is where my destiny lay. But the Swedes who sacked his temple... they paid for their blasphemy. Ukko's curse was on every one of them. Not one lived to see their homeland again; I was brought there by the men they had left on the ship. Their leader I strangled with a cord, and threw into the sea. The gods willed it." She stroked the dragon amulet. "I know it looks a poor thing. That is why I was allowed to keep it. But believe me, in the North this dragon is known and coveted. There are Danes and Nordlanders who would recognise it. Once, long ago, it was stolen by a Danish king, and only through all the cunning of

Ukko's priestesses was it recovered."

Never before had Kolfrosta made so long a speech; never before had she spoken about her past. Torfrida was bewildered; she had a thousand questions but could not put them into words.

"You wonder why it is so important?" said Kolfrosta, with a cracked smile. "Ukko's favour resides in this. It is said that, with the right words, it can command the dragon. The words are lost: but if they could be recovered…"

Her voice tailed away, and she slumped back on the pillow. Torfrida gave a cry and started up.

"Hush," said Edith. "She breathes: she is sleeping. It will be best to let her rest." She glanced at the dragon pendant, but said nothing about that: whatever Kolfrosta had entrusted to Torfrida, she would leave between them.

Spalding.

"Speak," urged King William, with a wave of his hand to the mud-stained scout who had just dragged himself into Ivo's hall. "What news of the rebels?"

The man bowed his head.

"There is fever on the island, sire," he said. "Some manner of shaking ague. Men are dying there every day."

"Excellent!" beamed the King. "It seems the marshes are doing our work for us."

"We need only sit back and let them die," put in de Warenne; but the King shook his head.

"I think we can do better than that," he said. "If we wait, the fever may pass; but now even those who are not sick are tied up caring for those who are, and their morale will be all but destroyed. No, the sooner we attack, the better."

"Attack?" echoed de Warenne. "A place of infection? The men won't go near it; they'd mutiny."

"Is discipline then so poor?" wondered the King. "No

matter. Perhaps it is a little early to enter the Camp of Refuge: but we may still attack it."

"With arrows?" wondered Ivo.

"No," said William. "Arrows do little good against buildings, and there is small point in lighting them when everything is damp. But in Anjou once I saw a catapult floated along a river on a raft. If we could bring an onager or two close to Hereward's camp..."

"But surely, sire, any raft big enough to support the machine, and not be overturned when it was loosed, would be too big to guide across the Fens," objected de Warenne.

"Usually, no doubt," agreed the King. "But the spring rains have raised the water in the western approaches. There is barely a reed to be seen above the surface. And there is no need to operate the machines from the rafts. We can land them to the west of Hereward's camp, where they will not look for us, and attack from there. A few stout men can defend the onagers against any counter-attack the fever-ridden rebels are likely to make. The aim is not to take the camp in one assault: only to weaken it." He waved a guard forward. "Send in Walter du Gast," he ordered.

The engineer du Gast was a slight, unassuming man of no background, whom Ivo and others had expected to quail in the presence of so many great nobles: but instead he bore himself with the confidence of the expert. He knew that he could only have been sent for to address a matter of siege warfare, on which none there could fault him. He bowed, and waited for the King to speak.

"Would it be possible to land two onagers to the west of the Camp of Refuge, and pound it?" William asked.

"Possible, certainly," agreed du Gast. "But we have no such engines at present. It would take time to build two, and unless we landed a substantial force with them they should almost certainly be lost."

"One, then," said William impatiently, ignoring the engineer's failure to address him by his title. "Could we build and land one?"

"Yes, but there would be a limit to the damage it could do."

"We need to strike while the flood and the fever are still high," insisted the King, "not to waste all summer building siege engines while the rebels recover and the Danes return. Could we land one by raft, flatten a few houses and storage barns – maybe let a stone or two go astray towards the abbey?"

Du Gast did not waste time in pretending to be shocked by the latter suggestion.

"It would be difficult to come within range of the abbey," he said. "Coming from the west, that would put us in considerable danger from counter-attacks. The abbey is east of Hereward's camp."

"But we could knock down a couple of barns, yes?" said William. "Hurt their supplies just before the hungry summer." Du Gast nodded. The King smiled. "Then set about building the machine at once," he said. "I want it ready within a week, less if you can do it."

Asbjorn was not pleased to be sent back into the place of infection. Death in battle he did not fear: but, Christian or no, the Danes still remembered the fierce faith of their forefathers, which taught that the man who died in his bed would not see Valhalla. The smell and the hopelessness that hung about houses of sickness repelled him, and he was seen to shudder as he stepped from his boat onto the soil of Ely.

But this was King Svend's will. Word had reached him in the North that the Scots were in retreat, and the Normans raiding into Lothian; and this he felt the men of Ely should know – especially since some might yet incline more to Edgar Atheling than to Svend Estridsson. Furthermore, he regretted not leaving a Danish presence on the island: for he placed but little trust in the monks or the islanders. With this in mind, he had sent Asbjorn and a dozen men back; and with some trepidation they now entered the Camp of Refuge.

Those of Hereward's men who were not sick or on guard duty had mostly been set to nursing work; the islanders, meanwhile, attempted to continue with normal life. It took some time before the Danes found anybody who could be persuaded to direct them to Hereward; but they were at last told that he had gone to the pilgrim hostel to check on the health of Kolfrosta. At the name of the Permian, several Danes muttered, and crossed themselves or made other, older signs against evil; their prince, for his part, felt much the same way about the hostel itself, but strove not to show it.

There was, Asbjorn decreed, no need for any man to accompany him in search of Hereward: they would do better to seek out lodgings for themselves. They replied that they would rather sleep in their boat, or if need be upon the ground, sobeit they were outside the camp; but none volunteered to join the prince.

He was met in the main hall of the hostel by Torfrida, who was still tending to the stricken warriors. She raised her hand in greeting.

"Prince Asbjorn!" she exclaimed. "We did not expect you... My husband is within."

"My lady."

Asbjorn inclined his head – then paused, and narrowed his eyes. Hanging around Torfrida's neck by a fraying leather strap there was a metal shape – one he recognised. The same shape was carved into a beam in the longhouse at Roskilde, with dark and ugly runes about it, warding against evil. It was unmistakeable. A copy..?

"My lady," he said, "where did you come by that?"

"This?" Torfrida flushed. "It is nothing..."

"Did it come from the North?" pressed Asbjorn. A thought struck him. "From the Permian woman?"

"My lord Asbjorn," said Torfrida warmly, "you forget your manners."

"My lady," replied Asbjorn, "I know that serpent. Its

232

image has been kept at Roskilde since the days of Gorm the Old. The skalds say it was given to him by Thor as a sign of favour, but was stolen by the sorcerers of Permia. If it came from the Permian it may be the same: and if it is the same it belongs to King Svend."

"You have forgotten yourself, sir," declared Torfrida, her weariness falling from her as her anger rose. "You are a guest here, and yet you dare -"

"He dares what?" said Hereward.

Torfrida turned stiffly towards him.

"He lays claim to this," she said, "this iron trinket of Kolfrosta's."

"It was Danish," insisted Asbjorn. "The Permians stole it."

"When?" asked Hereward.

"In the days of King Gorm -"

"A hundred years ago and more," retorted Hereward. "There are no witnesses. There could be a thousand such amulets: it's just a scrap of iron. Unless Kolfrosta were to confirm that it was Danish…"

"She declares it to be Permian," said Torfrida.

"Then there is no more to be said." Hereward peered at the amulet. For the first time, Torfrida noticed the dark rings around his eyes, the sheen of sweat on his brow, the unsteadiness of his gait. "It's a poor thing, anyway," he remarked. "What's its value?"

"It is said to be a symbol of the favour of Thor."

"Then it is hardly a matter to concern a Christian prince," retorted Hereward. Asbjorn narrowed his eyes, but said nothing. "What has brought you back to Ely? Has King Svend abandoned his raiding expedition?" The Dane shook his head.

"I am sent with tidings," he said. "The Scots and their pawn Edgar are in full retreat before Red Alan. We have taken much plunder on the coast, but -"

Asbjorn never finished his sentence: he was

interrupted by a mighty crash from somewhere without, and by the time he had blinked back his surprise Hereward was already barking a curt apology and heading outside to learn what had happened.

He did not have to go far. Less than a hundred yards from the hostel, an islander's hut had been smashed to splinters; amid the wreckage, pinned under a boulder twice the size of a man's head, was the broken, bloody body of a woman. The fire she had been tending had been scattered by the impact, and the tumbled thatch and planking, damp as it was, was beginning to smoulder; a poker was still clutched in her hand.

Hereward had barely arrived, and was still wheezing, clutching the single post that remained standing, when a second stone, larger than the first, sailed past him and thudded into the ground, spattering the bystanders with mud. It bounced, and rolled on for several yards.

"What's happening?" somebody wailed.

"It's devil's work," muttered Geric. "Rocks falling from the sky."

"This is man's doing." The assembled crowd looked round. Few there had heard Girolamo di Salerno speak English before; he had practised largely with the monks, and with Zainab, but now he felt confident enough in his fluency to use the language publicly. As usual, he had Azecier in tow; the boy frowned suspiciously at the English, understanding less than half of what was said. "The Normans must have an onager."

"An onager?" said Wulfric. "What's that?"

"It is a machine for hurling stones," said Girolamo. "The name means 'wild ass', because of the way it kicks. They're not easy to build, and they're not cheap. There are few who have the skill. But somebody must have."

"Can they launch stones at us from Spalding or Brampton, then?" demanded one of the monastery tenants. "That's devilry indeed!"

Girolamo shook his head.

"No," he said, "the onager's range is nothing like so far. It must be on the island, close by."

A third stone sailed over their heads, and landed within twenty yards of the hostel; and Hereward, losing hold of the post, fell to the ground.

"Look to Lord Hereward!"

Martin was first to Hereward's side, and felt for his pulse. He looked up, eyes widening: for the first time, the people of Ely looked on Martin Lightfoot and saw fear.

"It's the ague," he said.

A woman in the crowd threw back her head and began to keen. Everybody was jabbering, frenzied, panicking. Girolamo held up his hands for peace, but was ignored. At last he bellowed:

"Silence!"

All turned to the Italian.

"The onager must be destroyed," he said. "The Normans must have landed men to guard it, but not many, or they would be attacking on foot by now. The sun is sinking. Azecier and I can disable the machine easily enough, but we will need two good men to help us get to it."

"I'll come," Wulfric volunteered at once. Girolamo looked around for a second. Men shifted and gazed down at their feet.

Then Martin stood up.

"I will go," he said quietly. "See that Lord Hereward is taken back to the hostel and well cared for. All our hopes live in him."

The same low scrub to the west of the village on which Walter du Gast had relied to provide at least partial cover for his onager now allowed Girolamo, Azecier, Martin and Wulfric to approach the great wooden beast unseen. They were able to come within a few feet; two Norman footsoldiers were at that moment cranking back the stiff

235

wheels which drew down the arm of the catapult, while a third hefted another rock from a small pile to one side. A fourth soldier stood to one side, gazing towards the Camp of Refuge; and beside him a fifth man, dwarfed by the powerfully built soldiers, who had been chosen for their strength, stood looking on. He wore a light helm and a leather jerkin instead of a coat of mail, and Girolamo had seen him before.

"Walter du Gast," he muttered.

Two more soldiers stood by the edge of the mere, guarding a large raft with two punts lashed to it, and looking distinctly bored. Martin glanced at Girolamo, who nodded.

Drawing his axe from his belt, the Irishman hurled himself forward with a ululating cry, and caught the unoccupied soldier round the neck, sinking his blade into the gap below the Norman's aventail. The man with the stone dropped it, the two operating the wheels straightened up, those by the raft ran towards the onager, and all fumbled for their swords: but by this time Wulfric was among them. He cut down one before he was even drawn; as a second slashed at his head, he ducked, and the Norman's blade bit into the frame of the onager. As he struggled to retrieve it, Wulfric kicked him in the chest: as he staggered backwards, his helmet fell off, and Martin's axe sank through his chainmail hood and into his brain. The body fell against Martin, bearing him to the ground.

Girolamo rose, drawing his sword.

"Release the rope," he barked to Azecier. "I'll protect you." The youth hurried to the onager, and reached for the lever to release the arm; as he did so, one of the soldiers from the raft slashed at him, and he leapt backwards to avoid the blow. The sword struck the rope in whose tension lay all the power of the onager, and cut more than halfway through it; Girolamo drove his blade into the Norman's belly, and, gurgling blood, he fell – upon the lever.

The rope snapped at the moment of release, and the

onager shot backwards; Azecier, who had fallen awkwardly, was not able to avoid it in time. It careered over his leg, and only came to a halt at the very edge of the water, its wheels beginning to sink into the mud, while Azecier, his leg crushed, lay howling on the ground.

Girolamo glanced quickly around him, taking in the scene. There remained three Normans alive, two soldiers and du Gast; Wulfric, who had taken a wound, was fending off both soldiers. Martin was still struggling out from under a corpse; Azecier lay in a mire of blood and dirt; and the onager was past its axles in the ooze.

"Girolamo?" exclaimed du Gast suddenly.

"Walter," he said curtly, not lowering his sword.

"You fight with these barbarians?"

"You fight with William," retorted Girolamo.

"My work is devices, not causes," said the Norman. "William pays for the building of my machines. Will you let this piece of work be lost?"

"Call off your men, and we'll help you save it."

Walter tugged unhappily at his collar.

"I can't," he said. "They have orders not to let me or the onager be taken."

"Then why are you still alive?"

"Because you took them by surprise. Nothing else."

Wulfric was weakening. He had retreated two paces, and was holding his left arm awkwardly. Martin, finally free of the dead man, now made to help him: the nearer Norman, hearing his approach, turned to defend himself – and so showed his back to Wulfric. The tumbler at once ran the Norman through, at the same time stepping back to avoid the downstroke of the other: but as he did so, his heel struck against a root. At any other time he would have been able to keep his footing, but with the weight of the dying man dragging his sword arm down and his other arm wounded, he was not himself: and he stumbled, and fell. Before he could rise, the last of the Norman soldiers had driven his blade through the Heron's heart. An instant later, Martin buried his axe between the Norman's shoulderblades.

Azecier's cries were dimming to whimpers, as the ground about him grew redder. There were tears in Martin's eyes, and Girolamo felt a prickling in his own. Walter swallowed nervously.

"Girolamo -" he began.

"Go," said the Italian softly. "Go now. Back to William if you think he will spare you, over the sea if you can, or where you will – but go, and never let me look upon your face again. You have done evil enough here." The Norman engineer needed no further prompting; he turned and ran stumblingly to the raft, splashed aboard, and pushed hastily away from the shore.

Girolamo knelt beside Wulfric, and spoke a few words in a language Martin did not recognise: then he placed his hand over the Heron's face and closed his eyes.

Martin and Girolamo bore Azecier back to the Camp of Refuge between them; being only two, they could not carry both bodies, and it seemed best to take the man there was yet a chance to save. In the end, it made little difference: overwhelmed by shock and loss of blood, the youth was dead before they reached the fence. A handful of curious islanders, and those few of Hereward's warriors who were neither sick nor occupied in caring for those who were, had come out to see them home: and among them was Rowena.

"Martin?" she said uncertainly. "Where is Wulfric? Is he coming behind?" Martin could only shake his head wearily. Rowena frowned, puzzled; then, as she saw the salt streaks on Martin's cheeks, she opened eyes and mouth wide in a silent scream, before falling to the earth as if dead herself.

Within the Camp they were met by Torfrida, who bade two monks bear Azecier into the monastery church, and dispatched men to retrieve the remains of Wulfric and the Normans.

"Poor Rowena," she said. "To lose her husband so young, and with a child to care for." She shook her head sadly. "And Azecier – barely more than a child himself…"

"How is the lord Hereward?" asked Martin.

Torfrida blinked.

"He is strong," she said. "The fever does not go deep. Thomas says he will be well. Elfthryth is tending to him." She fingered the amulet of Ukko. "I… believe he will be well," she said uncertainly. "Tell him nothing yet of Wulfric and Azecier. I… I must speak with Kolfrosta."

"I knew," croaked the old woman hoarsely. She was unable now to sit up, or even look at Torfrida, instead staring blankly at the ceiling. "I knew the Dane would seek to claim the dragon; that is why I gave it to you. That you might know his nature. He is a thief and the son of thieves; do not trust him."

"What of Hereward?" asked Torfrida. "Will… will I lose him?"

"Do you mean 'Will he die?'" asked Kolfrosta. "All men die. But Tuoni will not come for Lord Hereward yet; he will see out the fever. It is already in retreat; Tuoni is appeased, he is leaving the island."

"Do you mean there will be no more deaths?" asked Torfrida. "Is the ague ending? Are all to recover?" There was no answer. "Kolfrosta?"

The ancient Permian did not speak, or move. Torfrida reached out, placed a gentle hand upon her old nurse's face, and closed her eyes.

"Well bides it with him who seeks mercy," she murmured in English,

"Balm from the Father in Heaven:

There, for us, stands the only fastness."

Ely, May, 1070.

The letter had been expected at Peterborough for months, but still came as something of a shock to Prior Herluin. He had enjoyed running the abbey; every discipline imposed on a wayward novice, every penny of tribute ground out of a reluctant tenant, had swelled his sense of power. But now it was to come to an end. The chapter had obeyed King William and elected Thorold of Fécamp to succeed the late Abbot Brand; the mother-house had confirmed the election; and now at last, Abbot Thorold was readying to leave Malmesbury and make his way to Peterborough.

The news was no secret; and though Father Wulfwine was no longer welcome at Peterborough under Herluin's regime, he and Brother Benedict corresponded when they could, making use of passing pilgrims and peddlers. It was not long, therefore, before word of Thorold's imminent arrival had reached Hereward at Ely.

"All the treasures of Peterborough," lamented Abbot Thurstan, "in the hands of Thorold."

"What do you know of him, Father?" asked Hereward.

"He has an evil reputation. A greedy tyrant, men say, who has sucked dry his previous houses. Of course, it is not godly to listen to such tales; but I have yet to hear any good of Thorold. And he is William's man, heart and soul."

"There is much gold at Peterborough, and many holy relics," put in Wulfwine. "Including the holiest." In the hidden tomb of St Edmund, two years before, Hereward had found a reliquary containing an alleged splinter of the True Cross: and it had been placed in the vaults of Peterborough, together with many another relic, both of local saints and of

240

Peter himself. "It would be shameful if they were used to enrich Thorold and his Norman kinsmen."

"Something must be done, then," said Hereward. "Before Thorold arrives; he will have soldiers with him."

"I will be no party to robbing the Church," said Thurstan hastily.

"Not robbing, Father," said Hereward. "Transferring certain items from one arm of Holy Church to another, no more. But we needn't trouble you with too much knowledge of it."

It would not be possible, they soon decided, to enter and leave Peterborough by stealth alone: the monastery was too well defended. A raid would help morale: since the slaying of Wulfric, Azecier, and the island woman Ethelflaed, nearly six weeks ago, they had had no chance to strike a blow against the Normans, and many ached for revenge. There was, however, a complication.

"We cannot do this without the Danes," said Martin heavily.

He was right. Though Svend continued his raids with half his fleet, taking Mariana with him on the basis that she was safer in his sight than out of it, Asbjorn, Harald and Knud were back on the island. The English might have been able to mount an unassisted raid upon Peterborough, but not without the knowledge of their Danish guests. To go without them would be an insult, and they could ill afford to lose the Danes' goodwill, with William's strength undimmed and the Scots pent up far beyond the Border.

"What do they care for the relics of Peterborough?" demanded Winter. "If we can't give a strategic reason for the raid, they'll want plunder. If we can, they'll still want plunder."

"There is a strategic reason," Hereward pointed out. "Keeping the treasures of Peterborough out of Thorold's hands. There's plenty of gold and silver plate there as well as holy relics – and much of the loot the bishops stole from Durham, too. The Danes no more wish to enrich our enemies than we do. And it'll help win the hearts of the people for King Svend. Herluin's already hated here, and Thorold's reputation is even worse; the men who rob them will be heroes."

"Even so," said Winter uncomfortably, "we're asking the Danes to tramp across the marshes to Peterborough, fight their way to the gold, drag it back – then turn it over to the monks?"

"We can spare them a little, can't we?" said Ulric. "The monks don't need it all."

"We will pay them compensation," said Hereward. "So much for every man killed, so much for every man wounded, no more."

"To take more would be robbing the Church, after all," added Leofric. "Asbjorn might not care about that, but Harald and Knud are God-fearing enough."

"We'll need their help to bring it all back, anyway," said Winter. "Do we have enough boats?"

"I can get you there dry-shod," declared Uluncas. Hereward frowned; he had forgotten the Gyrvian was there, so silent had he been.

"Dry-shod?" echoed Winter. "That's impossible."

"Impossible a month ago, but it's hardly rained a drop since. The Gyrvians knew every dry route across the Fens. I can get you to Peterborough and back without boats, I swear it."

"Could we bring horses?" wondered Hereward.

Uluncas shook his head.

"Not without doubling the distance, and even then it might not be safe. The way is too narrow, the ground too soft."

"So how do we bring back the relics? We may be pursued."

"The relics go by raft, with ropes to haul the raft over

dry patches, while the men on foot draw the pursuers," said the Gyrvian. "It's simple."

"You've done this before," Martin realised.

"Of course," said Uluncas. "It was how we lived. We never raided an abbey, of course…"

"No," Winter retorted. "Only peaceful villages."

"Enough," said Hereward.

"How many innocents did you kill?"

"Be quiet!" Hereward slammed his fist into the wall. "Uluncas is one of us now. He's proven himself well enough. The past is the past." He turned to Winter. "You and I were little better than bandits when we were young. We may not have killed, but how many barns did we burn, how many cattle did we drive away? And we never acted from need." He glowered round at the company. "We work together. We cannot let ourselves be divided. We are one! This is the Camp of Refuge!" He turned back to Uluncas. "Tell us more," he said quietly.

Drogo fitz Dudo reined aside to make way for the approaching troop: it did not immediately occur to him who they were. He had been told that the new abbot would ride with a guard – but this was a company, almost an army. There must be scores of horsemen snaking back along the road. At their head were two men on tall Franconians, towering over the soldiers, whose mounts were little more than ponies. The one on the left was armed *cap-à-pied*, his armour highly polished, and a cruciform brass boss nailed to the centre of his brightly painted shield. The other's burly form was squeezed into an ill-fitting hauberk which chafed his thick neck red, and his broad, pale face was twisted into a scowl; a plain steel cap perched on his hairless skull, a round, unadorned buckler hung upon his left shoulder, and a vicious-looking mace was tucked into his belt. Two vast wolfhounds loped by his side.

"M-my lord abbot?" said Drogo uncertainly.

"I am Thorold of Fécamp," replied the man with the mace. His gravelly voice was no more friendly than his expression. "Who might you be?"

"Drogo fitz Dudo, sergeant of the abbey guards at Peterborough." He fell into step beside the abbot.

"Sir Waryn here will command my guard," said Thorold, gesturing at the knight. "He has a sergeant, but he may find use for another – perhaps. What's your business here? Have you a message for me?"

"Brother Prior wished to learn the number of your retinue and the time of your arrival, that he might be better prepared to make you welcome in fitting style."

"How many of us are there, Waryn?" asked Thorold, glancing at the more soldierly figure who rode on his other side.

"All told, a hundred and sixty," said the knight. "We should come to Peterborough in four days – three if the servants on foot pick up their pace."

"You have your answer," said Thorold curtly. "Get back to your prior and tell him to have the tenants slaughter some oxen. We will expect a proper welcome."

"Of course, of course," said Drogo, slightly dazed. "We may have trouble finding housing for so many; but a feast for your men can be arranged outside the abbey walls –"

"For this rabble, yes," interrupted Thorold. "But Waryn and I will dine in the refectory."

"Sir Waryn will be welcome, of course," said Drogo, who had never been allowed into the refectory himself. "But the monastery cook will not wish to serve meat in the refectory. The Rule of St Benedict -"

"The Rule permits the serving of meat to the sick, does it not, to keep their strength up?" said the abbot. Drogo, who did not know, made a non-committal gesture. "Very well. A table will be set up in the infirmary, and Sir Waryn and I will dine there, with such guests as I see fit to entertain. And the cook will serve what he is ordered to serve, or else he will be replaced. Do you understand?"

Drogo nodded dumbly.

"Good," said the abbot. "Now, we understand you have had a little local difficulty with outlaws."

"The rebel Hereward Askilsson haunts the Fens," said Drogo, nodding. "The former abbot was in league with him, but Prior Herluin is a loyal subject and has naturally ended all contact with the wolfshead. He even captured one of his closest companions, but the outlaws surprised the monastery with overwhelming force and rescued him. He is a godless beast, this Hereward, who thinks nothing of assaulting Holy Church."

Thorold grunted.

"I heard of the rescue of the outlaw," he said, "although not quite as you tell it. Tell me, why was he not hanged as soon as he was taken?"

Drogo blinked.

"We, we had no authority…"

"Well, I have the authority," declared the abbot. "His Grace the King anticipated that this Hereward would attempt to prevent my instalment, perhaps even assassinate me before I reach Peterborough: hence my armour and this train of men – and my commission from the King. These are extraordinary times, and I have been given extraordinary powers. Any person who hinders my progress to the abbey or my taking of office and all its privileges is to be deemed an outlaw and may be put to death out of hand. Tell that to your prior; no doubt he will sleep easier for the knowledge." Drogo nodded dumbly, then spurred forward, riding ahead of the abbot's train, back towards Peterborough.

Hereward shielded his eyes, and peered out across the marsh, picking out the tussocks of grass that protruded from it, the clumps of reeds, areas where the mud was cracking in the sun, the trees once waterlogged whose roots were now exposed. Yet between them there were still treacherous-looking patches of vivid green, and here and there clear pools. It might indeed be possible to cross it on foot, but it would be a dangerous undertaking: and certainly they dare not take horses.

"Hereward?"

He looked round, his hand automatically reaching for the hilt of his sword: rapt in his contemplation of the Fen crossing, he had heard nobody approach. Elfthryth was standing only a little way off. She had pushed back her mantle, exposing her hair, brilliant gold gleaming in the sun: but the same action left her face unshaded. The fever had left her wan and thin; she looked a little healthier now, but had not quite her former childlike energy and effervescence. Life in the Camp of Refuge was harsh, and had aged them all, but it was startling to see the effect so plainly, so suddenly, in one so young.

"My lady Elfthryth," he said stiffly.

"You like to wander in the wild places, away from the abodes of men," she said, stepping up to his side. "So do I. It can be good to be alone; but not to be always alone."

"I hope nobody is alone here," he replied. "Ely is a family."

"For you, it is," she said. "Your family is here with you, and men like Winter and Martin who are brothers to you. I... I'm an outsider."

"Has anybody made you unwelcome?" asked Hereward. "This is a refuge for outsiders. Outlaws and outlanders, everyone who lacks a home elsewhere finds one here."

"I'm sorry." She lowered her eyes. "I must have sounded so ungrateful. Truly, nobody has been anything but kind. But... it has been so long... since I saw Dolfin. I don't know where he is; his father is Earl again, and at peace with William, but – I don't know if I could go back. To be in the King's peace, while you're still fighting here... I think I should hate myself, and Dolfin. I couldn't bear to hate him."

"I don't believe you have hate in you," said Hereward. "The latest rumours were that Dolfin was in Cumberland; there's fighting there, but people don't even claim to know what side he's on. It would be too dangerous to seek him there; but Gospatric will know how to reach his son. If you were to go to him at York, he could call Dolfin back from the Border. You'd be safe, and together, away from the war; there's no fighting round York any more."

"Because there's nobody left alive to fight," said Elfthryth. "You've heard the stories. I couldn't bear to live in a dead city, to see every day what they've done to us. Besides, when you and Svend join up again, you'll march on York, won't you? So the war will come there again."

Hereward said nothing, and avoided her gaze.

"Unless you don't believe there'll be a march inland," said Elfthryth suddenly. "Is that it? Is the war already lost?"

"No!" exclaimed Hereward, gripping her roughly by the shoulders. "It is not lost. It should have been won long ago, but it is not lost. The Danes have let themselves be distracted by plundering, and seduced by the sea, but they know well enough that we must needs fight the Normans on land, and they have the men for it. They came to make Svend King of England, and if they won't let their campaign go for nothing. We will strike a blow soon. But not in the North; we've failed too often there, and now there's nothing left to take."

"I hope you're right," said Elfthryth, shaking her head; "but how many more must die?"

Hereward folded her in his arms, clutching her head against his chest: and for a long time they stood, unmoving, by the edge of the mere.

"Full compensation for every man lost or wounded?" Asbjorn narrowed his eyes. "But no more?"

"No more," Hereward confirmed. "St Peter can spare what we need, but we're not barbarians."

247

"So why do we do this?"

"To save the relics. To humiliate Thorold, William's place-man. To show our strength. William thinks he has us beaten: let's remind him of what we can do."

"And you say he can lead us across the Fens? A half-crippled footpad?"

"Yes," said Hereward. "I've no doubt of it."

"Hmm." Asbjorn stroked his beard. "We could do with a victory before Svend returns. We'll join you." He extended his hand, and Hereward clasped it.

"Hereward."

He looked up; Torfrida had entered the hut. Asbjorn, withdrawing his hand, nodded curtly, turned on his heel, and left.

"Torfrida," said Hereward uncertainly. He did not recognise the hard look upon his wife's face, did not understand it.

"What is there between you and Elfthryth?"

Hereward's jaw dropped.

"There is nothing!" he declared. "Nothing but friendship. I knew her as a child…"

"She is not a child now."

Hereward sighed.

"In some ways she still is," he said. "Not everybody is as strong as you, Torfrida. Elfthryth needs protection."

"Then let her own husband protect her. Isn't that his duty?"

"Nobody knows where Dolfin is!" Hereward exploded. "What would you have me do? Turn her off the island, hand her to the Normans? She's under my protection here, under *our* protection, in the Camp of Refuge!"

"Hereward…" There was a catch, something close to a sob, in Torfrida's voice. "I believe you, I do, I believe that you are honest, maybe even that she is. But will you stay honest? How much longer can you, if you feel this need to protect her? She is not yours to protect. I am; your daughter is. I may not need protection, but I need *you*."

"Oh, Torfrida…" Hereward reached out, and drew her to him: she hung back only a few moments before melting into his arms. "I don't know what to do," he confessed, in a whisper. "I can't send her away. I can't bring Dolfin here. I would never betray you, but I know I've hurt you, and I can't bear to hurt you more. What are we to do?"

Torfrida looked up into his face.

"Is there nowhere she could go?" she asked. "To York, perhaps, or by sea to Edinburgh?"

"I don't know," sighed Hereward. "I don't know."

He looked up suddenly: he thought he had heard something at the window: but there was nobody there, and he put it from his mind.

Outside, Elfthryth, blinking back tears, stumbled back towards the pilgrim hostel.

The first watch of the night was ending when the raiding party felt solid land under their feet; it was a clear night, none so dark as they could have hoped, but there was no sign that anybody had seen them. The raft, which had stayed close all the way, occasionally having to be dragged over dry patches, was hauled up onto the grass. Ahead loomed the shadow of Peterborough Abbey.

"Which side are we to come from?" whispered Knud.

"There," answered Hereward, pointing. "The gate's at that end; it's the weakest point." Barred and manned the main gate might be: but breaching any gate would rouse the guards, and the postern was narrower and easier to defend once breached. The main gate it would have to be. The raiders greatly outnumbered Drogo's men, but they had to get inside to make their numbers tell. Asbjorn had suggested the use of fire, but Hereward would not hear of it: he was not a burner of monasteries.

"If only we had a ram," muttered Geric.

"We couldn't have brought it across the Fen," said

Hereward. "We have axes. We have ladders. We'll get through."

"How do we get there unseen?" wondered Harald.

"Hug the walls, stay in the shadows. It'll get us to the corner, and then it's only a few more yards to the gate."

"On the town side," Winter reminded him. "Within sight of dozens of houses."

"The townsfolk don't love Herluin, nor the Normans," replied Hereward, "and they won't attack armed men to save treasure for Thorold."

And so they filed along the wall, and turned the corner: and in a rush they hurled themselves towards the gate. A half dozen axes bit into the wood, and again, and again; two scaling ladders were hooked over the top of the walls, and men swarmed up them. There were but two men on guard within the gate; they at once beat upon a gong, but by the time Drogo and the rest of his men, struggling into their armour, had made it into the courtyard, the Danes were already leaping down from the wall-top, and the wood of the gate splintering on the inner side. As Hereward had predicted, no help came from the town. The bell was ringing now: but if Peterborough heard, if Peterborough saw, Peterborough did not stir.

Within moments it was unbarred, and the invaders surged in.

"Kill guards only!" barked Hereward. "Do not harm the monks!"

Asbjorn, wielding a vast double-bladed battleaxe, had already cut down one soldier, and buffeted Drogo himself to the ground; he turned now to Hereward.

"Where's the gold?" he growled.

"The plate is in the church – there," said Hereward. "The relics will be locked away, underground or in the high steeple."

"Hereward!"

Prior Herluin had stepped into the courtyard. The

monk was not a large man, but he seemed to loom, casting a long black shadow before him, and an apocalyptic anger writ upon his plump red face. His arms were raised, bearing aloft in his right hand a gilt crucifix, in his left a reliquary carved of dark yew.

"Hereward Askilsson, robber of the saints, despoiler of God's Church!" he declaimed. "Murderer, heretic and traitor! Cower now! Behold this holy thing, to which our house owes its name. Behold the filings shaved from the chains which bound St Peter in the dungeon of Herod, from which the angel of the Lord released him. In the name of St Peter I curse you. In the name of all the apostles I curse you. In the name of Jesus Christ I curse you. May you never know rest nor peace, in this life or the next. May crows peck out your eyes and may serpents eat your entrails. May chains bind you eternally, and may the fires of Hell consume you!"

Hereward blinked. He had never seen the monk so fearsome – or, indeed, as anything but laughable. Through all Hereward's childhood, Herluin would have given anything to frighten him; but whatever hells he promised, whatever beatings he administered, he had found the boy impervious to fear. Now he had at last struck a spark of fear from the man: but a spark alone it remained, from which no fire caught.

"Brother Prior," answered Hereward quietly, "you are unfit for your office and a disgrace to your order. I am here to take these and the other relics of this abbey into safekeeping, until such time as an abbot worthy to sit in my uncle's place rules here. You will surrender them to me."

He reached out, and prised the reliquary from Herluin's hand. The monk was, momentarily, too surprised to fight back: only when the box was gone did he suddenly swing the crucifix towards Hereward's head. It was Martin who caught him by the wrist, and tore the heavy cross from his grasp. The prior looked round wildly, eyes staring; then, with a sort of strangled sob, turned and fled.

"The church!" exclaimed Martin, pointing. The door of the abbey church had been broken down while Herluin was speaking his curse, and the attackers, Danes and English, had poured in, eager for gold: and now, from within, there came the faint flicker of firelight.

Hereward, cursing under his breath, broke into a run. As he burst through the remains of the door, he lugged Brainbiter from its sheath. He all but tripped over the corpse of a monk; ahead were men hooting, shrieking, gathering plate and candlesticks into their arms, while the altar cloth blazed. Wisps of burning linen were detaching themselves from the main cloth, some floating upwards in the smoke, others falling and smouldering upon the floor.

"Stop!" roared Hereward.

A few men glanced his way, but the frenzy did not cease. Looking wildly from side to side, he saw a man only a couple of yards away, a Dane, whose axe-head was stained with blood. Hereward glanced down at the dead monk, whose skull was cloven.

"Did you do this?" he growled.

The Dane shrugged.

"He was in the way."

He did not even have time to raise his axe before Brainbiter plunged through his beard and into his throat, and out at the back of his neck. When Hereward withdrew the sword, he finally had the attention of the men in the church.

"We are *not* here to slay monks!" he shouted. "Not even Herluin, God rot him."

"And why not?"

He had not noticed Asbjorn among the throng of looters: but the prince stood before him now.

"Herluin and his kind pray every day for King William," he said. "They marshal the hosts of Heaven against us. Is that peaceful? War is war. You chose to attack a monastery, and you complain when a few monks die?"

"We're not savages," snapped Hereward. "We're not

252

Gyrvians or Wish Hounds or Normans – nor vikings! We're the army of a Christian king. We do what must be done, but we don't do wanton murder."

"Then what was that?" demanded Asbjorn, gesturing at the dead Dane. "That man was my shield-bearer. You killed him."

"His blood price will be paid," replied Hereward, "just as if he had fallen honourably." He looked round once more at the arc of men before him, their helms and blades glittering red in the firelight. "But know this: any man who takes the life of a monk, or raises fire, or tries to secrete gold for himself, I will slay, and pay no blood price for." He fixed his eyes upon Asbjorn's. "Whoever he may be," he added.

There was a long, dangerous pause: then Asbjorn bowed his head.

"As you wish," he said.

The monastery was now effectively in the hands of the attackers. As it turned out, the relics had not been hidden, but were in their usual storage place beneath the abbey church; even the splinter of the Cross, whose presence at Peterborough was supposedly a secret, was with the rest. These and the gold were loaded onto the raft, with two men to pole and steer it; and, unpursued – for only two soldiers had survived the attack, and the townspeople of Peterborough had stayed in their houses – the raiders struck out for Ely, with Uluncas once more at their head.

Ahead, a lick of flame spouted out of the marsh, flickered, and vanished. Harald caught at Hereward's arm.

"What was that?" he demanded. Several of the men crossed themselves, whispering prayers.

"Just the marsh lights," said Hereward. "You get them sometimes in the Fens."

"Corpse candles," muttered Winter. "We've angered God." Another light flared, a little further off.

"The lights are our friends," said Uluncas. "They

guide our steps; they mark the treacherous places either side of the path." He grinned. "God isn't angry with us, He's pleased. He's sending His lanterns to light our way home."

As dawn broke, the monks of Peterborough were still on their knees, scrubbing blackened patches on the floor, or sweeping up broken glass and splintered wood; Prior Herluin trotted about from one scene of devastation to another, tutting, admonishing, pointing out what they had missed.

"Abbot Thorold will be here tomorrow!" he declared shrilly. "We must not let him find the place in this state! Is it not bad enough that we must tell him our relics are lost, our plate is lost, Hereward has humiliated us once again?"

"Brother Prior," said Drogo quietly.

"Yes?" snapped Herluin.

"The sky is light. It is St Clothilde's Day. The Abbot will be here today, not tomorrow."

Herluin blinked, and gaped; then, suddenly swaying, he caught at the sergeant's arm, and nearly fell.

"Today?" he echoed. "No; no, he must not come here today. Not today. He cannot – I cannot face him – I'll be degraded, lose my office – not today!" He stared wildly at Drogo; there were tears in his eyes. "Help me, Drogo," he said. "I cannot stand…"

The soldier gently guided the monk to a bench, and helped him to sit down; the old man slumped against the wall, his head on one side, breathing heavily.

"I can hear them," he said. "I can hear them coming, already – hooves clacking – they are here…"

Drogo pulled off his aventail, and listened. He could almost swear that Herluin was right. *Clip-clop, clip-clop…* No. There was nothing there. But soon enough there would be.

The Prior was still sitting crumpled like a discarded rag doll on his bench at noon, when Thorold at last did arrive. The gates were off their hinges, and unmanned; the Abbot and his train rode unchallenged, ungreeted indeed, into the courtyard.

"Is there nobody here to welcome your lord Abbot?" Thorold shouted. His voice echoed back at him from the walls. After a long pause, Drogo's head appeared around the inner door. Seeing the soldiers ranged behind Thorold, he bit his lip, then stepped out into plain sight.

"My lord," he said, bowing his head.

"Sergeant," said Thorold. "What has happened here?"

"The, the Danes –"

"Danes? How many? What did they come for?"

"I, I don't know how many… they came in the night… Hereward was with them. They've taken the relics."

"The relics?"

"The holy relics of St Peter, and many more; and all the abbey plate, pyxes and crosses, and -"

"They have taken my plate?" said Thorold quietly. "My plate and my relics? And you did not stop them?"

"They were too many, my lord, there was nothing we could do…"

"Nothing?" exclaimed Thorold. "Nothing! Where is your prior?"

"He, he is unwell…"

"Not wounded?"

"No, my lord, though there was fighting. Some were slain – all my men but one, and monks too…"

"Better for your prior if he had died," declared the Abbot. "Bring him out."

"My lord, I do not think he should be disturbed."

"Bring him out or I will send two of my soldiers," said Thorold. "I think he would prefer you, would he not?"

Drogo bowed his head, and slipped back into the monastery church, where he had left the Prior. Herluin was dozing on his bench; Drogo reached out, hesitantly, and gave his shoulder a gentle push. His eyes blinked open.

"Whuh?" he said. "What is it?"

"Father Abbot would speak with you, Brother Prior,"

said Drogo quietly.

"Father Abbot? He is here? Thorold? Oh, God – help me up…"

Drogo clasped Herluin by the elbow, and pulled him from his seat; without letting go, he steered him towards the door, and out into the courtyard, where he blinked in the daylight. Several heartbeats passed before he could see well enough to pick Thorold out from the shapes before him; as soon as he did, he fell down upon his knees, and blubbered:

"My lord, I am sorry! We were taken by surprise, there were too many, barbarian Northmen, heathens and enemies of God – they have wrought such blasphemy…"

"Be silent," barked Thorold. "You were Prior of Peterborough and acting Abbot. This man, Drogo fitz Dudo, he commanded your guards. The two of you bear the responsibility for what has befallen here." He turned to the knight. "Do you not concur, Sir Waryn?"

"It is beyond doubt, my lord," replied Waryn, inclining his head. "They have failed both you and our lord the King."

"And by their failure," Thorold went on, "have they not hindered me in taking up my office? It is not now the same office it was. To be Abbot of Peterborough today is a lesser thing than it was yesterday, and that is their fault. Are they not traitors within the terms of my commission?"

"The terms are for your lordship to interpret," answered Waryn. "His Grace made it quite clear that your discretion was to be absolute. Those you name as traitors are traitors."

"Then this is my judgement," declared Thorold. "The powers given to me by His Grace King William allow me to treat you both as outlaws and traitors, and so I deem you. You, Brother Herluin, come of a noble house, wear a holy cloth, and have in the past done the Crown some service: therefore on you I will not impose the gravest sentence. You will be stripped of your habit, and suffer thirty-nine lashes, before being turned forth from this abbey in a penitent's smock and with a begging bowl." Herluin groaned, and slumped forward onto the ground in a swoon. Thorold curled his lip, and turned to the sergeant. "Drogo fitz Dudo, you will be hanged until you are dead, and your body gibbeted before the gate of the abbey." He motioned four footsoldiers forward. "You two, take this man into custody; you, pick up that snivelling louse and wake him up."

Drogo was seized, disarmed and bound; the other two soldiers hauled Herluin into an upright position, and shook him roughly. When he remained limp, one of them pulled off his gauntlet, and felt for the old monk's pulse.

"He's dead, my lord," he reported.

"No loss," shrugged Thorold. "Go and tell the cook we're here; and you – choose a team of men, and build a gallows."

Folkingham.

In the division of the old manor of Bourne, once the home of Hereward's family, the lodge of Folkingham had been assigned to Gilbert of Ghent. It was a modest enough place: he had many grander properties, scattered across England and Flanders: but King William required his presence in Lincolnshire, and Folkingham was conveniently close to the King's camp without being in it. Gilbert felt more secure upon his own estate, even a small one, than under the shadow of his monarch and his fierce neighbour Ogier.

He kept only a small establishment there, and could not entertain large numbers, but it suited him not to give feasts; and it was a frugal supper of bread and dried beef that he was enjoying, with a mug of local ale, when he was informed that a lady desired audience. Intrigued, he ordered that she should be admitted: and she entered, cowled and cloaked, her face invisible.

257

"Show yourself, my dear," he said, gently.

She pushed back her hood, revealing a face which, though pale and somewhat drawn, was still quite strikingly beautiful; and thick, gleaming blonde hair under a flimsy grey mantle.

"You won't remember me, Lord Gilbert," she said. She spoke Anglo-Norse, with the accent of the Border country: and it was that which touched Gilbert's memory. It had been long ago, but he remembered the little girl at Roslyn; and, of course, he had heard that she dwelt now in the Camp of Refuge.

"Elfthryth?" he said.

Chapter 12: *Danegeld*

Lindsey, 491.

King Hrothmund turned his dagger over and over in his hand. Above him, his standard fluttered in the faint breeze.

"You know the price of our assistance," he said. "Lindsey will become subject to the Kingdom of Norfolk."

King Winta inclined his head.

"When the Britons are beaten," he said.

"Of course."

"If we lose the battle -"

"We will not lose," interrupted Hrothmund. "We have Wendel." His champion gave a low, wordless rumble of affirmation.

Back in Angeln, Winta had been told that any capable warrior who could get himself to Britain could become a king: the natives were weak and decadent, the east coast already in the hands of revolted German federates, a chaotic rabble who waited for their kinfolk across the sea to provide them with leaders. And part of that had proved true, even if Lindsey was somewhat smaller than the empires he had dreamed of. But the Britons had failed to live up to their reputation. Almost from the start, they had organised resistance to his raids into their territory, and even mounted counter raids: and then the new leader had come. His mounted company beneath its dragon banner was feared throughout the settlers' lands, their fearsome lance formation the one thing that could punch through an Anglian shield wall. And now for this whole summer they had been ravaging Lindsey. Settler villages had been burned; Winta himself had three times been routed in pitched battle. At last he had had no choice but to appeal to a stronger king. At least Hrothmund of Norfolk was a fellow Angle; it would have been more than Winta's pride could bear to have to submit to a Saxon.

Hrothmund's housecarles, twice the number of Winta's, were a fearsome force indeed, and none more so than the celebrated Wendel, of whom the scops sang that he was the son of a giant and could not be slain, save by one also of giant's kin; some even added that in the berserk rage he could change his shape, and fight as a mighty wolf or bear. Half a head taller than any other man there, he was deceptively thin – his strength not apparent at first glance; but Winta had seen him cleave a pig's carcase in half at one blow. About his shoulders hung the now balding skin of a bear he had killed in his adolescence, long years ago; his dirty, tangled hair mingled with its remaining fur as if it were a part of him. He wore no shield, carrying instead two swords, and struck as fast and sure with the left hand as with the right; his body was festooned with jewellery, gold armlets and chains, some bestowed on him by his lord to reward his victories, some claimed from his fallen foes of many nations; he even wore the gold ring of a Roman patrician. His bloodshot grey eyes were slightly crossed, but it neither hurt his aim nor made any man laugh at him – none dared.

Wendel was his own man now: he had seized himself a fortress, far to the south beyond Hrothmund's reach, which he called Wendel's Burh: and he acknowledged no king. But he never said no to a fight. And so, no longer as housecarle but as ally, he had once again joined his old ring-giver, for one more battle.

Winta held up before him his sacred amulet, so that all could see it.

"On the hammer of Thunor," he said, "and before all the gods, and these witnesses here present, I, Winta Wodning, King of Lindsey, pledge that, if we win today's battle against the horse-lords of the Britons, I will do homage to Hrothmund Trygilsson, King of Norfolk, and be his man; and I will acknowledge him and his heirs as overlords of the Kingdom of Lindsey for all time."

"Not before time," Hrothmund remarked. "Here come the Britons."

They had foregathered by the riverbank, in the path of the British company as it pressed towards the coast, seeking to either force the Angles back to their ships or cut them off and surround them on land. The land was flat here, and boggy, poor for any fighting men but worse for horses; but the Britons had local guides and seemed always to find the solid way. Under cover of the trees which clustered almost everywhere that the soil was thick enough for them to take root, the horsemen had advanced so close that the Angles could see the gleam of their eyes beneath the thick ridges of their iron helmets: they were on the far bank, but there was a wide ford here, obvious to all, for the track that passed for a road descended into the water on both banks. This time, however, the Angles were wide awake, well fed, ready armoured, and but one barked order away from forming the shield wall, still formidable even against these terrible horsemen.

The Britons were already assuming formation, and preparing to level their lances. Each lance was attached by two chains to the harness of its wielder's horse, so that the shock of impact should not carry the rider out of his saddle; and their heads were long and broad. The Angles had learnt to dread these vicious weapons. They trotted down into the waters of the ford, five abreast, and emerged at a canter, fanning out into an arrowhead formation. Winta gritted his teeth and braced his shield.

The Britons crashed against the shield wall like a wave, not upon a rock, but rather upon a wooden pier, built to withstand the waters but still vulnerable, still liable to crack. For a long few heartbeats the wall held: then, some weak link having faltered, it cracked, and collapsed. Hrothmund was bawling orders but he was not heard. The British leader, with his distinctive dragon-crested helm, drove through the Anglian ranks, trampling men, scything through them with a long Roman cavalry sword; his lance, its purpose served, dangled by his side where he had let it fall.

At this fearsome being, Wendel now launched himself, his two swords whirring. Those who got in his way, Angle or Briton, were hurled aside or cut down: there was but one thought in the great warrior's mind, to bring down the man in the dragon helm. Seeing him approach, the Briton made to meet him. The two kings swallowed hard. On this encounter the entire battle might hang. The Angles had still the advantage of numbers, and might yet win the field if only that dreadful horseman could be slain: and now there was nobody between him and Wendel, now he spurred forward as the Angle stood with swords upraised and crossed, now he raised his cavalry sword...

Then, very suddenly, the Briton tossed his sword into his left hand. As he caught it, and Wendel shifted his stance to meet a blow from that side, the Briton bent low in the saddle, and snatched up his dangling lance again: but he did not straighten up. Instead, remaining crouched over his horse's neck, he drove the lance forward, low as it was, beneath Wendel's defensively upraised arms: and that great broad blade burst from the Angle's back. Wendel was transfixed; he hung, a limp weight, on the point of the lance, dragged along by the forward motion of the horse, until the Briton unhooked the chains from the harness, and let lance and body alike fall to the ground. Wendel was dead.

"Bear his body from the field," barked Hrothmund to his shield-bearers. "The Britons must not take his head. He will be taken back to Wendel's Burh, for a princely burial."

Ely, June, 1070.

"The old folk down round Cambridge say Wendel's tomb was filled with gold," said Leofric. "And not only gold. For King Hrothmund took over Wendel's Burh and levelled the fortress, and forbade Wendel's people to bear arms again, lest they should turn against him: and so the weapons and armour of all his retainers were laid in the tomb with him. But they say also that there is but one entrance, which none has seen in hundreds of years; and that the tomb is watched by a Guardian – Wendel's ghost perhaps, or something else – that keeps mortal men from ever finding the treasure, until the proper time is come."

"That's a heathenish story for a deacon to be telling," remarked Methelgar. Leofric grinned.

"A lot of the old stories are heathenish," he said. "I grew up near there; Wendel's Burh is called Wandlebury these days."

"If there *is* a cache of arms and gold," remarked Hereward, "it could be useful to us."

"Chasing off after buried treasure again?" said Martin. "After what happened at Aylmerton?"

"At Aylmerton we had no knowledge of what the Pits were," Hereward pointed out. "This Wandlebury really is a burial mound; Leofric has seen it. Treasures have been found before. Remember St Edmund."

"Exactly," said Martin. "We were lucky there; it won't happen twice."

"Not only luck," said Hereward. "We had the clues the Abbot found in his chronicle; we knew where to look. Maybe there'll be a clue for Wandlebury too."

Leofric shook his head.

"In Wendel's time there were no monks to keep chronicles," he said. "Everything we know is legend and half-remembered rumour. And it isn't a burial mound. There's a fortress, right enough, though it's in ruins now – the legend is that he was buried inside the walls, so that Wendel's Burh should never be rebuilt. But nobody knows where. Enough people have searched for Wendel's tomb; they've found nothing."

"Then we wait," said Hereward decisively, "until we

do know something more."

They were gathered around a low campfire in the evening light, enjoying a round of Fenland ale; as silence settled over the company, Ulric Grogan stepped into the circle.

"Two Southrons have landed at the west end of the island," he said gruffly. "They wear wolfskins and they say they know Lord Hereward."

"Did they give their names?" asked Hereward mildly, swirling his ale in the cup.

"There was a rangy fellow called Bana, and a boy with green eyes called Ailnoth."

"Ailnoth!" exclaimed Methelgar. "Ailnoth Edricsson!"

"And Bana," added Martin. "What are they doing in the east?"

Ailnoth was the son of Wild Edric, the ferocious rebel leader from the Welsh Marches whom Methelgar had once served. Hereward and Edric had parted badly: but they were still both enemies of the Normans – until recently. Now, though Hereward could hardly believe it, it was said that Edric had submitted to William.

A couple of Ulric's subordinates pushed the two Marcher men forward. Both were looking lean and travel-worn: they had ridden for several days with little food or rest. Hereward stepped up to Ailnoth and embraced him; the youth was shivering. He seemed unwell.

"What brings you to Ely?" asked Hereward. "We hear strange things from out of the west. What has been happening?"

"It is all true," muttered Ailnoth, his eyes on the ground. "My father has betrayed us."

"I cannot believe that," said Methelgar.

"He lost his spirit when the Lady Rhiannon left him," said Bana. "He spoke slightingly of her kinfolk in one of his high moods, and the next day she was gone. Back into Wales, I suppose, or to her father's people in Dublin. Edric says she's gone into the Otherworld; he always did believe she was part elf. Wherever she's gone, she's gone, and all Lord Edric's strength with her. He gave her only one day to return – the next, he rode into Hereford and gave himself up. He wanted to be a martyr, all but begged them to hang him, but Brian de Penthièvre's too clever for that. He had him washed and shaved, and dressed up in a new tunic, and promised him that if he entered King William's service he'd never have to fight against Englishmen; and Edric agreed to it. He asked a day's grace before he'd swear the oath, and he rode up to the Bomere and threw his sword out into the depths. He said Lightning would never be borne in William's service; I think he was half expecting a hand to rise up and catch it, but there were only ripples on the water. Then Count Brian gave him a new sword and packed him off to the Border, to fight for King William against the Scots."

Hereward sighed, and shook his head, wondering at how a man might be so changed.

"What's become of his men?" he asked. "Does the Wild Hunt still ride?"

"It has not ridden since the Lady left us," said Bana. "But the camp in Haywood is still there, and many of the Huntsmen remain, poaching and scavenging for a living. That is why we are here."

"We need a new Huntsman," declared Ailnoth, for the first time looking Hereward in the eye. "One worthy to wear my father's cloak. One with a sword as famous as Lightning." He gulped, then said: "We need you."

Hereward gaped.

"Me?" he said at last. "Leave Ely, leave all that I've built here? It's impossible."

"All that you've built here could collapse any day," Bana broke in. "The Normans are closing in on you. It was all we could do to evade their patrols, with all our woodcraft."

"They can't penetrate the Fens, not yet," said Hereward. "And we have our Danish allies – many here, more further up the coast. The Normans can't put a ship to sea; they can barely defend the shores."

"What Edric built has already collapsed," added Methelgar, "or you wouldn't be here."

Ailnoth shook his head.

"The Wild Hunt never dies," he insisted. "When the new Huntsman comes, it will arise and ride once more."

"Why not you?" wondered Hereward. "You're Edric's son; the Wish Hounds know you, you're one of them. If they won't follow you, why should they follow a stranger?"

"You're not a stranger!" said Ailnoth fiercely. "You're a Wish Hound! You've ridden with my father, you're a Wish Hound until you die. And you're a legend! No man has fought the Normans as long and as hard as you. No man has done them such hurt. The name of Hereward is spoken throughout England! I haven't the gift of leading men, I never had. You do. You can do more good in the West than here. Our woods are easier to hide in than your Fens; and we have our Welsh allies behind us, a nation of free men. They've seen how English necks strain under the Norman yoke and mean never to feel it themselves."

"So their princes will do nothing to give the Normans an excuse to invade," answered Hereward. "The Welsh may have helped you in secret, but they won't defy William openly unless he attacks them first. But that's as may be. Whatever happens, this is where I fight. In my own land, and in my own way. I may visit the West again, if a time comes when I'm free to leave Ely: I want to help you, I want to give our people hope all over England: but not to stay there. Not to settle. This is my England, here in the Fens; and this is where I will defend it."

"My lord Asbjorn – wake up."

Asbjorn stirred, and blinked. For a moment he could not quite focus on the figure crouching over him; it was only the prick of steel at his throat which stung him into

266

wakefulness.

"Krakus!" he hissed. "Traitor! What are you doing here?"

"Traitor?" retorted the Obodrite. "Who made me so? I should kill you here, on the ground like a beast."

"Why haven't you?"

"Up," said Krakus. "We'll talk outside."

The Danes had been placed in the same barn where the attempt on Edgar Atheling's life had been foiled; Asbjorn lay near the door, and they had few bodies to pick their way across to get out into the open air.

"On." Krakus prodded, and Asbjorn walked on, beyond the torchlight, beyond the hearing of the many men sleeping outdoors, as far as the clusters of reeds at the edge of the camp. "Now: turn. Slowly." The Dane spread his hands, and turned to face his enemy.

"Why are you here?" he repeated. "Are you out of your mind?"

Krakus shook his head.

"I've come to my senses," he said. "You should come to yours."

"What do you mean?"

"Why do you think I haven't killed you?"

Asbjorn shrugged.

"You want something. What do you think I can offer you? You'll never marry my niece. You'll never come back to Roskilde. I couldn't help you if I wanted to."

"No," agreed Krakus. "But you can help someone who can help me. King William has a niece too; her name is Judith de Lens, and he plans to marry her off."

"To *you*?" said Asbjorn incredulously. Krakus' grip tightened on the haft of the knife, and he raised the blade momentarily; then he let it drop.

"I was almost good enough for Mariana," he reminded the Dane.

"What does he want?"

"What do you think he wants? He wants you to go home. He's ready to talk."

"Talk is cheap," sneered Asbjorn.

"Cheap at seven thousand English pounds in silver?" said Krakus. "Maybe more; that's his starting offer. How much plunder have you taken since you came here? How far have you advanced against the Normans? How many battles have you won? And how many men have you lost?" This was unusually articulate for Krakus; he must, Asbjorn decided, have been schooled in what to say.

"I would be guaranteed safe conduct?" he asked. "He would not take me as a hostage?"

Krakus snorted.

"Who'd pay to get you back?"

Asbjorn ignored the gibe.

"Where is William now?" he asked.

"He waits at Spalding."

"I will come to him, tomorrow or the day after – as soon as I can safely leave Ely. I make no promises, but I'll hear what he has to say."

"Very wise of you. Now, turn around, walk quietly back to the camp and go to sleep."

"Hereward!"

"What is it?" Hereward looked up; he had been mending his shield, which had sprung a couple of nails from the rim. "Who is that with you?"

Geric and Winter had returned from a hunt in the Bromeswold. But slung between them was no deer; instead, they supported a man, grey-haired, straggle-bearded, in a brown woollen tunic and ragged grey cloak, with leaves in his hair and his shoes and hose covered with thick mud. Though his head was hanging and his breathing laboured, he was clearly conscious. They dragged him to a stool, and sat him down; Winter knelt beside him, propping him up. He raised his head, and peered into Hereward's face. His own

268

visage was scratched and bloodied, and there was also, Hereward noticed, a red-soaked slash in the front of his tunic; but his piercing blue eyes were as clear as any man's.

"I come from Wandlebury," he rasped.

"Wandlebury!" exclaimed Hereward. The stranger nodded.

"My name is Weohmund. My family claims descent from Wendel. I see you know that name." He cracked a painful smile. "I never used to believe it."

"You need attention," Hereward told him. "You're wounded; we have skilled healers here…"

"In good time," said Weohmund. "I'm not dying." He coughed, and his whole body convulsed.

"Now," said Hereward. "You can talk while you are treated. Geric, fetch Zainab. Winter, help me get our friend to the hostel."

It was only when Weohmund's wound was washed out with wine and Zainab was binding it that Hereward let him speak on.

"I know where the entrance to the tomb is hidden," he said.

"Indeed?" said Hereward. "Then why not take the treasure for yourself?"

"Ha!" barked Weohmund. "Do you think one man could bring it all out unobserved? Do you think one man could hide it from the Normans?"

"You must not excite yourself," Zainab interrupted, pushing him back into his chair.

"Ralph Guader knows about it," said Weohmund. "It was one of his men who gave me this." He gestured at his wound with his good arm. "He has not enough men to watch the ruins day and night – not with the war taking so many of them away to the North – but if I return to Wandlebury, he'll know before I can bring the treasure away, sure as the Fen's wet." He shrugged, causing Zainab to lose hold of the bandage and mutter something in Arabic.

"But Guader does not know where the tomb is?" asked Hereward.

"Do you think he hasn't searched?" retorted Weohmund. "Do you think men haven't been searching for hundreds of years? Nobody's found a thing, and most of those who've dug there have ended up dead. There've been a lot of accidents there. They say there's a curse on it."

"A curse?"

Hereward raised a sceptical eyebrow.

"That, or the Guardian," said Weohmund. "Either way, you can't come at the treasure unless you already know how to get to it."

"And you do." Weohmund nodded. "And the Guardian will leave you alone if you dig in the right place?"

"I didn't say that. What do you know about the Guardian?"

"That he's supposed to watch over the tomb, and keep mortals away from the treasure until the right time has come."

Weohmund shook his head.

"Until the right *man* has come," he said. "Anyone who digs in the wrong place is the wrong man, and there's no need to ask his name; they get frightened off or killed and that's an end to it. But if you know the way in, it's different."

"And just how do you know it?" demanded Hereward.

"I *know*," insisted Weohmund. "That's enough."

"And if you dig in the right place, the Guardian won't challenge you?"

"No, the Guardian *will* challenge you. That's the point: he'll give you a chance to prove yourself."

"How? In battle?"

"Maybe," said Weohmund. "I don't know."

"And yet you're certain of the way in?"

"Wendel showed me."

"What?"

"Wendel showed me," he repeated. "I saw him as clear as I see you now, and he led me to the spot. The rest, about the Guardian, I know from my father."

"You… dreamt this?" said Hereward cautiously.

"Dream, vision, what's the difference?" Weohmund winced as Zainab pulled the knot of his bandages tight, but he did not let the pain interrupt his oration. "I *saw* him. I saw the fortress, the path, the two elder trees… I saw the way, and he pointed it out."

"If Wendel chose you," said Hereward carefully, "doesn't that mean that you are the one destined to find the treasure? In which case there's not much point in anyone else trying."

"Who said anyone else was going to try?" asked Weohmund irritably. "I'll open the tomb, but I'll need your help to bring the treasure away. And I'll need to stay here anyway – I'm an outlaw now. I gave two of Guader's men cracked skulls. You can make good use of the weapons…"

He gasped suddenly, and fell back in his chair.

"God's teeth, woman," he muttered to Zainab, "what's in that poultice? I'm as weak as a drowned mouse."

"You are exhausted," she said. "The need to tell your story kept you strong; now you need sleep. Your wound was ugly, also. I do not think it was infected, but you were lucky it did not remain any longer untreated."

Weohmund blinked. He seemed already half asleep. Hereward stood up, and lifted the older man bodily, like a child, and laid him upon the bed in the corner. Within moments, he was snoring.

"How soon will he recover?" Hereward asked quietly.

"He will be on his feet the day after tomorrow, if there is no infection," said Zainab, "and I saw none. But sometimes, a wound that looks clean can fester, even after it is treated."

"There is no fever? Nothing that could explain… the way he was talking?"

"I was attending to his wound," she said. "I confess, I

271

did not listen much to what he said. There is perhaps a touch of fever, but very little; I do not believe it would affect his mind."

In fact, Weohmund was walking, if a little unsteadily, the next morning; and by the second day insisting he was fit for the expedition to Wandlebury. Zainab warned that any major exertion so early could reopen his wound; but he scoffed, and declared that she did not know Wandlebury men.

"You really mean to go?" said Martin. "After Aylmerton?"

Hereward nodded.

"You and I, Leofric and Weohmund, no more. We'll take horses; we can be there before night, even avoiding the Cambridge road."

"And how do we bring the treasure back, if it's there?" demanded Martin.

"We'll find a way. We don't know yet if there is a treasure. We'll be back tomorrow or the day after. What harm can happen in that time?"

"We could be taken."

"Guader hasn't enough men. I doubt he's even in those parts himself; more likely he's with William."

"There is the Sheriff of Cambridge," Martin reminded him. "From what Leofric says, Wandlebury's not ten miles from the city."

"We'll take our chances with the Sheriff," said Hereward. "If Weohmund has truly found the tomb of Wendel, it won't only mean gold and arms. It will be a symbol, a sign. Wandlebury is part of the foundation of England. If Guader finds the treasure, the Normans will have conquered our ancestors. If we do, Weohmund's dream may give the people hope, show them that Svend is the favoured one, the destined King."

Spalding.

"The Prince Asbjorn Estridsson."

Asbjorn strode into the hall. Two shieldbearers flanked him; it must have been harder for three men to sneak away from Ely than for one, but Krakus had predicted he would be too proud to come alone. Their swords had been removed at the gate, but they still wore full armour; Asbjorn himself wore a shining hauberk, and carried his helm under his arm, but bore no shield. He cast a supercilious eye over the array of Norman nobles at table before him. Though it was barely midday, they had eaten and drunk heartily, enjoying the St John's Day feast; some were already sprawled snoring across the tables..

"Which of you is William the Bastard?" he asked, speaking Norse. They looked blank. Krakus raised his bleary head, and gestured at a stout, steely-eyed man with red hair, sitting midway along the central trestle.

"That is the King," he said. "You will address him with respect."

Asbjorn inclined his head to the King, who returned the gesture. The half-slumbering form to William's left grunted and stirred.

"This is the lord Ivo Taillebois," said William, gesturing at the swinish sleeper, "and the Baron William de Warenne." He indicated the man on his right, who nodded curtly. "The Baroness Gundrada." Gundrada gave a thin-lipped smile. "And Sir Ranulf de Gavray, who will interpret for us." William motioned forward the knight, a thin man with sharp cheekbones and white-blond hair cropped close to his skull, who repeated the introductions in Norse. "Can you speak for King Svend?"

"I will undertake to speak for him," said Asbjorn. "He doesn't want a long war." Sir Ranulf spoke rapidly in French.

"I will be blunt," said William. "You have been a

273

serious inconvenience to me, but you have failed to take and hold any significant territory. You have squandered the chance of a Scottish alliance and I now have Malcolm Canmore on the run. You have wasted your time in raiding because you dare not face me in open battle. You will never conquer England this way, and you know it. Nor can Svend afford to winter away from Denmark with all his fleet, when he is menaced by enemies closer to home." Asbjorn glanced pointedly at Krakus, who grimaced. "In the past," William continued, "Danish invaders have accepted payment to depart from England. It happened so often that the Danegeld tax was instituted to pay for it. I see no reason to depart from custom. If Svend really wanted my crown, he would land his army and set it against mine. Am I right to conclude that he would accept a payment to remove his fleet from my shores?"

"Yes," declared Asbjorn. That needed no translation. A ripple of interest ran through the hall.

"You are certain of this?"

"Absolutely."

He was. William was right, raiding would never conquer England. What Denmark needed was a full treasury; and if it could be got without sacrificing more men, men who were needed should a war against the Obodrites come to pass, so much the better.

"Excellent. Then it remains only to settle the price. I understand that His Grace was offered five thousand pounds to go to war so as to make Edgar Edwardsson King, and rejected it. I offer seven for peace."

Asbjorn shook his head.

"I will not consider less than twelve."

"Eight," said William.

"Twelve," insisted Asbjorn.

"I am thinking only of convenience," said William. "You will want to leave as soon as possible; you can hardly remain on the Isle of Ely now. I have limited money to hand; if you force me to raise more, your departure could be delayed by weeks. And the sooner you are gone, the sooner I can leave. I have a war to finish in Scotland, building works in London, any number of things to attend to; I am growing sick of the air of Lincolnshire."

"You knew you'd have to haggle," countered Asbjorn. "You must have raised more than eight. How much is there?"

"Ten thousand," William admitted. It was not worth lying.

"Very well," said Asbjorn. "Ten thousand… and the head of Krakus the Obodrite."

Krakus leapt to his feet, snatching up a knife, and sprang across the table, kicking aside a platter of pork. The nearer of Asbjorn's shieldbearers raised his round shield, and struck the hurtling Obodrite in the face with the boss; he collapsed groaning to the ground. Several Normans reached for their weapons: but the King held up his hand.

"Peace!" he said. "I will have no fighting here." He looked to de Gavray. "What did he say?" he asked. The knight told him; William chuckled.

"You are immovable on that point?" he said. De Gavray translated; Krakus sat up, still moaning, and rubbing his jaw.

"There will be no peace without it," declared Asbjorn. "If Krakus is alive when I leave Spalding, you can eat your ten thousand English pounds."

Sir Ranulf spoke again in French, and William gave the slightest of nods. Krakus was by now struggling painfully up; even as he attained his feet, two sentries seized him, and cast him back down again. One grabbed his shaggy hair, and hauled it forward, forcing his head down and baring his neck; at another nod from the King, Sir Ranulf almost casually drew his sword, and slashed downwards. It took two blows to sever the Obodrite's head; his body remained crouched, blood spurting from the neck, for a long moment before it toppled sideways. There were several gasps, and more than a few diners turned distinctly green.

Asbjorn smiled grimly.

"Now," he said, "before I go back to remove my men from Ely, I should like to see that silver."

The four horsemen had left the flat Fen country and entered the low hills of southern Cambridgeshire. The ruins of Wendel's Burh were visible ahead, a great crumbling wall ringing the summit of the largest hill, here and there obscured by clusters of trees. Next to that, Ivo's tower at Spalding or any Norman castle they had seen would have been dwarfed.

"It was old when Wendel came," said Leofric. "They say the giants built it."

"It looks as if it could still hold out an army," remarked Martin.

"From this distance," agreed Weohmund. "But it's all tumbled down and broken. Rebuilding it would mean building a new castle. And besides, people are too afraid of the Guardian."

"We'll have no trouble getting inside, then?" said Hereward.

"None. There must be a dozen places where you could get across the wall if you needed to, but we can go through the main gateway. The gates rotted to nothing hundreds of years ago."

"The sun's nearly set," said Leofric.

"Good," said Hereward. "This work is best done by dark. And there's a good moon tonight; we won't lack for light."

It was completely dark before they reached the gateway. There was a sinister air to the gloom-shrouded fortress: Hereward could well believe that there was something uncanny here, and even Martin glanced anxiously from side to side, wondering what watchers the avenue of trees that lined the approach to the gap might hide.

"The ground within is too rough for horses," said Weohmund. "We'd better dismount."

"And leave them here?" asked Martin. "The path looks smooth enough to me."

"The path is, but it goes up to the inner ring. Wendel's tomb is to the right, across the slope. It's uneven, and full of stones and roots."

"Is it within call?" asked Hereward.

"Oh, yes. It's not much more than fifty yards, if that, between two elder trees and by a breach in the outer wall."

Hereward turned to Martin.

"Then you and Leofric can hold the horses here," he said. "You can watch for any pursuit, and we'll call if we need help."

Martin bit his lip, but did not object. It was good policy to guard the gate: this was surely the way any pursuers would approach: but his heart misgave him.

Hereward and Weohmund dismounted; Weohmund opened the bundle tied to the back of his saddle, and took out the mattock he had brought to open the tomb; and, leaving the horses with Martin and Leofric, they went ahead. As they turned right, into the shadow of the wall, darkness fell upon them: the moon was still visible, but no longer illuminated the ground before them. They had almost to feel their way along the rough ground.

"Should we light the torches?" wondered Hereward.

"When we come to the spot," answered Weohmund.

It seemed they had gone considerably more than fifty yards when, at last, rounding a bend in the side of the hill, they saw ahead the two elder trees. Beyond them lay a large oval stone, set into the hillside, with a number of smaller stones strewn around. The area was out of the shadow, and the moonlight fell directly upon it.

"There," whispered Weohmund. "The stone."

"You are the one who must open it," replied Hereward. Weohmund nodded, hefted the mattock, strode up to the stone, and struck the turf above it.

Hereward fingered Brainbiter's hilt, and glanced

anxiously from side to side. An owl hooted somewhere within the inner ring of the fortress. He was certain there was somebody watching them.

The minutes passed; slowly, Weohmund cleared back the turf and moss, exposing more of the stone; then, suddenly, the mattock blade struck through, finding a gap behind the stone.

"I'm through!" he exclaimed. "I'm through!"

Bracing his foot against the slope, he hooked the blade of the mattock behind the stone, and heaved with both hands, throwing all his weight backwards: but the gap was too small, the stone still too strongly bound into the hillside. It did not move; and Weohmund, losing his grip, fell backwards, and tumbled down the slope.

"Weohmund!" exclaimed Hereward.

A voice out of the darkness answered him:

"Who disturbs the sleep of Wendel?"

"Who's there?" demanded Hereward, drawing Brainbiter. He looked around; he saw nobody.

"Who disturbs the sleep of Wendel?" the voice repeated.

"I am Hereward, son of Askil, Lord of Ware, Steward of Bourne, and captain of the Camp of Refuge," he declared. "Who questions me?"

Down the slope above the stone there bounded a dark shape, a long cloak flapping behind it. It landed, cat-like, before Hereward, and straightened up. The figure was several inches taller than Hereward, and wore a cuirass of boiled leather studded with iron; his cloak was of coarse black wool; he bore a wooden buckler and a broad-bladed sword; and the front of his helm was a blank, featureless steel mask, behind which his face was entirely hidden, even his eyes in shadow behind the two black holes.

"If you would come to the treasure of Wendel, you must come through the Guardian."

"So be it," said Hereward, raising Brainbiter. The

Guardian struck, and their swords met.

How long they fought, Hereward could never afterwards say. It felt as if time had been slowed, as if the air was thick as water. They were very evenly matched: every blow either struck, the other parried perfectly. Hereward began to feel that the Guardian knew where his every blow would be aimed.

At last, as he grew tired, Hereward's guard slipped: and the Guardian lunged forward, stabbing with his point. Hereward brought Brainbiter up too late to ward the blow off entirely: he knocked it from its course, but it struck him upon the shoulder. His light Saracen hauberk held firm, and the blade did not pierce his flesh, but the blow jarred through his shoulder, and he staggered, gasping in pain. The Guardian stepped forward, raising his sword: and Hereward, with a sudden access of strength, hurled himself forward, throwing all his weight behind Brainbiter, and drove it through the leather armour and into the Guardian's heart.

The masked man groaned, and slumped, first to his knees, then sliding backwards off the blade, dark blood trickling from the bottom of his visor. Hereward leant on his sword, gulping the air. Hearing a noise further down the slope, he snapped to attention.

"Who's there?" he demanded.

"Weohmund. I hit my head…" Weohmund was half climbing, half crawling up the slope from wherever he had been lying under the shadow of the wall. His hair was bloodied; so too was the front of his tunic, where his recent wound had burst open.

"The Guardian is dead," said Hereward. "He was a mortal man… he is dead."

He sat down upon the slope, clutching Brainbiter; Weohmund hauled himself up and sat beside him. The night had taken a chilly turn; and in the east, the first faint glimmerings of dawn were already visible.

"Are you fit to dig?" asked Hereward, looking at his

companion's injuries. Weohmund put a hand to his chest, and winced.

"I don't know," he said. "Not now... I need a little rest. Just a little."

"I could dig," said Hereward. "It makes no difference now." His left shoulder was still aching, but his right arm was good. The mattock could be wielded with one hand, though it would be slow.

Weohmund shook his head, then grimaced as pain shot through it.

"I was chosen," he said. "There may be more than the Guardian to face."

"My lord!"

Hereward looked up. Martin was hurrying towards them from the gate – and there was somebody with him, not Leofric. As they came closer, Hereward frowned, recognising his cousin Geric.

"Geric?" he said, struggling to his feet. "What has happened?"

"The Danes!" exclaimed Geric. "They are leaving! Boarding their ships and leaving! They may already be gone."

"Gone?" echoed Hereward. "What is this? Gone where?"

"Gone from Ely, that's all that I know," said Geric. "They've cleared out the barn, bundled up their arms, loaded provisions in boxes and they're leaving. They won't answer questions, won't talk to anybody, and if we stand in their way they knock us aside. We couldn't stop them without fighting them, and we daren't do that; they're too many."

"Leaving?" said Weohmund, frowning. "What does it mean?"

"It means William," said Hereward grimly. "It means Danegeld. We have been betrayed; we must return to Ely."

"But the treasure!" protested Weohmund.

"The treasure can wait," said Hereward. "William may be planning an assault on the island; Ely is worth more than whatever lies here."

There was no Norman assault; but by the time they returned to Ely, every Dane had departed. Once again, Hereward found Lysir at the western edge of the island; there was no boat to be seen, but no doubt, like Uluncas, the one-eyed man knew the dry paths across the Fens.

"The Danes are gone," he said flatly. "William bought them off, and they left, every last man, and took the Peterborough plate with them. First Gospatric, then Edric, now this… at every turn we are betrayed."

"Kings and earls may fall away," said Lysir, "but the people love you. There are still many who have not given up, all over England."

"Perhaps they should," said Hereward. "Perhaps we all should. What strength do we have to set against William's? What good can we do without an army? The Scots are beaten, the Danes are gone, the earls are eating from William's hand. What's left?"

"England," said Lysir. "Thousands of free souls. And there is still the Camp of Refuge – and other places."

"We can hold the Normans off here, but without the Danes we can hardly strike against them," answered Hereward. "Perhaps Ailnoth was right; perhaps I should go west and lead the Wild Hunt."

"Perhaps. Though I told you once before, the Wild Hunt is with you as long as your enemies fear you. They still do."

"Do they?" retorted Hereward. "I should think they'd be laughing at me now. At least Edric had Wales at his back. Here we have nowhere to retreat, and now no friends."

"You still have friends," said Lysir, "of many nations."

"And worthy people they are too; but they bring no fleets, no companies of horse. Diarmait, Malcolm, Svend, every foreign king has failed us."

"And you need them?"

"I hope not," said Hereward. "I *will* go to the West, and the North – what's left of it – and see if men can be raised; we need a revolt all over England, so the Normans have to divide their forces. We will need a hundred Camps of Refuge, ten thousand robbers and raiders; if kings and princes will not help us, we must help ourselves." He sighed. "I never did learn if there was truly a treasure at Wandlebury; if there is, no doubt Ralph Guader will take it."

"No," said Lysir. "The Guardian will not let that happen."

"The Guardian is dead," said Hereward. "I killed him."

The old man shook his head.

"You killed one man," he said. "The Guardian does not die so easily. Perhaps whatever lies at Wandlebury must lie undisturbed a little longer."

"This way, my lord – there!"

Adalbert pointed eagerly between the elder trees. Ralph Guader raised a quizzical eyebrow.

"Where?" he said. "I see nothing. The hill is as it was."

The soldier peered the way he had been pointing. The stones lay in their old position against the hill. The turf clung around their edges as if from months of growth, and there was no sign of any disturbance. He glanced to his right: yes, there was the crack in the wall where he had perched hidden, after making his way round outside the outer ring.

"But, but – I don't understand…" he spluttered. "I saw them open the barrow!"

"Nobody has opened anything here," said Guader. "And what of your dead man? Where is he?"

Adalbert swallowed.

"He is – gone, my lord," he said.

"So it appears," sniffed the Seigneur. He turned to his captain. "This man is either a dreamer or a drunk. Flog him and don't let him waste my time again."

Upon that, he turned, and strode back towards the gate, where he had left his horse tethered. In a copse a little way off, there stood a silent figure in a black cloak: and he watched the retreating Norman from behind a mask of steel.

In his mother's tiny cottage in Brampton, Starkad Arngrimsson seethed and plotted; while in Kent, Sir Ascelin de St Valéry stepped ashore, confident that in England he would make the fortune that had eluded him in Flanders and Picquigny.

Hereward stood on the edge of the island, gazing out across the flat expanse of the Fens. Faces flitted through his mind: Christian, Brand, Lewine, Wulfric, Azecier, Toli. He stretched out his arms, Moses-like, towards the waters, and began to chant:

> "Sooth, I may not think
> Why my soul is not darkened
> When I think upon all
> The life of men in this world,
> How fairly they fly the floor,
> The mighty thanes:
> So this Middle Earth
> Each day a little
> Droops and falls;
> The halls are worn down,
> Their lords lie
> Bereft of joy,
> Fallen all the throng
> In their pride, by the wall."

He let his arms fall to his sides, and stood there, still, for he knew not how long: then Torfrida's hand stole into his.

Afterword

Christian and Zainab

Christian is inspired by a hermit of that name, who is alleged to have died some decades after the events depicted. He reportedly maintained that he was King Harold, and had escaped Hastings exactly as my Christian claims – borne away to be healed by a Saracen woman, then disguising himself as a pilgrim. Obviously they cannot be the same man, since mine dies in 1069: but, for the purposes of the novel, we can assume that the hermit – if he existed – must have heard of this Christian and taken on his identity. (Or, rather, his false identity, since that Harold survived the battle is wildly unlikely.)

Zainab's back-story is simply the most plausible explanation I could think of for how the "Saracen woman" of the hermit's account came to be present in England some thirty years before the First Crusade.

Krakus and the Danish invasion

Krakus is fictional, but that Prince Kruto of Wagria could have had a brother who sailed with the Danish fleet in 1069 is none too implausible. Kruto was the last pagan prince to hold sway over the Obodrite Confederacy, after overthrowing the Christian Gottschalk in 1066. Gottschalk's sons Henryk and Budivoj fled to Denmark and Saxony respectively; in 1074, Budivoj and his Saxon army were lured into a trap and massacred by the Wagrians, but in 1075 Kruto met his end when he attempted to assassinate Henryk at a banquet: his own wife, Slavina, helped Henryk to murder her husband instead.

How far Hereward was involved in the events of 1069

284

is not known. The *Book of Ely* makes him a central player, and I have drawn on its account. Certainly, he must at least have liaised with the invaders: however, it is not until Svend's arrival in early 1070 that Hereward enters contemporary chronicles.

Genealogical issues

Long established but largely erroneous traditions have entangled the family of Sheriff Turaud with the House of Mercia. Turaud himself has variously been described as the nephew, full or half-brother, or even (with wild disregard for chronology) the father, of the Countess Godiva: many genealogical websites still baldly refer to them as brother and sister, as if there were no doubt in the matter. However, since his name, though Norse-derived, is Norman, and hers Anglo-Saxon, it is highly unlikely that they shared both parents: that they were either half-siblings or, as I have made them, aunt and nephew, is much more plausible.

Lucy of Lincoln used to be thought of as the daughter of Alfgar Leofricsson and sister of the Earls Edwin and Morcar; since equally mistaken traditions made Hereward Alfgar's brother, she appears in Kingsley's novel as the hero's niece. In fact, however, she was not a member of this family, but of Turaud's. I have followed the general modern consensus in making her his daughter, although some, particularly those who maintain that she was born after the Conquest, have argued that she was in fact his granddaughter or great-niece. In any case, Edwin and Morcar were not her brothers but probably, if Turaud and Godiva were related, her second cousins. Since I have made Hereward's mother a sister of Godiva, he is in this novel Lucy's first cousin once removed: but this relationship is not necessarily historical. The name of Turaud's wife is unknown, although she was certainly William Malet's daughter: later sources variously call her Beatrice or Alvarissa, and I have plumped for Beatrice.

The *Gesta Herewardi* mistakenly asserts that Frederick van Oosterzele and William de Warenne were brothers. Most likely they were in fact, as depicted here, brothers-in-law, Frederick being the brother of de Warenne's wife Gundrada. The alternative tradition concerning Gundrada's birth – that she was the daughter of Queen Mathilde, either by King William or by an otherwise unknown previous husband – will not hold water.

The Harrying of the North

Harrying was an accepted practice in medieval warfare: however, the scale of what was done in the North of England in the winter of 1069-70 was absolutely unmatched, and even pro-Norman chroniclers were deeply shocked. Orderic Vitalis remarks that "I have often praised William in this book, but of this act which condemned the innocent and the guilty alike to death by slow starvation I can say nothing good… Such savage murder should not go unpunished." On his deathbed, bringing to mind his sins, William was said to have been more troubled by this than by any other atrocity of his ruthless career. The death toll is reckoned to have been in the region of 100-150,000; if it happened today, it would unquestionably be called genocide. It would be decades, if not centuries, before the North recovered.

Hereward will return in DOOM OF BATTLE.